lives in Hampshire ~~~~~~~~~ sons and works part-time ~~~~ a legal secretary for criminal defence lawyers as well as writing freelance 'human interest' features for the national press. She has written erotic short stories and novels for various publishers and magazines for twenty years and this is her fourth erotic novel.

Primula also offers a critique service for aspiring erotic and romantic writers through the online Writers Workshop.

PRIMULA BOND

The Diamond Ring

AVON

AVON

A division of HarperCollins*Publishers*
77–85 Fulham Palace Road,
London W6 8JB

www.harpercollins.co.uk

A Paperback Original 2014
1

A catalogue record for this book is
available from the British Library

ISBN 978-0-00-752413-6

Set in Sabon LT Std by Palimpsest Book Production Limited,
Falkirk, Stirlingshire

Printed and bound in Great Britain by
Clays Ltd, St Ives plc

ACKNOWLEDGEMENTS

To all at Avon Books and Lightbrigade for the expert advice, encouragement and enthusiasm which helped me complete this trilogy. To the team at Writers Workshop for giving me the opportunity to run an erotica workshop at their writing festival, which, as well as forcing me to assess and analyse my own work, gave me the rewarding experience of being treated by other writers and readers as a serious author. To the bloggers who have invited me on to their websites to talk about myself and my characters. And finally to all the readers who continue to buy my books and take the trouble to befriend me on Facebook and follow me on Twitter to tell me their thoughts!

For my family

'Age cannot wither her, nor custom stale
Her infinite variety: other women cloy
The appetites they feed: but she makes hungry
Where most she satisfies; for vilest things
Become themselves in her.'
    William Shakespeare, *Antony and Cleopatra* 1606

'Whenever I'm caught between two evils, I pick the one
I've never tried.'

Mae West

'J'ai bien besoin d'avoir cette femme, pour me sauver
du ridicule d'en être amoureux.'
Pierre Choderlos de Laclos, *Les Liaisons Dangereuses*

Le feu plus couvert est le plus ardent.

French proverb

CHAPTER ONE

The silky blue and green strands of the feather ripple as if they're still attached to something breathing. The sharp quill end pecks a dot of blood from Gustav's finger. It's been bent awkwardly to fit inside the envelope that has just been delivered, but as he shakes out the plume it unfurls to its full majestic length.

'Peacock feathers symbolise bad luck. Everyone knows that. They're beautiful, but deadly. A curse. So why is this package addressed to me?' Gustav frowns at the feather, turning it this way and that. 'A week ago this building was still being refurbished. Barely anyone knows the gallery's open and in any case the business is in your name, not mine. So who just posted it through this door? Who knows I'm here?'

The feather shimmers playfully, catching flashes of light from the dimness outside. Gustav's questions hum and buzz as he examines it. The oval eye set in the middle is distinctly outlined, as if it belongs to an ancient Egyptian goddess immortalised on the wall of her tomb.

The mellow atmosphere we have just been enjoying with our band of friends and clients to celebrate the unveiling of the *Serenissima* gallery has disappeared. The excitement of our engagement shelved. The pleasure of making up with my cousin Polly when she turned up unexpectedly is forgotten. The exquisite, planned, pleasure of making out with my handsome new fiancé in the window, watched by a clutch of voyeurs, has dissipated.

I may still wear Gustav's scent between my legs but the joy has evaporated like so many torn cobwebs. And it's all down to Gustav's brother. Pierre Levi.

The last time I saw this feather it was pinned to a tricorn hat, and that tricorn hat was on Pierre's head. It was part of the elaborate disguise he had carefully picked to attend the Valentine's Day ball in Venice a month ago.

I'm going to have to tell Gustav everything before Pierre does. Right down to the fact that in the mêlée of masked strangers Pierre convinced me that I was dancing with Gustav. And that's why I walked so willingly into his arms.

The peacock eye is the only fixed point on the wavering fronds. And it's fixed on me.

It's late March. The Carnivale was only a few weeks ago. But like a fool I thought that was long enough to put such a potentially disastrous encounter behind me. I thought that with Pierre now ensconced and occupied far away in LA I could hide the sordid encounter still haunting me, the truth that Pierre and I share still whispering in my ear. The truth which could still drive me and Gustav apart.

But now Pierre has sent this feather, this visual prompt, and yet again he's timed it perfectly. Only an hour ago he was part of the jolly proceedings when he phoned the gallery, pretending to congratulate us on our engagement. But all he really wanted to do was remind me that far from being separated by time and space, the diamond ring glittering on my finger means that he and I are more inextricably linked than ever.

It will be your turn to choose, Serena, Pierre said on the phone. *If you don't want to have any more to do with me, you know where the door is.*

In other words, the only way to avoid Pierre is to walk away from them both.

And just to make sure I understand, just to keep me in line, it turns out that Pierre is physically close by. He's been watching, waiting for the moment to deliver this coded symbol. Knowing that I will instantly recognise what secret the feather represents.

That Gustav's own brother tried to fuck me.

I rouse myself with an awkward shrug, aware that Gustav is waiting for me to speak.

'New York must be full of freaks who get off on scaring people. Maybe it's from someone who saw my voyeur exhibition in London and thinks I'd find this funny. Or someone who disapproves of my erotic themes. Someone with a grudge, maybe a member of the Club Crème who was at that stag-night shoot in January and doesn't want my shots to be circulated?'

The feather's breeze kisses my face. Every dip and sway of it reminds me of Pierre in that gondola, the way he was moving, what he was doing to me.

I back up against the glass door. 'All I know is, you need to get rid of it!'

'Relax, darling! I was only teasing about the curse.' Gustav continues waving the feather like a conductor's baton. 'Look at it another way. Maybe some people would see this as a good-luck charm intended for you. Not for me. Maybe Ernst and Ingrid Weinmeyer sent it, even though they were here just now. They are your most loyal patrons, after all. Maybe they feel honoured that we invited them to the opening of our cool new gallery. Or Polly meant it as a keepsake while she's off wandering the globe in search of herself?'

3

'It's not like you to stand around proffering useless theories, Gustav!' It comes out sharper than I intended, and heat floods through my face. 'It's just some creepy hoax, OK? Designed to sabotage our happiness.'

'Nothing and no one will ever do that.' He flicks the feather against my face and holds it there, still pondering. 'Then again, peacocks spread their tails as part of the mating call, don't they? So maybe it's highlighting my machismo? My success in ensnaring the cutest photographer in the western hemisphere, first with a silver chain, then with a golden locket, and now with this diamond ring?'

The fronds feel as if they're stuck to my cheek. Flimsy, yet weighted with menace.

I flick it away from me and scrabble for the door handle. 'Let's just get out of here. Go get dinner and start making some wedding plans!'

'Nothing I'd like better, Serena, but first things first. What on earth is wrong?' Gustav swings me round to face him. 'One minute my sexy seductress is doing incredible things to me right here on this couch. The next minute a harmless feather is making her tremble as if it's a loaded gun!'

'Oh, Gustav, that's exactly what it is. I wish I didn't have to tell you this, but—' I finally manage to open the door. 'I know the bastard who sent it!'

I realise I was wrong about those furtive footsteps I heard on the pavement a few minutes ago. I knew that more than one person was watching as I straddled Gustav, lowered myself slowly on to his hardness, dangling my bare breasts to brush against his lips. There were several people watching as I took charge, and that turned me on all the more.

So when a sleek grey Porsche parked up, I didn't halt my sexy display. I guessed the person getting out of the car to join the fun was simply the attractive girl I'd spotted earlier when I took a chilly evening stroll along the High Line. I'd

4

been surveying the surrounding apartments through my zoom lens, in my customary sniper's style, and her dark-skinned, curvaceous figure had caught my eye as she rose naked from a rumpled bed.

So when I glimpsed a black belted trench coat and beret getting out of the car and joining the crowd, I reckoned she was simply returning the compliment and had diverted her journey to watch *me* in action, watch *me* playing with my lover. I was even tickled that we shared a taste in outfits. I wanted her to stay, to breathe a little quicker as I started to rock and ride my lover just as I had watched her riding hers.

Because, you see, I like to watch, but since I arrived with Gustav in New York and started taking on more outrageous commissions, sometimes joining in, I've discovered I like to *be* watched, too. Sometimes I like to be the voyeur, viewed.

The clatter of the letter box didn't distract me as Gustav and I shared our climax with our audience. I wasn't fazed by the gunning of the engine as the woman pattered back to the sports car and it pulled away from the kerb.

Now I know that she wasn't acting alone.

'What bastard? Who are you talking about?' Gustav tries to stop me dashing outside. 'There were several people watching us out there. You didn't care then. Why are you so worked up now?'

'He couldn't man up and do it himself. He didn't want us to spot him so he got someone else to do his dirty work. He was waiting in the car.' I slip out of his grasp. 'He must have shifted into the driver's seat after she got out.'

'Who?'

I spin round like a dog trying to find a comfortable sleeping place.

'That's just it. I thought I knew who the woman was, but she's just some sidekick he persuaded to dress up like me and then deliver his bloody feather.'

5

'Serena, you sound like a demented Miss Marple! The woman in the coat was just a passer-by who got an eyeful.' Gustav steps into the cold to try to get hold of me. 'I meant, who is this bastard you keep harping on about?'

Normally I would love the idea of Gustav being so wrapped up in his pleasure that he was oblivious to the world around him. But this is no joke.

'He's probably still parked around here somewhere, watching us. Maybe he's laughing his head off. We have to find him, Gustav!'

I jam my beret more firmly on to my head and start to run in my lacy dress and my biker boots up the sidewalk towards the corner, where a set of overhanging traffic lights swings in the cold night breeze, permanently stuck on red.

Gustav is chasing after me. As I reach the corner I half turn. I don't want him to be with me when we locate the car. My foot catches and I stumble off the kerb. A truck blares its horn and swerves round me as I stagger into the road.

'Stop this nonsense, Serena! You got a death wish or something, charging at the traffic like that?' Gustav hauls me back to safety as the truck driver swears and gives us the finger. 'What do you mean, "He's probably nearby"?'

'I'm talking about your brother Pierre. That feather is from him! And it's more than a message. It's a warning!' I twist away to peer up each street radiating from the intersection, but all I can see are a couple of yellow cabs cruising for fares in the distance. 'He wants to tell you something terrible about me.'

I start to shiver violently. Gustav wraps his arms around me and guides me back towards the gallery. The open door is swinging and banging against the wall in the sudden sharp wind.

'My brother's in LA, you silly thing.' Gustav pulls me into

the porch. 'He's creative director of that pilot they're shooting. It's the breakthrough he's been waiting for!'

'How do you know he's there?'

'Wild horses wouldn't drag him back to the East Coast. He promised to prove himself to me within six months, and that's exactly what he's doing. He's progressed from sourcing costumes and props for fashion shoots to designing stage sets and directing theatre productions. He was already pretty cocky, sure, that's why he had all the cast and crew calling him "boss" during that burlesque production you recorded at the Gramercy Theatre. But now he's hitting the big time, and the best bit is that you were part of its inception. It's your material that was used for the pilot's original pitch.'

I stand limply against Gustav and close my eyes. Only a heartless bitch would want to quash his joy at sharing in his brother's life again after a five-year estrangement. So how do I tell him that I'm here not to praise Pierre, but to bury him?

'I know it sounds crazy, Gustav, but you have to listen to me. Pierre's not the paragon you think he is.'

'None of us are.' Gustav ruffles my hair. 'I know he's a rogue and he treats women like dirt. He's young and still has a lot to learn. But he's determined to better himself, and I'm proud of him.'

'Maybe that's why you can't spot all the shit-stirring.' I sigh and turn away to hide the redness in my cheeks. 'He thought you and I had broken up after that showdown in February, when Polly went berserk and showed you those awful photos of us apparently kissing. Pierre tried, and failed, to take me for himself. Then when I warned him on the phone earlier to back off, he declared that if I don't want him in my life then it's up to me to leave. I hung up on him. But the feather was already on its way as evidence to ruin me.'

'Evidence of what? Why would he risk everything, just when it's going so brilliantly for all of us? He's got the job of his dreams. I've got you. We're getting married. There's such a rosy future ahead of us.' Gustav combs my hair away from my sweaty brow. His quiet voice almost calms me down. 'It's thanks to you that Pierre and I are close again. You kept us talking when it looked as if we would never get over the past. He and I are done with hurling insults, Serena. Pierre's not playing any more games.'

'Isn't he?'

'No. If there's something bothering him he'd come out with it. I can't believe he would bugger about with enigmatic feathers!'

'There's nothing enigmatic about it. He's always one step ahead, don't you see? I don't want to keep anything from you. I'm trying to be honest, but I'm scared. Oh, God, Gustav. I'm so scared!' I try to pull away again, my voice splintering into sobs. 'I know that horrible feather is from him, because Pierre was wearing it in Venice!'

'I'm not talking about this out here. It's bloody freezing.' Gustav stops. The street lamp casts shadows over his face as he looks down at me. His black eyes glitter like moonlight on a deep pool. 'What did you just say?'

This is how he looked on Halloween night last year, when he stepped out of the darkness of that London square and into my life. There was something vampirical about him, the black bristles trying to push through his white skin, the sharp bite of his teeth into his lower lip when he was concentrating. He already seemed to know me inside out. But instead of scaring me that night, he thrilled me. And he has been thrilling me ever since.

I try to flatten myself against the wall.

'Pierre was in Venice last month. He was at the Weinmeyers' ball. He was wearing a tricorn hat, and in that hat—'

8

'Was a peacock feather that is working some serious voodoo on you!' Gustav shakes his head. 'He wasn't there, Serena. You were the one adorned with peacock feathers, not him. I found you all bedraggled and lost on that bridge, remember, trying to find your way home?'

I nod wearily. 'In every sense of the word.'

Gustav's smile is fading. 'I'd flown all the way from New York to surprise you. I was cursing myself for being so quick to believe your cousin. Of course you'd never go kissing my brother behind my back. But you'd flown off to Venice all on your own and I was desperate to find you.'

The weight of what's to come might break me. 'You were too late. You should have been there the whole time. Then none of it would have happened. You were too late.'

Gustav pushes his hair out of his eyes.

'No, no, no. Nothing awful *did* happen, darling. My flight was delayed, and to make matters worse Pierre called me when I landed at Marco Polo airport and kept me talking, and that's why I never made it to the ball. But I wasn't too late. I was just in time to persuade you to forgive me. And best of all, Venice will forever be the most special city in the world. We've even named this gallery after it. Because that's where you agreed to become my wife!'

Gustav's smile flits across his mouth again. He's remembering how he extracted the diamond ring that had been nestling inside the golden locket around my throat, got down on one knee and asked me to change my name to Levi.

'Hear me out, darling. Just listen. Before you found me on that bridge' – I clasp my hands together in a kind of prayer under my chin – 'Pierre made me do something terrible!'

He opens his arms and I walk into them.

'You're rambling now. Pierre has nothing to do with this. The peacock headdress was part of *your* costume, darling.

We tossed all the feathers into the lagoon outside the Danieli Hotel.'

Oh, I love him so much. But his soft voice is already losing its hypnotic power.

'You're going to hate me, Gustav, but – Pierre *was* already in Venice when he called and kept you talking. You can be anywhere in the world when you're on a mobile phone, can't you? He knew we'd had that row about Polly's photographs. He'd *caused* it, for God's sake. He even came to you at the apartment after I'd fled, and fessed up.' The wall behind me feels as if it's shifting and breaking apart. 'It was no secret that I was booked to go to Venice for the Carnivale. He orchestrated everything. Stopped you getting to the ball, instructed the costume lady to hire me the correct green velvet dress so that we would be a matching pair. He even planned the peacock feathers to identify me amongst all those masks. I had five feathers in my hair. He had one, in his hat. *This* one.'

'Honey, this is gibberish.' Gustav lets the feather drop on to the doorstep of the gallery and cages my face in the grip of his fingers. 'Pierre was nowhere near you. He was in LA. He's there now!'

'He's not in LA, Gustav. He's right here in Manhattan. I'm certain of it.'

Hot tears of shame and fear blind me, but instead of asking any more questions Gustav nods to himself, as if that's settled. He reckons I'm definitely unhinged. He pushes me back inside the gallery. My newly hung collection of Venetian photographs, the elegant bridges arching over khaki water, the deathlike masks processing in the distance, are obscured by the darkness. He doesn't turn on the lights. Nor does he sit down on the couch where we were lying together just now.

He walks over to the desk and picks up our coats. He has his back to me. He pauses, staring up at the only image that is illuminated, of the arched green shuttered window. A bright red row of geraniums are planted in a box below it, and a thin white hand is reaching into the flowers to pinch off a dead petal.

'I can't stand seeing you so worked up, darling.' Gustav turns over his phone. 'Let's ask the man himself.'

I galvanise myself. One more effort to make him understand.

'No! Gustav, listen to *me*, not him! Then you can never accuse me of concealing anything, and he won't be able to hold it over me.'

'Concealing *what*? Holding *what* over you? How has our wonderful evening, our gallery opening, our engagement, our dinner reservation, how has it all just imploded?' Gustav punches in the area code for Los Angeles. 'I want to know what Pierre has done to scare you like this.'

I grab the phone from him, prising his fingers off the casing. I pathetically hold it behind my back, as if I'm stronger than him.

'We're getting married, so there can't be any secrets or lies. The reason I was so bedraggled and my dress was torn when you found me on that bridge in Venice was because I was running away from him.' It's a hoarse whisper, but we can both hear it perfectly. 'He followed me. He tricked me into thinking he was you, Gustav. We danced together at the ball, and then we went outside—'

'Let me get this straight. Everyone at the ball was masked, weren't they? You must be mistaken. You think it was Pierre, I get that, but in fact someone else had their eye on you. Now you're frightening me, *cara*.' His black eyes are shadowed with a fresh anguish that I haven't seen for months. 'The man you went outside with was some chancer. My God, Serena. You were molested by a random stranger, and you've kept that from me ever since? That's why you were in such

11

a state when I found you. And that's why the peacock feather has sent you into hysterics!'

Gustav easily removes the phone from my fist, puts it down and eases my arms into the sleeves of my green leather jacket as calmly as he can before putting on his own coat. Then to my horror he picks up the discarded feather from the doorstep and bends it to fit inside his pocket.

'You may be listening, but you're not hearing me, Gustav! I wish it *was* a stranger who molested me!' I try to grab the feather out of his coat. 'Pierre Levi couldn't have been further from my mind. I assumed *you'd* come to get me, knowing Polly's stupid suspicions were a load of rubbish. I assumed *you* were the man in green velvet! I would never have gone off with him otherwise!'

Gustav pushes me back outside into the cold dark street and locks the gallery door. We stare at each other.

'Gone off with him?'

Different images are flickering through our minds, leaving scorch marks across the happy optimism of an hour ago.

Gustav is starting to see me with my arms around another man. A faceless, masked stranger. That's as far as his imagination stretches, for now, but in my mind, all too clearly, it is the reality. Exactly who I was with. Who was carrying me, a willing victim, through the shadows. Who was bundling me into a covered gondola so that we were alone and far from prying eyes.

Above all, I can see myself with Gustav's brother, falling with him into the cushions, ripping at each other's clothes. Turned on. Wet. And ready.

'Answer me, Serena. What did you mean when you said you'd "gone off with him"?'

Gustav presses redial and lifts the phone to his ear.

'We were dancing and I was calling your name, but then he – the man I thought was you – disappeared so I was running round outside the Palazzo Weinmeyer frantically searching, all the way to Piazza San Marco, thinking I'd lost you again!' I batter feebly at Gustav's arm, but he holds the phone away from me. 'Then you appeared again, the man with the feather, so I let him lead me away from all the chaos and noise. I peppered him with questions. He didn't speak, but I thought the silence was all part of your game. Then we were on the cushions – we were alone together in this gondola. That's when I realised it wasn't you and I ran away.'

Fear bubbles up, silencing me. Gustav is staring at me, but there's a familiar stony stillness in his face as he waits for Pierre to pick up.

Just then Dickson the Driver glides up to the kerb in the new navy blue Range Rover. I have never been so glad to see him.

'There must be some sort of explanation. Some mistake.' Gustav opens the passenger door for me, but his eyes are fixed on the middle distance, waiting for his brother to answer.

'Mistaken identity on my part, sure—'

'But if he *was* there, maybe on Pierre's part, too. Have you thought of that? He may have thought *you* were someone else! Christ, the way he goes through women he must have one in every port.'

'You're clutching at straws, Gustav. You can't trust him. He won't give you a straight answer.'

But what's the point? The battle lines are drawn once again. And what if he chooses to believe Pierre over me?

Then Pierre will have won, silly. The familiar internal commentary of my cousin Polly, silent for so long when we were estranged, murmurs once again in my ear. *You have to fight this tooth and nail.*

Gustav frowns when voicemail kicks in at the other end of the phone.

'I can't let this happen. The rug is being tugged out from

under us again, Serena, just when everything was looking so perfect.'

I reach out for him and run my hand down his anxious face. 'Gustav! Honey. Everything *is* perfect. I only told you all this because Pierre reckons he has something to impart, when really it's something and nothing. Nobody tugged any rugs.'

Rocked the boat, though, didn't they? Polly's commentary is in full swing now. *Ruffled some feathers!*

Gustav holds my hand against his chest and looks down at me. He's so serious. So pale.

'It's not long since your cousin was waving those photos of you and Pierre under my nose, Serena. I know I was too quick to anger that time, and I've said I'm sorry, but surely you can see how badly this affects me? I need to see Pierre. He set me straight about Polly's photographs and I need him to do it again. I won't rest until I hear his version of this Venice business. It's only fair.'

Gustav cuts off the phone without leaving a message and places me firmly into the car as if he's a cop and I might make a run for it. Dickson starts the car and we move smoothly away from the gallery. Why do I feel like the condemned woman?

'No, it's *not* fair. I'm your fiancée and I've told you what happened. He's your lying brother. You can't believe a single word that comes out of his mouth!' I snap the seatbelt so fast that the metal takes a bite out of my finger. 'Let me count the ways. He ran away with your wife and didn't speak to you for five years. He came back into your life with all these accusations. He strung Polly along and then dumped her. He told you he wanted to forgive and forget, then he kissed me and tried to steal me from you. Now he's suggested I leave you. You should be listening to me, Gustav. You need to believe *me!*'

Gustav turns to me, takes me by the shoulders and gives me a little shake. His black eyes bore into mine until they blur and go out of focus.

'I *am* listening to you, Serena. I will always listen to you, so long as you're telling me the truth.' His lips are pressed hard in my hair, but he's not entirely with me. 'Pierre deserves the chance to explain himself, too. So if he sent this feather as you say, and he's not in LA – as you also say – then we can do this face to face. And I know exactly where to find him.'

CHAPTER TWO

The diagonal journey across Manhattan is like a parody of a car chase. We are in a rush to find Pierre, yet the evening traffic is against us and we are crawling rather than careering. The set of Dickson's broad shoulders as he steers skilfully through the one-way grid system would normally make me feel safe and secure. But the atmosphere in the car is too tense.

Gustav keeps trying his brother's number. I pray with all my might that Pierre is nowhere to be found, because he's the one Gustav will listen to next. I've told him we sneaked off together, and then I realised my mistake and ran away, but how can I tell my fiancé how perilously close Pierre and I were to shattering everything?

Pierre won't hold back. Oh no. He'll rehearse every gory detail. The ripped muslin drawers, the velvet buttons flipping open his velvet breeches, my legs pulling him towards me as I urged him to hurry, the rope he tied round my wrist to keep me there. He won't tell Gustav how I stopped him. He'll put his own spin on it and say we went the whole way. He'll convince Gustav that we've committed the worst possible deception.

16

We pass Katz's Deli where Sally faked her orgasm in front of Harry – God, if only life was so simple – and cross over Rivington Street.

I can't work out where we are. According to Polly, when she did some digging to find out more about him, Pierre lives in an apartment still owned by Gustav's ex-wife Margot. But Polly said it was in Soho, not the Lower East Side, which is where we are now. It's an area I've never been into, and after the almost eerie quiet of the Meatpacking District late at night, this place is still humming with neon-lit stores and cafés. Dickson drives behind the main drag and pulls round into a narrower street. The engine of the car sounds intrusive and loud bouncing off the tall, looming tenement buildings, where iron fire-escapes zig-zag across the red brick walls above the back entrances of bars and restaurants.

Polly was wrong. After all, she has never been here. Pierre never invited her to stay, even when, for those intense few months over the winter, they were lovers. Dickson, however, knows exactly where he's heading. This might be Pierre's apartment now, but Dickson must have driven here plenty of times in the past when someone else was in residence. When he had that other passenger in his car.

'I hoped I'd never come to this godforsaken place again. Despite what Polly thinks she deduced, Margot has no hold over Pierre any more. She walked out of that apartment and out of his life six years ago, so the fact that he's been living there all this time means he's even more boneheaded than I thought,' mutters Gustav half to himself as the car stops. He steps out into the cold night air and shudders as if someone has just thrown a bucket of iced water over him. 'I guess staying there rent-free swung it for him. But I should have sold it when I had the chance rather than let Margot keep it.'

There's the clatter of cutlery and barked orders from the

surrounding restaurant kitchens. The primaeval heartbeat of club music thumps up from somewhere underground. But this street has a dark silence all of its own. It reminds me of the ghetto area of Venice where I wandered with my camera last month, thinking of Gustav. Thinking of Manhattan. Thinking it was all over between us.

The city noises clang and echo in my ears. The tall buildings in this narrow dark street are bending over, intent on crushing us. My fiancé turns his back on me, still clutching his mobile phone, and glares up at the mostly unlit windows in the building above.

I can no longer escape the series of disasters that has brought us to this narrow dark street. Maybe to the metaphorical end of the road.

The reason Polly had the incriminating photographs of me and Pierre which so infuriated Gustav was that she had been stalking us. The reunion of her boyfriend with his brother Gustav meant that when Pierre dumped her for no apparent reason after the New Year, Polly thought I could help her. So when Pierre commissioned me to shoot a storyboard at the theatre where he was working, that seemed like the perfect opportunity. Polly asked me to find out what was going on in Pierre's head and ask him if he would take her back.

But instead of trusting me to carry out my mission, she decided to spy on Pierre and me in the Gramercy Hotel bar. And if she'd heard how graphic the conversation became she would have pounced on us sooner.

When I interrogated him about my poor cousin, Pierre decided not only to share but to shock. He laid out his entire sexual history in intimate detail. I was given chapter and verse about the volcanic sex he and Gustav's ex-wife Margot indulged in after they had run away together, and how ultimately it destroyed him, because when she chewed him up and spat him out six months later, he realised no other woman would ever match up.

He had spent five years searching for the perfect specimen. Polly looked promising when they met at a magazine shoot. She was sexier than most, prettier, funnier, and English like him. They even shared a flair for fashion and style. But in the end, despite her connection with me and Gustav, she was the latest in a long line of casualties. Women who would never satisfy him.

Except that then, fired up by my slightly drunken attention, Pierre hinted that someone new might have come close. Me. He helped me into my coat as I prepared to leave, and knowing I was flummoxed by his insinuations he ran his lips across my mouth, and that's what my cousin saw.

So Polly took this as hard evidence that *I* was the reason Pierre had dumped her. His own damaged psyche was too complex to grasp. And when she stormed into our apartment, Gustav chose to believe a couple of grainy photographs over my emphatic professions of innocence.

That was the night my world caved in. Polly thought I'd gone behind her back with the boyfriend she still wanted. Gustav thought I'd been unfaithful with his own newly returned brother. I was incandescent that the pair of them could have so little faith.

So I went alone to Venice. Vulnerable. Broken-hearted. The perfect target for Pierre Levi. He came after me, impersonated his brother and got within an inch of penetrating me.

But I need to focus on what's happening now.

I follow Gustav towards the apartment block, but before I reach him I see that parked outside the entrance is a sleek grey Porsche.

'Let's go home, Gustav. Better still, let's get that table you booked at La Lanterna before it goes to someone else. We've got plans to make! We can just walk away, and you and Pierre can carry on as you were. He got it wrong, that's all. He'll be like a cornered animal if we go storming in there. He'll lash out.' I tug on Gustav's sleeve, aware that I'm mewling like a kicked kitten. 'You won, and he lost! Think how embarrassed he'll be!'

Gustav stares at the apartment building, his arm hanging by his side. 'Embarrassment won't cut it! He could try shame. Remorse, if it's true that he tried to take advantage of you. Sorrow, for upsetting and confusing you like this. And as for winning and losing? Serena, this isn't a competition!'

'It is to him, Gustav! That's just it! He's desperate to be your little brother again, but he also wants whatever you've got! That's how it's always been. He wanted, and took, Margot—'

'She stole *him*, you mean. She knew exactly how to hurt me the most. He may have been a willing participant, but he was still a kid.' Gustav's face is set in a series of hard lines as he takes another step across the pavement. 'Going after my girlfriend six years later is totally different.'

Yet again I regret saying anything. I slide my hand up to his face, lay it on his cheek. I can feel the muscles flickering with tension around his clenched jaw.

'We can drop this now. What's important is that you and he have made up. You're brothers. So he's jealous. He looks up to you. He wants what you have. Gustav, you've both worked so hard to get back to where you were. Don't spoil it.'

'He's the one who's spoiling it. Just when my life was settled again. Just when I wanted to sit down and start thinking of where and when we might get married. Why does he never learn? Why did he have to mess with you, of all people? Why does he have to trample all over other people's happiness like that? He had his own chance of romantic bliss with your poor cousin, and he blew it. He can't have you. No one else will *ever* have you!'

We stare at each other out there in the street. The possessive words thrill me, but the new rage in his voice terrifies me, too.

'I thought you were angry with me, Gustav. But if you're not, let's just – let's just get away from here.'

'I'm angry with everyone and everything at the moment. You think your life is finally on track – lovely girl, successful businesses, brotherly love restored, rosy future – and then a feather, of all things, wafts in out of nowhere and turns it all upside down. What you've said, or tried to say, has really shaken me up.' He takes my hand and pulls me after him. 'But it's Pierre who has crossed a line.'

As we pass the Porsche, I touch the bonnet. The metal is still hot.

Gustav pushes open the big glass-panelled front door of the apartment building. We step out of the dark street into an even darker hallway. But there's a certain faded grandeur to it, with high ceilings and period cornices. The wall-mounted lights flicker and crackle, making it even gloomier.

I try once more to stop this.

'Pierre can't help himself. Margot fatally corrupted him. I was a juicy challenge, just because I'm female. He was arrogant, and I was stupid. Darling, I'm so sorry. Your relationship with Pierre will survive this. No harm's done. He'll be hunting some other woman by now.'

Pierre's boast comes back to me. *Anything with a pulse and a pussy will do.*

'You're not "some other woman". You're *my* woman.' Gustav pulls me roughly towards him and kisses me. 'Thank God he didn't get what he wanted. But if I let it go, all that communication closes off again. Don't you see? He needs to know he can't shit on me.'

Our footsteps ring on the hard floor as we walk to the bottom of the stairs. I peer down. I can just make out the Victorian-style geometric pattern of terracotta blue and white mosaic tiles. Gustav takes the first stair then changes his mind, doubles back and calls the lift instead.

Panic rises like boiling milk inside me. 'That feather, Gustav. Maybe it's not a taunt, or a threat. Maybe it's an admission of defeat.' I hop from foot to foot as he punches the buttons on the old-fashioned lift. We hear the thick metallic clunk far above our heads. 'His way of apologising?'

'You're not going to deflect me from this conversation, Serena. Pierre and I spent five years not speaking to each other, letting the misunderstandings fester. If we get this out in the open, especially with you here as well, we can clear the air. It's the only way.'

Gustav puts his arm round me to usher me into the lift and closes the squeaking scissor gates. The lift creaks upwards, passing landing after deserted landing until we reach the top.

'At least ring the doorbell to warn him,' I whisper, though the building is silent as the grave. 'We can't just turn up unannounced!'

'Watch me.' Gustav shakes out a key and shoves it into the door with a decisive rasp. 'You know perfectly well that I deal best in situations where I have the advantage.'

'We know you're here, Pierre!' I call out as the door swings stickily open. I'm still clinging on to the last vestiges of hope that a couple of seconds' warning will keep him on my side.

There is no answer. Gustav pushes away from me into the warm, musky darkness.

So this is the love nest.

I hover by the door, waiting for Pierre to show himself.

I fear that instead of admitting to Gustav that he tried to seduce me, and that in any case I rebuffed him, he'll stand there, gloating over the feather and all the havoc it's caused. How he danced with me in Venice. How eager I was. How far he got. How far he wanted to go.

I feel the sour draught from the stairwell licking across my face as I wait in the dark entrance of the flat. I'm a trespasser. If I go inside, the rip tide will suck me back to that night. How can I ever explain my dirty excitement, how I relished the roughness of this strange, silent *faux* Gustav, how I lifted my skirts for him, opened my legs, his breeches open to display the extent of his excitement, that peacock feather dancing above my head, how I was begging for it, oh, how close we came to destroying everything?

Gustav is crashing about somewhere in the flat. I venture inside and feel my way down a hallway. An internal door gives as I fall against it, and a light switches on.

I'm standing in a black-painted bedroom strewn with clothes and shoes and belts, as if someone has just upended a suitcase. There are no pictures on the walls. Only a series of red-lacquer-framed mirrors. The ceiling is also totally mirrored. A black-painted carved bed dominates the space. It's unmade, with scarlet pillows dented and punched and scarlet satin covers slipping off the mattress as if someone has just woken up and thrown them back. Hanging off the posts are handcuffs, whips, long chiffon scarves, executioner-style leather masks and muzzles as well as bejewelled and feathered Venetian masks.

There's a scent in the air, but it's not Pierre's heavy, headachy scent, which I would know anywhere. It's floral, with an exotic eastern tang of lemongrass and something else. The nostril-pricking aroma of female excitement. Gustav will be able to smell it, too. Maybe even recognise it.

I stare at the bed and remember what Pierre told me

23

about this very room. As we sipped those strong fig cocktails in the Gramercy Hotel, he described the scene nearly six years ago when Gustav found his wife sitting on his brother's face – just as she had threatened to do if Gustav ever crossed her – and threw them both out. After a few days in a London hotel, Pierre and Margot had come to New York and lived in this flat. She had kept him here for six months, tied most of the time to this very bed.

A draught of cold air rushes over my face. The thick curtains billow and I cross the carpet strewn with discarded underwear and stockings. But as I lean out to shut the window, the night air clutches at me. The hot, cluttered room behind me is shoving at my back, urging me to plunge into the dirty alleyway below.

Don't be ridiculous. Polly's in my head again. *It's not haunted. It's just a bachelor bedroom done out with a taste-less penchant for Chinese brothel motifs. Which is odd, given Pierre's a designer—*

Well, it feels haunted to me. I close the window and lean my forehead on the glass. I miss Polly. I wish she was right here, like when we were kids, telling me what to do next.

There's a tiny creaking sound. The door to the double wardrobe, painted in shiny red lacquer, is half open. I go to push it shut, but an internal light flicks on.

I expect to see a jumble of Pierre's trademark leather jackets and jeans hanging there, but instead there's a rail of immaculate men's shirts, arranged through the colour spectrum from jaunty pink through deep blue to snowy white. Each sleeve has a sharply ironed crease and is buttoned to the neck.

The clean laundry smell of starch contrasts with the slut-tish mess and manky scent of the rest of the room. The shirts sway under my fingers on their smooth wooden hangers. The last one is a white dress shirt, such as you

24

would wear for a wedding, and as I separate it from the others I see that a silver grey cravat is tied round the wing collar, fastened with a simple silver pin.

It glistens in the light dancing from the tasselled lampshade above my head. I can't resist pulling the shirt closer to look at the tiepin.

This doesn't belong to Pierre. Because engraved on it are the entwined initials GL.

'My brother has obviously moved some of his dancers in here. Two or three, judging by all this paraphernalia. So it's group sex he's into now!' Gustav calls from up the hall. 'None of his stuff is in evidence, but there's knickers, make-up, theatrical costumes everywhere. The place is a tip.'

Where have I seen those initials before? I know they stand for Gustav Levi, but where have I seen that style of engraving? I turn the pin over, and a cold hand claws at my heart.

Across the back is the tiny inscription *M and G. Forever.*

Gustav is in the corridor, muttering something about a wasted journey, but I can't move. This is the loving inscription from a bride to a groom, promising permanence. Encapsulated in those curly silver words is their relationship, their marriage, their life. When he was *her* groom. Not mine.

Everything Gustav has told me about her, the things Pierre told me about Margot and what she did to him with her whips and handcuffs; it all comes back to me. Those deep voices merging with story after story, trapping me in this overheated, over-furnished, stinking reminder of Margot Levi and the sexual power she had over both the Levi brothers.

When she had reduced Gustav to a debauched, diminished figure after five abusive years of marriage, Margot took Pierre. Her willing, besotted prisoner. She was the cougar. He was nineteen, easy meat. He'd lusted after her all the time she was married to his brother, fantasised about her when he heard them moaning in the night, and when at last he had her to himself, he probably thought it was for ever too.

PL and GL.

I let the shirt nestle back softly against its fellows and close the cupboard. I step backwards and fall back on to the bed. Margot was insatiable, Pierre told me. She couldn't get enough of him. She would straddle him, or get him to take her from behind, several times a day, tying him, whipping him, drugging him either with dope to make him hornier or Viagra to make him harder, teaching him everything she knew about her world of punishment and pain, the world she once shared with Gustav.

GL.

Pierre couldn't resist tormenting me with the notion that Margot's particular brand of poison still flowed in Gustav's veins, too. That after living with, and being married to, a mesmerising, demanding dominatrix like her, no woman would ever be enough for him.

The woman they both loved once writhed on this bed. I can see her black hair twisting like wire, the nodules of her spine flexing as she knelt up, impaling herself on the hard length of her sex slave. GL, or PL.

It's the same image that tortured me in the chalet in Lugano where Gustav took me last winter. I blundered into Margot's boudoir, thinking it had been cleared, but her stuff was everywhere. Her leather basque and boots invited me to try them on. Her collection of whips hung on their hooks, ready to deliver punishment. In my confusion that day I thought I might become stronger by dressing myself up in Margot's clothes and in a way I did because, although Gustav went mad with anger when he found me, the anger turned, very quickly, into lust, and that's the night when he first fucked me.

I know where I've seen those initials before. I yank open

26

the wardrobe again. The same style of engraving was on the silver cufflink I found in the master bathroom in Lugano. Gustav declared that a cufflink without its pair was worse than useless. He told me that he had disposed of it, along with every other gift from Margot.

I snatch at the sleeve of the white dress shirt. One cuff is unfolded and bare. Fastened in the other is the missing link.

This place feels like a shrine to the unholy trinity of GL, PL and M. And I don't belong.

I used to feel excluded like this as a child. Every day I came home from school to be ignored by unloving parents, knowing that in other families my friends were being welcomed into warm homes full of light and food. All I could do was stand in the darkness outside.

But I'm an adult now. I'm going to marry Gustav. I'm supposed to be in control.

'Why is Pierre storing your shirts here?' I slam the cupboard shut. 'Your *wedding* shirt, for God's sake?'

There's no sound. Not even from the street outside. Nothing, then the creak of floorboards. I peer down the dark red painted corridor.

'Pierre's not at home, Gustav. This feels all wrong. Let's just get out of here.'

Still he doesn't answer. But the peacock feather that was in his pocket floats through the air from the room opposite the front door and drops to the floor.

'I've been counting the days till you were in my boudoir again instead of that freeloading brother of yours. Or should I say *our* boudoir? Cat got your tongue, Gusty? I always did have that effect on you!'

A woman's throaty voice, perforating the silence. The accent has a Germanic rasp and she pronounces his name 'Goostie'.

A pair of spike-heeled red sandals steps through the open front door. The brief hope that they are attached to a harmless young dancer flickers and dies. A dancer wouldn't be able to afford Jimmy Choo.

I'm about to meet the third member of the triumvirate. My legs give way beneath me and I crumple in the doorway.

The pointed toes stop right in front of me. She is wearing red stockings with a silky sheen. They crease very slightly as she lifts her foot.

'You like the shoes? Sexy as hell, aren't they? A little fetish, no? Gustav gave me these, when we got engaged.'

One pointed toe hooks itself under my chin.

'Stand up straight.' The voice segues from a croon to a snarl. 'Slouching there like a slut.'

My face is levered upwards, leading my eyes up the long, skinny legs, past the red stocking tops and under a black trench coat where I catch a glimpse of a bare, waxed snatch glowing white in the shadows.

Margot Levi stamps her foot back on the floor. She puts her hands on her hips in an aggressive, questioning gesture as she swivels to face Gustav who is now standing in the corridor behind her.

He takes an unsteady step nearer. 'Don't you dare speak to Serena like that!'

She throws her head back and laughs. It's a deep, rattling sound which seems to suck the breath out of her.

'Still so angry and masterful, Levi. You used to leap to my defence in just that way!' Margot points at me. 'She too pathetic to stand up for herself? No, don't answer that. I can see she's just out of nappies! God, you two have goaded me for long enough.'

She is wearing a black beret just like mine. She pulls it off and tosses it with perfect aim on to a coat hook. Her black hair is plaited into cornrows, which she quickly coils into a bundle at the back of her head. A collection of dreadlocks falls over and conceals one side of her face, but the slanted black eyes glitter through the screen of hair. The cheekbones are still razor sharp and painted with the same theatrical matt white foundation she wore the first time I set eyes on her.

Margot has been creeping round the edges of our lives for weeks. Pierre made out I was going mad, but I'm certain now that she was dancing with him at the burlesque theatre the day I did the commission.

She tips her head sideways, the better to study me, and slowly starts to unbutton her coat.

Why on earth did I think I could avoid Margot for ever? I've seen her face repeated a hundred times over in the sketches that lined the walls in Lugano. I've seen her in a video she uploaded when I stupidly left my iPad at the theatre after that same shoot. She filmed herself holding a wedding bouquet of edelweiss, those almond-shaped eyes blinking flirtatiously.

This is for you, Gustav darling. Remember these pretty bridal flowers? Remember this wedding music? Remember me?

And it was her I saw at the Weinmeyers' Venetian ball, dressed all in white with a gold mask, watching me. Watching Pierre as he pranced about in green velvet and peacock feathers and came to claim me.

'No greeting for the love of your life, Gusty?' she demands, pulling the black trench coat off her shoulders. She's not topless underneath, thank God, but wearing a scarlet, sheer, see-through blouse and a red leather skirt.

'You wouldn't know true love if it took you up the arse!' Gustav growls in a voice I don't recognise, slamming her against the wall as he pushes past her. 'I'd hoped I'd never breathe the same air as you again.'

He pulls me against his chest. I can hear his heart drumming crazily. Despite those ugly words, I realise he's not just trying to protect me. I'm a shield protecting *him*.

'Ah, my love, you have no idea. You see, we've been sharing the same air for months now. I know for instance that you have a silly flag hanging from that telescope on top of your apartment building. I know you kiss goodbye at the corner of the Dakota building every morning when you go your separate ways to work. Touching.' Margot lets out a harsh sigh. 'And when I'm not watching, I'm eavesdropping. Because my minion planted a bug in your apartment on New Year's Eve, oh, and another in your gallery when the builders were in there. You're going to be late for that reservation at La Lanterna, by the way!'

'Go back to your desert island, Margot. Get out before I do something we both regret.'

His words hiss out, half-smothered in my hair.

'Oh, Gustav. What's happened to you? You never used to scare so easily.' She laughs quietly behind us. 'I'm not here to harm you. Why would I? I adore you! We were bound to come together again eventually. And you know how beautiful it is when we come together.'

The floorboards creak. The front door slams shut. Gustav groans and holds me so tight I can't breathe.

And then Margot must have moved into another room, because music starts to play. Edith Piaf warbles in an old, scratchy recording from what must be the sitting room. Heavy curtains rattle shut across the window, the metal rings jostling and clattering. The French sparrow declares, quietly at first, then louder as the dial cranks up the volume, that she regrets nothing.

'As for ordering me out? Impossible, I'm afraid, since this is my property, acquired from you in that very generous divorce settlement.' There's the pop of a cork being drawn

30

from a bottle and the heavy chink of crystal glasses. 'Oh, by the way, Gusty, did you like the peacock feather? My little visual joke? I went to all the trouble of posting it myself, even though your little tart was, ah, distracting you at the time.'

Gustav lets go of me and marches stiffly into the next room. 'And?'

'And it worked! You're here, aren't you? My pet, come to heel. And it's not just any feather, my love. It's the feather in your little brother's cap.'

I hurry after him, dreading what she's going to say next. 'So if Pierre didn't send it, how did *you* get hold of it?'

Margot has arranged herself like a queen on an oversized armchair upholstered in purple brocade. She is brushing the feather against her face. She turns briefly in my direction, glancing at my breasts, then turns back to Gustav.

'I came here straight from Venice. There was no sign of Pierre or any of his things, but I found this feather. Lovingly arranged in that vase.'

We all look at a delicate flute on the mantelpiece, twisting and turning in waves like a whirlpool. It's hideously ugly, veined with rainbow colours, but I recognise it as Murano glass.

'So where is he?' Gustav has reached her side of the room and stands over the big chair, the gas flames licking greedily at his legs.

'My little puppet?' Margot waggles her fingers like a clown. 'I couldn't care less.'

Everything about her, the white face, the red slash of lipstick, the cruel amusement, the ironic musical backing track, is reminiscent of The Joker. Neither Gustav nor I can speak.

'He's served his purpose. Six years ago he helped me humiliate you, Gustav, and now he's helped me again.' Margot's eyes slither in my direction but fix on the golden locket, not my face. 'All it took was a call from me supposedly out of the blue last autumn, when I heard this ginger-haired tramp was worming her way into your life and into your wallet. He was shocked and pretty hostile at first. We'd both abandoned him, after all. But once I applied the soft pedal and promised that I was a changed woman, that it wasn't him I wanted, that I was simply heartbroken after six years without *you*, Gusty, he was ready to listen. He told me he was leading a normal life, chasing normal women, but that's pure bravado. It was only a matter of time before he was crawling between my legs for an encore. Anyway, the breakthrough was when I told him I knew where to find you. He admitted he missed you desperately but hadn't the bottle to start searching, and that was my cue. I convinced him that this little tart was in the way and he would never get close to you without my help.'

Every word sounds as if she's spitting pips.

'How did this work?' demands Gustav. 'The mechanics of it, I mean?'

I stare at him. 'Don't give her the oxygen, Gustav!'

She cuts through me. 'Night and day I've been texting Pierre. The bird on his shoulder. The voice in his ear. I had to keep reminding him whose idea it was to broker this reconciliation; I had to keep him on your tail. I was his prompt, suggesting what to do and say. Right through Christmas. Even on New Year's Eve, when he was in your apartment. Those initial bitter exchanges between the two of you came mostly from him, I might add. His way of saving face, I suppose. He was desperate to get close to you again, but making amends doesn't come easily to him. He had to air his own myriad grievances before you could be brothers again. I'd forgotten how petulant he could be. All *I* wanted was for him to get rid of *her*, but oh dear. Look. She's still here. The bare-legged waif and stray.'

She stops. There's a pause between music tracks, no sound except the hiss of the gas fire. I want Gustav to look at me, but his eyes are fixed on Margot.

She points the feather at me, but her eyes are on him.

'Six years is long enough without you, Gusty. The idea was for Pierre to get back in touch with you, pave the way, deal with this thorn in the flesh, and then I would step in. He could be part of our future or not, whatever he chose.'

'So you and Pierre are not together?'

'We never really were. Not six years ago. Not now. You're the only one for me, Gustav. Oh, I promised him some sexy fun when I contacted him again, so long as he played ball the way I wanted it, but that only worked the first couple of times. Enough to reel him in, but he was faltering almost from the start. He wasn't even grateful that I'd helped him find you. It proved quite traumatic seeing you again and he went on the offensive. That aggression, those fights! He could have blown the reconciliation completely. Then it came together too quickly, and this redhead runt – she's different from the others. He wanted her. I told him he had to keep his prick in his pants, at least until I'd got you safely back, Gusty, so Pierre came up with the rather brilliant idea, at least in theory, of wheeling his randy friend Tomas into the mix to deflect any mischief away from himself.'

She pauses, separating the strands of the feather with a long fingernail while the words sink in.

'Tomas?' repeats Gustav, making the connection just as I fear he will. 'I know that name. Serena? Who is he?'

'No one important.' I feel myself blushing scarlet but there's no way out of this one. 'Tomas is the guy who – he's the guy you saw at the Club Crème. Who participated in that stupid striptease I did after I'd photographed the stags' night. Then he went and told Pierre all about it.'

Tomas, who had come on to me back at Pierre's Halloween

party. Whom I rejected. And now I know why Pierre and Polly kept going on about him at New Year, suggesting he join us in a foursome when Gustav's flight home from Lugano was delayed.

I swallow and glance up. Gustav doesn't seem to be listening. He is watching Margot as if she's a praying mantis.

'That's the one. Cute. Blonde curls. He carried out his first task at the Club Crème willingly enough. It could have worked, except Pierre was too jealous and told Tomas he wasn't needed any more.' Margot sighs. 'Your brother was no good. He kept stalling. He became agitated around this little tramp, so I had to keep him sweet in my own inimitable way. I've still got it, Gusty. I was thinking of you the whole time he was in my bed. You remember my bondage trick with the blindfold and the horsewhip? But even while I was pleasuring him, he was harping on and on about how he liked your little tart. He didn't want to hurt anyone. He felt bad about what he was doing. You and she were the real deal, he said!'

'And so we are,' says Gustav in a very low voice. 'Pierre's absolutely right.'

'Touching. Nauseatingly so,' Margot mocks. 'But where the brotherly love thing gets so biblical and amusing is that he couldn't stop thinking about her. He liked your little redhead *way* too much. So you see, however close you boys become, a woman will always drive a wedge. Women are Pierre Levi's drug. His downfall. The more *verboten* she is the better. A lesson learned at my knee, of course. That's why on New Year's Eve he came rushing over here from your happy little reunion at the apartment, telling me he wasn't happy with the plan, or indeed with me for dreaming it up, but then within ten minutes he was tied to the bed next door with his bottom in the air. He just can't say no.'

'Even so. He knew where his loyalties lay. Your plan didn't work, Margot. Nothing will work.' Gustav snorts. 'You can stir that cauldron all you like. But it's a total waste of time.'

'I was beginning to think I would have to bring down the house of cards myself, certainly. And then what do you know? Paranoid Polly comes up with those photographs!' Margot claps her hands gleefully, making me jump. 'Hilarious! You all started falling out. I couldn't have planned it better myself! I was poised to strike, and then he—'

'You're boring me now. I don't want to hear about your warped thinking. Pierre isn't answering his phone.' Gustav clenches his fists. 'What have you done with him?'

'Look at me, Gusty. Look. At. Me.' Margot licks her finger and runs it over her painted eyebrow. 'He's a grown man who regularly works out. You really think a petite creature like me could hurt him?'

'Absolutely I do.' Gustav takes a step nearer, then pulls back as if she might burn him. But now he's too close to the fire. 'You are capable of murder.'

Margot falls back in her chair theatrically, fanning herself with the feather. She even glances across at me, finally catching my eye with an exaggerated expression of conspiracy, as if to say, did he really just accuse me of something so dreadful?

'Amazing that you boys both emerged from the same womb. Pierre Levi isn't worth the effort. I've dispensed with him, but that doesn't mean I've killed him!' She rests her finger thoughtfully on her chin as her eyes fix on my golden locket. 'The last time we were face to face he was alive and well and extremely rude. You were there, too. I surprised him at his scruffy little backstreet theatre, but under cover of the music and lights he told me yet again that he couldn't do it. He told me the deal really was off this time. He wasn't involving Tomas or anyone else. *Finito*. He said he'd fallen for his brother's girlfriend. And then he went off on a date with her.'

'Not a date. He and Serena had a business meeting, which ended with an over-affectionate farewell. His own admission.' Gustav allows himself a grim smile as he folds his arms. 'I must say I never thought Pierre would have the balls to tell you to take a hike!'

'That boy doesn't have balls, Gustav. Not like you. He's weak, and he's bitter. That delicious spunk of his has all dribbled away. You know how I like my lovers. Obsessed. Besotted. Enslaved. Not half-cocked or lusting after someone else. I mean, how insulting is that!' She snaps her eyes back to Gustav. 'Oh, for God's sake. He's gone. OK? My information is that he's slunk off to LA.'

'Now he can leave us in peace!'

It's out before I can stop it. I clasp the back of the velvet sofa blocking my way into the over-furnished room. Gustav's black eyebrows draw together as if he's forgotten I'm there. He turns at last to stare at me.

'Bravo! Spoken like a woman with a very guilty conscience!' Margot's catlike eyes and mouth tilt up in a triumphant smile which seems to stretch her skin until it looks too tight.

And there's something different about her face. I've committed that face to memory, God knows, with and without such heavy make-up, but even allowing for the passage of time, something *structural* has changed.

'He hasn't slunk anywhere. He's in LA for work.' Gustav clears his throat, but he still sounds as if he's chewing on pebbles. 'He hasn't sent the feather. He's done nothing wrong. So he's probably just delighted to have escaped from you.'

'He's done plenty wrong, Gusty.' Still smiling, Margot starts to count off on her fingers. 'Ask your precious jailbait.'

I stare at those bony older-woman's fingers. The same

36

fingers I saw at the burlesque theatre when I was filming the finale. Margot was reaching out of the wings to grab Pierre. I remember now that he didn't looked pleased or even surprised to see her. Just hypnotised as they sketched a tango before the lights snapped out again.

But if he was terminating their arrangement as they danced, then something he said to me later that evening doesn't ring true.

If Margot was here, I'd take her right now in front of you. I mean it. And she'd go with it. She doesn't care where, when, who, what.

Margot's voice punctures my thoughts. 'The idea was to isolate your little plaything by drip-feeding terrible things about your past, dangle juicy young Tomas in front of her, whatever, all the while staying squeaky clean himself, but instead Pierre ripped up the agenda.'

'Agenda? You make it sound like a committee planning world domination.'

'There's no other way of achieving your goal. You know that. But a plan is only as good as its execution and its fulfilment. Pierre lost his head. No amount of brotherly love was going to stop him from having a crack at this girl once the opportunity arose. And *voilà*! The two of you unexpectedly part, she storms off to Venice, he loses all loyalty except to his loins, and he goes in for the kill. All his own idea. And to be fair, even though I had no active part in it, his scheming in Venice nearly succeeded in toppling Saint Serena off her perch after all. Except the spineless little shit didn't follow through.' She stops, clamps her bright-red lips shut and closes her eyes as if in pain. 'If you need a job doing well, just finish it off yourself. Which is why I am here.'

Gustav walks over to the fireplace and runs his finger along the mantelpiece, empty save for the horrible little vase and a trio of oversized black glass candlesticks. His hand is shaking. His black hair falls over his face as he stares into the fake flames for a moment.

'Just so I don't have to stay in this room a moment longer than necessary, let's get this clear. You are saying this rapprochement with Pierre started off as a ruse? He came to find me in London, pretended to end our estrangement, purely on your instructions?'

Margot's eyes snap open. Even her false eyelashes seem to radiate gleeful evil.

'He's changed a lot in the last six years, Gustav. A consummate performer! All that time he spends hanging round in theatres has paid off, fondling those petticoats, trying on those masks, watching how others make a profession out of lying.'

'Not to me. He hasn't been lying to me.'

'*Especially* to you! If he was in this room with us now he'd be lying to save his sorry scorched skin.' Margot lifts her chin in the air and presses her hand to her breast to imitate a pretentious actor. 'He's weak, like all of you. He couldn't keep it up in the end. Either the act, or his cock.'

Gustav stares up at the ceiling, his mouth drawn tight. I follow his gaze. The ceiling has the same ornate cornicing as the lobby downstairs, but there is a large, urine-coloured stain running across it.

'I don't buy it. My trust in him has been right. You may have cooked up this situation, and I suppose I should thank you for that, but you've lost your touch. In fact, all of this has backfired. I *knew* it was genuine, however shaky it felt initially. Pierre and I have been building bridges. We've talked about things nobody else knows about. It's meant the world to both of us. You can't fake that.' Gustav coughs and tries again. 'Thanks to you, we're closer than ever.'

'And so will you and I be. See? What goes around comes around. It was only ever a matter of time. No one else matches up to me, and you know it!' Margot puckers her lips ready to take a sip of red wine but pauses, waving the glass in front of her mouth. 'Remember when we bought this dear little place? How we celebrated the purchase in front of this fire? You were my true love, taking me up the *arse*, as you put it in your charming English-gent way just now. Ooh, so rough and hard, just the way you always did. Just the way we liked it. I was on all fours for you, I was your dirty little bitch. Right where you're standing!'

'Don't change the subject!'

Gustav clenches his jaw as I let out a stifled cry, but he can't look at me. It's as if by pinning her down with his glare he will find a way of shutting her up.

But she's said enough already. It can't be unsaid. We are all her puppets.

It's all here, in a fragile nutshell. Their marriage. The damage Margot did when she made enemies of the two brothers. The chaos she's caused and is still causing, whether or not Pierre has followed her lead. The ugly exchanges between the brothers, the stammered confessions, Gustav's weary acceptance of his own guilt, his desperation to have his brother by his side again, Pierre taking matters into his own hands in Venice, his clumsy apology to me on the phone at the gallery, everyone trying to hold the fragile peace together. Even though it hasn't gone according to her plan, it's still blindingly clear.

Margot has stage-managed it all.

'And see how cosy I made my little den since I took it over again?' she goes on, sure of her captive audience now. 'My special Manhattan collection of whips is still here. Your cute ass has been striped red by each and every one of them!'

My beautiful, clever, strong lover is locked in a staring match with this woman as if she's one of those mythical creatures, a basilisk was it, that can kill you with one look.

I follow his gaze towards her glossy red mouth, the seam of red wine wet between the plump lips that don't quite meet. They have that swollen look of collagen injections. That must be what's different about her. As her throat jumps to swallow the wine, I can imagine those lips wrapped round Gustav's hardness, sucking on him, swallowing his juices. Has he noticed the papery skin on her neck? The artful pussycat bow of the see-through blouse, tied to hide the slight droop under her chin? It's probably wishful thinking on my part, but up close she looks like she might just disintegrate at any moment.

'What about Polly?' I whimper, trying to carry my voice across the room to get Gustav's eyes off his ex-wife. 'She and Pierre met by pure chance through work. Not even you could have organised that. Not even you could know we were cousins.'

'Adoptive cousins, wasn't it? Weren't you the baby they found chucked in the mud?' Margot keeps her eyes on Gustav. 'Your connection with Polly was a delightful coincidence, it's true. So marvellous when everything ticks like clockwork. Tick-tock, she led Pierre right to Gustav. Tick-tock, another woman rocked Pierre's world and she was history. And tick-tock, she got all paranoid, did an even better job of breaking the two of you up than I did!'

Gustav doesn't silence her horrible words. He doesn't stop her gaze running slowly down his body, over his stomach in its aubergine cashmere sweater, over the belt of his jeans. He doesn't stop his ex-wife licking her lips as she ogles the crotch of the man who once walked her up the aisle.

I dig my nails into the fabric of the brocade sofa, scratching for a thread to unravel. 'Polly and I are like sisters!'

'You weren't thinking of your *sister* when you were cavorting with her boyfriend in Venice, though, were you?'

Margot runs her long pink tongue across her lips and stands up, but she moves towards Gustav, not me. 'The heavens were smiling on my scheme, as they always do!'

Gustav shakes his head slowly. It's as if she's injected him with tranquilliser so that he can barely move, even when she steps closer.

'Listen to yourself. *My scheme.* You're the one who's lying. Every word that comes out of your mouth—'

'Turns you on. Don't deny it. You're getting hard now, seeing me again. I'm willing to bet your entire fortune, Gusty, that I could make you come, right here, right now, within seconds. I practised endlessly on your little brother. All I had to do was crook my finger. He was in my panties as soon as you could say "boner". But it was only ever about you. Getting you to notice me again. Admit it. You're horny as hell just hearing my voice, Gusty. You're remembering how good we were together.'

Gustav shakes his head. 'I'm wondering what I ever saw in you. It's gone. That sexiness. That exotic beauty. Even the fact that you were older than me added lustre to it all. There was something transgressive about that, too. The naughty nanny. I'm sorry, Serena. This isn't supposed to hurt you. It's supposed to prove how deluded this woman is, because look at her now! And in Pierre's case you were old enough to be the wicked stepmother. No wonder he doesn't want you any more. Where's all that lustre? You look – shrunken.' He lifts one of the candlesticks and rubs it thoughtfully under his mouth as he holds her gaze. 'As if someone's let all the blood out of you.'

'Blood flows thick and fast in these veins, I assure you, Gusty. Like the waters of the Nile. Once tasted, you'll always come back. And you were always coming back for more. Right up until that last night when you told me it was over, but still you couldn't help yourself. I could reduce you to a whimpering heap with a huge erection just by arching an eyebrow.' She sniggers. 'I'm doing it now.'

With a stage conjuror's flick of the wrist, she reaches down beside the fireplace where there's a stack of pokers, and whisks out a long white plaited whip like something the Snow Queen of Narnia might use to speed on her reindeer. She runs the handle of the whip across her mouth in an echo of what he's doing with the candlestick. Then she licks it.

'You're *my* whimpering heap.' She runs the flicking end of the whip down Gustav's stomach, down his fly, tickles it between his legs. Then she fans her hand out and grabs him there. 'And here in your trousers, this is *my* huge erection.'

They stand stock-still. She has possession of him. He is staring at her as if someone has carved them both out of ice.

But I'm not made of ice. I'm burning hot with rage. 'Gustav! Stop it! Why are you looking at her like that? Get away from her!'

'I'm just searching for whatever captivated me all those years ago. You really were the archetypal temptress, Margot.' Gustav's eyes rake over his ex-wife's face almost tenderly as he gropes for the words. 'You came straight out of all the best and worst of fairy tales.'

Margot's mouth lifts expectantly. Her fingers curl round the now visible bulge in his trousers and start to squeeze. 'And now?'

'Ephemera. Ether. Emptiness.' He spits into the fire and makes it flare angrily. 'Time has been very cruel to you, Margot. You're not even the wicked witch.'

And as she opens her mouth to reply, he hurls the candlestick into the grate. It seems to tumble in slow motion before smashing against the marble hearth, lethal black fragments flying into the fireplace and out into the room.

'This is a waste of time,' he growls. He encircles her wrist

42

with his long fingers, his knuckles bone-white as he squeezes. Then he drops her hand and steps away to the other end of the fireplace. 'We'll get more sense out of Pierre.'

Margot tucks the whip under her arm as if he's no more harm to her than a fly. She flips open a carved wooden box on the mantelpiece and pulls out a long black cigarette, places it between her lips, lights it. When she blows smoke in his face, he doesn't flinch.

'You're right about one thing, Gusty. All that crap about blood being thicker than water. He was so happy to be seeing you again. Genuinely able to forget all the angst between you. Where he went wrong is when he fell in love. That wasn't supposed to happen. Love spoils everything. He was only supposed to get her out of the picture.'

At last Gustav tears his eyes away from her and they both look at me. There's a distance in his eyes that's opening up a gulf between us again. I have to say something to bring him back to me. I seem to take in a lungful of the pungent, aromatic smoke from Margot's cigarette as I speak. 'Pierre's not capable of loving anyone.'

'So you say. But you're a bit of a sprite yourself, aren't you?' Margot blows a couple of smoke rings at me. 'You sense things before they're real. You saw me dancing at the theatre in Gramercy Park. And then you saw me at the Weinmeyers' ball.'

'Serena?' Gustav's eyes glitter. 'You never breathed a word!'

Spots start dancing in front of my eyes. Every time Venice is mentioned we come a step closer to the exact details of what happened, or nearly happened, with Pierre.

I slide over the arm of the sofa to land in the deep seat. I feel dizzy. Actually, I feel stoned.

'I couldn't be sure it was her. Everyone was whirling around in strange costumes and masks. At the theatre, and at the ball. I just told myself I was obsessing.'

43

'Not quite the whole picture, though, is it, sweetie? Lots of things you haven't confessed. You obviously didn't pass on my loving video message, for instance, even though it was intended for my husband?' Margot blows out another thin plume of smoke and winks at me. 'I would love to be a fly on the wall when you eventually have *that* particular interrogation!'

'How has this conversation started revolving around Serena?' Gustav pushes Margot back down on to her armchair, as if by making her sit he can somehow reduce her power. He pushes his face into hers. 'She's already told me what happened in Venice. Pierre tricked her into thinking he was me. And that's precisely why we're looking for him!'

'He's good at hiding, especially when he's licking his wounds. He'll be frustrated, and furious, and you know how dangerous that can be! But what he did in Venice was all his own idea. Any damage that causes in the future is out of my hands. He rushed in where fools fear to tread. As for me, I was just monitoring his wild goose chase so I could choose my own moment to strike. Call it surveillance, since we're talking campaigns. And you'll be needing me more after this, Gustav. Much more. That feather was far too subtle a message, but I was only trying to help.' Margot pouts her swollen lips. 'You had to know. He's in love with your girlfriend.'

The smoke, or maybe it's just the haze of words, is making me increasingly faint. Margot's gaze has barely left Gustav's face since we all came into this room. Jealousy coils unpleasantly inside me. She's hungry for him, as I would be. She's been starved.

'And who can blame him?' Gustav murmurs, so quietly I'm not sure I've heard correctly. 'I would go mad if I couldn't have her.'

'That's just it. He *has* had her. Every inch.'

Margot runs her fingertips delicately over the red dents left on the white skin of her wrists and smiles. Is that some kind of coded message? Is that how it used to be between them? Or is she just relishing the pain he inflicted on her? This is a woman after all who relishes pain in all its sexual darkness. It's her speciality. Her trade.

I try to sit up straighter. 'Pierre may want me, but he will *never* have me.'

Margot laughs harshly. 'There's no gloss you can put on this, sweetheart. I'll tell Gusty, since you're plainly not going to. You went skipping off into the night with Pierre. You allowed him to rip off your silky drawers. Ooh. I wonder what happened next?'

The two sculpted white faces are staring at one another as if I don't exist. They waver and blur, almost seem to merge, as my eyes fill with hot, hopeless tears.

'I told you before, Gustav. I thought I was with you, but then I felt the scars on his back!'

There is a long silence, peppered only by some exploratory drops of rain ringing off the metal ladder outside the window. A police car makes a whoop in the street below then shuts off as if it's changed its mind. There is a burst of angry voices, also silenced abruptly. Maybe they've all sought shelter.

At last Gustav turns towards me. But his hands are still on the arms of Margot's chair and her wrists are still striped with his red fingermarks. His voice hits me from across the room. 'You got close enough to touch his skin, Serena. Which means—'

'That they were naked. History repeating itself wouldn't you say, Gusty darling? Pierre did what he does best. Pilfers your women.'

Margot lifts an arm and swipes Gustav aside. She stands gracefully and walks over to the window. She stalks like a heron, or a flamingo, picking her high-heeled claws across the carpet. She has a dancer's gait, the balletic twitch of the buttocks as she walks, but I notice she presses at her face as she pulls the curtain back. Sheets of rain are whipping across the glass.

I get up and dart across to Gustav, take hold of his hands and pull him round to face me. His eyes are too deep to read. I cup his chin in my fingers, our gesture to calm each other down. I need him to look at me.

'Yes, my hands were under his shirt. I felt his scars and kicked him where it would hurt the most, and I ran away, up on to the bridge, and that's when you found me!'

Margot's sharp laugh cuts through my words like a knife. Although I'm trying to get Gustav to focus on me, we both swivel towards her.

'Oh, look at that innocent face, all flushed and indignant! But she's no angel. She's had two Levi brothers in her knickers, after all! Just like I have! So just you wait, Gusty. We belong together. And you'll be grateful I made you see the light about this little bitch.' She points the feather at us again as if it's a wand. 'You should know that they were fucking in that gondola, Gustav. I saw them.'

The rain outside turns into a torrent, bouncing off the railings, smacking on the awnings on the shops below us. Drumming on the window behind Margot.

I keep my hand in Gustav's and move very close to him. The fire is too hot behind me, sweat is prickling up under my hair as I shake my head, over and over. I've handed her this on a plate because I was too cowardly to go the distance and tell him every detail.

Very slowly, Gustav curls his fingers into a cage around my hand and lifts it towards his mouth. He rubs his lips almost thoughtfully across the tender skin before he speaks.

'Good try, Margot. Your best ever. But, bizarrely, you've

46

just advanced Pierre's case. If Serena has unlocked something in him, something tender, something not even you could winkle out of him, well, that has to be a good thing, right?' His voice is quiet, but humming with the determination and strength that drew me to him in the first place. 'I know and love this girl better than I've ever known or loved anyone. And I would know if she'd had another man. I would sense it. God knows, I would smell it on her.'

Margot is silent for a moment. Her white face is a bland, hard mask of disdain. She takes a long drag from her cigarette, then jabs it at us. 'That's very touching, Gusty, but you've been totally hoodwinked.'

'Thanks to you, I know that Pierre likes his sex rough. He's bragged about it. But see?' Gustav lifts my wrist and the silver bracelet he gave me in the very early days, to which he used to attach the silver chain, glints in the firelight: 'I was in bed with Serena that night. We made love in the shower the following morning. I went over every inch of her. He never left a mark.'

Margot blows out the smoke she's been holding inside. I notice a slight redness in the whites of her eyes, despite the heavy black kohl make-up. That cigarette aroma is herbal, all right. She's smoking some kind of weed. And it seems to have taken the sting out of her tail because, instead of the nasty cackle I expect, she simply holds up her pinky finger with its long black nail and makes a winding motion around it.

'She's got you wrapped round here, Levi. She could have been personally trained by me!' She takes another drag of the joint. 'Christ, if I didn't want her wiped off the face of the earth I'd hire your little girlfriend myself.'

It's Gustav's turn to laugh mirthlessly. He holds my hand up, fans my fingers out to show her the beautiful diamond ring.

'Hasn't anyone told you? That proves that you and Pierre haven't spoken in the last six weeks. So either those listening devices you planted are faulty or they're non-existent. She's not my girlfriend. Serena is my fiancée now.'

Margot's thin neck snaps backwards as if he has slapped her. The hand that isn't holding the cigarette clutches at the curtain and the rings rattle along the pole as the drape takes her weight.

Her black hair seems to writhe on her head like Medusa's as her slanted eyes half close with fury, and that's when it hits me. What's happened to her face. She was painted to look like a swan the first time I glimpsed her in the flesh, when she was dancing with Pierre at the theatre. Her eyes and eyelids and brows were all painted black, with black lines swooping down her nose to make her look like a bird. But now I see it's not just warpaint. Her nose looks as if a carpenter has gone at the sides with a plane, shaving off the natural sweep of the bridge until it's almost flat, then tapering straight down between her eyes in what an 'aesthetic practitioner' would describe as a ski slope, but what anyone with a pair of eyes would call a beak, complete with unnaturally flared nostrils.

'Your funeral. And believe me, that's how it will end. It's plain as that hideous carrot hair that she and Pierre are perfectly suited. Same age. Physically, they're extremely compatible. She's not worthy of you. You'll see. There will be no wedding.'

Now it's my turn to let an evil smile creep across my face. I turn my hand deliberately slowly in front of me, letting the facets from the diamond ring shoot out their multicoloured lights.

Gustav threads his fingers through mine and starts to lead me towards the door. I look up at his dark, troubled face, searching for the calm triumph that has been there ever since we got engaged.

And after his lovely words, it's returning, like sunshine after rain. But still, *still* he's staring at Margot. And she is staring back at him, her red mouth stitched shut at last. Without the power of words, it looks puffed, bruised, and petulant. Her eyes have sunk back in their sockets as if she's looking up from the bottom of a pond, but there's still a sick flame flickering there.

I've seen that look before, in a wild animal that is about to die.

'Watch your back, Gusty. I'll be everywhere, in your dreams, in your nightmares, until I'm the only thing you can see. And if that doesn't work, I'll haunt this little bitch instead,' she hisses through those lips, bunching the curtain up in her fingers. 'Don't say I haven't warned you. I wanted this to be friendly, but you've made that impossible. If you go with her now, there'll be no happy ever after. For you. For her. For any of us.'

The floorboards creak as we reach the door. Suddenly Gustav lets go of my hand and walks back to her. He snatches the feather from her and runs it slowly over her sharp nose and swollen lips. There is deadly affection in the gesture, and I want him to stop it. Margot goes very still as the feather strokes her, her eyes red hot with longing.

He steps away and holds the feather low over the gas flames.

'You're sad. Insane. And nothing to me.'

The fronds start to crisp and curl, and then a blue flame runs up the quill, burning off every remnant of life or colour.

'I can wait. When she brings you down, I'll be here to pick up the pieces.'

But Margot is not watching him as he guides me out of the door, or the feather as it burns. Her black eyes are fixed on me. The coolness has gone. In its place is poison.

And as we leave there's a sucking sound behind us. Margot starts screaming.

'They were fucking in that goddamn boat, Gustav! Your brother fucked her!'

CHAPTER THREE

Her voice screeches down the stairwell. Somehow we've crashed out of the apartment and Gustav is pulling me past the lift. The gates are gaping open, and we're flying down. Cracked, peeling doors open to investigate the disturbance as we pass each hallway. I don't see the faces of Margot's furious neighbours. I only catch their anxious murmurs, a child's piping question, mostly male splutters of indignation.

But we're not stopping. Not until we're at ground level, spinning through the door and out on to the street.

Gustav lets go of my arm and falls against the wall, resting his hands on his knees as he bends to catch his breath. I step away from him, terrified that his ex-wife's poison has worked.

Dickson is nowhere to be seen. I run a few steps, first one way, then the other. The rainstorm has cleared this end of the street. Even though the rain has eased off now, and there's plenty of life passing along the main drag, down here it's so deserted you'd think a crime-scene cordon had been put up to block the traffic. And it's not only the lack of cars that makes it so quiet. There are no people.

I come to stand in front of Gustav. I daren't touch him. I try to zip up my jacket, but my hands are shaking too much.

My legs are bare beneath the little lace dress, and I realise I am absolutely freezing.

Still he's bent over. His glossy black hair is a curtain separating us. His shoulders are hunched up round his ears, and I can see that his fingers are digging hard into his thighs.

I stretch out my hand, not sure where to place it. The hopeful glance of the diamond on my finger nudges at my dulled senses.

'Gustav? Honey? Talk to me.'

He shakes his head, lifts one hand to silence me.

When we first met and started working together that authoritarian gesture was not to be argued with. He was the master. I was – if not the servant, definitely the underling. He had pulled me out of nowhere and made me into a star. So I liked the dominance. It defined our roles and our rules. Conversely, it also showed me how to break those rules when I wanted him to notice me – and it was when he really noticed me that the gas under us was lit.

As we grew closer and I got the measure of him, recognised that he needed me in his life as much as I needed him, I could occasionally mock his authority, or turn it to my advantage. He'd be using the silver chain to anchor me, but I would be the one wanting it and wriggling with impatience, waiting for him to come into me as hard and fast as possible. I'd be squealing with pretend resistance, but really I'd be wet for him as he pushed me on to my hands and knees.

Icy fingers trail down the back of my neck. That's what he did to Margot. Took her *up the arse*, right in front of the fire, the night they bought that squalid little apartment.

As if he can read my mind, Gustav's head swings up and his black eyes fix on me. They are the only part of his white face showing any signs of life, and I can read the questions, accusations and the pleading that move across his features like clouds before a strong wind.

His ears will be ringing with Margot's parting words. So before I have to start grovelling, again, deny everything, again, I try to obliterate what she's said with the first thing that comes to me.

'I won't be quiet, Gustav. I have to know. Do you still want her?'

Gustav straightens, keeping his eyes on the ground. But just as he opens his mouth to say something, just as relief sweeps through me that he will at least hear me out, believe what I say over Margot's lies, we hear the lift gates inside the apartment building clatter closed.

'She's coming after us!' I squeal, backing away and staring wildly up towards the lights on the main street, down to the darkened end of this one. 'Where the hell is Dickson? Oh, God, she knows everything. She knows where we live!'

Gustav grabs me, but instead of breaking into a run he yanks me down the dark alleyway edging the building. He slams me against the cold, damp wall beside a huge dumpster and I yelp as I land in a cold puddle.

'She'll find us, Gustav! We'll never be free of her!'

Gustav clamps his hand over my mouth. Voices spill out of the main door where we've just been standing. Margot's smoky drawl, the voice I've quickly learned is the one she uses when she's certain she's in control, has risen to a hysterical, childish pitch and is spewing a stream of what sound like German curses. Someone, a man, is trying to interrupt her.

'She's got someone with her!' I mouth into his hand. Hot tears prick at my eyes and start to fall. 'Do you think that's Pierre? After all that crap she's told us, maybe he's been with her all along?'

Gustav cocks his head for a moment. The voices mingle in a hubbub of yelling, then go silent. Gustav's hand is covering my nose as well as my mouth, and I can't breathe.

He shakes his head.

After several minutes we hear the scrape and tap of Margot's shoes, but instead of coming this way her footsteps are muffled by the front door of the building once more clanking shut.

We're safe here. For now. She would never sully herself or her expensive shoes by searching for us in a filthy, dank alleyway full of trash. But this isn't the end of the story. Not by a long chalk.

Margot is out to finish us.

I struggle under Gustav's hand, but he presses it harder over my mouth, banging my head back against the wall, and now his black eyes are glaring as if he wants to bore a hole right through me. With his free hand he pulls mine away from where I'm bashing at his chest. He thrusts my hand down his stomach, down over the front of his jeans until my fingers clamp over him.

He's hard as rock. He's so hard that I can feel the heat throbbing right through the denim.

The shock is like a punch in the guts.

Margot has done this to him. Not me. The dangerous allure that once attracted him to that woman was oozing out of her just now. Everything about her, those red stockings, the wet red lips, the laser eyes, the knowledge that she was naked beneath that leather skirt, those gloating, filthy reminiscences she was so desperate to share, has brought it all back. Christ, if I can't look at her without seeing the two of them going at it, what memories must be boiling inside Gustav?

I nip viciously into his palm to get him off me, but he doesn't budge. His eyes glitter with the grim determination he employed to overpower me in the early days. He continues to press my hand over the big thick bulge inside his pants. I can feel a sob choking me, but also the sharp twist of desire deep inside me as I touch him.

All at once he moves his hands away from my mouth, leaves my fingers on his crotch and shoves one knee between my legs so that they are forced apart. My legs are shaking as I stagger slightly, but he's not going to help me. He's going to have me. He pushes his hands under my little lace dress and sinks his fingers into the soft flesh of my buttocks, lifting me quickly so I don't have time to feel the cold. I scrabble to keep hold of him by wrapping my legs round his hips and now I'm slicking open for him, moistening against the denim jeans despite the dizzying mix of fear and fury as my dress floats up round my waist.

Gustav pins me against the cold, flinty wall as he starts to unbutton his fly. His breath is hot on my face, his lips parted to show the glint of his gritted teeth. Our eyes lock as footsteps pass beyond the entrance to the alleyway. I lean in and bite his bottom lip, suck up the droplet of blood.

Once tasted, you'll always come back.

He shoves me harder against the wall so that the cold bricks scrape into the tender skin on my lower back. My lovely leather jacket is going to have scratches on it, too. I kick my boots against his butt as he starts to bite my neck, but he just shoves me more brutally to keep me still.

His fingers dig deeper into my butt cheeks, prising them apart, and then his fingers are in the damp crack between, searching and sliding towards my centre. I grip his shoulders as we both feel the wetness beneath his fingers, a mixture of the seething sweat of fear and the curling cream of excitement.

I open myself wider to swallow his fingers, grinding against his jeans, winding my fingers in his silky hair to pull his head to me so that I can kiss him. He groans unevenly, licking and biting his way up to my mouth as his fingers grapple with my weight and then they slide inside me, releasing my urgent, musky scent, driving me wild with wanting.

As he kisses, or rather takes chunks out of me, he mutters under his breath, so rapid and angry it sounds like a foreign language.

He's saying *bitch, bitch. Bitch.*

I reach down and flip undone the last remaining buttons of his fly and wrap my fingers around him. This man belongs to me. This hard-on belongs to me. This precious part of him is mine, and it's going into me now.

I grunt like an animal and he lifts his head, lips wet with saliva. We stare deep into each other in the darkness. I'm holding on to him, but I'm quivering violently with the effort of gripping him and with the ferocious desire to have him.

'She was lying about me and Pierre, G. You must believe me. We never went that far. You know she was lying.'

I'm aware that I've just said G, his brother's pet name for him, but just then it seemed to fit perfectly. I can't take it back. So I kiss him to shut myself up, not biting this time but pressing my lips on to his gorgeous mouth, pushing my tongue in to open him to me. He pauses, as if he is about to break this long silence, but then his tongue snakes hungrily around mine.

Kissing is better than talking, however violent and angry it is. I am still gripping him but he needs no guidance. He pulls his hips back and then slams himself up inside me, so rough and hard against the wall, jolting me violently so that my teeth bite through my lip.

He pulls out, allowing a breath of cold air to wash over my bare skin in the brief pause, then with a muffled groan he thrusts inside even harder. I wrap myself like a limpet around him and I make it easy because I'm so wet and ready. He moves inside me, so smooth compared with the painful rasp of brickwork on my spine, and my body closes tight around him. Then our bodies are stuck together, just as they should be, and we're ramming it, swearing into each other's ears like a whore and her brutish punter in the alleyway.

One of those enormous, noisy fire trucks that looks like a toy roars down the street, choosing the moment when it reaches the entrance to our alleyway to sound its horn and wind up its siren. We both jump in alarm as the sound invades our space, but the renewed commotion of the city around us doesn't stop us rutting like a pair of dogs.

In an apartment a few metres above us, my lover's ex-wife is pacing up and down in her hot, stuffy sitting room, dragging her fingernails across the fabric of the thick curtains and showering curses on our heads as we start to come.

I grind against my Gustav and feel his teeth biting into my neck again as he shudders to his climax, and I suck him in, keeping him inside me until I've no more strength. We slither down the grimy wall in a tangle of limbs until we're sitting amongst the cans and pizza boxes and spilt beer and Coke and cat piss and who knows what else, needles and condoms probably.

We collapse, panting and exhausted, on to the dirty paving stones of this backstreet alley.

The fire truck has gone and the street is quiet again.

'No is the answer,' Gustav says into the night quiet. He rakes my hair roughly off my face so that he can see me clearly. 'I don't want her back.'

I keep my eyes on the gold crinkle round one iris that gives him that wolfish look.

'But she wants you, Gustav. She has your things in the flat. Shirts. Wedding gifts. She won't rest till she—'

'I don't want anything of hers. She leaves me cold. I feel stone dead inside when I look at her, compared with the passion that burns me when I look at you.' He shudders. 'She was sexy as hell, Serena. Pure lust blinded me to the reality of how rotten she was. Hard to believe it now. She physically repels me. But back then it was a need, greed, hunger, an itch, I don't know, a virus. It wasn't love. Never love. You couldn't love someone so empty and cruel. I've told you I was besotted with her for a few short years. She could have me on my knees just by raising her eyebrows, and on my knees is where I ended up. That's not love, is it? How could it be? It's not even as meaningful as hate. It's just – emptiness. I was broken. I lost Pierre. But at least I was free. There's a vital piece of her missing, *cara*. There always was.' He bashes his fist at his chest. 'Was it the ice queen who had a chip of ice where her heart should be? Margot doesn't get how normal mortals live. How far you can go before you stop being forgiven. She doesn't get any of that.'

I nod. I feel safe with my face cradled in his fingers like this, but now that the cold is creeping into the space left by the heat of passion, I don't feel sexy any more. I feel dishevelled and anxious. And the lies about me and Pierre are still circulating like vultures in the air.

'Margot was up here for a long time.' He taps his forehead. 'But she'll never be in here.' He taps his heart. 'That's where you live.'

He winds my hair round his fingers and pulls my face tight against his.

I cling to him, shivering with fear and cold and exhaustion.

And then his phone buzzes.

'Leave it! Leave it!' I cry, trying to stop him getting to it. 'Don't answer it!'

Gustav keeps his eyes on me as he untangles his fingers and takes the phone out of his pocket. I can see the fire ebbing from him, replaced by a steady distance.

Margot's eyes, slicing into me just now. Not looking at Gustav. Looking at me.

The eye in the peacock feather.

'Is it Margot?'

He shakes his head, still studying the screen. 'Not even she can hack into my phone. It's Pierre. He's seen my missed calls.'

I open my mouth. Shut it again. I step back from my lover, feel the cold, dirty air rushing between us as he frowns and texts something back.

'What did he say?'

He presses *send,* still not looking at me. Waits for the reply, which comes rapidly with another double buzz. He reads it, starts to text a reply, then changes his mind and drops the phone back into his pocket.

At last he looks at me again.

'Pierre is catching tomorrow night's flight out of LAX.'

I nod, then take his face in my hands and rub my cheek against the hard plane of his jaw, feeling the rasp of his harsh bristles. 'This is me. In your heart. In your head. I'm yours for as long as you want me.'

He doesn't smile, but squeezes me, hard. 'So prove it by swearing something, Serena. On that diamond ring.'

I hold myself very still. 'What do you want me to say? And why do you need me to swear it?'

'Before I ask Pierre this question I want to hear it in your voice, your words.' He lifts me to my feet, tugs my lace dress around my cold, shaking knees, straightens my jacket. 'Swear to me that my brother has never been inside you.'

Instead of soothing me, the massaging jets are irritating me. The Jacuzzi's too big to wallow in alone. You could easily drown beneath the frothing surface, and no one would know for hours.

Gustav is already up and dressed. He was out nearly all day yesterday. We barely spoke, and this morning he's been out to buy food and is now doing his chef thing, preparing mussels in a creamy white wine and tarragon sauce. I woke up late in our empty bed after a second restless night peppered with dreams of a hot, cluttered flat. Margot Levi was standing behind a judge's bench wearing a black gown, like a bat, handing down death sentences. Then she was dancing out of an enormous mahogany wardrobe wearing a very short bridal gown, pulling the petals off armfuls of white roses.

Waking up wasn't the relief I needed. I was aching and stiff and I needed Gustav.

I wander into the kitchen to find him buttoning up his whites. He knows it turns me on to see him pretending to be Gordon Ramsay. He looks so gorgeous. He hasn't shaved since we got back from Margot's apartment two nights ago, so his face is shadowed with what I call his bandit beard. His glossy black hair keeps falling over his eyes as he bends over the steaming pot.

'*Moules marinière*? A little extravagant for lunchtime isn't it, honey?' I murmur, coming up to him and winding my fingers through his hair. 'Doesn't that smack of the prodigal son?'

Gustav lets me secure his black hair, which has grown just past his collar, into a silly ponytail so that it won't fall into his eyes, but he keeps watching for the pops to pierce the rolling water. So preoccupied.

'It's Pierre's favourite.'

I step over to the coffee machine and pour myself a cup. But it's not caffeine I need. My heart is clattering along too fast as it is. Valium. Dope. I need some kind of sedative.

I close my eyes and try to count down my heart rate. 'How long is the flight from LA?'

'Less than six hours. He's been on that plane while you've been asleep. He'll be landing at JFK any time now.'

I gaze up through the skylight to the bright blue sky. There are no clouds. No white streams carved in the ether by departing or arriving planes. What are the chances of Pierre just, well, not showing up?

Gustav is testing each mussel. He runs his fingertips over each ridged black shell and without looking he rejects any bad ones that are open too early, casting them with perfect aim into the bin.

I look away, back up to that blue sky. Spring has arrived overnight. That late-March brightness, the hint of sunshine, the promise of warmth, should be filling me with birdsong and thoughts of weddings and honeymoons, but instead I only have the sensation of sliding too fast along a walkway.

I can't get off. Although I don't want to get off. Not if Pierre is waiting at the other end.

When he makes his way through the airport he'll step on to one of those conveyor belts and move steadily towards us. He'll have minimal luggage. No luggage, preferably. He's not stopping long.

I blow across the surface of my hot coffee.

'Gustav. Stop a minute. We've barely spoken in the last two days. Be honest. Are you angry with me for stirring all this up with the feather and Margot and Pierre?'

Gustav holds a shell above the boiling water, ready to drop it in. He glances up at last. The reflection from the cooking pot makes his black eyes look as if they are bubbling, too.

'All of the above. Also none of it. My darling girl, so sweet and so sleepy. I wish you'd never gone to Venice on your own and yes, I know that was my fault, too. But since you ask, I'll admit it. I'm still rattled by what you've told me. What Margot said.' He drops the unfortunate shell into the water and picks up another. 'Seeing her is like ripping at an old wound when you thought the scar had healed and finding it's as raw as ever. But also I'm nervous about Pierre's reaction when I confront him. He's capable of fighting to the death just for the sake of it. Bizarrely I want him to corroborate every vitriolic thing she said. Then at least it will all be clear, and we can start again.'

The shells start raining down into the water.

'Except the bit about me.' I take a sip of coffee and it burns my mouth. 'If he just admits the truth about what he was playing at in all this, no one need be angry or nervous. Ever again.'

We smile at each other for a long, simmering moment across the steam. Then Gustav lifts the lid, ready to clamp it on top of the pot.

'And if you don't get out of my favourite shirt and into some decent clothes I will have to work off this tension by ravishing you right here. Right now.'

I duck away before he can come round the counter, and run back into the bathroom.

Now I'm standing in front of the full-length mirror, sweaty yet shivering. My breath puffs rapidly on to the glass as I study my naked reflection. I'm no fatter, no thinner. My breasts are still high and full, the red nipples hardening as soon as I think about them. My waist is tiny, my hips feminine, my legs long. The curves that were hidden for the first twenty years of my life. It wasn't so much Gustav who changed me. It was Crystal, our assistant, who I suddenly wish was here.

It's thanks to her that I dress this body up like a proper grown-up woman these days, not like someone who has just crawled out of a horsebox.

I'm no different from two days ago. My eyebrows have been groomed professionally so that they somehow follow and refine the line of my cheekbones. My eyes are hazy and big with anxiety and fatigue, and the bright light in the bathroom gives them a darker hue, a kind of laurel-leaf green. They are staring back at me as if peering out of a dark well.

There's a shadow behind them, as if someone else is in there with me, looking out.

What is different is my mouth. It's always full, but it's come up bruised and crushed. The lower lip is swollen from where I bit it hard as Gustav pinned me against the wall. Kisses that felt like punches.

I pick up a comb and start to drag it listlessly through my hair. I relish the snag when it catches at the roots. One by one, I start to curl tendrils of my hair round my fingers. I have a new long fringe, and trim only the ends of my hair now, so it still flows to my waist.

I'm up high, like Rapunzel in her tower. I glance out of the window as I comb. From here I can see the Hudson River. The sun is nearly overhead. It's the first time since we arrived in New York at Christmas that I've seen the sparkle of it on the water and the deep sharp shadows cast from the high buildings by the stronger light.

I'm about to squeeze styling gel on to my hair, just as Crystal has nagged me to do to banish the frizz, and then I stop. No. No hairstyling. I turn back to the mirror. No make-up, even. I don't want to look as if I've made any effort for Pierre. I don't even want to be here, except that Gustav has insisted. It's about the only thing he's said to me, with the new gruff edge that's been in his voice and his manner, since we left Margot's lair.

My stomach tightens. If I can push that woman to the perimeter, just for a few minutes, I can dwell on what happened when we got down from her apartment to *terra firma*. Gustav shoving me through the rain and into that filthy alleyway, pushing me up against the wall beside the dumpsters.

I turn and look at the vivid red scratches scoring my back as if he's been whipping me, right down my butt and my legs. They are stinging from the soap. I flinch as I run my fingers over each one. My eyes are drawn back to my neck, which has a ring of angry red bite marks around it.

I look as if I've been raped.

Tears rise up in my eyes. I can't hold on to anything positive right now. I can't hold on to the sexiness of being fucked by Gustav like that. It was just him and me, and it was earth-shattering, but something else was driving him.

And hovering around us still, like a cloud of mosquitoes, is the triumvirate, that exclusive threesome of Gustav, Pierre and Margot.

'He'll be here in about half an hour.'

Gustav's hands are on me. I'm in front of the mirror with my eyes closed, resting on my forehead. He has a soft white towel and he dabs it gently over the scratches on my back, over my arms, down my legs. Between my legs.

'Your hands smell of fish,' I murmur, leaning against him.

'And you feel tense as a wire brush,' he replies, running his warm hands over my sore skin until it starts to prick up in goosebumps of pleasure. 'You still brooding over that meeting with Margot?'

'That, and everything else.' I try to wriggle away, but he places his hands over my breasts to keep me still. 'I don't like any silence between us, G. But I don't have anything sensible to say, either.'

Despite everything that's whirling away in my brain, my body has other responses. My nipples shrink and poke against him, sending urgent messages of desire down my body.

'Silence is fine, so long as it's not secretive. You're shaking, *chérie*. What is it?'

'Where were you yesterday? You didn't leave a note.'

'This isn't like you. Not far.' He goes very still, his hands still clamped over my breasts. 'Yesterday I had to attend to something that cropped up at work. You were dead to the world nearly all day. And this morning I was in the French delicatessen.'

64

'I was afraid when I woke up and you weren't here. You didn't see the look your ex-wife gave me.' I keep my eyes closed. 'She says she had this place bugged, though you've not been able to find anything. But still, she knows where we live, Gustav. She knows everything about us. And she wants you back.'

'She can't hurt us. I won't let her. But would it help you to know that I've taken the practical step of issuing photographs of her to all employees, at all our business premises, and told them she's banned from coming anywhere near? Likewise, I've detailed the guys downstairs to question any visitor who claims to be a friend of ours.'

'She's the mistress of disguise though, isn't she? A burly doorman with a photofit isn't going to stop her if she really wants to get to us.'

Gustav runs his hands thoughtfully over my breasts, making them swell with longing, then moves one hand lower, down over my stomach.

'She's past it, Serena. All she has in her arsenal is angry words. She's incandescent that we're getting married, but she can't touch us now. I want you to see this diamond ring as your talisman. It tells you I love you. It tells her she has no place in our lives. And it makes me more determined than ever to get a date in the diary.'

He breathes into my hair and I smile weakly. 'So if nothing can touch us, why do we need to see Pierre?'

'To make things absolutely crystal. I want to get back to the way we were. And then I want to focus on our engagement, and our future.'

I lean against him. 'He has never been inside me, Gustav.'

His hand finds its way home, between my thighs. One finger starts to run over the damp crack.

His fingers part me. 'You're all tight and tense, like a jittery mare. How about I find another way to relax you?'

'We haven't got time!' I start to push him off, but Gustav's black eyes are gleaming behind me in the mirror. His glossy hair is still secured in the ponytail so that the scary beauty of his face is accentuated. Despite his soothing words, he's looking at me as if he's far away. As if he's never seen me before.

If it wasn't so terrifying it would be unbelievably sexy. Strangers in the steamed-up mirror.

He catches my hands and slaps them up against the glass, and then I hear the rip of his zipper.

'There's always time.' He kicks my legs apart, bends me over, and then his hardness is there, nosing its way into the damp softness. I stretch my arms so that the mirror is at arm's length. His hands leave my body and press down on mine again. Our reflected eyes lock as he pushes further into me, then pauses. There's that question again, flickering far back in his head.

Is he asking where I've been? Or is he asking who I am? Or after the roughness and haste of the other night, and the scratches on my back from the brick wall in the alleyway, is he seeking permission?

'Just be gentle with me, Gustav.' My knees buckle. 'I don't want to talk any more.'

'I don't want you to talk,' he mutters into my hair. 'I just want you to come back to me.'

My fingers squeak against the mirror, clawing for purchase, but there's nothing to support me, just a smooth slippery plane of unforgiving glass. My mind goes as blurry as my reflection as the desire loosens and envelopes me. My lover, my husband-to-be, draws back to enter me with the strange new force that possesses him. His fingers tangle with mine up against the mirror, my arms press us both back as if we are resisting our own open-mouthed reflections, as if someone at arm's length is doing this to us.

66

He pumps harder, faster, and I push against him, away from the mirror. He is saying something through gritted teeth, like he did the other night. Only this time it's not *bitch, bitch, bitch*. It sounds like *mine, mine. Mine*.

All too soon the warmth of his climax starts to gush inside me as my body squeezes tight around him. I hold him there, bucking against him, and just as I come there's the melodic tone of our doorbell singing round the apartment, interrupting, clashing.

'Oh, God, he's here. Spoiling everything.'

I bow my head between my arms, panting for breath, my legs shaking like a newborn colt's as Gustav sweeps my wet hair away and kisses my neck. He's still inside me.

'Whatever he did to you, just remember that you're mine now.'

He pulls out of me, zips himself up and backs out of the bathroom, still looking at me in the mirror until he's out the door and hurrying along the hall to let in his brother. I gaze at the space he's left, my body still clutching for him, still throbbing, longing for him to stay inside me.

Slowly, reluctantly, I get myself dressed and check my reflection again. No make-up. No scent. I'm putting on no jewellery or pretty dresses or high heels to honour this state visit of Pierre Levi.

I pad down the apartment towards the sound of the brothers' deep voices. I pause at the entrance to the huge, light-filled sitting room. All you can see from this angle is the sky. For a wild moment I long to be a bird flying up there, far away from this room, this apartment. Even this city.

'Hi, Serena. Thanks for – it's good to see you. You look – you look a bit feverish. Are you OK?'

I'm fine. My fiancé just took me from behind in the bathroom, that's why I'm all flushed.

67

I ignore Polly's off-stage prompt, afraid I might start to snuffle inappropriately.

The two men are standing on either side of the long mantelpiece, separated by the suspended, and unlit, fireplace. My eyes skate over them, unwilling to settle on either, and especially not on Pierre. Although they are already holding glasses of beer, there is too wide a space between the brothers, something awkward in their stance, the way they swivel quickly towards me when I come into the room as if I might offer some light relief.

'Hello, Pierre. You got here quickly.'

I take the glass of Chablis that Gustav hands me and sip from it as I walk past him towards the window. The wine flows through me and I know it's making my face even redder. On an empty stomach it hits the spot instantly. The tension doesn't release its grip, but it loosens a little.

'Just in time, by the look of it, sis. Have you been in a fight? My God, if anyone has hurt you—'

I round on him before I can stop myself. 'I told you on the phone the other night. Don't ever call me that!'

I avoid Gustav's eyes. Thank God I decided against a skirt and high heels. I've pulled on a slouchy pair of harem pants – glorified pyjamas really – and a creamy cashmere sweater and kept my feet bare. Even so, I'm prickly and self-conscious as I settle down on the wide windowsill, my favourite spot in the apartment. You can see Central Park from here. There's a new dusting of pale green on the treetops. My senses are vibrating like the antennae of those minuscule insects you see on wildlife programmes. Anticipating the predator.

'You look comfortable there. That's where we watched the fireworks on New Year's Eve,' says Pierre. 'Kind of where this all began.'

I turn my back on the fledgling spring day that has arrived

overnight and allow myself to look at him. No green coat. No velvet breeches. No peacock feather. Just a new hangdog expression.

Before I know what's happening, I have flown across the room and smacked him, hard, across the face.

The sound ricochets around the room. Pierre takes the blow with barely a flinch. Just a momentary closing of his dark eyes. The silence ticks by as we watch my handprint come up in livid stripes.

So much for growing wiser. I shouldn't have done that. I daren't look at Gustav.

'Nothing began,' I reply coldly, backing away from him. 'Not between you and me, anyway. Come on. You know why you're here, so let's just get on with it.'

'Serena, please.' Gustav clears his throat. He starts to walk towards me, eyeing his brother as if he might bite, or make a run for it. He changes his mind and stays where he is, halfway between us. 'She has a right to be angry, though, P. That bitch Margot has told us everything.'

'I can't think what she's told you. I haven't spoken to her since that night at the theatre. I thought she'd long since left New York when I told her I wasn't playing ball.' Pierre's knuckles whiten as he clutches his drink. 'She was grossly insulted, of course, rained down curses on my head. On all our heads—'

'Which is why I'd abseil into a volcano rather than be in her presence again.' Gustav keeps it very quiet. 'But into her presence we were enticed. It transpires she did leave New York, but only to track your movements in Venice. She sent us your peacock feather as evidence of your gatecrashing the Carnivale ball and pretending to be me. It spooked us, as intended, but we – Serena – thought it was from you. From your Venetian costume.' Gustav gestures towards the caramel suede sofa facing the window. 'Sit down.'

'You've told him everything?' Pierre doesn't move, but fixes his eyes on me.

'Of course I have. That's why you're here,' I reply, edging round the other sofas back to the windowsill. 'Your brother wants to hear it from you.'

'I know Margot instructed you to do whatever it took to remove Serena from the equation so that you, and she, could get close to me. She made out the twisted argument that Serena would somehow block any reconciliation between us, which would be funny if it wasn't farcical.' Gustav sighs and gazes at me, the flame in his eyes so hot Pierre can't possibly miss it. 'All this girl has ever done is support our efforts. But then at the first sign of trouble in our relationship you took the idea and ran with it. You fancied my girlfriend for yourself.'

I rest my fingers on the window for a moment. 'That sound like a fair summary to you, Levi?'

Pierre plonks himself down and pushes his body into the corner of the big sofa as if trying to make himself smaller. One knee jerks up and down so much that he puts the glass down on the table.

'Yes, I was in Venice. And yes, I was with Serena. But all I want is for us to be friends,' Pierre pins his eyes on me as he touches the red mark. 'I come in peace.'

My hand still stings as I study his face. He's lost some of the chunkiness around the neck and shoulders. The aggressive spiky hair has relaxed into surprising wild curls and the Californian sun has already tanned him. He's smart, and clean, surprisingly so, in a lightweight blue suit.

Goddammit, he's looking good.

But the best thing is that now he looks a lot less like Gustav.

Now he's here in front of me, I let myself feel it for the last time. Pierre's weight. The give of the cushions beneath us. His hands on me—

'When you say *with* Serena' – Gustav takes a step towards

70

Pierre, then veers round him and walks to the other end of the room – 'did you want her for yourself?'

Pierre's eyes slide over to his brother. There's a strange calmness about him I don't remember seeing before. And a tinge of sadness. But that could still be fake. As Margot said, the guy lives and works with actors. This humility is probably assumed, like everything else about him.

'What has she told you?'

'I'm asking *you* to tell us the truth, P. It's not up to Serena to defend herself.'

Pierre puts his head in his hands and it's a relief to have that glittering black stare extinguished for a moment. 'I mean Margot. What has *she* told you?'

'That you fucked my fiancée.'

The vicious words scatter around the space. Pierre and I flinch simultaneously. My head knocks against the thick glass window pane, setting up a new aching throb through my body. Pierre keeps his eyes on me, as if we are two naughty pupils being chastised by the headmaster.

Gustav's eyes move from me to his brother and back again as he starts to pace back towards the sofa.

Pierre collects himself and sits up straighter. He pushes forward slowly. He fixes his eyes on me. On the bites on my neck. My bruised, unpainted lips. My hair, tied in two loose plaits. He folds his arms. He could say anything right now. Absolutely anything. And it would all be over. This triangle taken apart, brick by brick. The three of us would never see each other again.

'Serena was so beautiful that night, G. You should have been there.'

Pierre has taken aim and shot us.

'What the hell kind of answer is that?' Gustav gasps, grabbing at his brother's folded arms to wrench them out of the defensive position. 'What did you do to her?'

71

Pierre catches Gustav's hands and pushes them away from him.

'I wanted her. OK? I admit it. Look at her. She's gorgeous. I'd fancied her since – oh, God, I was going to say since that evening she and I spent talking in the Gramercy cocktail bar, but if I'm honest it was as early as New Year's Eve, when I showed her the scars from the fire. Nearly every woman in my life has been repelled by my body, Gustav. You wouldn't know what that's like. But Serena? She just looked as if she wanted to help.'

'One of the many reasons I adore this girl.' Gustav folds his arms now. His legs are slightly akimbo, like a soldier. He glances across at me. 'But she's mine. Not yours.'

Mine, mine. Mine.

They are both studying me as if I'm an exhibit in a trial. There's unabashed admiration in Pierre's face, and pure, possessive love in Gustav's. I jam my hands between my knees and say nothing.

Pierre stands up, takes a couple of paces and kicks at the basket of logs beside the empty fire.

'I have a vacuum in my life, Gustav, where a good woman should be. And don't talk to me about Polly. I feel rotten about that, and one day I'll tell her so. But Serena – the attraction grew worse after that day we spent at the theatre. Then we had those cocktails at the Gramercy Hotel. Serena wanted to know why I'd dumped her cousin, but even when I went off on a tangent, blaming Margot, blaming my scars, blaming everyone and everything for making me such a shit, she still listened. Anyway, when I arrived at your apartment a few days later to return the camera equipment she'd left behind at the theatre – and yes, I admit I'd deliberately locked it away as an excuse to visit her – you'd obviously had some kind of row, and she'd taken off to Venice. Alone. So I took a chance. I'm a chancer,

G. You know that. Only this was the most dangerous gamble I'd ever taken.'

'You're not telling us anything we didn't already know, P.' Gustav growls. 'Did you fuck Serena in Venice?'

Margot's words, screaming at us down that dark stair-well.

They were fucking, Gustav!

Pierre hesitates, then turns back towards us. I wish he wouldn't stare at me like that. As if somehow I can save his life.

'Serena was a vision. The gown matched her eyes, as I knew it would. I'm experienced enough with costume fitting to be able to estimate her vital statistics, and boy, she spilled out of it in all the right places. OK, sorry, you don't want to hear that. But it wasn't just me who was captivated when she floated into that ballroom, Gustav. Nobody could take their eyes off her. And she hadn't a clue – at least, not until the other guests started groping her! There she was, with her mask and her camera, and the five peacock feathers in her headdress like a beckoning hand. I had organised every detail so that I could have her. I pretended to be you, I made sure we were in matching costumes, I didn't deny it when she kept calling your name. I knew she'd never go with me other-wise, and oh, God, I was so close to having her—'

'You're making me feel sick. Just be a man and tell me exactly how she sussed out you were tricking her. And tell me whether you passed the point of no return.'

Pierre pauses and looks at me. He scratches his tanned cheek.

I can remember the glitter of his eyes that night in Venice. It was all I could see of his face. He bruised me when he slammed his gloved hands over my mouth to hush me, but that roughness excited me all the more. I can remember the noises outside the gondola, the carnival revellers, the wash of a passing boat, our gasps as we pulled at each other's clothes—

'Pierre, you know what to do. You know what to say. You've come all this way,' I murmur, turning my hot cheek to lean against the cool glass. 'But if you lie to Gustav now, just like Margot did, so help me, your life won't be worth living.'

A message, a kind of shooting star, flares between me and Pierre. We're in this together. We were the only ones there on that Valentine's night.

'Serena is as innocent as she ever was. She did nothing wrong. I tricked her, because I wanted her. Her only sin was thinking I was you and responding just as she would have responded to you. She was over the moon! She thought you'd come to carry her home. She was so thrilled, so eager, so passionate, so sexy – in those few precious moments, even though I knew it was false pretences, even though it would only ever be the once, I got a taste of how it would feel to be you—'

'No, no, don't listen to this, Gustav. Please!'

But Gustav steps forward, his fists up again. 'I'm warning you, Pierre!'

'It didn't happen. OK? Nothing happened! I didn't fuck her! We were disturbed, and Serena pushed me away the moment she felt these bloody scars on my back. They're my brand. They always spoil everything. She kicked me right in the bollocks and then she was out of the boat like a bat out of hell.'

Gustav stares at his brother, then down at his fists. He uncurls his fingers, one by one, and flexes them as if they hurt. Then he opens them, as if letting something fly away.

'Which is exactly what Serena told me.'

'*Voilà*.' Pierre joins his own hands together and taps his mouth with his forefinger before pointing it at me. '*Mea culpa*. She's obviously been terrified of telling you how close we came, but none of it, not one moment, was her fault. And I'm so, so sorry. I've had time to think about this, time away from Margot, time away from you. I tried to do a terrible thing. I won't blame you if you banish me from your life again. But it only happened because she thought I was you, Gustav, you lucky bastard. Serena loves you.'

Gustav slowly unfolds his arms and bends to straighten the log basket. He picks up his beer glass and stares into the amber froth.

'Do you love her, though? Did you fall in love with my fiancée?'

Pierre rubs his hands over the new black curls, making them bounce and stand on end. He stands like that for a moment as if pressing thoughts into his head. Then he slaps his hands down.

'Look at her. I think she's incredible. Beautiful, talented and wise beyond her years to have entranced you the way she has. I was blinded. Knocked off my feet. Exactly the same way you were. But ultimately I think I'm incapable of loving anyone, G.' He shrugs, unaware that he's echoing the words I used before. 'Except you.'

Gustav nods, a mixture of sadness and weary amusement playing round his mouth.

'In which case I feel sorry for you, Pierre. And angry. But I'm angry with myself more than anything. I took my eye off the ball. But this isn't about me. It's down to Serena to forgive you.'

Pierre hesitates, then walks across to the window. His musky scent reaches me before he does: attractive, strong, yet my temples are throbbing painfully before he reaches me and holds out his hand. I remain motionless, the window hard and cold behind me.

'I'm sorry, Serena. I behaved atrociously to a lovely girl who didn't deserve it. I took a chance, like I always do, and put you in a terrible position. But maybe I did you a favour—'

'Pierre!' Gustav growls, putting his beer glass down with a smack and taking a step towards us. 'That's not the way it's done!'

'—because I only demonstrated, if it needed demonstrating, that the two of you are still unbreakable.'

Pierre's hand is firm, unwavering, in the air in front of me. There is a long silence, so deep I can hear the fridge humming in the kitchen and two birds arguing on the roof above us. I feel light and insubstantial as I take Pierre's hand, feeling his fingers close around mine, and shake it.

'You did something very dangerous, Levi,' I say quietly, and glance over to Gustav. His eyes are shining with delighted relief. 'But for Gustav's sake, and for the sake of our future together, I want to achieve some kind of harmony between us. You're a boneheaded bloody idiot, but fine – I forgive you.'

Pierre bows like a pageboy. 'And I'll do everything I can to make it up to you.'

I let him kiss my hand but as he lowers it again the pale-blue cuff of his shirt sleeve peeping from his blazer triggers fresh questions in my overactive mind. I snatch my hands away and shove them under my legs.

'Pierre. This may sound like a silly question when we're all being so serious, but why did you keep Gustav's shirts, all pressed and starched, in your cupboard when you were living at Margot Levi's apartment?'

'It's no secret that I was squatting there. I never pretended it was my place! But as for keeping G's clothes, I left in a hurry for LA, and although some of my winter gear is still there, that's all. Believe it or not, that apartment has always been more like a monk's cell for me. I barely spent any time there. Preferred to sleep in other people's beds. Sorry. Maybe that was a bit inappropriate.' Pierre straightens and shakes his head. 'Why would I hoard Gustav's shirts after years of not seeing him? We're not even the same collar size!'

There is not one iota of comprehension as the brothers shrug at me. I tap the side of my head.

'Don't look at me as if I'm mad. I wish I'd never mentioned it now, but – Gustav's wedding shirt is there. Wing collar. Silver tiepin. And the missing cufflink that matches the one I found in Lugano. The one with the initials GL engraved on it.'

Any animation in Gustav's eyes dies. He touches the cuffs of the maroon shirt he's put on today. 'So Margot took the shirts. And the mementos. I told Dickson to burn them, or take them for charity, but—'

'You threw away that other cufflink, though, didn't you? There was no point keeping just one, you said.' I stand up now. 'And when I got so upset about it, you assured me you had disposed of every gift from Margot.'

'Calm down, *chérie*. There's not so much as a long black hair of hers left in any of the houses.' Gustav nods, but his eyes have that closed-off look again. 'She's got nothing and no one in her life. She's like Miss Havisham, hoarding old shirts and mismatched jewellery as if it will bring me back. Come on, girl. Rise above Margot's morose obsessions.'

I let my head fall back against the strong, cold glass. 'I'm sorry, Gustav. Seeing those things, those *wedding* things, just creeped me out, that's all. That whole place made my skin crawl.'

Pierre hesitates, as if he wants to sit down next to me, then to my relief he goes to stand next to the suede sofa on the other side of the room.

'Guys, I don't want to sound the alarm bell, but this

obsessive insanity is what I've been living with for months. I'll be too far away now in LA to help, but I'm warning you. The ball you need to keep your eye on is Margot.'

'I won't have her name contaminating my day.' Gustav steps abruptly towards the kitchen. 'I have lunch to get sorted.'

'Margot is on a mission, G. If she can't have you, she'll make sure no one will. She won't rest until Serena's out of the picture.' Pierre follows Gustav and grabs his arm. 'I'm not your nemesis. *Margot* is. She's the danger you need to watch out for.'

CHAPTER FOUR

The gallery looks bright and optimistic in the daylight, but like every other morning for the last month I wonder when I unlock the door if I'll find it ransacked. Will the photographs from my 'Windows and Doors' themed exhibition be ripped off the freshly painted white walls? Will the simple elegant frames be snapped, the glass smashed? All my images shredded and obscene graffiti sprayed on the walls?

I've done my best to hide my worries from Gustav. I feel safe when I'm with him, in those strong arms, looking into those steady black eyes. But when I'm on my own I'm terrified. And to make matters worse I've been hiding something from him.

He says she's barred from the condo. Banned from the gallery. The apartment has been swept again for bugs and – surprise surprise: there were none. Although they did find one in the gallery office phone. She can't come anywhere near us or he'll call the police. So when does it become acceptable to turn fretting into snooping?

I wasn't really snooping. I left Gustav and Pierre to go for a walk together after our tense conversation and a few nervy bites of lunch, but thoughts of cufflinks and shirts went on nagging at me after they'd gone out. I knew Gustav would be furious and Pierre would think me neurotic. But the madness of Margot was infecting me. I couldn't get her whispered threats out of my ears, the smell of her clogging perfume out of my hair, even the air in that apartment out of my skin. The fact that she had taken precious items engraved with Gustav's initials from Lugano made me feel sick. She'd kept them somewhere for the last six years, brought them back to New York, lovingly unpacked them, washed and pressed them, hung them in their old wardrobe as if, as he said, she was waiting for him to come back.

So here I was, facing the fear, or so I thought, opening one, then another of the battered antique cigarette boxes that Gustav keeps in his dressing room, and, after I'd sneezed away the old tobacco dust, there it was, glinting amongst some old coins, as if waiting for me to find it.

The cufflink he said he'd thrown away, whose mate is now snugly fastened in the shirt he wore to marry Margot. He'd kept it.

So he forgot about it. Big deal. Polly's opinion was brisk. I dropped the cufflink as if it was red hot, and banged the box shut.

Say what you like, Polly, but that cufflink makes her, their life together, a tangible presence. She's a face, a voice, I have seen and heard and will never forget. A jealous, deranged woman collecting treasures from her marriage to my fiancé. And don't tell me, Polly, that they're just shirts and trinkets, because to me they feel like armour. Weapons of war. However mad that makes me sound, I want her gone.

Leave it for now. Just leave it. Don't let her get to you. Don't stir things up between you over a piece of junk. And yes. You do sound mad.

So today, like every day since I got my act together,

everything in the gallery is in place. The main picture of the pale hand extending from between green shutters to dead-head some scarlet geraniums still holds centre stage on the main wall, now adorned with a red spot to indicate that it's been sold. Actually to the local art college. The other pictures still hang in groups according to the city – London, Paris, Manhattan – where they were taken.

Dickson has nailed the title of my new venture, *Serenissima*, above the door.

That name isn't just an emphatic version of my own. It's a gift from my patrons the Weinmeyers and the moniker applied to the city of Venice at the height of its unique, feminine splendour.

One of the larger images shows a row of blank *palazzi* windows, Gothic arches set into crumbling red walls, with a tattered gold curtain flapping through a broken pane like a lolling tongue.

Here's a church in a quiet *campo,* a broad carpet of sunlight leading the way across a worn step into the dark recesses. And there is the little costume shop in Campo San Barnaba where Crystal, sent by Gustav to watch over me, accompanied me to hire the ill-fated green gown for the Weinmeyers' ball. The display in the hire-shop window is crammed with cruel, mirthless masks suspended behind the smeared glass like decapitated heads on spikes.

I switch on all the spotlights, and with the glare comes a kind of epiphany. Time to embrace the day. Time to push aside the lingering fear that our life will always be a series of pitfalls, an identity parade of other enemies lining up to trip us up. Time to dismiss the discovery of a single tarnished cufflink and let Gustav's calm belief in me make me feel ten feet tall. If he can forgive my recklessness in going off with a masked stranger after a ball in Venice, and my stupidity in believing that stranger to be my boyfriend, then I should be able to get past that hideous scene in Margot's flat, too.

Every day we talk and we talk, and we are closer than ever. But still I'm not sleeping. Thank God Gustav is coming back this evening after another business trip. His second in four weeks. I sleep better with him next to me, warmed up and worn out from sex. Last night I sat cross-legged on the wide window ledge of our bedroom and stared for hours over the dark oblong of Central Park.

The world feels fragile somehow because Margot is on the planet. She may not be visible, but she's everywhere. Gustav seems to think that by facing her he's laid a ghost. Pierre disagrees. He reckons the diamond ring has made her all the more determined. And I just feel uneasy. All the time.

Manhattan Island feels way too small.

I nip out of the gallery to get a coffee. We're well into April now. There's real warmth in the air. Why not focus on all the good things? Green shoots and flowers are sprouting on the High Line above this street. I'm the owner of a great new gallery and my second exhibition is selling fast. I've got a rich, handsome, passionate man who makes me feel like a sexy, low-down princess every day and wants to marry me before the year is out.

By the time I've got my coffee and my pastry and wandered back to the gallery I am feeling much more like Carrie in *Sex in the City*. Before tackling my schedule of phone calls, I assess each photograph and its position on the wall. It's time to view the few unsold images through a potential buyer's eyes. I mustn't lose my resolve. I'm even wearing a sassy new Chanel suit, smoky pink bouclé tweed with a silky white blouse, and cherry-red brogues, to make me feel more like a boss.

The steady flow of visitors results in the sale of the remainder of the images, so it's late afternoon before I get to the penultimate of my list of phone calls. I'm speaking to the tutor of the large art college who bought my 'Hand Plucking Petals' photograph. I'm dictating another advertisement, trawling for raw new photographic, figurative or abstract talent amongst her students for my next show. Then I'm going to call Crystal in London and ask her to come out here to work for me.

'The younger the better, so long as they need a real break,' I tell the tutor at the other end of the phone, who is enthusing about the fledgling talent she has both in her current intake and amongst the freshers who will be arriving in the autumn. 'I was given a chance by Gustav Levi, who launched a solo show for me not long after I graduated. I want to do the same for others. Yes, I hope to expand back to London, maybe next year, but Manhattan's my base for the moment.'

The little bell above the door tinkles and I curse softly under my breath. I can't get this woman off the line and I really want to close up and get home. I have all the ingredients of something really healthy and juicy to prepare for Gustav tonight. Chorizo casserole and butter beans cooked in lashings of marsala.

The gaggle of female voices bursting into my gallery is so noisy I can't hear myself think. I make sure the art tutor has my details then hang up and turn round. Three stunning blondes are pushing through the door, unwinding pashminas and shaking lustrous hair out of barrow-boy caps as if they're settling in for a session.

'Wow. What a cool place! And you look a million dollars, Serena! Very stern and businesslike today! Glad to see you're still doing the risqué shots, spying on people through their windows, but we were hoping you might have included some naughtier ones from your past commissions?'

The tallest of the girls comes towards me with her arms out. I'm still trying to work out who she is and what she's talking about when she pulls me against her soft breasts, swelling through the tight pink sweater she's wearing under her open jacket. She tilts my face up to hers and gives me a long, soft kiss, right on the lips. She twitches excitedly as the others giggle and start walking around the gallery, studying the pictures.

I extricate myself from the girl's embrace as politely as I can and pull my jacket closed.

'I'm sorry to appear rude, but I don't—'

'Recognise us with our clothes on! Of course! How stupid of us!' The girl skips over to her friends, reaches into the enormous bag one of them is carrying, and pulls out a huge white dildo. 'This jog your memory? Or any other part of you?'

I snort with laughter as one of the others bends over the desk and sticks her bottom up in the air. They all go straight into their act without the aid either of a backing track or any kind of stage direction. The tallest girl tosses the dildo around her head in a series of skilled and hilarious cheerleader moves while the second girl starts kissing the one bent over the desk. She runs her hands to the top of her friend's legs and yanks down her silvery tights and knickers to reveal a pert bottom. The bent one arches herself eagerly as her friend's fingers wander under her little miniskirt as if to soften her up.

Their tongues flicker in and out of each other's luscious mouths, moaning like proper porn stars. I tiptoe across to the door, glance outside and decide to lock up in case someone influential comes into the gallery and is shocked by the entertainment.

Just as the kissing girls start to exaggerate their moans and squeals, the cheerleader smacks the ass of her friend still bent over my desk, kicks her legs further apart and makes as if she's going to ram the dildo up her cute white butt.

I clap my hands like a schoolmistress to stop them. 'OK, OK, I get the picture! But this is a gallery, not a strip club!'

The cheerleader presses her friend between the shoulder blades and shoves her face down on the desk, sliding the dildo further up between her cheeks. 'And for your information we're dancers. Not strippers. You want us to stop? We won't stop, or leave your establishment, until you tell us where you've seen us before.'

'OK, you win!' I laugh helplessly, flipping the 'closed' sign over the gallery door and lowering the slatted blinds. 'It all comes flooding back. It was the Club Crème. You were performing for the Robinson stag night and I was taking photographs. It's the midtown private members-only club where anything goes—'

'And everyone comes! We know it's all hush-hush in that silly club but we were hoping you'd smuggled out some shots of that night. Something we could include in our CVs?' They all shriek in unison as the dildo gives a final playful jab at its victim's ass before the ringleader pulls it away and licks it lasciviously. The other two snap out of their roles and hoik their panties up again. 'You can do that for us, can't you?'

'No, I cannot! Top secrecy is the Club Crème code! I'd never work in this town again if the press got hold of some of those shots! Admittedly, I was paid handsomely by the Robinson brothers to shoot their mate's stag night, and boy, was that poor groom debased by you lot!' I shake my hair in front of my face. 'Actually, you did more than debase the groom. I went a bit crazy with the stags after the shoot, and then, to punish me for misbehaving, Gustav bought a dildo off you!'

'Not much of a punishment!' giggles the girls' ringleader. 'We sold him our favourite!'

'And we specialise in using oversized ones,' chime in the others. 'Bet it made your eyes water!'

The three of them jiggle and dig each other in the ribs as they straighten their minuscule clothes. They seem to fill the gallery with their swishing blonde hair, spray-tanned limbs and a kind of chirruping dawn chorus. They check their reflections in each other's hand mirrors and then sway across to the couch in the window to sit in a row, like tropical birds on a wire.

They obviously take their work home with them. The dildo-wielding may be their signature act when they're on stage, but I bet they enjoy using the toys on each other when they're at play, too.

My body gives a dirty little kick deep inside. I know damn well how good a woman's naked skin feels. Her mouth. Her nipples between my teeth. I have an inkling of what that's like because I was kidnapped, for half an hour, by a couple of dancers at Pierre Levi's burlesque theatre after that shoot back in February. When everyone had gone, they dragged me behind the scenes backstage, set up my camera to film us then ravished me with their mouths and fingers.

I cross my arms firmly across my breasts. My body prickles with a mixture of remembered pleasure and remembered anxiety. It was fun, an eye-opener – and a leg-opener – but I still suspect that Pierre was not only hanging around to witness that impromptu girl-on-girl display but set the whole thing up. Well, if he thought it would serve as another ploy to turn Gustav against me, it backfired. Gustav loved the footage when I showed it to him.

I perch on the edge of the desk facing the girls, and try to look serious.

'OK, lovelies. I'd love to talk about my sex life with you all day, but that's not why you're here. What can I do for you?'

'Well, it *is* partly why we're here. We only saw you working behind your camera that night at the Club Crème, but we've heard about you going a bit crazy with the stags, as you put it. So we wanted to check you out for ourselves.' The second girl, the one who just pretended to take a dildo up the ass, speaks up. 'Word on the street is that you're just as smoking hot as us professional strippers.'

The third girl kicks out petulantly. 'Dancers, please. We're artistes!'

We all giggle again. It's as if they've blown fresh air through the gallery.

'So much for confidentiality. And look, you're fantastic artistes. But this is my place of work. It's a gallery, not a pole-dancing club. I'm not about to join your troupe if that's what you're after.'

'Well, that's just it. We might have a commission for you,' says the first blonde, the one who kissed me on the mouth. 'But first, to prove that we girls aren't solely about tits and ass, I've brought a portfolio of my own work to show you.'

The pink folder she pulls out of her enormous bag of tricks feels rather light when she hands it to me.

'I'll look at it with pleasure. May I keep it for a day or two?' I start to unzip the case, then pause. 'So as well as rumours that I'm "smoking hot", you've also heard about my new gallery and that I'm actively seeking new talent? You seem to know an awful lot about me, er—'

'Chloe!' They all sing her name together. 'And they're not rumours.'

'Fine. I'll look at the portfolio tomorrow, Chloe, if that's OK. I'm closing up now because I have to get back home and cook dinner!'

They all stand up slowly and stretch like cats.

'Cooking dinner at home on a Friday night? What are you, fifty years old?'

'None of your business how I choose to spend my time!

87

Now if you don't mind—' I move to the back of the gallery to start switching off the lights. These girls must be at least three or four years older than me. So why do I suddenly feel like the sensible big sister? I pause. 'But before you go. Who was it who told you all about me? Did someone send you?'

They finish their stretches and start draping their silky scarves around their necks.

'One of our new colleagues met you at the Theatre B.'

Half the lights are out now. The three of them are illuminated by the spots over the door.

'Theatre B?'

They are smiling at me. Glossy cupid's-bow lips spread over those even white American teeth, but there's a couple of beats of hesitation before Chloe, the leader of the pack, continues.

'It stands for Burlesque. Midtown. Gramercy Park. You did a day's work when Pierre Levi had invited the Hollywood guys in. I guess you must have so many commissions, but you were shooting a storyboard, a day in the life of a burlesque show.'

I swallow, try to keep my face straight.

'Of course I remember. Fantastic Moulin Rouge décor, costumes, music.'

'You must be stoked to have him as a future brother-in-law.' They all nod enthusiastically. 'We hear he's going places. The cameras are rolling.'

I lock up the back office carefully and gather my things. 'So is it me personally you're interested in, or is it what I can do for you at the gallery?'

'Both! The world of theatre and dancing is such a small one, you see. Everyone talks about each other. Our friend told us how she dragged you backstage when the shoot was over and introduced you to the delights of girlie sex. Oh, look, guys, Serena Folkes is blushing!'

A confusion of shame and exhilaration swirls inside me as I recall the heated atmosphere of the Theatre B, as they call it. The scented changing rooms recreated on the stage. The dancers arriving for work in their street clothes and then transforming themselves with costumes and make-up into painted, show-stopping can-can girls. The illusion, to give Pierre his due, cleverly created to make us believe that we had all been transported to *fin de siècle* Montmartre.

And, permeating the whole day, Pierre's dark, disconcerting presence. So different from the cowed young man who flew all the way from California on his brother's orders to shake my hand and say sorry. Or is he?

'Some of those lucky girls have gone off to Tinseltown to make their fortune.' Chloe's voice interrupts my reminiscences. 'And we've been left behind. For now. But while we're resting, we're working in this amazing new bar. It's called Sapphix. The clue's in the name. It's a bit like the Club Crème, but not so exclusive. And not so secretive.'

'So not really the same.' I start to move across to the door. 'I mean, is it girls only? Do they keep boys out altogether?'

'Oh, the gorgeous ones who hang around the doors are occasionally allowed in once the scary boss has checked their credentials!' The girls are all talking at once.

'Sounds fun.' I flick off the last light, leaving just one to illuminate the main photograph above the desk. 'But I really can't—'

'We know you've used a dildo. We know you're not nearly as innocent as you look! But really the club's cool. You drink, you dance and you forget all your cares!'

They are all clustered round me like a shoal of silvery fish. I fling the door open and hold my arm out to usher them out.

'Hey, girls, I'm glad you've got a great new job. You deserve to do well. You're amazing strippers – I mean dancers. But you're telling me all this why? Did you say something about a commission?'

'You're obviously not selling Sapphix to her, Chlo!' The second girl nudges their ringleader in the ribs. 'Get to the point!'

'You look as if you've got the world on your shoulders today, so we reckon we've come along just in time! We want you to come down and check out our club. You can let your hair down! And if you're worried about taking time off from running this place and spoiling your husband's dinner, think of it as a brief. Publicity for the club. We can be your new client!'

'Venturing into the world of hospitality—'

'It'll be fun!' They giggle again as I lock up the gallery. Our breath puffs in joined-up clouds on to the window.

On impulse, I take a picture on my phone of my three abductors all whispering and fidgeting around me, and send it with a text to Gustav:

Remember that scene in Love Actually *when the gauche English guy travels to America seeking adventure and is picked up by four gorgeous gals? Well, these are my new friends, honey. But I'll still be home in time to meet you!*

The girls run into the road to hail a cab that cruises past while I wait for Gustav's reply. His response comes quickly.

Your kidnappers look cute, naughty and familiar. I know what they like to do with a length of silicone and latex. Don't worry, plane delayed. Just make sure they leave you in a fit state to pleasure your fiancé when he gets home.

I hesitate for a moment. Maybe I should go home and make myself beautiful for him. But the girls are herding me towards the yellow cab.

'I give in. I may be the owner of a smart new gallery, but I can't afford to turn down work. So OK. We'll call this a commission. Because God knows, I could do with letting off some steam!'

And then I turn to my gaggle of admirers and crook my elbows for them to lead me astray.

There is so much gossip and chatter in the cab that, although we're still somewhere in Manhattan, I have no idea which area we have come to. When the car comes to a halt, we pile out on to a scruffy narrow street which seems to be buried almost entirely under scaffolding. A brave row of spindly, leafless trees lends sparse softness to the acres of grey tarpaulin flapping in the sudden aggressive breeze.

The girls trot across the pavement and drag me down some basement steps, noisily assessing my vital statistics as we all tumble past display cases showing flashing neon images of stripping starlets. And then we're in the warm, noisy embrace of the already rammed, brothel-red, chandelier-lit Sapphix Bar.

The heat and noise of voices and music envelop me, and I cease to give a damn about anything. I don't know what made these girls think I had the world on my shoulders. Maybe it was the severe suit, my hair up in the kind of tightly pinned knot that Crystal would be proud of. Maybe it was something in my face. Maybe they are mind readers. I could use some female company. My handful of trusted friends who saw me through thick and thin when I was a troubled, lonely kid are all back in Devon, England, leading their own lives. Or maybe I'm spending too much time with Gustav and not enough time around other females. My cousin Polly is meditating in Morocco and virtually uncontactable. Crystal – if you could call her female – is looking after the London properties. And every time I see Ingrid Weinmeyer, she paws me like a hungry cat.

We're not about to sit down and chill out, it would seem. The girls pull me round to the back of the bar where a statuesque waitress with chocolate skin barely covered by a sparkling white bikini spins shot glasses from a bullet belt slung across her body.

'Remember me, honey? I was one of the dancers at Theatre B when you were shooting that storyboard for Pierre Levi back in early February?' she cries, pouring a neat line of liquid into each glass. 'My girlfriend and I had a taste of you behind the scenes. And I've still got your panties from that day as a trophy!'

'Oh, God, of course I remember! Your world really is far too small for my liking,' I say with a pout, wagging my finger at the other girls. 'Is nothing sacred?'

'Certainly not your panties!' The blondes all laugh and slap their long slim thighs. 'You think her man has a clue what Serena Folkes is like behind that wide-eyed look?'

'If Gustav Levi is anything like his wicked brother Pierre, he'll handle her just fine.' The black girl leans down, breasts spilling from her tiny white bikini. She studies me hard as she hands me a glass. 'Everyone knows about you and Gustav Levi, honey. You and he are the hottest couple outside showbiz. And I'll bet he's happy to see his girl swing with girls as well as boys. No faking that cute little climax once we'd got our hands on her, I can tell you.'

I pick at the pins in my hair to loosen them. 'You owe me dinner for that little escapade. Remember? You and your girlfriend grab me at the end of a long day, ravish me with fingers and tongues as a none too subtle introduction to lesbian sex, oh, and also you film it – I reckon dinner's the very least you can offer me!'

They all kick their legs out again, shrieking with glee.

'Sure. Whatever madam wants. But first, a tequila tasting to get you in the mood. Stocking this really good stuff was my idea. The new management didn't have a clue. Just told me to get on with ordering it in. So listen up. This liquor is not your usual tacky "mixto" tequila. This is a hundred per cent agave. Tell me what you taste. And mind you sip it like real Mexicans. Don't shoot.'

We hold our glasses up, pinkies in the air, and drink.

'Lime!' shouts Chloe.

'Citrus, definitely!' shouts the second girl.

'Oranges,' I murmur, relishing the ooze of warmth invading my veins.

'Good. That's a blanco. You can drink it with delicacies such as ceviche dressed in lime, chilli and coriander. So. Here comes another.'

The girl stands in front of us and spins another bottle out of her holster twixt finger and thumb, like a pistol. 'This is a lightly aged reposado. You can eat strong cheese or hung meat with this. Totally different taste.'

'We like well hung meat,' chortles one of the others.

'Cinnamon,' I murmur, draining my next glass. 'God, it's making me hungry!'

'I can taste honey!' calls out Chloe. 'Ooh, making me horny!'

Any stresses and strains the girls thought were bothering me have vanished, washed away by these first fiery tequila shots. I slam my shot glass down on to the chrome and, as I reach for a third glass, a thought strikes me.

'Shit! In all the excitement I've left my camera behind at the gallery!'

The girls stop as they're about to knock back the third round, and exchange looks. Chloe jumps to her feet. 'I've an idea! You can sing for your supper, then! Or rather dance.'

'You have to be kidding! You owe me, remember, not the other way round! I'm no one's performing seal, and if I'm not working, at least let me relax!'

We all down another row of shots, and then they're off their barstools and surrounding me. I stare round in confusion as they bundle me off my chair.

'Not any more. We've been told to get you to work, and if you've left your camera behind then you have to pay for your drinks some other way. Come on. Let's get you out of these boring clothes and have you looking like a proper ho!'

We tumble through a glittery curtain into a small, hot changing area consisting of wall-length mirrors and tiny pink fluffy bathroom stools. They push me down on one of these while they peel off their clothes. Unlike the performers at Pierre's burlesque theatre, who draped themselves and fondled each other as they undressed, applying lipstick to each other's mouths, navels and nipples, transforming themselves as part of the performance, these girls are brisk and on a meter.

I feel like a spare part without my camera to hide behind. The girls pour themselves into smooth, sequinned leopard-print bodysuits. I remember the costumes so well from the stag night at the Club Crème. The music throbs louder at the front of house. The girls stop talking at last, concentrating on painting each other's faces with gaudy shading to accentuate their eyes and bright red lips.

I can't tell the difference between them now. They are standing in a row, each one back-combing the next one's hair into a lion's mane.

'Is it just the three of you here?' I ask, remembering the crowded stage at the burlesque theatre.

'The boss was supposed to complete the line-up.' I think it's Chloe speaking, with her mouth full of hairpins. 'That was the idea when we were hired. Problem is, it turns out she's not as young as she makes out, though we'd be fired on the spot if we said as much. There's something wrong with her, anyhow. Collapsed on the first day of rehearsals.'

There's too much noise. Too many voices. I put my hands over my ears and glance round the little space for some kind of back door, but the three of them turn to me now, bending from their waists, rotating their necks and knees sinuously as they sketch their stretches, their huge cartoon-cat eyes unblinking as they surround me again.

'Sounds like you've all been muddling along for the opening nights of your routine? You must be pretty nervous, then!' I take off my jacket, but sweat continues to trickle between my breasts and down my back, making my crisp cotton gallery-owner's shirt stick to my armpits. I try to pluck it away from my overheated skin, but I seem to be getting hotter by the minute. I realise they haven't answered me. 'Wait a minute. You're looking at me like that – why? Oh, God. I thought I was off the hook, but you little bitches are serious about me getting up on my hind legs, aren't you?'

'We told you. You're here to work, and now there's a gap in the formation, we need you in the chorus line.' They advance on me and start unbuttoning my shirt. 'And if you're sexy enough tonight, maybe you can understudy for Chloe when she goes off on her holidays!'

And that's how I find myself blinking in the light from my phone camera as they take a picture of me dressed in a sparkly white bra just like the tequila lady's. I'm also wearing white lace hold-ups and a tiny white tutu like a cygnet in the *corps de ballet*. They go to put the finishing touches to their own attire, strapping leather suspender belts round their waists to add to the oddness of their costumes.

I peer through the glittery curtain at the back of the stage. It's little more than a podium. I can't think how the girls are going to move at all, let alone gyrate and dance in such a small space. They have deliberately dressed me differently from their jungle motif, because I am playing a 'victim' and must therefore stand out.

My role is simple, apparently. All I have to do is stand there, or lie there, and take it. They won't tell me what 'it' is.

I start to think that maybe, if I don't open the curtain any wider, it won't happen, but Chloe puts her arm round my waist and sweeps the curtain aside to point out the audience. The club is full now of beautiful, chattering, drinking, scantily clad women, although there's also a handful of men lounging in a darkly lit booth on the opposite side of the room.

'Oh, there's the boss. She's like the queen bee. And those guys with the bulging crotches are her drones.'

I follow her pointing leopard paw. And see that I've walked straight into a trap.

Because the queen bee enthroned on the velvet banquette, wearing a long sheath dress in red snakeskin, a red lace net over her face, looks exactly like Margot.

'Chloe! Tell me I'm hallucinating. Is that Margot Levi? Because if it is I can't be anywhere near her!'

The lookalike hasn't seen me yet. Or at least she hasn't acknowledged I'm here. I may be wrong about who it is, but I still want to get out. I turn frantically to beg Chloe to help me. But Chloe's speaking to the barman.

This is no coincidence. It really is her. Margot sent those girls to entice me here with a story about taking photographs of her new club. I don't blame them. I like them. And God knows, they need to know what – who – they're dealing with. But now that I've been tricked into dancing with them, she'll organise some serious degradation to alienate me from Gustav. This could be what Pierre meant. That she will toy with me and threaten me, hurt me over and over again until she's driven me away.

I could escape now. There must be some kind of fire exit. So why am I rooted to the spot? I stare at her, at her spiky body and shadowed face. Then I look at myself.

I look pretty damn hot, actually. Just like my new friends said. I'm in character as a cygnet from *Swan Lake*. I can use this. I'm damn well going to work it.

My legs are long and elegant in the white stockings. I fluff up my tutu, run my hands up the tempting inches of visible thigh to leave them showing. I flex my foot so that the stocking rides up and down. Then I run my hands up to the frilly knickers that the girls said looked so much sexier than going commando.

I dig my fingers into my sweaty palms. My body stiffens. This is not fear flooding through me. It's cold, hard resolve. She's got me here. I'm in costume. I'm on my marks. She wants to use this to hurt me, or show Gustav I'm cheap and unworthy, but I won't let her belittle me and I won't give her the satisfaction of running away either. The girls have made me look hot. Really, really hot. How can this possibly work against me?

The show's about to start and the atmosphere in the club is quietening down in anticipation. The DJ is mouthing something at one of the dancers as they parade out from behind the curtain to take their places.

Look over here, Margot. See my white painted face watching you. Masking my fear. Taking that fear away, at least for the next few minutes.

Sure enough, she looks up. She lifts her sharp chin above the shaven head of one of the young men, whose mouth is wandering down her stomach while another lifts her red dress. She fixes me with those slanted eyes, glaring down her narrow beak, and she nods, as if giving the signal to drop the guillotine.

The icy calm washes through me once more. It won't be Serena Folkes who's belittled tonight. The girls beckon to me, but I reach behind me and take out my phone. They make rude gestures. I put up one finger to ask them to wait.

Making sure everyone can see me, can see that any plan to humiliate or blackmail me isn't going to work, I hold the phone up. I take a photograph of Margot, and then I text Gustav's number, attaching Margot's picture and a selfie of me in the white costume and adding the name of the club.

I want him to be here. Not just to protect me. I want him to see everything that happens when Margot is around.

Then I'm ready to begin.

The girls have brought a row of barstools up on to the podium and arranged them beside a metal shelf to represent a bar laid with a wine bottle and four glasses. They strike louche, masculine poses with their elbows on the shelf, flicking at the strange white belts they are all wearing. Chloe sits astride a stool with her legs spread, just like a man. All of them ogle me.

The volume is jacked up. It's some kind of tribal house music, the kind of repetitive, hypnotic beat that pumps inside so that your heart jumps against your bones. I strut across to the pretend bar, kick the 'guys' aside and down a glass of wine in one. It's not pretend wine, though. It's another glass of tequila and the room tips slightly.

Chloe takes my arm and pulls me to stand between her legs. She looks me up and down, her face set in a hard, masculine leer. I glance out at the audience. If Margot wants to teach me some kind of lesson, she can think on. My lesbian cherry has already been popped.

One of the other girls pours another tequila, and as I lean to sip it, my breasts swell heavily over the edge of the tight bra. I arrange myself so that the audience can see my every move, one white thigh crossing slowly over the other, my hand stroking leisurely down my throat. It's hard to see through the dazzle of footlights at the edge of the stage, but I can feel those hungry female eyes burning. My fingertips brush my breast and because I'm so wrought up, this lightest of touches sends a bolt of excitement sizzling through me.

I glance over at the mistress's booth. I can just make out her eyes above the dazzle of lights, but her toy boy is obviously licking her now, because although she seems to be

98

staring at me, there is the half-closed, blank expression of a woman being sucked off.

I can't remember where the entrance to the club is, so I won't even know if, or when, Gustav arrives. Maybe that's for the best.

I turn my head so that now all I can see is Chloe. And as if someone else is directing me to follow orders, I take one breast, already squeezed halfway out of the tight bra top, and let the nipple pop out and harden in the air. Chloe's eyes flash with surprise, and she turns her grin into a masculine leer of desire as she sees what I'm doing. One of the others comes closer to me and mirrors the action on my other breast, tweaking and rubbing the nipple, and a fist of excitement clenches inside me.

Chloe gives a very faint nod at the two others and they retreat out of sight. She clinks her glass with mine and runs her finger over my wrist, sending a faint shiver of electricity up my arm.

So this is how it feels to be a proper performer. This is Serena the show-off, getting wholeheartedly into character. I so hope Gustav gets here soon. I so hope he understands, when he sees Margot, that his role is to show her he's mine and I don't give a shit for her and her games. This is me, showing her what I'm made of. I glance over at the bar. If Gustav is here, surely that's where he'll head if Margot doesn't somehow waylay him first?

The barman isn't serving anyone, however. He's ogling me, polishing a huge balloon glass over and over as if he's in a trance. Then he reaches up and turns a small metal handle, and a filmy muslin curtain drops down between the stage and the audience. The arc lights shift around and shine brightly from the back of the stage. We're going to be shadow dancers.

Chloe stands up, leaving the stool between us, and pulls

me closer so that our faces are touching. She runs her lips over mine. I jerk away, but she pulls me closer and probes my mouth with her tongue, flicking it exaggeratedly so that the audience can see what our outlines are doing.

I wonder where the others are. Is this going to be a real-life sex show, just the two of us? I let her kiss me. It's not so unfamiliar. Emilia Robinson, sister of the Robinson stags, got me into a threesome with her Latina bridesmaid when I was supposed to be shooting a 'bride preparing for her wedding day' montage in her boudoir. The tequila-shooting barmaid kissed me like this when she seduced me at Pierre's theatre.

This behaviour is allowed. Gustav and I agreed long ago that pretty much anything goes, so long as he is there to watch, or he gets to see it on film. This is for his benefit, too, when he arrives.

As Chloe kisses me, someone, presumably the barman, the tequila girl or the other two dancers, fixes the curtain in place so that it stretches taut to make our silhouettes ultra-clear.

I am just a shadow now. I can do whatever I like, and no one will know me. No one except Margot and Gustav. I just have to trust that he's here, and that he's watching.

There's a sudden whoop of applause from the audience. I struggle to pull away from Chloe, but she has my face locked between her hands and she continues to kiss me, pulling me to lie across the stools.

The music descends to a much sexier, deeper beat. Somehow more threatening, too. My nipples scrape across the bar seat as Chloe continues to pin me down, and as I smile up at her she whips a wispy scrap of chiffon round my wrists and ties my hands to the foot bar of the stool.

Chloe does her Bond girl shimmy, raising her arms in triumph like a boxer, and the audience cheers and whoops to see me tied so elegantly yet firmly. Then one of the other dancers grabs Chloe away from me in a show of possessiveness, and as we are dragged apart I see why the audience are yelping with such delight. The newcomer has a huge white phallus strapped to the belt around her waist. It's protruding like a huge hard-on from her groin and bouncing eagerly. It must look shockingly sensational against the curtain.

This other dancer runs her hands over Chloe's breasts, holds them up and pinches her nipples into sharp points to poke through the flimsy net-like fabric of her leopard-print body. Then she rips it neatly at the waist so that it slithers like a second skin down her legs, leaving her bottom and pussy totally bare.

Chloe starts to smile as the other dancer gropes and fondles her, and then other hands start touching me. The third girl must be behind me now because my tutu is flipping up to my waist. A white dildo slides down my face. It waggles comically to show me what I'm in for, and the audience wave their arms in the air and dance about with delight.

The other girl presses up behind Chloe and with her fingers she parts her to reveal a sudden redness. I wonder if they've run lipstick up the crack to make the colour show so vividly and, if so, why, when the audience can only see us in monochrome? A finger disappears inside Chloe and I start rubbing myself against the stool in response.

The girl behind me mirrors the action of her mate, so that her fingers are on me, too, fingering me, fluttering and tickling round to explore my softness, making me wriggle, making my body clench with desire, and then suddenly her fingers are inside me, stirring up new, impatient tremors.

Is Gustav here yet? What's he seeing? What's he thinking? Is this gamble going to pay off? Or is it going to go horribly wrong? Has Margot grabbed hold of him? Is he going to be turned on or is he going to castigate me, when we get home later, for shaming myself, and him?

The little tremors start to knit together more urgently now, tangling with this new anxiety, and the result is a sticky wetness that makes me fidget between my legs. My nipples brush against the leather seat, then my breasts are squashed down as my bottom tilts more visibly in the air.

I glance at Chloe, and my stomach gives a lustful twist. She is being bent over in the same way as I am. Our faces are close up. Close enough to kiss. The other dancers keep us in place as they grasp their big thick dildos with their free hands. I can't see what my assailant is doing, but the dancer behind Chloe is stroking her dildo lovingly over Chloe's bottom before making it pump and jump like the real thing.

As I gape at the enormous phallus about to plunge into her, my own warmth is pulled open. A hard, long shaft nudges between my buttocks. I grip the stool as it circles blindly under me, searching for my centre. It brushes over my clitoris, and when the contact makes me jerk backwards, it deliberately repeats the action for the benefit of the eyes watching us. The surface of the shaft seems to be slightly ridged, so that there's a kind of catching sensation each time it touches or scratches me. The slightest contact sings just that bit longer.

God. This is good. Doing it in front of a crowd feels shameful and dirty, but so good. Remember to keep it exaggerated and stylised. Remember that I'm just an outline.

A tiny voice is trying to insinuate that I still have time to behave decently and stop this. But the other, stronger voice, aimed at Margot Levi and any challenge she cares to throw at me, refuses to give in or stop anything.

And you, if you're here. Watch me, Gustav. Watch how dirty I can be. I can be so much dirtier than her, any day of the week. She can't touch us.

As if it can hear me, the phallus rubs harder against my

102

body, whipping up the warmth as it edges closer. I tip myself up invitingly, but still it's determined to tease.

Chloe's invader is more brutal than mine. A hectic flush suffuses her cheeks as she is suddenly thrown forwards. Her mouth brushes mine as the dildo slams into her.

Even though the music is deafening you can still sense the excitement that rips through the audience now, swaying like a cornfield then jumping impatiently as they watch the show.

I force my focus inwards, concentrate on moving sensuously. I tip my bottom higher in the air, arch my throat so everyone can see the invitation. I push at the dancer behind me to invite her to go ahead and do it to me, and she manipulates her dildo to follow my movements, the blunt head of it still hovering millimetres away from my centre.

'Look at you. You're loving this,' Chloe yells into my ear as our faces push towards each other again. 'You lowdown little ho.'

'Think Margot would approve? Come on, girlfriend, don't look so surprised. You must have known your boss and I were connected, otherwise why would she ask you to entice me here? But maybe you didn't know she's my fiancé's ex-wife?'

My new friend doesn't insult me by coming on all innocent – which might be because, far from being belittled, I'm stealing the show. Instead she grins conspiratorially.

'OK. Busted. She made out you were intimately acquainted. But I don't know why she asked us to bring you here. Some grudge you guys have? But I'd say she's made a big mistake. It's backfiring, because you make her look washed-up.' Chloe flicks her tongue over my lips. 'You could be the permanent star of this show if you wanted!'

And then she's pulled back and temporarily lost to me. I watch her bucking back and forth across the hard little stool, her small tits bunching and swinging over the edge of the seat as her friend rogers her with the dildo. Her mouth opens wider, her blue eyes unblinking, as she gets right into it. The dancer behind pulls her weapon back and pushes it in, hard. High, keening cries escape from Chloe as she's penetrated.

'What are you waiting for?' I yell to the dancer behind me. 'Go for it!'

The chiffon ties stop me twisting round. I can't even glance over my shoulder. In any case, there's no response, other than more pushing and pulling. The dildo is creating sensations which go so far and no further. The head has yet to enter me. For some reason my dancer is fixated on rubbing it back and forth to set my clit burning. Maybe she isn't so experienced, or maybe she's waiting until Chloe's been thoroughly seen to, but I crave the spotlight now, because the more tentative she is, the more determined I am to show the audience, and Margot, who is tonight's diva.

I bring all my acting skills together to mime my frustration. I stamp my legs apart and together again, and gyrate my butt, and the audience are clapping along in time with my gyrations, but the girl behind me is strong, because every time I rise too far she pushes me back down across the stool and then, as if to punish me for showing off, the dildo is whipped away, catching my clit in one last tease. It leaves me sore and throbbing, and aching for it to come back.

I struggle and kick with fury, but I'm kicking thin air. Watching Chloe being aroused by that brutal thing has made me greedy, but my dancer and my dildo have gone.

Oh no, they haven't. Here they are again. Chloe's eyes, just about to close as if she was on the point of coming, widen at the person behind me, then she winks at me before she is thrust violently forwards to keep her in line.

I'm grabbed by the hips, and there it is again, oh, heaven, warmed now by its contact with my body and edging into place, and then when my dancer pulls me back against her groin, the dildo pushes right up inside me. It's big, and hard, but maybe because it's so deep it's lost the unbending brutality and that ridged feeling. It has a lifelike feel, throbbing and pulsing, and as the delicious sensations expand inside me my legs turn to jelly.

Chloe's assailant rears back with her white weapon, the length of it nearly out altogether, and then she thrusts it back in. Both girls seem to be focused far more on me and my dancer than on each other. Their eyes keep flickering to the person behind me and sly grins split their faces. Natural to make me the star turn, I guess. It's probably part of the act, since I'm the newcomer. The little ingénue in her white fairy costume, dragged on stage all protesting and innocent, yet let's all witness the animal awakening.

'Gotta keep up!' gasps Chloe as we rock towards each other.

'Just watch me!' I flash back.

But now Chloe loses herself again. As her friend and the music dictate their rhythm, Chloe starts to come.

And I'm thrown forwards once again. The metal feet of my stool scrape across the floor as my legs are spread wider. My forehead knocks against Chloe's bare shoulder. I can sense rather than hear her groaning as I race to catch up with her, but I'm dependent on the girl behind me and this curious dildo, which is so lifelike and so responsive that instead of being rigid its super-sized length has swollen to fit me.

Wild, fierce lust climbs through me, jagged and sharp, goading me in this wild display. As the shaft speeds up inside me, replicating the thrusts of a real man, I cry out like Chloe did, letting the moans shiver through the music. My hands scrabble to keep a hold of my madly rocking stool and I don't care if Chloe's acting or not. We are both, for our own purposes and the crowd's, coming brilliantly together and my dildo even seems able to simulate its own bursting climax.

We are both held down for a moment longer until the applause, and the music, start to fade. The audience waits as the dildos are slowly pulled out of us. My tutu is pulled down over my bare bottom, but the show isn't quite over, because Chloe turns on her dancer, holds the dildo up like a spoon and makes her assailant lick it clean.

I remain tied to the stool. I am still just a stark outline. They are waiting for me to straighten up, snap out of it, presumably so the curtain can go up and we can take a bow. Margot is still watching and she isn't going to witness any weakness in me, even though I can't move.

But now the two dancers are unclipping the curtain, the barman is winding it up to the ceiling, and Chloe and her mates are bowing to the crowd. They all start roaring with laugher as I'm revealed to the audience, still bent over the stool, the skirt barely covering my sore ass. I know I look helpless, and there's a moment when I feel it, too. Weary of fighting for my life. For my man. But I can't let it show. Not for a second. Not while that woman's hateful eyes are on me. And especially not if Gustav is somewhere in this club, watching how his girl is fielding Margot's latest grenade.

Chloe pretends to forget about me, then skips across to untie my wrists.

'Bravo, Serena!' she says, laughing and lifting me upright. 'You and your man were brilliant!'

But instead of lifting my hand or directing me to curtsy for the finale, she leaves me standing there in the middle of the stage. She and her dancer carry the stools to the side, sit astride them, take cocktails from the barman, and the lights all go out, leaving me in a single spot.

'Time to take a bow, Serena. You've done what you set out to do.'

The deep voice in my ear makes my whole body buzz. A trickle of juice tickles my inner thigh. My knees threaten to buckle as I stare up into Gustav's black eyes, glittering with pride and triumph.

'You crazy, crazy man!' I squeal, bashing uselessly at his chest as he ostentatiously buttons up his jeans, and the audience break into rapturous applause as they realise they've been had. 'Who knew you could impersonate a dildo!'

'Can you impersonate something inanimate?' He lifts me up on to my tiptoes to kiss me. 'And talking of inanimate objects—'

He jerks his head in the direction of the raised area where the queen bee was holding court earlier. I glance across in time to see Margot rising to her feet, shoving her companions away from her. Her white face is drawn tight beneath the red lace netting. Her mouth is an uneven buttonhole of fury.

The only part of her that is alive is her eyes, which blaze as she draws one red fingernail across her throat.

'Ignore her and kiss me!' Gustav turns me towards him.

I flush, itching to turn back and see what Margot is doing. 'I did it for you!'

'You exhibitionist little slut! You didn't even question who, or what, was inside you!'

Before I can answer or apologise or explain, he tilts my face up in the big hands that were holding me down just now, and the audience goes wild as he kisses me.

The last light snaps out, leaving us in the dark.

'Too late to be angry with me now, lover.' I pull away from him, my lips warm and wet as I jerk my head out towards the dance floor. 'Whatever I did just then, I did it to show Margot.'

We stand together on the stage, searching the blur of

faces as people resume their conversations, buy more drinks, demand new music. But the banquette on the far side is empty.

Margot has slunk away. For now.

CHAPTER FIVE

'Being engaged suits you, sugar. You are positively glowing!'

Ingrid Weinmeyer folds me into her pastille-scented embrace as I step into her panelled hallway over on the East Side of the park. I close my eyes and let her hold me. Despite the kinkiness that lurks beneath her porcelain exterior, despite her penchant for enticing uninitiated young peaches into threesomes with her and her randy husband, this woman is the nearest thing I have to a mother figure. Or maybe an aunt. Otherwise, what I have agreed to do later would be way too incestuous.

'Hey, honey, put her down. You don't know where she's been!'

Ernst Weinmeyer takes his turn to greet me, folding me into his burly arms. This embrace doesn't feel quite so natural. I can't shift the memory of his long, surprisingly slim erection nudging hopefully at my backside the first time I ventured into this house and nearly ended up as the tasty centre of a Weinmeyer sandwich. Nor can I forget that same erection, barely concealed beneath his white toga, nudging into my back at the ball in Venice, demanding to take me from behind in front of all his masked, euphoric guests.

Despite those memories, or perhaps because of them, I hug him back. I've shed a lot of inhibitions, been inveigled into several compromising situations, since the first time I was propositioned by this powerful couple. I smile demurely, twine my bare arms around Mr Weinmeyer's neck and press myself coquettishly against him, the silky black lace of my dress rucking up slightly against the bulge inside his exquisitely cut dinner trousers.

Keeping my eyes on Gustav all the while.

Back in January I came here to take the couple's portraits that are tonight being showcased in their house. This rich, influential couple enticed me down to their basement boudoir and tried to get me into bed with them. It later transpired that I was one of the few people who had refused their advances and lived to tell the tale, at least professionally. Not only that, but they have continued to harbour me under their wing, sung my praises to anyone who would listen and flown me over to Venice to film their annual masked ball.

But there's something else I owe them in return for their custom, their generosity and their kindness, and we all know it. I owe them no less than my naked body to do with what they will.

'You know exactly where she's been, Ernst. With me. Day and night.' Gustav steps into the hall after me, and taps his host on the shoulder. 'But we're all here to admire Serena's professional work tonight. So while she goes and checks the exhibition, why don't you deflower that rare Scotch you were telling me about? I've been thirsty ever since you mentioned it when we last bumped into each other.'

'Ah, yes. At the Club Crème. What a night that was! My God. This girl was magnificent then, and she still looks good enough to eat. She may still have much to learn—' Mr Weinmeyer kisses my hands before handing me over to his wife. His handsome, slightly thickened features glow with a

110

mixture of pride and lust. 'But she's a hundred times more stunning than the first Mrs Levi, and of course these younger models have so much more torque!'

Gustav tries to hide the flare of anger in his eyes by pushing his black hair off his forehead. 'Be careful what you say, Ernst!'

Ernst spreads his arms out and for the first time I recognise the primitive surrender in the gesture. The symbolic dropping of fists and weapons and the subconscious exposing of all vital organs in defeat. I daren't catch Gustav's eye. But I have to admire Mr Weinmeyer his deft diplomacy.

'Relax, Levi. I only meant that Serena is the jewel in your crown. How do you ever let her out of your bed in the mornings?'

'With immense difficulty, I'm sure!' Mrs Weinmeyer sashays back into the circle and slaps at the men. 'Unless he had someone even more delicious to play with! *Comme moi!*'

'You are the toughest act to follow in the land.' Gustav bows over her hand. 'I'm always up for play, and variety, Madame Weinmeyer. But there will never be anyone more delicious or beautiful than my fiancée.'

'You're a betting man. How much would you be willing to put on that?' Weinmeyer claps him on the back and starts to lead him to the back of the house. 'On me producing one day a filly even more lovely?'

'You can keep any new blood for your own nefarious devices.' Gustav winks at me over his shoulder as they walk away, sending me a blatant horny message. 'But I'd put every single penny I own on that being an impossibility.'

Fresh desire, never far from the surface, no matter how often I'm satisfied, clutches at me.

'My God, Peaches. Your eyes!' Mrs Weinmeyer stares at the two of us. 'I don't think I've ever seen a woman glow with passion like that. I am just green with envy!'

The manservant takes my Tamara Mellon leopard-print coat and my hostess hands me an elegant flute bubbling over with champagne.

'Loving the dress, sugar. Florentina, yes?' She raises her glass and then to my astonishment downs it in one. 'We fully expect to be guests of honour at your wedding, by the way. When is it to be?'

Her cornflower-blue eyes water slightly as I start to giggle, and she makes me down my drink in one before her butler refills us.

'Of course you're invited. And I don't know yet. Gustav says before the end of the year.'

'You have a say, you know, sugar. Why don't you surprise him?'

We chink our glasses together. 'Now what a marvellous idea, Mrs Weinmeyer!'

She lifts her shoulders with pleasure then wraps her long thin fingers round my upper arm.

'Now I want to show you what we've done with your marvellous films and pictures before everyone arrives. Come and see how we've mounted your Venetian series. We've decided to make it a series of moving images, as if we're all at the ball again, and that will lead us through the rooms until we reach the main drawing room and the *pièces de résistance*, those private photographs you took when the three of us were here in the winter.'

She starts to lead me into the first of the elegant *salons*, but I stop in my tracks. 'This is completely different from when I was here before! The place was crammed with all your priceless furniture and paintings, Mrs Weinmeyer! Why have you cleared it?'

She takes a step in front of me and then, with a slight cluck of annoyance when she sees I'm not following, turns on her pin-sharp heel.

112

'Well, we wanted to create the correct space to show the images. We didn't want anything here that would distract from the exhibition! In fact, we asked Gustav's advice on that.'

I bite my lip, harder than I meant to. 'You could have asked my advice! This is my work, after all!'

'You seem a bit on edge, sugar?' She puts one hand on her hip, and the other holds her glass up to her lips as she waits. 'But technically, you know, this is our work. I mean, we've paid for it. And the reason we asked Gustav's advice rather than yours is because we wanted you to have a surprise.'

I raise my eyebrow knowingly. 'So that's where he's been sneaking off to some evenings. Secret meetings with you!'

'Oh no, cupcake. We just spoke on the phone a couple of times. Now. I hope you like what we've done here.'

She picks up a remote control and waves it elegantly in the air. A group of people in period costumes and masks seems to emerge from the wall by the door and starts to parade across it, followed by others, moving, dancing, laughing, the figures spreading up to the ceiling, down to the floor, across to the corner and on to the main wall, until the whole room is inhabited with projected life and colour and music.

And here it is, that extraordinary Venetian ball in that extraordinary city. On that extraordinary, almost fatal night. Thank God I can react to these images as an art installation now – *my* hard work – rather than viewing them solely as the prelude to Pierre's tricks. My stomach might tighten a tad as I examine the sequence. I certainly won't welcome the sight of a figure hovering in the shadows, dressed in green velvet. But at least Pierre's mask has been ripped away by the conversations Gustav has forced us all to have.

Every so often the parade of dancing figures is halted by a

still photograph, a couple caught spinning in a waltz, a violinist holding his instrument high under his chin, or a sinister hooded figure on the sidelines, sipping that lethal punch, and then the dance continues to accelerate, becoming, as it did that night, wilder and louder and more degenerate.

Somewhere in real life the doorbell rings, heralding the first guests, but Mrs Weinmeyer comes to me, takes my hand in her cool fingers and waltzes me through to the next room.

'We thought it would be an entertaining way to entice everyone through the rooms towards the portraits. I know you would normally oversee the printing and production process, sugar, but we sent it to a graphics studio because we wanted to make this as hallucinogenic as it was on the night. Remember how surreal the ambience was? See how we've over-tinted everything, so that costumes and make-up and faces are even more brilliant! Remember the effects of that punch we were all drinking? We never admitted what special substances we spiked it with, but it was magic, wasn't it? Made you see everything edged so clearly? We wanted to recreate that with this tinting expert Gustav knows. Hope you're OK with it?'

'It's the perfect treatment of the film. I wish I had this kind of expertise!' I breathe out at last, determined not to be precious about the way they've altered my work. I turn in circles to follow the progress of the film. 'It's fabulous!'

The story of the Weinmeyers' masked ball progresses across the walls. A soundtrack of waltz and minuet accompanies the initial sedate greetings and curtseys at the beginning of the evening and gradually drowns out the brittle chatter.

The second room shows the stage of the ball where the women were being thrown into the revolving centre of ersatz Eightsome Reels to be touched and fingered until plucked from the fray by the winner to be ravished. Now the music whines and charges from mad polka to frenzied

114

folk dancing, to accompany the change in tempo and mood of each frame.

As we reach the door to go into the third room, Mrs Weinmeyer's grip on my arm tightens. 'And now, *la crème de la crème*! I'm so thrilled to have the wonderful Serena Folkes exhibited here. I can't wait for you to see how glorious the family album display looks! All Cecil Beaton and classy in here, all bordello and bawdy in the final room!'

'You sound like a tour guide! All these French superlatives! What's the hurry though?' I laugh, tripping slightly on my vertiginous Louboutins as the Venetian revellers circle chaotically behind us. 'The guests are only just starting to arrive.'

We're about to enter the next room when the baroque colour and music around us fade and we are enveloped by a new, muted realm of shadowy blue and purple Gothic shades. A moody, sombre track winds through the air in here, impossible to pin down. More an idea than a tune. This totally alters the Venetian mood that was just capering over these walls.

The walls still seem to be alive. But different figures move sinuously across them now, and at first I can't make out the detail.

And when I do, I wrench my hand out of Mrs Weinmeyer's fingers.

Because as the purple light bleaches to reveal the exhibition, it's plain that the well-dressed characters being silently fucked and whipped in the orgiastic film now creeping across the walls of this mansion on the Upper East Side, obliterating my Venetian images, come directly from the loop that used to be installed in Gustav's old house in Baker Street, London.

I can't tear my eyes away, even though my heart is galloping. You'd think Manhattan would be far enough away from all that shit, but no. The power of film can reach you anywhere. Gustav and Margot Levi recorded these orgies in that house

115

towards the end of their marriage. I knew the films were for sale to erotic art collectors, and I knew the Weinmeyers were putting in a bid for the collection at auction. But stupidly I assumed I would never have to look at them again.

However, the loop has been resurrected right here. The deceptively harmless carousing at a London house party, guests' arms raised in bacchanalian delight, descends from decorum into debauchery as bodies prostrate themselves on sumptuous couches or rest in poses too awkward for real sleep. Then there's the realisation as you watch that, just like the *lupanare* frescoes painted on the bordello walls in Pompeii, these solemn participants are being coaxed into group sex.

The first couple are half-clothed on a big bed, stylised like a classical Titian, complete with slave girls whispering in the corner. They are joined by another couple kissing messily and pulling at each other's remaining garments. In the next frame a woman is on her back and a man is thrusting into her while other people gather round to watch, including the slave girls.

A familiar heat starts to trickle through my body. I'm vaguely aware of people gathering closer to watch, voices exclaiming, heels clicking rapidly towards me. I fold my arms around my body to stop anyone touching me. My eyes travel over the faces, the mouths, the hands, the naked bodies in the film. It all comes back to me. Not only the display itself, but all the sensations that consumed me the day I first saw it. Despite my resistance, despite not wanting to respond to anything that involved Gustav's past, watching these people pleasuring themselves excited me. They reminded me of the nuns I'd spied on in Venice, drifting round their cells and flagellating themselves with the shocking slap of knotted leather on their downy skin.

The scenes progress into a no-holds-barred orgy,

beautifully composed and patently not simulated. This is sex by numbers. The hands, fingers, mouths, are everywhere. One woman's face is contorted with abandon as she's groped and penetrated by two men. Other women are open, the men are erect, they're all gymnastic in their positions, beautiful in their physiques. It's art, but it's unadulterated sex, too.

And the display is starting to work on me just as it did when I first saw it. Introducing that same coiling mixture of dread and arousal. The underlying menace in the film, because of its history and the person who masterminded it, is echoed by the chills running through my own limbs.

Mrs Weinmeyer is beside me now, plucking at my arm and twittering. I flick her fingers away.

'What is this doing here? I saw this display once before, and once was enough. You know what associations this has for me, Mrs Weinmeyer, both personally and professionally!' Despite the heat curling within me, my voice is reedy with rage. 'Why have you – when you told me you were buying the Baker Street footage for your erotica collection I specifically said – I *begged* you never to display this pornographic crap anywhere near mine!'

I have no idea whether I've just managed to offend one of the most influential people in this city, but right now I'm past caring. The last sequence flickers on to the wall in front of me. It's the most powerful of them all and the one I've been dreading. There's the empty bed, the empty room. Except for a woman on all fours, on the floor.

'This is an absolute travesty!' Mrs Weinmeyer pulls me back to her. 'Sugar, you have to believe me! This display is nothing to do with us. We had no idea—'

I shake my head and stare instead at poor Crystal. The permanent installation, Gustav called her, when I was so shocked to see her taking part. Her jet-black hair is pinned up in its usual severe knot. She's wearing a high-necked white

117

blouse and even a string of pearls round her neck. She grips the edges of the bed with long claw-like fingers, and lifts her bottom.

I need Gustav here. Now.

When I saw this film the first time, it turned me on. I'm getting wet now, despite my disgust and fury. What the hell is happening to me? When he saw how I responded to the punishment being meted out to his erstwhile guests, or rather Margot's clients, Gustav described me as an exotic flower, ready to open. And we went home, and he whipped me, and everything bad came flooding out of me.

Crystal continues looking into the camera, her face white as a mask, her eyes black holes. This was shot more than six years ago, yet she looks exactly the same. Only her red mouth, with its strange little smile and snaky tongue, shows any kind of animation.

Another figure steps into the shot. Dressed entirely in black leather, including a cat mask. Dominatrix gear, black leather, studded collar. The figure is holding a thin black switch, like a riding crop, with a bunch of fine leather tassels dangling off it.

In real life the room is filling with scandalised yet fascinated guests. Mrs Weinmeyer leaves me, darts about trying to explain the montage to her guests, then comes back to me, speaking at me, but I can't hear her. I'm too horrified to speak, or move.

On the film, Crystal spreads her arms and legs in a star shape. The black-clad creature plants its high-heeled boots on either side of Crystal. Her bottom and thighs glow in the dead lighting of the interior. Then the creature lifts its arm. All I – we – can hear is the whip, slicing the air as it comes down on Crystal's buttocks. The stroke rings out like a cruel gunshot and Crystal's flesh quivers under the blow.

Sweat springs along my spine, under my arms, under my hair, as I watch.

'Don't you move, Crystal, or you get double.'

The dominatrix's voice hisses out of the film. She leans down and strokes Crystal's butt cheek, where a livid red stripe has come up. She strokes as if she is preparing a rare steak, but then steps back and swipes the whip down a second time, squarely on the second cheek.

I squeeze my legs together as the dampness pricks up down there, too. I try to resist the urge to feel the fire of punishment on my own skin, to beg someone to liberate me. I don't need that any more. But on the screen Crystal flicks her head as her bottom jerks involuntarily, and I understand every single response.

Again the frail flesh quivers under the blow, and again there is a tantalising glimpse of her sex as she bounces off the floor. The dominatrix kicks at the back of Crystal's knees so that she rises higher, thrusting up her bottom, decorated now with three pink stripes. The whip strokes Crystal's bottom almost tenderly. Yes, it would be tender as well as cruel. Sweet, as well as sour.

The whip swipes down once more. The blows have raised her flesh into weals. One hand has come up brazenly between Crystal's legs and she is touching herself, moaning as she waits for her mistress to strike her, her face tilted heavenwards as she sways, one long white finger pushing in.

I can feel heat spreading through me, the thrust of the finger's invasion, as the film fades. Then the loop begins again. The start of the party, the laughing faces, the sumptuous beds—

'You have to believe me, sugar. I have no idea how this film got here. We bought it at the auction but we haven't even collected it from the shipping company yet, let alone set it up to play in here, and we definitely have not superimposed it on your Venetian study.'

Mrs Weinmeyer's face swims in front of me yet again. I

119

realise my eyes are full of tears. Her lips are moving, her blue eyes wide with alarm.

'I thought you were my friend, Mrs Weinmeyer.' I let her keep hold of me now, mostly so I won't shake too visibly. 'You promised.'

'And I meant it. This is a terrible mistake. Someone has swapped the reels and we need to stop this one immediately and find yours. Someone is in very deep shit. Let's just try to look calm and dignified for our guests, yes, while we sort this out? Time for the main event. Let's lead everyone through to the next room to see our family portraits.' She tries to fix a pink smile on to her face, but it's sinking down on one side as if she's had some kind of seizure. 'You're the guest of honour, Serena. Everyone's waiting.'

I still don't move. Many eyes are on me, people who are eager to see my work. There's a weight of good-natured expectation in the room. I can't let them think this film is my creation.

'Where is Gustav?'

Mrs Weinmeyer's fingers flutter up to the pearl choker around her neck. 'He's with Ernst and the Robinsons, in the study. Best they stay there, for the moment.'

The volume of murmuring and footsteps increases in the room around us. I know I should show some manners and acknowledge these well-wishers and potential clients. But I can't.

'Please can you get him here? Now.'

She tries to look dismayed, but the Botox won't let her. She gestures at one of the waitresses then tries to steer me through the next doorway. 'And so. It's time to shine the lights on your lovely sexy portraits.'

I take her spindly wrists in my fists and pull her close to me so that I can still focus on her and no one else. I've got to be careful here. Very, very careful.

'I can't just ignore this,' I say very quietly. 'You know how I feel about Baker Street. What they did there, what they filmed, has nothing to do with my vision. However sexy it is, however voyeuristic, I don't want it connected in any way with what I have done for you. This is a total professional embarrassment. And on a personal level—'

'Do please take another drink, ladies and gentlemen! I'll be with you in a moment!' Mrs Weinmeyer smiles round at her guests then wriggles away from me as the butler bustles in. She snatches a bulky remote control off the silver tray he has produced. 'Sugar, no one will think any the worse of you. We'll fill them with vintage champagne while we get your Venetian montage on again and move them through to the final room. I'll get Ernst out here to restore order. After he's finished throttling the technician.'

She punches clumsily at the buttons on the remote and aims it at the walls. At last the film freezes and we both close our eyes with relief.

'Such an exquisite work of art, though, isn't it, Ingrid? I'm so proud of it.'

Another voice cuts through the whispering around me.

'I thought I was switching the thing off!' Mrs Weinmeyer bashes the remote against her mouth. We both swivel round. 'What's going on?'

Just to the left of me Margot appears, projected on to the wall and superimposed over the film. Behind her, the freeze-frame captures the moment when the dominatrix's black leather leg is kicking Crystal's legs open.

Margot's black eyes are more catlike than before. The upward tilt at the corners makes her look permanently satisfied, as does the wide red smile. I can only see her top half. She's wearing a tight white sheath dress, but the deathly pallor I noticed at her apartment the other night is dusted expertly with blush for the benefit of the cameras.

121

'How did she get in there? This is like one of those Big Brother propaganda films!' Mrs Weinmeyer drops the remote and the batteries rattle out over the polished parquet. 'What does she want?'

Margot's black hair falls in a thick sideways sweep over the side of her face that was concealed before, but she looks plumper in the cheeks. Amazing what lies a camera can tell. I steadfastly refuse to touch up my images in post-production, but whoever did her make-up for this has made her look less cadaverous. Smug. Like the cat that's got, or is about to get, the cream.

The other guests glance from screened Margot to real me. Like unruly children they ignore Mrs Weinmeyer's surprisingly nimble efforts to wave everyone through to the final drawing room like a sheepdog.

'Where's my invitation, Ingrid?'

Gustav's ex-wife takes a step nearer whatever or whoever is filming her so her face is in close-up. Mrs Weinmeyer's eyes go circular with shock.

'You didn't invite me to this cosy little private view, just like you left me off the guest list to your Venetian ball. But I gatecrashed anyway.'

There's a weird fizzing pause as if Margot is actually waiting for us to reply through Skype or a satellite. As if she can really see us and hear us.

'You know what happens in fairy tales when people are left out? Revenge. I'm here to inform New York's high society that Serena Folkes is an upstart. Her pieces are cheap snaps compared to the power unfolding in my film. Are the great and the good all gathered? Very good. So, hello, lords, ladies and gentlemen! You're transfixed, aren't you? The film you have just seen is not just a beautifully choreographed orgy. It's a testament to my marriage. We were never apart, you know. He wouldn't leave me alone. Always watching, touching, sketching. Gustav even features in this film. If you rewind you'll find him in the scenes where the woman is being done like a doggy by two guys. He was too shy to show his face, bless him. But it wasn't his face we were after!'

I press the diamond ring tightly into my finger until it hurts. Mrs Weinmeyer hurries towards the doorway with her arms out like a traffic policeman, but her guests are flowing around her as if she's a leaf in a stream.

'So here I am in your house anyway, Ingrid, enshrined with my husband.' Margot smiles, biting the tip of her tongue. 'I let Gustav keep that footage, against my better judgement. Anything to keep him happy. He must have enjoyed this constant reminder of our time together. But I still share the copyright. He needed my permission when it came to selling it at the auction.'

My permission. I sway slightly and reach behind me for something to lean on. There is nothing there. Just empty space.

'You communicated – you and Gustav have spoken in the last few months?'

'She's not real, Serena! She's a display. That's all. We can switch her off.' Mrs Weinmeyer picks up the remote and clumsily tries to stuff the batteries back into it. 'And that's not how we acquired the film. Will someone please go and get Ernst?'

There is nothing in this room to cover the image of Margot, which has gone still. Maybe it's finished. I try to push through the guests back towards the hall to find Gustav, but Mrs Weinmeyer catches me and steers me backwards towards the drawing room door where the final part of the exhibition is still in darkness, waiting to be unveiled.

'The butler is sorting this catastrophe. Margot Levi has ruined our expensive investment. But that doesn't matter now. I think we've managed to freeze it. Come, Serena. Let's distract everyone. Give them what they've come to see!'

My ankle tips slightly in the high shoes, but I start reluctantly to follow her.

'You can erase films, burn letters, deface photographs. But I'm locked away in here.' Margot starts again. She is tapping her black eyebrow. 'You may be in his bed, but I live in his head. And you'll never evict me.'

As she elongates the word 'evict', I look again at the tapping finger, manicured with flawless black nail varnish. The knuckles are gnarled and the veins are ropey under the papery skin. That clever theatrical foundation on her face has a translucent glow to it, intended to cover every wrinkle and blemish.

I break away from Mrs Weinmeyer and sure enough I can see that trying to break through the blanket of panstick on Margot's skin there are uneven bumps and dips. Like the surface of the moon.

'I'll wipe that pretty smile off your face one day, Serena. Because I was paid handsomely for my permission, I can tell you. Everything Gustav asks of me he must pay for.'

Every lady who lunches and her wealthy walker is swirling round us now, laughing openly behind their champagne glasses, glancing round the walls, at me, at Margot. My urchin's fingers are itching to do some damage. I so wish she was real. If I didn't have to be on my best behaviour tonight I would lift her slight frame and hurl her through the window just like I used to hurl heavy rocks over the cliffs when I was a child, watching them splash and sink into the grey waves.

'Come away.' Mrs Weinmeyer finds her voice. 'This is your moment, Serena. Everyone is gathered.'

I've snapped the stem of my delicate flute and Dom Perignon is fizzing over my fingers.

'There are other ways of winning, Serena.' Mrs Weinmeyer detaches herself from her guests and pinches my arm, hard, above the elbow to turn us away from the film. 'Take a leaf from my bible. Never lose a shred of dignity, even when your worst enemy appears.'

'So, how did I do?' I hang my head, watching the champagne dripping to the floor.

'Brilliantly. I'm proud of you, and I'm deeply sorry. You must understand Ernst and I had absolutely no idea – I'll do whatever I can to make this right.' Mrs Weinmeyer winds her arm round my waist and pulls me close. 'But Margot Levi is back in town, sugar, whether we like it or not.'

Gustav rushes in at last, the men all gesticulating and questioning.

I beckon him over. This is my night. Not Margot's.

But he senses it before he sees it. He's tensing, like a hunter. Or the hunted.

In some control room somewhere in the Weinmeyer mansion, someone has finally frozen the film. Margot's face is huge on the wall. As we all stare, a black hole appears in the middle of her face, spreading outwards, wavery and black, obliterating her like a burn, and then there is blankness. The screen reverts to being a mushroom-painted wall.

We all wait, dreading Margot's reappearance, but when the butler makes an OK signal to Mr and Mrs Weinmeyer, I let go of my hostess, steady myself and pull Gustav through to the final drawing room. Before the Weinmeyer portraits are finally illuminated, I rest my head briefly on his shoulder, smile sweetly up at him for the benefit of the crowd and press my mouth against his ear.

'Since I've known you, Gustav. Since we've been in New York. Have you ever spoken to Margot about the Baker Street sale?'

The still simmering hatred in Gustav's eyes, even as he pulls me close, holds a dire warning for us all.

Don't ever be the cause of that look. Because the daggers in his eyes will kill you.

'That woman took everything, including my brother, and kept on taking. I bought her out of all the properties in the divorce settlement except the one here in New York. I took Baker Street and the house in Lugano, and in return I expected her to take care of Pierre. Look how that turned out. So no. From the day she walked out until the night you and I went to that downtown apartment, I have not exchanged a single word with her. All sales are dealt with entirely by the agents.'

I allow myself to relax a little. Gustav's eyes are calm again. I have to trust him.

I am called forward by Mrs Weinmeyer to flick the switch and illuminate the series of erotic photographs I took of her and her husband in the New Year. Talk about being thrown in the deep end. It was my second commission in New York and I was instructed to capture our hostess ensconced in their basement bordello of bliss, ecstatically riding our host.

As one by one the portraits are illuminated, there is a mingled sigh of shock and appreciation from the audience. Everyone shifts forward to examine their writhing, naked hosts a little more closely.

Mr and Mrs Weinmeyer stand close in their Siamese-cat pose, and as one they nod at me.

I nod back, and an understanding passes between us. They have to make amends. They must use their considerable influence to make this debacle, and Margot Levi, go away.

And they can start by taking me down to their basement and entertaining me until I lose the ability to think. I made them a promise, months ago, but they will be doing *me* a favour tonight, not the other way around.

Giving them my body for the night may be the only way to drum Margot Levi out of my head.

'She's nearly ready for you, Ingrid!'

Ingrid finishes fluffing up her hair in the mirror and stands up. She looks softer and younger with her pale yellow hair falling round her face There's just a touch of lipstick to bring colour to her face. She is wearing a powder-blue short negligee and her slim white body is totally naked, and totally waxed, beneath.

She tiptoes across the thick carpet. She takes my arms and stretches them across the bed so that my stomach is pressed down, my head supported by the mound of pillows. Then she clips my wrists into the fluffy handcuffs attached to the hook in the wall.

'Perfect. Keep her bound. Oh, look, Ingrid. Such a lovely bottom. That's what they call their asses in the UK, you know. *Bottoms*.' The strong male hands run over me. I am totally naked and, now that they've tied me down, I'm totally helpless.

I close my eyes. It's so late. The guests didn't want to leave, there were so many comments and questions, and then the Weinmeyers and Gustav had to talk me down. Now I'm so tired. I'm tired of being charming and sociable on the outside, and being eaten up by anger and worry on the inside. The fighting spirit that kicked in at the Sapphix Bar has taken root and, like Jack's beanstalk, the tentacles have grown that little bit more this evening.

I love Gustav with all my being, but I hate him, too, because his association with Margot has infected me now.

My legs are pushed further apart as the big hands stroke my thighs, moving higher.

'Tell us how you want us to say sorry, Serena?'

I don't want to talk. Mrs Weinmeyer is kneeling next to

me and when I turn my head my eyes are on a level with her crotch.

'Empty my mind. Whip me. Hurt me.'

Fingers knead my butt cheeks, fingers spread wide as if to measure me, pinching and squeezing the plump white flesh. I squirm slightly, but that just raises my bottom higher in the air.

Mrs Weinmeyer laughs and bends down, still holding my wrists. She pushes her face close to mine.

'When can I start? She's so cute. And so tasty. God, we've waited nearly six months for this!'

'Any time you like.'

A hard slap smacks down on me.

I wriggle and twist but I'm pushed down again, my face buried in the pillows. Soon my head will be empty. The more transgressive they want to be the better. We've done this before. Gustav has seen me naked and manhandled by other people. We had a deal not long after we arrived in New York, triggered by these very Weinmeyers in fact. When I showed him the footage I'd taken of them in their bed, and admitted that they'd asked me to join them in a threesome, he was both appalled and aroused.

And so was I. That's when we agreed that I could explore certain scenarios, with particular emphasis on girlie encounters, so long as Gustav was there to keep an eye and enjoy proceedings himself from the sidelines.

But this is different. I'm not the naïve flower I was then. I've proved myself as a photographer, as a voyeur, as a lover. I'm Gustav Levi's fiancée. But in getting to this point I've been tripped up, trapped and tricked. In the last six months, faces from his past have scattered obstacles in our path and threatened us both. We've been tested to the max. And tonight I'm very angry.

Margot Levi is far too close for comfort now. Christ, she

was visually plastered over this very house an hour ago. We can't get rid of her. Now, as she would put it, she's *in our heads*.

Mrs Weinmeyer kisses my mouth.

'Keep still. I'll be your mistress, if that's what you want.'

There's a sharp kick between my knees and my legs collapse apart. The hands go on smoothing the tender skin on my butt as if flattening a bed sheet. I can feel goosebumps coming up on my skin as he strokes, and shivers twitching deep inside. I want tonight to be beaten out of me.

'You feel so good, Serena. Positively addictive. I wonder if that man of yours will let us do this again before he walks you up the aisle?'

There's no response from anyone else in the room. My silence is taken as consent and the person behind me slaps my butt. I'm silent. It doesn't hurt enough, yet.

As I shake from the hard slaps, Mrs Weinmeyer starts kissing me, taking my hot face in her hands and pushing her tongue into my mouth. I resist at first, or at least I don't respond, but when her tongue tickles the tender lining of my lips, I shiver and suck tentatively, making her kiss me all the harder.

'I need to be thrashed,' I mumble through her kisses. 'But I want this to be the last time. When we're married I don't want to punish or be punished. I want to be normal. I just want to love.'

'Beautifully put, *cara*. And I doubt I will ever have cause to punish you.' Gustav chuckles from close behind me. 'So we'd better make this a session to remember, especially as our friends have waited so patiently!'

My eyelids flutter as I gasp for air. When I open them again, Mrs Weinmeyer has pulled her mouth away. She has positioned herself a few inches from my face. She is pale and hairless, waxed so completely that her parts are blue-white, almost see-through. I've been touched, and I've touched, but I've never looked so intimately at another woman before. I jerk against the handcuffs and they bite into my wrist. The sharp pain flashes more intensely through me.

'I bet your Gustav doesn't normally waste time spanking you, eh? I bet he normally just gets on and fucks you!'

'I told him to hurt me!' I manage to growl. 'He should be doing what he's told!'

Out of the corner of my eye I see Gustav's arm, the shirt sleeve rolled up, lift in the air, palm flat. I open my mouth to scream, but my voice is just a puff of hot breath. His hand comes down really hard this time, the sting instant and sharp. I judder and squeal as it burns.

'Poor Ernst is going to be livid he missed this!' Mrs Weinmeyer's voice has descended into quite a heavy Austrian accent. Attractive, but moody. 'He wanted to be in control tonight, and it's all gone wrong. Not just because of that contamination of our Venetian series, but *entre nous* he feels just a little humiliated by those last private pictures in the exhibition. They're stunning, and classy, but what do they show? Me, tying him up, blindfolding him. All our associates have seen that. He wanted to be the master tonight. He wanted to take command.'

The vision that sails before me just then, of Mr Weinmeyer standing on the prow of a ship wearing a tropical naval uniform that's a tad too tight, momentarily erases the other pictures in my head. I snuffle into the pillow and earn myself another smack.

'But poor Ernst has had to summon everyone into his office upstairs and castigate whoever allowed Margot to get at our precious film. Maybe we should bring them all down here for a good whipping, eh, Serena? You should be the one slapping everyone, not lying there like a little virgin victim. On the other hand, you're all mine tonight. I like you like this!' Mrs Weinmeyer adopts the persona required of her and pushes herself into my face. I breathe in her aroma of sex and some kind of rose-petal wash. 'So now, sugar pie, you're going to lick me. Can she lick me, Gustav?'

There's a pause. Gustav's hands spread over my bottom and squeeze it.

'She'll do whatever you ask her to do tonight, Ingrid. That's what releases her, and gives me my girl back. Just wait until I've punished her some more. I've got my own pleasure to come, don't forget.'

I tug against the handcuffs. I need to see Gustav's face. And I need to breathe.

There's another harsh slap on my butt. 'We're waiting!'

Gustav's voice is gruff. More like the voice he uses when he's conducting business. We are performing together. We're in public. Not surprising he sounds different. Slightly forced. Slightly formal. But sexy.

I force myself to breathe more deeply. Focus on what is happening. Use it to obliterate Margot's spooky appearance earlier this evening. That nasty word she used to describe me. *Cheap.*

'Spank me again!' I yell, tipping my ass in the air. And it comes, stinging then spreading into a warm glow.

Mrs Weinmeyer spreads her legs.

'Smack the little bitch, Levi!'

This time the slap is much harder. The sting spreads over the already tender spot and radiates deeper, and though I try to ignore the pain, the very act of struggling against it is kicking me into another zone at last, away from everything real.

Gustav grunts with satisfaction. He's the commander tonight. I wriggle harder as he does it again, harder. My body rubs against the bed. A vicious flare of excitement sears through me.

'I hope you feel good about yourself, sugar, because you're behaving like a little whore in front of your boyfriend.'

Gustav starts smacking the other butt cheek. The hot, vicious slap, then the angry heat spreading through me, feels fantastic. He's only using his hand. I know they don't do whips down here in the Weinmeyer bordello.

'Smack me again!' I yelp, rubbing myself harder against the bed. 'I'm so dirty, and naughty! Slap me again!'

'This will teach you.' Ingrid is beneath me now and she takes me by the hair and pushes my face into her body. She is very wet. 'Lick me, sugar!'

'Such a lovely white butt, all sore from my hand.' Gustav mutters. Their voices are like soft chants weaving around me. 'I'm going to fuck it.'

He runs his finger up my butt crack and pokes at the neat, tight hole. I tense instinctively, but Mrs Weinmeyer takes that as her cue to push my mouth into her so that I'm smothered in soft petals of female flesh.

Each time Gustav slaps me, Mrs Weinmeyer thrusts herself into my face. Weakly, and to get some breath, I stick my tongue out and take a tentative lick. The taste is foreign, yet familiar. Sweet, yet salty. Inviting, yet so, so dirty. I savour it for a moment and smile to myself. Something else added to my list of never-befores.

Now Gustav's fingers are opening me up. I hear his zipper go.

'Oh, my God. Am I finally going to see the great Levi schlong?' Mrs Weinmeyer is very quiet in the muffled velvet room, half-moaning. 'Oh, my God! Look at it! It really is as stupendous as me and my girlfriends have all fervently imagined!'

'We're lucky girls tonight then, Mrs Weinmeyer,' I murmur as I dreamily start to lap at her. 'Normally my fiancé watches, but now we get the best of both worlds because he's here, and he's taking part!'

Gustav chuckles again and mutters something obscene to her in German, presumably concerning the size of his *bratwurst*, and the bed dips as he lowers his trousers. Then he's pushing hard where his fingers have opened me up.

Mrs Weinmeyer stops rocking my head for a moment but tightens her grip on my hair. 'Just before you do her, Gustav honey! You did set up the camera to film?'

There's a kind of flurry of activity around me. I can hear Gustav unclipping the small camera case I carry everywhere with me. I'm still muffled by Mrs Weinmeyer's crotch and everything sounds as if we are under water. She and I go into a kind of trance, rocking together as Gustav goes to set up the camera to film this latest entry in my diary of debauchery.

'Now we can both taste her together. Christmas and the Tooth Fairy have come all at once, darling. Make it up the ass, Gustav,' purrs Mrs Weinmeyer as she settles my head between her legs again. 'Go where it's really tight. That way she'll be all the more forceful with me.'

And here he is. My man. His hands take my hips and boy, he's hard, so hard. What's going on in his head? Is Margot there all the time, like she said? Is that why he's been even more masterful with me?

Or is he hard from watching me, his girl, fulfilling a promise she made to these kind, impatient people, and seeing her bare butt, her lips and tongue working on another woman?

Please God, let it be thoughts of me, not her, that are turning him on tonight.

Gustav is stiff as a rod. I tip my ass towards him. My human dildo. We did this once in the lift at the gallery in London. That was another first. Up the ass. And in a lift.

As I push towards him, Mrs Weinmeyer pulls me towards her. I like feeling used like this. There are no thoughts jostling

133

in my head any more. I'm just a piece of meat, built for pleasure.

Gustav pushes harder and I close instinctively against him, but he eases me open and pushes me again, up the bed and into Mrs Weinmeyer. He thrusts harder at the tight ring and I'm opening, and he is in. My body is packed tight, burning and full, utterly helpless. I'm pinned like a butterfly.

He starts to rock, his balls knocking against me. Mrs Weinmeyer, who I guess has been staring awestruck at the great Gustav Levi kneeling on her bed, naked from the waist down as he takes his fiancée, lets out a moan as if I've done something unexpected.

'You are in so much trouble making me do this!' he growls in my ear.

The burning up my backside makes me light-headed with euphoria. I lick my mistress harder, savouring the taste of her, savouring how this must look. Savouring another new lesson. As I lap faster and she starts to lose control, I locate the nub of her clit with my tongue and try nibbling and sucking at it, and that hits the spot because she yelps and squeals and then she starts to groan and swear. The harder I lick and bite, and the hotter and wetter she is, the hotter and wetter I am. The pleasure pulsates somewhere inside, I can't tell which part of me, and it's growing, and coming closer.

Mrs Weinmeyer pulls at my hair. The pain sends sick desire shooting through me. I suck at her, and from the spasms I know I'm doing it right. She rubs herself faster over my nose and mouth, tilting her hips wildly to get my tongue deep inside her, and as soon as I push it up her she comes, groaning and writhing against my face

Gustav isn't ready. He wants to go on and on, his fingers deep inside the other part of me to keep me impaled, and as soon as Mrs Weinmeyer comes and falls away from me, whimpering and shaking with dying pleasure, Gustav claims me properly, pushing my face back into the pillows so that my bottom is offered higher for him to swell inside, to pump harder and deeper.

I gasp for air as he shudders inside me at last and I come, waves of sensation breaking over me, holding him tight inside as I collapse beneath his weight, my breath creaking in my chest.

My arse sore and battered.

My head empty of everything except my debt paid to the Weinmeyers, performed to perfection with my future husband.

CHAPTER SIX

'*Les Liaisons Dangereuses*.' The sexy French voice caresses my ear. 'What an incredible theme for your next commission, Serena. A contemporary take on that classic tale of sexual shenanigans, all being filmed in a glorious château.'

'Don't stop with the gorgeous accent. I love it when you go all continental!'

He laughs softly and licks and nibbles the back of my neck, making me shiver even though we've just shared a very hot shower.

'Zeez are my roots. I don't know why I haven't brought you here before.'

'To the penthouse at the Georges V, do you mean?' I press my forehead against the cool glass and stare across at the Eiffel Tower shrouded in early-morning May mist. 'If we had your telescope I might just be able to spot the *pension* I stayed in last time I was here.'

'You're the budding star who scored an all-expenses-paid trip. What I meant was, I should have brought you to Paris sooner. It's where I grew up, after all.' Gustav combs his fingers through my hair and lets it drop, tickling my spine.

'And this commission will be a piece of cake. After all, you've done a similar day-in-the-life before, for Pierre.'

I open the door to our balcony. There's a faint chill as the spring rain paints the slate rooftops and wide streets a silky grey.

'Do we have to talk about your brother?'

Gustav lifts my wet hair off my damp skin and twists it into a plait.

'Yes, we do. You're going to be related to him just as soon as I can get a gold ring on your finger. Also, this gig is down to the enthusiastic response of his Hollywood bosses when they were shown your pictorial record of his burlesque show.'

I put my hand outside. The rain is so gentle I can barely feel it. 'I can't shake off the suspicion that he's been pulling strings. To make up for all the trouble he's caused.'

Gustav steps on to the balcony, out into the rain, so that he can face me. His hair is slicked back from the shower and he's naked but for a huge white towel draped dangerously loosely around his hips. He hasn't shaved yet and the morning's shadow sculpts his gorgeous features. He's shivering, but he takes my shoulders and shakes me.

'If he could twist people's arms on your behalf, he would. He won't rest until you are a hundred per cent convinced he's not a two-faced schemer. But it doesn't work like that in the tough world of film. So knock this chip off your shoulder, Serena. When are you going to realise your own worth? It's your professional talent that has brought us over here. Not Pierre. Not me. This French film company booked you after they saw the pilot of Pierre's show. It gave them the idea to run a similar storyboard for their own production. The Theatre B was a stepping stone, yes. But so is every job, surely? One body of work leads to the next.'

I open my mouth to respond, but Gustav puts his hand over my mouth to silence me and pushes me back into the room.

The breakfast tray is resting on our vast bed and I start picking apart a croissant. 'Well, if that's true, I'll thank him when I next see him. If I'm honest, these nerves are about Margot. She's like a bad smell, G.'

Gustav picks up another towel and starts rubbing his hair with it.

'Why are we even talking about her? You're her nemesis, Serena. Snow White to her Wicked Queen. The more beautiful you grow, the more her mirror has to give her the cold hard truth. That she was never the fairest.'

I shake my head, smearing butter on to my pastry. 'Honey, this is real life. Not a fairy tale.'

'Come on, cynic. Every day with you is magic,' Gustav says with a twinkle in his eye as he throws the towel into a damp heap on the floor. 'We've shown her we're unbreakable. No one in New York will give her the time of day. With any luck she'll have flapped away on her broomstick by now to pick on someone her own size.'

He drains his coffee cup then carries the tray over to place it outside the door.

'Look. Pierre may have been the catalyst for this job, but, as he said in his emails before we flew out here, your work sells itself. It's visual; a portrait, an impression, a story. So when it's on display, in a gallery, or in a boardroom, whether it's personal or public, by its nature it has an audience. The audience sees it, and likes it, and wants a piece of it. Just as I saw you, and liked you.' He wanders back to where I'm sitting, folds me into a tight bear hug and nips my neck. 'And wanted you.'

I pull my shoulders up and giggle as the sharp pain rouses me.

'Where would I be without you?'

'Not in Paris, that's for sure!'

I tip my head sideways to expose my neck a little more. 'I meant, without you putting things into perspective for me, G.'

'Did you know you're using that nickname more and more? I love it.'

I lean against him, watching a finger of sun running down the side of the Eiffel Tower before being snatched back into the clouds. If I continue looking straight ahead I can pretend we're on holiday. But in an hour, the film company's car will arrive and whisk me away from this dreamy room.

'I noticed the first time Pierre called you "G", during that awful row before Christmas. You'd not seen each other for five years. There was so much hurt, Margot had done so much harm, all of it was pouring out of both of you, but when there seemed nothing else to say Pierre reached out to you. He called you "G". One tiny letter, but it shows how close you were. Are. It seems to calm him every time the temperature between you starts to rise.'

'And it's yours to use, too, whenever you feel anxious.' Gustav starts to touch each bump of my vertebrae with the tip of his tongue. 'So let's focus on today, and why we're here. Thanks to that call from Château Cine, Serena Folkes is back in her voyeur's saddle.'

I let his words soothe me. 'Tell me more about these sexual shenanigans, then. These dangerous liaisons.'

'The clue is in the title, and as a *cadeau* for my clever fiancée I have acquired an original edition of the book the film is based on.' Still kissing me, he produces from behind his back an ancient book with a yellowing jacket. 'I sneaked off to a sale at the antiquarian bookshop yesterday. Only a handful of copies were available and they went like hot cakes. Philandering Frenchmen buying them for their *petites amies,* no doubt. But I've also bought a convenient translation so you can research the story in the car going to the location.'

'I'm not your mistress, buster! I'm your fiancée!' I slap at him. 'But thank you.'

He holds the book away from me playfully. 'It's a naughty, twisted, sexy tale full of scheming and intrigue between older characters, who set out to corrupt their innocent young counterparts. But it's a complicated *ensemble.* Before the studio limousine whisks you out of town to the château where they are filming, you'll need to read the cast list to work out who's who, and who is going to do what to whom.'

'Hmm. Maybe I'd better do some homework now. They've commissioned me to do what I do best, which is turning stalking into an art form. I'll just be lurking in the shadows as the film takes shape. The filmers filmed. This shoot shouldn't be too difficult if all they do is stand around plotting and then have sex!'

'And you know what will happen if you don't blend into the background?' Gustav hands me the little book. 'They'll want you to join in!'

'Honey, I'm trying to be serious! Today it'll just be me and my camera.'

I open the book and look at the list of *dramatis personae.* Gustav has drawn a tiny sketch of my face alongside the date and the words *Serena. Ma chérie. Ma femme.*

I smile up at him, speechless for a moment. He kisses me again and pads away across the thick, luxurious carpet.

He reaches for his clothes, which in last night's haste were left crumpled over a chair. 'I still feel a little regretful that instead of being your rich lover bringing you on a dirty weekend, I'm just here as your hanger-on.'

'So allow me to enjoy pulling rank over you, Monsieur!' I put the book down. There's a sudden flurry of rain ricocheting off the overhanging roof. The tulips out on the balcony boxes, apparently driven fresh from Amsterdam every day, bend their heads under the shower. 'Although I may not be able to concentrate on my work if you're lounging beside me in that biker jacket and scruffy jeans.'

'These jeans, do you mean?' I turn to see what he's talking about, and see him bending to pull one black trouser leg up over his tight boxers. My stomach lurches as the part of him that delights me, night after night, is packed away.

'Why are you putting those smart ones on? They turn you into Gustav the entrepreneur, not Gino the bag carrier. I liked it at that hilarious Robinson family shoot when you pretended to be my sexy Latino assistant, doing all the heavy lifting, and ended up watching me being fingered by the daughter of the house! Aren't you coming to hump my equipment?'

'Not today, *chérie*. I have to go out of town for a meeting with some Italian associates.'

'Another meeting? You never said. When will you be back?'

He pauses as he's about to do up the trousers. 'Late, *signorina*. They want me to take the high-speed train down to Florence to view the site. We've been discussing this project for weeks now. But don't look so despondent! Tomorrow I have a much more exciting appointment with a certain jeweller in the Quartier Latin. He has some very special measurements to take.'

I run across the room, jump into his arms and he staggers with me back to the enormous queen-size bed. 'Our wedding rings! Oh, my God, Gustav! It's really going to happen! When can we do it? When are we going to get married?'

He rolls on top of me and starts peeling the fluffy towel away from my flushed, damp skin. As my breasts are revealed and the nipples sharpen into tight points, I grab at his waistband and start undoing the button of his jeans.

'I don't want to rush anything, but hey, why not sooner rather than later? Can you think of any significant dates? How about Halloween?'

'The anniversary of our meeting! That would be amazing! But five months isn't much time to get things organised!'

'We could just elope.'

I smile as I grow heavy with desire. 'Our life is one long elopement!'

He kicks the trousers away and lets me pull off the clean boxers. Oh, God, there's nothing like a super-luxurious hotel room with a panoramic view over the rooftops of Paris, a historic wine cellar far below, and a sparkling blue bathtub big enough to practise your lengths, to turn you on.

And talking of lengths. My lover's hardness springs free, jabbing into my stomach as I wrap my thighs around his hips and pull myself up against him, feel the tip of him nudging at me.

'Gustav Levi, even if we elope I can't get married without a dress, can I? Polly would kill me if I did it in jeans or a bikini. She has her heart set on making the wedding gown, and I don't feel happy about planning anything until we've mapped out her part as seamstress, but how can she if I'm in Paris and she's in Marrakesh?'

Gustav fans his hands out over my bottom and pushes me hard against him. We pause for a moment, breathing softly into each other's faces, taunting each other to see who will move first, who will crack and give in.

'A minuscule complication, Serena. One I'm sure you'll fix somehow. But for now? Let's shut that beautiful sexy mouth of yours.'

His black stare rakes over me as he pulls his haunches back. I wait, luxuriating in the way he devours me with his eyes. He pauses. He's not going to be gentle. He's still loving, but he's rarely gentle these days. He rocks his hips against me and slides straight in, straight up. The rain patters more insistently against the window. The poor tulips dip their heads in the spring storm as my fiancé and I arch and move in delicious slow rhythm.

I ease myself across his thighs, press closer to him so he goes in deeper. My muscles tighten around him. His hands loosen slightly on my hips as his face softens. We are totally enclosed in this circle of love and luxury. So gentle, so familiar. So real.

His black eyes glitter with fresh fire and he moves faster, banging me against him in a spiral of excitement until his eyes half close with the effort of holding back. The release comes quickly and we fall together into the snowy sheets.

The studio limousine takes me away from Gustav and away from the magic of the hotel, out on to the bustle of the Champs-Élysées. We drive along the north side of the Seine for a while, past the spot near Notre Dame where I took the photographs for my Parisian series of young lovers that the Weinmeyers now have in their house. Or did have, before they installed the ruined Baker Street footage.

But instead of crossing over the famous river, we plunge underneath it, and when we re-emerge from the tunnel we have left all those landmarks behind us. We are in another land, the land of grey, flat *banlieues,* where even the telephone lines seem to sag with boredom.

I get out the summary of *Les Liaisons Dangereuses* and stick my iPod in my ears.

I wanna kiss you in Paris.

I read a little about the story then close my eyes and think of the big, rumpled bed Gustav and I have just climbed out of. How many hours will it be until we can be back there again? When I look up again about forty minutes later, the car is driving slowly along a nondescript village street. There's no apparent life except a couple of teenagers trying and failing to kick-start their mopeds. The rain has stopped, but the clouds hang heavily over the landscape as if waiting for an excuse to puke up a fresh load.

'*On arrive!*' declares the driver as two enormous black gates set in a long grey wall at the far end of the village street open electronically. We cruise up a long, straight gravel drive policed on either side by dark green topiary clipped into the shapes of cockerels and spaniels and flying fish.

The château is a mini version of Versailles. The large grey bricks are seamed with watermarks, but the pointed turrets give the building an impressive, majestic air. I tuck the book into the pocket of my faded denim jacket and get out of the car. I stare up at the long, blank windows, and the château stares back at me. The driver waves me up a set of stone steps extending along most of the façade and leading to the main double doors, which are standing open. I walk through a cold stone porch and straight through an internal court-yard. On the far side is another door, this time modern, double height and glass.

I've arrived in an echoing stone hallway complete with sweeping double staircase, a number of ominously closed doors and a glassed-in corridor leading away into the distance, offering more glimpses of garden. It's all very cool and grand, but still no one appears to greet me. If it wasn't for the coils of black cable snaking between arc lights, several unmanned film cameras balanced on enormous gantries, and the rows of overloaded electrical sockets, I would think I'd come to the wrong place.

'*Excusez-moi?* Are you lost?'

A door on the left of me opens just as I'm lifting my hand to knock, and a slim girl appears beside me with huge brown eyes and crimson-dyed hair cut in the kind of gamine crop only French girls like her can carry off.

'*Bonjour. Je m'appelle Serena Folkes,*' I say, holding up my camera case. '*Je suis ici pour photographier Les Liaisons Dangereuses?*'

'Ah yes. They are filming now. Well, they are always filming.' She waves a clipboard over the cold deserted hall and beckons me to follow her. Today I'm wearing a leather miniskirt and cowboy boots, and a striped Breton sweater which keeps falling off one shoulder. She runs her hand down my arm. '*T'es très française!*'

As she opens the doors, a wall of breathy, sexy music hits us. It's the lowdown, gravelly, slightly jungle beat of Madonna's *Erotica* complete with moaning, persuasive voice and orgasmic sighing. I've just been listening to it on my iPod. It winds into your ears, right down into you, makes you want to sway, until you remember that you're not dancing in an underground nightclub in the early hours, but toiling in a château in broad daylight. More studio lights are set up in here, filling the room with an artificially bright glare so that, although it's raining outside, it looks like a hot summer's day in here.

The girl leads me across the back of a rectangular, parquet-floored *salon* with pale gold and gilt walls whose cornices and coving are alive with vines and cherubs clambering all over the walls and ceilings. The room shares the proportions and period detail of the ballroom at the Palazzo Weinmeyer in Venice. The bright gold of the figures picks up the artificial sunlight being beamed around the room. When this is screened, the scene will be bathed in a warm, golden glow, like an advertisement for Hovis or Bisto.

The girl, who I realise is holding my hand now, puts a finger to her dark-painted mouth. I can't see past the next semicircle of cameras grouped halfway down the room. Various cameramen in nondescript dark clothing are training their lenses or moving their wheeled apparatus towards the far end while a couple of spindly lads lay a train track down the centre of the floor.

The runner and I walk down the garden side of the room where ceiling-height glass doors lead on to an ornate patio and a lawn sweeps down to a lake.

Everyone is staring at a vast stone fireplace with flames the size of a bonfire flickering in the grate. It's all very baronial, except that there is no wooden furniture, tapestries or aloof aristocrats. Instead, there is a huge TV screen above the mantelpiece, as wide as the chimney breast itself, showing what looks like a window spattered with raindrops, and grouped around the fireplace is a set of very modern, low-slung white leather sofas.

Instead of the aloof aristocrats you'd expect to see striking poses in tailcoats and powdered wigs, I can now see two men, one on either side of the fireplace, leaning pugnaciously out of their leather chairs and having a blazing row. One is handsome and silver haired, and wearing faded jeans and a washed-out cotton shirt. The other is in a kind of sharply tailored tawny mod suit with a tie-less white shirt buttoned up to the neck.

The silver-haired man picks up a bottle of red wine from a big glass table stacked with other bottles, cakes and candles, and starts waving it around as he snaps and snarls at the younger man. Everyone else in the room stands very still, arms crossed. Just watching. I make a face at the girl.

'Maybe this wasn't a good day to come!'

'Not rehearsal. This is real. Real shoot I mean.' She smiles, waving her clipboard at the actors. 'The cameras roll twenty-four seven. Like documentary. But also like reality.'

I glance back at the set. Cool idea.

The runner girl nudges me. 'That's the Vicomte de Valmont, the old guy, the one who makes all the trouble in the story, and he's fighting with Comte de Gercourt.'

I glance at her. She's clutching the top of her clipboard and staring at the grey-haired man. He has filled his glass so full that red wine spills on to the wooden floor.

I lean closer and whisper. 'You're going to have to explain the plot to me again.'

'All you need to know is that they all want to have sex with each other. At least, that's the simple version of the story.' She blushes, then pulls me behind one of the cameras and points at a third person I hadn't even noticed. 'And there's Cécile, the innocent character. That's the one they all want. Even the women want her.'

The male characters may be after Cécile, but at the moment the character is being ignored. She is young, around the same age as me and my new friend the runner, and she's perched at the end of a third long sofa which faces the fireplace and the blank TV screen with the raindrops. She is dressed in a long grey overcoat and thick black tights, and the knees in those tights are pressed tightly together. Her white fingers are hooked round her knees and drawing them towards her so that her feet in their polished black loafers are lifted off the ground. She has an angular, pale face with not a scrap of make-up, and pale hair the colour of sand pulled behind a drab grey Alice band.

She reminds me of Sister Perdita, the little nun whom I stalked and watched in her secluded convent in Venice last year, flagellating herself in her cell to atone for her sins.

'She doesn't look as if she should be in a film about sex. She looks like a nun!'

'C'est ça! Très bien!' The runner girl starts to smile but tips her clipboard over her mouth to hide it. 'She has come out of the convent to be married, but the old guy, Valmont, has a bet with his ex-mistress that he can take the little nun's flower.'

Now it's my turn to snuffle with laughter. The runner girl

147

is about to pull me away when the screen above the fireplace, unnoticed by the arguing men, suddenly illuminates, sending a dazzling white glow over the room, and there is Madonna, enacting the sunlit sexual fantasies she recorded in her infamous book of twenty years ago. She and her acolytes are writhing and dancing and moaning as she sings the lyrics to *Erotica*. The screen is alive now with a stream of artistic, erotic footage, part blurred, part paused, part sharply in focus. Mostly in monochrome. Girls pressing together on a windy beach, mouths on each other's necks and faces, but eyes on the camera. Two naked men bending over a stripped girl in a school gym.

Do as I say.

Below the TV screen, the two men are standing. They have their backs to the fireplace, so they are not seeing the bodies arching on the screen above them. They pay no attention to the thrusting breasts, the bondage straps wrapped around pert buttocks, the opening mouths and those greedy tongues poking and licking as the music suggests all kinds of naughtiness.

I begin to see how reality and fantasy can merge within a film set, especially with the surreal touch of highly sexual music distracting them even when they are not speaking. I want to capture this concept. A film within a film. I notice that a cameraman is placed on a slightly raised platform at the side of the room, filming the filmers.

The watchers watched.

I bend to open my camera case, and as I do so a crumpled photograph flutters out of an inner side pocket. It's the picture of me and my cousin Polly taken at the top of the Rockefeller Center last January. It shows us supposedly balanced precariously on a construction girder swinging out over the rooftops of New York City. Polly must have tucked it in there when she came to the *Serenissima* gallery's opening night to say goodbye.

I smooth out the creases. They run symbolically between the two of us, the white paper showing through the cracked image, like the graphics of a zigzag dividing a once happily married couple. The worst weeks of my life were when Polly and I fell out over that misunderstanding about Pierre. Now, looking at her white, pinched face pictured on that day up the Rock, I experience an overwhelming urge to be with her.

I grab my phone and send her a text. She rarely gets a signal from her Moroccan retreat, but I desperately want to communicate with her anyway.

Am somewhere near Paris, standing in a château full of mad people pretending to act out an old epistolary French novel, who wouldn't know real life if it bit them on the bum. Still. Am being paid. Wish you were here, Pol. U OK?

I press 'send' and glance around me. Everyone, except the dancers gyrating in the video above our heads, is standing completely still. The crew are fiddling with knobs and switches on their equipment, murmuring to themselves. The runner girl is staring at me. The two men by the fire are watching the young nun girl, and the young nun is watching the screen.

Let my mouth go where it wants to.

I used to sit in my old boyfriend's caravan in a muddy field near the cliffs in Devon, watching this film on YouTube. I also watched the video accompanying the track *Justify My Love*, over and over again. The singer's lust oozed out of her as she beckoned her wide-eyed companions to lick and pleasure her and each other. Like the singer, I couldn't get enough of it.

I'll hit you like a truck.

I place the photograph back in the case. I'll follow up the text and try to call Polly as soon as this shoot is done.

I'll teach you how to—

Suddenly the clapper-board is operated and someone yells 'And action!' So they still use the technicalities to compartmentalise the scenes that will eventually be screened. I guess the undercurrent, the flowing of fiction into fact and back again, will be incorporated later. As the slate clacks, the music on the video screen changes to the opening of *Justify My Love*. Someone can read my mind.

The young nun girl, Cécile, sits up on the sofa. She's lit by the fake sunlight, but she could be me in that draughty, cold caravan on the cliffs, waiting for her bulky boyfriend to come back from the pub. She's staring at the horny pop star up on the screen, all milky skin, mussed-up bleached hair and black eye make-up as she squats in a hotel corridor and touches herself.

No, not like that.

Cécile's hand is running down the side of her face. A silky strand of hair escapes the stern hairband and falls over one eye. Her finger hooks into her open mouth and she bites down on it.

The silver-haired man, Valmont, suddenly notices me and the runner girl gawping in the background. He slams the bottle of wine down on the table and calls 'Cut!' The crew appears to pay no attention. They continue filming, and holding up sound booms, and checking monitors.

All part of the illusion, then. Saying 'cut' in real life doesn't work, either.

Cécile's hand has run down over her breast. Her feet drop to the floor and she parts her knees. On the screen above the fireplace, the superstar lies back on a hotel bed and opens her stockinged legs for a wide-eyed, beautiful, androgynous young man.

I don't wanna be your sister.

Valmont extricates himself from the scene and comes towards me. He shakes my hand. His eyes are a bright Paul

Newman blue, the same colour as his faded shirt, but he's several years older than Gustav.

'*Bonjour.* Serena Folkes? I am Alain, the director. You will see that name on your invoice when I pay you. But while you are on set I am the Comte de Valmont.'

'Valmont is the villain of the piece, right? So you're one of the protagonists as well as directing this film?' I ask, flipping off my lens cap.

'Yes, and no. It's not so simple.' Alain waggles his hand to show *comme ci, comme ça*. 'I don't think the word "villain" is correct. The way Malkovich played Valmont he had a streak of evil, but in real life the man is charming.'

'You mean the actor is charming, or the character?' I frown as I get out the larger Canon.

'Both, actually.' The director lifts his hands. 'He is one of my idols. He directed a stage play of *Les Liaisons* which deliberately blurred the edges. It was designed like a rehearsal studio. The actors all watched each other, even if they were not in a scene, which gave it the claustrophobia and awkwardness of a masterclass. And the letters were transmitted by text and iPad. I wanted to go further with that idea. Not the iPads, but the illusion. Install the cast in a comfortable château then ask them to almost entirely improvise. They know the outline of each scenario. But since everyone in the story is tricking someone else, or two-timing, or spoiling things, why not have the cast doing that, too, even when they're off set learning their lines or resting?'

The young girl beside me starts to cough. 'Which means they will be having much sex, *mademoiselle*.'

I glance at her. Her angular face has gone bright pink, as if the words came out by accident.

The director's piercing blue eyes laser through her.

'*C'est ça!* So because they have total freedom I have one

rule to keep them focused. All actors are addressed as their character for the length of the shoot.'

'I guess that's what they call the method?' I remark, and Valmont nods approvingly. I touch the runner's arm. 'Can you show me where to go next? Can you come with me, er—'

'*Je m'appelle Cécile*,' she replies quickly, flipping at the paper on her clipboard.

'Another Cécile?'

She tries to navigate towards the window, glancing again at the director. Alain, Valmont, whatever his name is. 'They call me Cici.'

'Our pretty assistant has the same name as the virginal heroine. Sometimes I use her, to make them interchangeable. I forgot to mention that the crew are subject to the same rule. They are here to organise filming and lighting and sound, and record our work, but they can also take part if they like, or be dragged into a scene if someone demands it. I'll decide in the final edit if it fits.'

I glance down at my Canon and select a medium range lens. 'This has to be the most interesting brief ever. So, *monsieur*. Just so I'm clear before I set up. No real names. Everyone in character, all the time?'

'Don't question it. Don't fight it. You are the voyeur photographer. The bee on the ceiling.'

'Fly on the wall?'

Valmont smiles. 'You can eavesdrop, spy through curtains or half-open doors, listen to conversations and seductions. There are cameras in every room, some with operators, some not. We are living the story. Everyone sleeps and eats under the same roof. We are locked in this château until we start scratching at the cage to get out.'

'Something will blow soon,' Cici murmurs. 'Some of us already are half-mad.'

152

I screw my lens on. 'You live here too?'

The director whispers something into the girl's hair and she blushes.

'Of course she lives here,' he says, ruffling her hair into little spikes so she looks like a new-hatched chick. 'Nobody leaves until it's in the can.'

He takes a pen off Cici's clipboard and writes something on the paper. She peers at it, and her elfin face goes bright red again. Then he waves his hand to dismiss us. The nun Cécile and Gercourt remain exactly where they were, one standing by the fire, one sitting on the sofa with her hand now thrust between her legs. Not moving, and not speaking to each other.

My runner girl leads me towards a door beside the fireplace, and as I pass this part of the main *salon* I take a few more shots. Gercourt and Cécile keep perfectly still while Alain/Valmont peers for a moment into the monitor of one of the big cameras. Then the two of them turn stiffly towards the maestro as he re-enters the scene with an assertive click-tap of his Church's brogues on the parquet.

The clapperboard goes again and everyone jumps to attention. Valmont takes up exactly where he left off, roaring at Gercourt.

I can already feel a little of Château Claustrophobia's insanity infecting me, and I'm going to reflect this in my approach. I intend to entrap the viewer. Then trip them. Let them think they are in a domestic scenario, witnessing a real argument, then pan down to a trail of wires and cables snaking over the floor. A pair of head mikes hanging off a trolley handle.

As Cici and I retreat, I exaggerate the exposure to show how the natural sunshine is bleached by the glare of electricity.

Cici shuts the door behind us. 'I tell you the story as we go. The original *Liaisons* was written in the form of letters.'

We are in another dusty hallway. Delicious cooking smells waft towards us from the end of a long stone passage, but Cici leads me away, up a flight of stairs winding up to a wide landing dominated by a beautiful arched window. From here you can see over the formal gardens and the lake, the high grey wall bordering the property, and the haze of Paris just beyond.

'So, the *histoire*. Valmont and Marquise de Merteuil hatch the plot. They were lovers once. Maybe sometimes they still are. But La Marquise wants to make trouble for Cécile, *la petite religieuse*, because her mother has brought her out of the *couvent* to marry Comte de Gercourt, and he, Gercourt, was once the lover of La Marquise but he is now bored with her. So she is angry.'

'So the Marquise is the scheming older woman.'

My God. The Margot character. Which makes her ex-lover Valmont who? Gustav? Or Pierre?

'*C'est ça*. She wants Valmont to take the flower of Cécile so that she will be too dirty for Gercourt. But Valmont is not interested. He desires another woman, Madame de Tourvel. In fact, he sleeps with her and falls in love with her. She is his weakness.'

'So Valmont is not such a villain. He knows how to love.'

'Well, it's strange love, because he still takes Cécile also.'

'But a love story nevertheless. Do you think they'd have the energy for all that playing around and infidelity in real life?'

'The energy, yes. The endless time, no. There is much *ennui* in this story. They don't have enough to do.' Cici rips at the corner of her call sheet. '*Moi,* I believe they would all end up killing each other!'

I laugh and go to sit on the broad window seat for a moment and stare at the distant pencil prick of the Eiffel Tower. My Gustav was a baby, a child and a teenager in that city. What did he look like growing up? All the family photographs from that time were destroyed by the fire that killed his parents.

His silky black hair was probably too long, probably the bane of his mother's life. He was not yet shaving properly, but already kissing girls and smoking Gauloises and gabbling in French to his friends, swinging his long leg over a bike or a *mobylette* to scamper off over the cobbles to school or college. He must have been cute, fresh and naughty.

I get out my phone. There's still no answer from Polly, so I text Gustav.

These people could be you. Us. They are living and breathing this film. It's giving me the creeps!

Cici touches the diamond ring that sparkles as I hold my phone up to the light. 'Beautiful.'

My body tugs with longing for Gustav. He's too far away today. If he's going to be late back tonight I'll keep busy for as long as possible.

Cici taps my arm and beckons me to follow her. She leads me up to the next floor, which consists of smaller, cosier servants' quarters, and the next hour is spent taking photographs of secondary cast and crew up here, mostly sleeping, eating, gossiping, playing card games or, oddly, knitting.

The final door on this floor gives way to an enormous bathroom under the eaves, and in the rolltop tub by the window a big man with a bushy beard is lying back in the greenish water. Above him the spindly white body of the nun Cécile, wrenched from the drawing room to the attic, is partly obscured by clouds of hot steam as he holds her above the water long enough for me to get several fantastic silhouette shots, before he lowers her on to his huge, erect penis.

'That's the dirty gardener, Artolan! The actor has done Shakespeare in Stratford, would you believe?' Cici whispers.

'But here, finally, with the help of Cécile, he is getting clean.'

The craziness of this scenario starts me giggling helplessly. I snatch up my unopened camera bags, and Cici collapses into laughter too as we run down another set of stairs and into another wide corridor which passes over the main *salon*.

One side of this corridor is bordered by glass walls overlooking the garden. The other is flanked by closed double doors.

'So who lives along here, Cici?' I ask, catching my breath. 'Are these VIP quarters?'

'This is the wing of Valmont and the Marquise de Merteuil.' She stops laughing. 'But sometimes we sleep along here, too.'

We pace slowly past a set of closed double doors and approach a second. The old floorboards creak beneath our feet.

'So tell me more about those two. What schemes do they cook up that are so awful?'

'Madame La Marquise is mad on sex. All the men on set she likes. How do you call it, she's *un couguar*?' Cici tries to close the second door, which is slightly ajar. 'Don't go in there, *mademoiselle*. La Marquise is a diva. My boyfriend says she's fierce if she's disturbed. She might be sleeping or – otherwise occupied.'

The rain has stopped and the real sun is shining through the huge windows behind me, trying to push its light into the dark room. The pervasive music from hidden speakers all over the château is now a kind of funky salsa overlaid with a remix of Nina Simone's *My Baby Just Cares for Me*.

My phone vibrates. Gustav has replied. *Je suis Valmont, qui trouve son amour véritable.*

Valmont finds his true love. I text Gustav back. *Et alors? Qui est ton amour véritable?*

156

He answers immediately. *Toi, bien sur! Tu es la Madame de Tourvel.'*

'Serena, come away, *s'il te plaît.'* Cici starts pulling at me. 'You must be hungry. Chef is making *coq au vin.* Good for photographs.'

'In a moment, sure. But I'm intrigued by what happens in these rooms. Can't we just explore a little more? Tell me what happens in the end of the book?'

The girl shakes her head, ripping at the corner of the sheets on her clipboard.

'Please, *mademoiselle.* Let me show you the catering! Fantastic catering we have.'

'I'm a professional voyeur, Cici. I seek out the naughtiest, most private activities which should be hidden. I explore everywhere. The darkest corners.' I push open the door with my foot. 'And I suspect the bedrooms will be more interesting than the kitchen.'

At first, like the *salon* downstairs, this big room looks empty. Bare floorboards, shutters half closed at the windows, a *lit bateau* with a white muslin canopy hanging like a waterfall from the ceiling.

The music is piped into here, too, and changes to a slow, sensuous Argentine tango. Now I can see that it's not entirely empty. There is someone dancing near the window. From here all I can see is a sinewy woman's back and tendrils of wild black hair falling down as she winds her arms above her head and shimmies on long bare legs across the dusty floorboards.

She's wearing a short baby-doll negligee in black or dark navy, I can't see in this light. She moves beautifully to the Latin arrangement of the music. If you were walking down a backstreet one steamy night in downtown Buenos Aires you might spy a woman like her, through a chipped blue door, being undressed, then laid across a bar and ravaged.

157

I lift my camera and take a couple of shots of the way the light slants across her body from the wooden shutters. As I pan round the room, I spot a film camera and a couple of folded up studio lights parked in the corner. No obvious cameraman, but the dancing woman is not alone. A surfer dude is sitting astride a bentwood chair, leaning his chin on his arms. From here he looks stark naked. He has long blonde hair which would be girlish if he didn't have beautiful swimmer's shoulders. When he stands at a silent gesture from her, all vestiges of femininity vanish, because there's a huge bulge visible in his tight tartan boxers.

Cici grabs at my arm. 'You have to stop them! That's La Marquise. And the boy – he's my – he's Danceny!'

I step further into the room and the boy sees me. The dancing woman must have noticed him glancing across her shoulder, but she doesn't turn. In fact, she steps closer to him and starts running her hands up his body.

Cici gasps. I can hear tears catching in her throat.

'Remind me. Who is Danceny in the story?' I whisper. 'Why are you so upset?'

'Danceny is the young man who the little nun Cécile falls for. But La Marquise, this cougar, she sleeps with him, too.' Cici keeps tugging me like a child. 'But that actor is my boyfriend.'

I hesitate. Cici is waggling her hand frantically from behind me, trying to catch the boy's attention. He looks directly at both of us, his face expressionless.

As the dark-haired temptress runs her hands over him, caressing the bulge in his shorts, Danceny keeps his eyes on poor little Cici. It must be agony for her to see this, but I suspect this goes on all the time. I also suspect that Valmont has rammed home that if she doesn't like it, she knows where the door is.

There's no one directing this scene, and no one filming, at least as far as I can see.

'But you're disobeying Valmont's rule, Cici! You must leave your life behind while you're in here, *n'est-ce pas*?' I press my mouth against her hot cheek. 'So what do we think? Are these two rehearsing, shooting a scene, or are they just having a quick screw while they wait to be called on?'

She leans her forehead against mine for a moment. 'All what you say. But also none of it. Valmont says we can do whatever we like while we're here, but *ça ne marche pas*, because we must stop or start the moment he tells us.'

I watch the woman's hand diving into the boy's boxers now. 'What you're saying is, you have to go with the flow?'

She shrugs sadly. '*Qu'est-ce que ça va dire?*'

'Er. In French you'd say, *suivez le mouvement*? That's what is happening in this château. Reality and illusion, flowing seamlessly.' I pinch her cheek to try and get her to smile back. 'Either you enter into the spirit of it, or you walk out.'

I train my camera on the couple again. The woman has a sensational body, and now I'm seeing more clearly through my viewfinder I'm certain I recognise her. The tumbling black hair, the flex of muscle in her spine, the tempting rise of her big breasts in the flimsy little nightie. I've seen this body before.

I step closer to the bed. The floorboards creak loudly again. I'm not sure if the couple has heard my footfall through the music, but even if they have, surely Valmont has warned them I'll be filming today. The boy knows I'm here, and the woman isn't bothered. The little satin garment rises up over her naked buttocks as she hooks her leg round the boy's thigh. His eyes shift away from Cici and fix on the woman who is charming the pants off him. Cici gives a kind of strangled sob. The woman turns, her hands gripping the boy's shoulders, and her black eyes flash over her shoulder. First annoyance, then a questioning raise of her eyebrows, then a big, pleased grin spreads across her face. I can almost feel her warm, wet lips fastening on to mine.

With a jolt, I realise it's the same girl I espied through my long lens when I was walking along the High Line in Manhattan a few weeks ago, the night Gustav presented me with the *Serenissima* gallery. She was being filmed having sex with an anonymous guy in a rumpled bed. Her CV must be well thumbed by casting directors looking for uninhibited actresses, and boy, she's perfect for this scenario. Ripe, exotic, and naughty.

She winks at me. She's a woman, not a girl. Her eyelashes are long and thick like spiders. Her mouth is a juicy honeytrap of thick red lips and I want those lips. I want her. Shockingly. Desire plunges inside me. And she knows it. Sliding her hands down to the boy's hips, she turns to face me fully, rubbing her bottom against his body like a pole dancer, opening and closing her knees for my benefit.

I return her look, aware that my mouth has dropped open. I lift the camera. That's my message to her. I can't have her. Not now, anyway. I'm working.

The boy's eyes are half closed as she rubs against him. She bends forward, her big breasts dangling like tempting fruit. Showing herself to me. I remember the erotic pop video on its endless loop downstairs. Those hungry open mouths, those girls and boys greedy for each other. My hands are sweaty as I adjust the apertures for more light.

Danceny can't hold on any longer. As La Marquise fondles her own breasts, pushing them together, running the flats of her palms over the nipples so that they poke through the silky nightie, the boy spins her around, hoists her up off the floor so that her legs wrap around his hips.

'Cici,' I whisper, trying to distract her. 'Could you unzip my tripod bag for me, please?'

The girl bends to do so, still sniffling. She's been involved with this production for long enough. Surely she knows the score? I can see why she's possessive over her tasty boyfriend, though. He may be young, but he sure works out. He bears the voluptuous weight of La Marquise as easily as if she's a fresh baguette and throws her on to the bed. They sink into the whiteness, the pillows bouncing round them as if eager to join in, and I switch to film because the slow motion stills will look fantastic.

When they stop bouncing, La Marquise manoeuvres herself on top of her prey. Her strong thighs grip him. Her hair flies back as she tosses her head triumphantly. She's in the same controlling position as when she rode on top of her lover in that loft in New York.

'Ça suffit, mademoiselle. Viens.' Cici hisses. She's beginning to annoy me now. 'We can find other people in the château to film.'

I shake my head. She can talk the talk, but when it comes to her own feelings the poor girl can't face walking the walk. If Cici has a problem, she has to button it. I'm just here to do a job, and her feelings have to go on the back burner for now. But I can't tear myself away.

La Marquise is pulling the boy's boxers down now, kissing her way down his hairless torso and flat stomach. Her face is buried against him, but he can't help glancing over at us. At me, actually. Is he a brilliant actor or is he genuinely struggling with a mixture of remorse for his jealous young girlfriend and exhilaration at being fondled by the sexiest woman in the film business?

His erection thumps out of the boxers and La Marquise cradles it in her fingers for a moment, twisting her long black hair back behind her shoulder with the other hand. The two of them are perfectly positioned in profile against the slatted window. The light is more diffuse here, perfect for the atmosphere. I'm guessing there's a courtyard or a more shaded

161

area of the premises beyond. On my side of the room the light through the still-open door is coming through stronger now that the rain has eased.

And so in perfect profile Danceny's erection thrusts upright, manifesting its impressive proportions. No wonder little Cici wants that treasure to herself. The woman is massaging it, hard, as if she's throwing pottery.

A long-ago conversation with Polly comes back to me. Actually referring to Pierre, when he was this age. When he was lusting after Margot, his out of bounds sister-in-law.

You know what they're like at that age. Always hard, and always grateful.

And thinking of Pierre, he fits the Gercourt profile. La Marquise's secondary lover, employed to create mayhem. But as I watch the couple, I realise that Pierre's name no longer makes me panicky or anxious. He's forgiven. Better still, he's far away.

I'm working. I must push those Levi brothers out of my mind. I peer through the camera again. Danceny is hard enough now. La Marquise is going down on him. She pulls him into those red, shiny lips of hers, her teeth nipping. She's sucking and he's responding, thrusting into her face.

My fingers start trembling. Time to screw my camera on to the tripod. Cici is silent, not offering to help. I turn round and realise that whatever nonsense she spouts about the liberating ethos of this shoot, it's proving too hard for her to swallow. Poor Cici has left the room.

Once the camera's fixed on I can take the pictures without spoiling the shots with too much shake. I check the apparatus is secure and I'm lifting my meter to test the dimness in here when the light alters, because a door has opened on the far wall.

Danceny notices, and moans with frustration. But he can't move. For the benefit of the intruder who has just come in,

La Marquise tightens her grip on the young man's hips and sucks harder, then works her way back up to the tip, sucking and licking his sweet length until he jerks and cries out loud.

A dart of desire shoots through me again, stronger this time. I watch the woman's mouth, working on the boy, and I imagine those lips working on me, kissing my mouth, working down my throat to my breasts, her female mouth on my female breasts, on those other parts of me other women have only really skimmed over in my little experiments.

I could practise on her what I learned with Mrs Weinmeyer.

Look at her! As she leans over the boy, sucking him, her fingers wandering beneath him and jabbing into other parts of him, she works her heavy breasts and nipples against his body, rubs herself against his legs. The moist sound effects carry over the music. It's changed yet again to an almost monastic humming, accompanied by a drumbeat. The woman's wide, brown bottom flexes eagerly against her toy boy, showing him how a real woman feels.

Another man has come through the far door and simply merged with the shadows, because he is wearing a beige suit. It's the character called Gercourt. I look at my watch. I've been up here for ages.

The newcomer walks straight over to the bed and stands above the lovers, watching them. He's close enough to touch them. But he folds his arms, and his face is expressionless.

I take a shot of the curves and shapes of the two lovers on the bed contrasting with the ramrod-rigid watching man. La Marquise gives the boy one last, long suck, letting the length of him, still stiff, slide out past her teeth, along her tongue and into her waiting hand. Without turning her head, she murmurs something to the newcomer Gercourt.

I remember how astonished I was when I saw her in that New York loft, mounting her invisible lover in the bed, all the time offering a running commentary to the crew hanging around her. This woman has to be the coolest thing since red-hot chilli.

As if reading my mind, she glances at me. All three of them glance at me. The boy in fresh embarrassment, rising up on his elbows to push her off. Gercourt coldly. La Marquise with another languorous wink. Then she clambers back on top of her boy, pressing him gently down on his back, tilting herself over him.

'*C'est magnifique,*' she croons at him, showing him the length of his shaft encircled by her fingers.

She grins, not at the boy, but at me, as she rises on her knees and aims him inside her, pausing, letting me focus and shoot, the stiffness about to enter the softness. She lowers herself inch by inch, sighing loudly now, and a muscle twitches in Gercourt's cheek.

I watch the woman teasing herself, teasing her lover. I know how that feels. That agonising slowness, forcing yourself to put off the delicious moment for as long as you can bear, knowing that you will want to screech with delight when it's inside you. And that's what she does, flinging her arms in the air like a flamenco dancer, sweeping her hair up. Her spine undulates as she alternates between rising up on her knees and falling forwards on to her hands. When her nipples swing over his mouth, her curtains of dark hair conceal them both.

Gercourt can't hold back. That gorgeous female bottom must be a red rag to a bull. I don't care if this is rehearsed, or being secretly choreographed by Alain, or being filmed by invisible cameras. Lust runs riot in this château, with no boundaries. The naughtier the better. The more combinations, the better.

It's perfect material, and it's perfect for the narrative.

Gercourt unzips his narrow trousers. The boy Danceny's eyes widen in alarm. Maybe he thinks Gercourt wants him.

But La Marquise simply tosses her head and rides the boy more furiously.

Gercourt steps round the bucking bodies and kneels on the bed behind La Marquise, pulling her butt cheeks open, running his hand over her rump. Then he settles himself, angles himself like a weapon, and with no niceties he thrusts up that other part offered to him, forcing a long, low, juddering groan from her as he enters.

She's not so in control now. She falls forward, and Danceny takes advantage of her distraction by pulling at her breasts, taking one nut-brown nipple into his mouth and biting it, hard, just as Gercourt at the rear rams himself in.

So this is the question answered. The composition of two men and a woman, framed by my viewfinder, showing me what goes where, and into whom.

Somehow I can't see Gustav agreeing to me trying it.

Should this be happening, or is this going too far even by Valmont's standards? Is La Marquise being overpowered, or do they all know full well she can take whatever's coming to her, whoever, whenever? However?

La Marquise starts to mutter to herself as the pace increases, a kind of crooning, puffing stream of consciousness in a language I don't recognise, but the two men are silent, intent upon filling her.

I take a couple more splendid shots of the intricate threesome, zooming in on a sequence of intimate close-ups.

Now it's time to retreat. I pick up my equipment as best I can, my legs trembling as I drag it noisily from the room. For all I know, they'll stop as soon as I'm gone. Someone else I haven't seen will call 'Cut', and either they'll stop or they'll finish in their own good time. But so what? I'm not here to shatter the illusion. I'm here to encapsulate it.

Even the music seems to have stopped now. I wander down the wide corridor, back the way we came. Cici's clipboard has been left on the window seat on the landing. I pick it up and carry it down the stairs and down the corridor she told me led to the kitchen. That's where she must be.

I can smell garlic and onions and wine as I approach. Maybe the casserole is ready. Something metallic crashes to the floor behind the kitchen door, accompanied by whispered curses.

I push open the door.

Cici is in here all right. She's half sitting, half lying on a big scrubbed pine table, and it looks as if she's just knocked an entire plate of steaming vegetables to the floor. Behind her, through a rubber curtain, I can see other white shapes blurred by steam, arms waving, knives flashing, utensils gleaming. I hear the slamming of oven doors.

In this section, the dining area I presume, Valmont is standing between Cici's long white legs, peeling her dark woollen stockings and tiny white knickers down to her ankles while she unbuttons his faded jeans.

I lift my smaller camera, still slung round my neck, and take a few more shots. I'm well into my stride now. Cici and Alain are kissing. Her young face is so fresh and clear against his greying, grizzled bristles.

The rubber curtain clatters aside, making me jump. The large man from the bathtub, dressed now in a lumberjack shirt and mud-spattered gardening trousers, pushes through. He mutters something at Alain, who nods and then lifts his hand to dismiss us both before pushing Cici on to her back amongst the bread and the fruit and the bottles of beer. She's ready to be properly skewered.

I grin at Artolan, the dirty gardener, and he scowls back as if he's never seen me before. Despite the filthy clothes and still-wet, matted hair, he has perfect white teeth and clear grey eyes. I'll mark him down as the Dickson/Crystal character from my own life. He points towards the door to indicate that I'm to leave the way I've just come in. No food for me, then.

I pack up my camera, remember to place Cici's clipboard down beside her. As I grab an apple from the fruit bowl beside her head, I can see the *billet-doux* that Alain/Valmont scribbled on there earlier.

In five minutes I'm coming to fuck you.

CHAPTER SEVEN

My work is done. Artolan is ignoring me, stumping through the lobby back towards the *salon*. Fine. I can't wait to get my ass back into the city to wait for Gustav.

'*Excusez-moi?*' I call out, trotting after the gardener as he flings open the door to the *salon*. '*La voiture?*'

He shrugs like the Gallic stereotype he is and leaves the door swinging open. I follow him into the *salon*. The sun has gone down now but it's still bright in here.

The music has shifted to the Gainsbourg and Birkin song *Je t'aime,* with erotic stills spooling across the screen above the fireplace. A different group of people is standing around the fireplace, drinking beer straight from the bottle. The conversation appears to be perfectly polite, judging by the calm modulation of the voices, except that the women are swaying their bodies slightly to the sensual music, rotating their heads. They are all mouthing the whispered endearments, imitating the cracked breathing of the girl in the film.

I take out my small camera, still slung round my neck. I want to know if the group by the fire are quoting the lovers on the soundtrack. Are they inviting each other to enter them, to come, just like those singers? If so, it's very subtle. They're not even touching at the moment. They're just drinking, quite suggestively, from their beer bottles, but otherwise nodding and smiling in civilised mode.

Scanning the group, I zoom in first when I spot La Marquise. She must have rushed down here pretty damn quick. She's still flushed and tangle-haired from her recent threesome, and still wearing the tiny negligee. She's thrown a matching navy silk dressing gown loosely over herself. The dirty thought darts into my mind that she must still smell of sex.

I pan over to the nun-like Cécile character. She's still in her grey coat, but her sandy, watery hair is loosened from the severe grey headband and flowing back from her fine face. She mouths '*Moi non plus*' at La Marquise, who runs her tongue sensuously over her large red lips in response, before fellating her beer bottle.

There's a third woman I haven't seen before and who isn't singing. Madame de Tourvel, *peut-être*. Straight out of Sixties sex-bomb central casting with her Bardot bleach-blonde hair backcombed into a puffy bun, her eyes heavily outlined and her lips a shell pink, although incongruously she's dressed in a severe pink bouclé Chanel suit.

She can't take her eyes off the only man in the group, who has his back to me and is hidden by one of the cameras pushed up close to the scene. All I can see of him is black hair and broad shoulders. But that's all I need to see.

The three women are pushing close to him, eyes gleaming, mouths open, tongues flickering as if they want to eat him. Not even bothering to compete for his attention or push each other out of the way. They are all after him, and they'd have him here, now, one at a time or altogether, if no one objected. My God. Are they bored already of the lovers all over this castle who are there for the taking at the drop of a clapper-board? Or is this yet another staged scene I've walked into?

Valmont is still humping little Cici in the kitchen. The cameramen in the room are hunched in a corner staring at a monitor and sparking up some very strong-smelling cigarettes.

La Marquise spots me through a gap in the camera apparatus and her big eyes gleam. She gives me one of her long, slow winks, her long eyelashes curved like Bambi's. A fidgety warmth fills me as she starts to walk towards me. The Bardot woman steps into her place as if they're all part of some kind of roundel dance. She puts her hand up to touch the man's face, fingering a lock of his curly black hair.

And when I realise who the man is, so unexpected, so out of context, yet so apparently at ease, I'm so shocked that my finger presses the shutter before I'm properly prepared. Goddammit. We all parted on polite, if slightly shaky, terms back in March, but Pierre Levi and I are certainly not best buddies. I'm not ready to see him again, especially on my own without Gustav here. What's Pierre doing all the way over here in Paris? Why is he standing in this very château?

'Before your handsome friend whisks you away, I am so glad to meet you at last,' murmurs La Marquise in a husky French accent with a tinge of North Africa, pouting a kiss in my viewfinder. 'I am Maria Memsahib. I've seen you before, yes?'

'You're not allowed to use your real name here!'

'I don't give a shit for Valmont's silly rules!' She produces a white card with curly Arabic script in gold writing and bites it at the corner. 'I can use whatever name I like!'

'I saw you filming a sex scene in New York, didn't I?' I keep the camera up to hide my confusion. 'You were in a loft near the High Line?'

'Yes. And later that evening I saw you making love with my old friend Gustav Levi in the art gallery.'

170

She winks again. She has my attention.

'You know Gustav? How come?'

My hands are shaking as I take another blurred close-up of her then let my camera drop down on its strap round my neck. As the group disperses, my 'handsome friend' turns and spots me. He lifts his hand in a mock salute.

Maria Memsahib slides her card into the pocket of my jacket. Her tiny negligee rucks up as she pulls me against her haunch.

'Pierre has grown into a fine young man, yes? Are you not pleased to see him? I knew the Levi brothers in London.'

'I'm just a little thrown, that's all. I thought he was in LA. I had no idea he was planning a trip over to France.' I'm about to remove her hand from my waist, but then I pause, partly to delay having to greet Pierre. 'How did you know them?'

'Their place in Baker Street. His wife found me waiting tables in Marylebone and invited me to a private party. I thought it was a casting. And in a way it was. I was perfect as her mini-me.' She rests her warm face against mine for a moment. 'I was young and stupid, *signorina*. Gustav was the only strong, steady presence in a crazy, unstable situation. You must give him a very big kiss from me.'

She was an ingénue, rescued by the dashing knight. Just like I was, less than a year ago.

'She's not his wife any more.' I lift my hand and show her my diamond ring.

'Lucky, lucky you. But he is even luckier.' Maria Memsahib examines the jewel and nods slowly. She brushes her mouth against my cheek as if to kiss it, but she catches the corner of my mouth instead. 'He has had a lucky escape.'

Pierre is crossing the room towards us now. I turn slightly away from him, keeping my mouth against Maria's so she can still hear me.

'What happened to you in the house? Did you – oh, God, I feel sick asking you this, but – did you ever, you and Gustav—'

'He's a gorgeous man, *signorina,* but we never were naked together. Not fully. You see, I prefer women.' She laughs at my shocked expression and kisses me emphatically on one cheek. As she kisses the other, she whispers in my ear, 'I am an actress, darling! Of course I can pretend. But you can't. I saw how you looked at me. There is more you would like to try, but you hide it. You look so sweet, but you know, there's a proverb here in France. *Le feu plus couvert est le plus ardent!'*

'The more hidden the fire the more ardently it burns?' Pierre translates the phrase as he approaches. 'Hi, Serena.'

'What are you doing here?' I hiss as he loops his arm around Maria's shoulders.

She pats his face fondly. 'So good to see you, Pierre. We were talking about our muses just now, weren't we? What about yours, *mademoiselle?* The singer up there. Is she one of your heroines?'

Painfully aware of Pierre's unexpected presence, and his highly amused expression, I follow her gesture. The video has looped back to the scene where the singer is on a hotel bed spreading her legs for a dark young man as another masked man watches.

I can't look at it with Pierre standing right here.

'Tell us, Serena.' He speaks quietly. 'Who floats your boat?'

The blush is so unexpected, and so hot, that my hair starts to prickle.

'I have two idols. Madonna the singer, and maybe because I never had a real mother, Madonna the mother.'

'From the profane to the sacred, and back again. That sure sums you up.' Pierre takes my hand and leads me across the *salon* towards the outer hallway and the front door. 'But

172

do you want to know who my muse is? Who knows? It could be you.'

'Don't be ridiculous. What are you doing here, anyway?' I demand, shaking his hand off me as soon as we're outside in the hazy twilight. 'In Paris, I mean? Why aren't you in America?'

'*Mademoiselle!* I need to catch you!' Cici runs out of the château after us, her dark hair still ruffled and her clothes not quite done up properly from her hasty session on the kitchen table. 'The car will be here in a moment. But Valmont wants you back here tomorrow.'

'I'll be here. And Cici? I'm glad to see you looking so much happier now!' I nudge her gently in the ribs. 'Alain must be doing something right!'

She gives me a shy smile as I take the papers she hands me. The only sign of the director is a fresh love bite beneath her ear. Pierre gives a little bow which makes her blush prettily.

'This is my world too, Serena.' He watches her skip away. 'I know Alain and some of the guys working here. He's notoriously secretive, it's always closed sets with him, so this was the perfect excuse to take a peek. And no, I know what you're thinking – I did not bribe them or influence them to hire you. They were already blown away by your work. They certainly didn't know we were related—'

'Which reminds me. I need to call Gustav.' I realise how harsh my voice sounds, and I take a deep breath. 'Does he know you're here? In Paris, I mean?'

'Of course he does. I haven't come to France to see you, so you can quit worrying. I'm here for a totally different reason, which will become clear when he gets back tomorrow.' The car crunches over the gravel. 'Gustav has been delayed in Italy, so he asked me to fetch you. He thought it would be more friendly.'

I take out my phone and Maria Memsahib's card drops

out on to the ground. I look at the phone. At the card. And at Pierre. I feel Gustav watching us from wherever he is, willing us to be civilised with each other.

'You gave me a shock, Pierre, so I'm sorry if I was rude. It's kind of you to come. But my God. What a surreal end to a very surreal day.'

'Well, I'm here as long as you need me.' Pierre waves to the driver and goes to open the door. 'I'll wait here while you phone the big man.'

Gustav picks up on the first ring. 'Hey, darling! How's my budding star?'

Tears of longing prick my eyes. 'Missing you, honey. Where are you? Why aren't you coming back?'

'I'm about to sign on a very important dotted line.' He laughs softly at the other end. I can hear the chink of glasses and excitable Italian voices. 'I'll be with you as soon as I possibly can, darling. I'm aching for you.'

I glance over at Pierre, who is texting on his own phone. He has a new beard, close shaven to his face, which makes him look even slimmer than last time, and somehow older. Despite the casual T-shirt and sweater thrown over his shoulders, some of the old menace is restored.

So he's found a new mask.

'Gustav?' I ask, biting the corner of the business card where la Memsahib nibbled it herself just now. 'What happened to La Marquise de Merteuil in the end?'

'You mean you haven't read the book yet?' Gustav laughs again. 'She came to a sticky end, like all the bad guys. She caught smallpox and went into hiding because her beauty was ruined.'

The journey back into Paris takes forever. The car is far too silent. The lack of conversation far too stark. Finally I can't bear it any longer.

174

'Pierre. I want to be friends. We will be friends. But let me get my head around everything.'

He glances at me. I'm expecting some kind of wisecrack, but he just folds his arms and looks out of the window at the dark countryside washed by the rain.

'Are you really over Margot?'

We turn to each other at the same time, equally surprised by the question that has burst out of me.

'Unequivocally. She revolts me. But why do you ask?'

I shrug and turn away. 'I wish I hadn't now. I hate hearing her name. But she never leaves us alone. She's been watching us in New York. Gustav's pretty cool about everything, but I feel she's still threatening us. She tried, and failed, to humiliate me at some new venue she's opened, the Sapphix Bar. And she completely ruined the Weinmeyers' private view of my work by recording herself speaking over the Baker Street orgy.'

Pierre frowns, but he returns my gaze totally calmly. His eyes are steady. His hands rest on his knees. His legs in the navy chinos are relaxed, not twitching like I've seen them do when he's agitated.

'I warned you to watch out. She's stepping up her game. I still think she's dangerous.'

Remember, he works surrounded by actors. He could be pretending. But something in his demeanour is giving me confidence. I sit back against the car seat.

'Explain to me, then, just so I'm clear. Why, when we were drinking cocktails at the Gramercy Bar, did you tell me that you still got hard thinking about her? Even though you had just told her to get lost. You were hard at that very moment. Just talking about her. You said that you could take her right there in front of me if she was there. So. One more time. Do you still want her?'

The car pauses at a crossroads, dropping an uncomfortable

quiet over us. I look at the traffic lights, and wait for Pierre's derision. But again there's this thoughtful pause.

'Be careful using such explicit language, Serena. You're straying into flirtation country.'

I fling round at him. 'Those were your crude words, not mine!'

He shifts round to face me and flattens his hands on the seat between us.

'Look. We can't wipe out history, however unpleasant. Gustav and I were enthralled by her once. First him, then me. She had us both by the balls. But she's history. I told her as far back as New Year's Eve that she disgusted me, and not long afterwards I bailed out. So what I said that evening about wanting her was pure bravado. I said it because I was alone with you at last. You were listening to me. You're always so' – Pierre pauses, searching for the right word – 'you always listen. I had to be crude like that, otherwise I'd give myself away.'

'Give yourself away?'

He opens his mouth to say something, then thinks better of it. His fingers lift and smack down again.

'I wanted to impress you, I suppose. Or horrify you. How clumsy was that? But I want to be a better person now, Serena, however unlikely that sounds. I went along with her plan for too long. Those couple of months over Christmas and the New Year, and then my stupid, dangerous behaviour towards you in Venice nearly lost me everything, all over again. How did I think I could live my life without Gustav? Making up with him has made everything feel right. And then there was you – I didn't want her meddling with either of you. And I still don't.'

The car takes us through the deserted village and out the other side.

'You know, when I was at her apartment, and I found

Gustav's wedding shirt in the wardrobe, I felt like the three of you were a unit, and I was the outsider.' I finger the diamond ring thoughtfully. 'I had this awful jealousy, not only of her, but I resented your brotherly closeness. I never had a brother or a sister. How do I know I won't be the outsider again one day?'

His face softens, obviously relieved that I've dropped the subject of Margot.

'Because you're as close to Gustav as you could be. Me being his brother won't change that. Just think. You've got an extra pair of hands around to catch you if you fall.'

We smile uncertainly at each other. There are more buildings outside now. More lights. 'So what about you? When are you going to find someone of your own?'

Pierre shakes his head, the smile fading. 'Look at my track record! Poor Polly. That was my idea, by the way, to break it off before she got in any deeper. I know it was cruel and clumsy. But she's too nice – she's your cousin for God's sake! I couldn't be involved with her any more. I can't be involved with anyone. The one sorry truth in all this is that despite loathing Margot for what she's tried to do to all of us, the fact is that I've tasted her. I've had her in my bed. I've been her slave, I've even managed to reject her. But Margot Levi has ruined my chances of making it with any other woman.'

Now we're passing flyovers and tower blocks on the outskirts of Paris. I look at Pierre's hands resting on the leather seat.

'If she's done that, then she's won,' I remark, placing my hands next to his. If I try really hard I can expel from my mind, once and for all, everything that those hands could have done. 'And as we're stuck in this car for a few more minutes, answer me one more thing. What about me?'

He pulls his hands away and pushes them through his unruly hair.

177

'What do you mean?'

'Venice. What were you *really* playing at? Margot said you went after me because you'd fallen for me. What did you think would happen once I realised my mistake?'

He turns away. 'I didn't think. Not past the moment you were in my arms. That was all I wanted. I've just said that Margot has ruined my chances with other women, and it's true, but I'll never stop fighting that influence. From the start you seemed like the one woman to break that curse. But you were Gustav's girl, so there was no hope. Didn't stop me wanting you, though. Badly. In fact, the feelings didn't even have a name.'

'Margot called it love.' I realise my voice is hard and cold, but I can't let him draw me back into dangerous territory. 'But I said you were incapable of feeling love.'

'You were right. I love Gustav, but otherwise there's not a lot going on in here.' Pierre bashes at his chest. The same gesture Gustav used when we were scrabbling around in the alleyway beneath Margot's apartment, to show me that I lived in his heart. 'All I can tell you, since you are demanding answers, is that I tried my best to put the feelings to one side and focus on the fact that Margot's plan to separate you and Gustav was futile and wrong. I hoped that if I told her to forget it, to leave us all alone, I would work out a way of watching the two of you go off into the sunset, try to be a good brother, and then get on with my life. But I'm not a logical person, Serena. All my good intentions went out the window when I thought you were alone in Venice. I was consumed afresh by the desire to have you. To take the risk. Taste you. Just once. And it felt so good, Serena. Just for that tiny moment.'

'How could it have felt good? Those awful, dangerous desires – they weren't even romantic. You were possessed. It must have been agonising. But what you tried to do to me

178

was potentially so disastrous – and for what? It wasn't *real*, Pierre!'

The car plunges under the Seine and the silence elongates for the length of the tunnel. We rise slowly in a traffic jam, and when we emerge the familiar turrets and spires of Paris sprout against the velvety night sky.

'You really want to go over this again? I knew I'd regret at least not trying, OK? That's how I operate. Led by my loins. Act first, think later. Deep down, I knew you'd reject me. And the silver lining is, there will never be intimate memories of your sweet body to torment me.' He rubs his beard. 'I'm working hard on myself, I can tell you. That's what we do in LA. We have therapy. We talk. We acquire a shiny new persona. And we distract ourselves. The women over there – boy! I wanted you, and now I don't. It was an addiction, as mindless as that, and I'm done with it. Eventually I will revert to thinking of you purely as a very attractive photographer who soon will be my sister.'

'I so want to believe you, Pierre.' I pause as the car speeds past Notre Dame and up towards the Champs-Élysées. 'That those feelings are gone, or at least going.'

'Believe me, Serena. No more mania. No more danger.' Pierre pats at his empty heart again. 'The only love I have now is Gustav.'

As the shops and hotels and cars flash past us, so the things that man in the gondola said and did start to fly away, too. The mask peels off to reveal the young man who shares Gustav's features. Who doesn't want to fight any more.

The car stops outside my hotel. Pierre gets out and holds open the door for me.

'I don't suppose – a nightcap?'

'Don't push it, Levi!' I retort, lifting out my camera bags. 'But thanks for meeting me. And thanks for the chat. We've made progress, yes?'

'Gustav would be proud.' Pierre tips an imaginary cap. 'I am at your service, *mademoiselle*. Always.'

I wonder if there's anything as depressing as the prospect of sleeping in a beautiful hotel room alone? The more sumptuous and well earned the room, the more lonely the night.

For a split second I forget that Gustav won't be here, leaping to his feet to greet me. For another split second I pray he'll surprise me anyway.

As I walk into the room and throw my jacket over a hook, there's another split second of regret that I rejected Pierre's suggestion. What better way to toast our tentative new friend-ship than with a dram of Irish coffee? But that would have been utter madness. We've said enough for one day. And I haven't forgotten that he has also said, more than once, that he can't trust himself around me.

I unpack my camera bags and take out the Canon to examine today's labours. If I concentrate on that, maybe the night will pass quicker. Maybe Gustav will tiptoe back after all, ruffling my hair with kisses while I'm asleep. The first image of the day lights up. Thick black cable, snaking across a parquet floor.

But I stop. Something's not right. My neck is prickling. I sniff. There's an unfamiliar scent in here. Not the flowers. I asked for non-scented flowers because lilies make me feel sick. It's floral, with an exotic eastern tang of lemongrass and something else. The nostril-pricking aroma of female excitement.

I walk around the corner. Ahead of me are the twinkling lights of Paris, spread like a carpet beneath my balcony. I stretch and yawn and turn to the bed.

It's been slept in. Or played in. The duvet has slipped halfway off. One pillow has the dent of a head in it. Two others are placed in the middle of the mattress.

180

We never left it like this. Gustav normally straightens the bed. And, hang on, but shouldn't it be pristine in a hotel like this? I reach for the phone to call housekeeping, and then I see them. Red shoes. High heels. Pointed toes. One upright, one lying on its side.

A tiny, pleading voice in my ear. A gift?

But then they would come in a shoebox, with a ribbon. Not thrown on the floor. There's no imprint of sweat on them, but the strap curls as if round an ankle and there is a ridge under the tiny buckle. These have been worn. And then they've been removed. The last item taken off before their owner fell into bed.

Other thoughts are flapping about like moths seeking a flame. I touch the white sheet. It's still warm. I snatch my hand away and spin about. My heart is banging. I'm not thinking. I don't know what I'm searching for. Is he still here? Are they both here, out on the balcony, or hiding in the bathroom?

The happy, confident fiancée I was a few seconds ago has gone.

Gustav has lied. He's not in Italy. He's been in our hotel room with someone who wears fuck-me Jimmy Choos.

I stare down at the shoes, kicked so carelessly to the end of the bed, not even covered by the fallen duvet. Pierre's words of warning, back in New York, come back to me.

I'm not your nemesis. She is. She's the danger you need to watch out for.

Gustav wouldn't do that. He would never go with Margot in our hotel bed. We're engaged. Tomorrow he's going to size our wedding rings. There must be some other explanation. She's been here, tricking me into thinking this. That's it. That's the answer.

Is he still in Paris? Or has he left me, gone to London or back to New York? When he rang me was he in some noisy trattoria to make it sound as if he was in Florence?

Dismay and devastation are hovering, but they haven't got hold of me yet. Something else is approaching to swell and fill this emotion-vacuum.

Anger, that's what. Mindless panic shoved aside for sub-zero fury.

I punch at Gustav Levi's number on my phone. Voicemail. I punch it again.

'Gustav. Where are you? Ring me. Now.'

I stare at the phone, listen again and again to the formal message left in his deep voice, and then I punch in another number.

'Pierre? I don't know what to do!' I whisper, tears queuing up to choke me. 'Help me!'

There's a sharp rapping at the door. Pierre is there, holding his phone. 'You rang?'

We step forwards simultaneously, ridiculously holding our phones to our ears as if they're transmitting life support.

He looks bigger and broader than before, and for some reason he's got his blazer slung over his shoulder as if he's been indoors for some time. What's he doing? I should be creeped out by it, but I'm not. Quite the opposite. Relief floods through me. Right now, if he wasn't totally off-limits, I could kiss him. His face is a crumpled picture of concern.

'What the hell?' I begin. 'Are you staying in the hotel too?'

He shakes his head. 'No, but – you called for help.'

I gesture behind me. 'The bed's all rumpled, it stinks of sex in here, and there are these shoes – I don't know if I'm going crazy, all that talk in the car of mania and danger is getting to me, but I think Margot's been here.'

Pierre steps past me and goes straight round to the bedroom. He puts his hand over his eyes.

'Shit.'

The horror in his voice is the last thing I wanted to hear.

I point at the wrinkles in the sheets. Down at the offending items on the floor.

'Those are her shoes. See? Not mine. She's the only person I know who wears those slutty heels. She was wearing them when we confronted her at the apartment. She practically kicked my teeth out.'

Pierre turns and takes hold of me. His fingertips rest on the balls of my shoulders. He's being very careful not to come closer, I can tell, but even so, his hands are warming my skin through the silky jersey T-shirt. He pulls me a little closer, but not close enough to kiss me. My eyes are on a level with his. He's shorter than Gustav, and although he's lost weight, his stockiness is emphasised by the new beard. The resemblance between the two brothers, thank God, has faded.

Nevertheless, we are too close. I can smell his heavy cologne. We haven't been as close as this since Venice. I should pull away. But this closeness is comforting me. If I move, I'll have to start thinking again.

'Can't you smell it?'

'What?'

'Her horrible, cloying scent?'

Pierre shakes his head. 'No. My sense of smell isn't great. The fire, you know.'

'Well, I can. She was here. Messing up my bed while I was working at the château. And she wouldn't have bothered to come up alone. So she must have been with Gustav.'

'You need to stop winding yourself up like this. What did you say earlier about Margot? That I was letting her win? Well, you're doing the same.' Pierre clears his throat. 'You've got it all wrong, Serena. You're engaged to the most decent man on the planet. You don't honestly think my brother would cheat on you?'

I press my hand against his chest. One of the buttons on his shirt catches my fingernail and I twist it on its thread.

'He's been going off on all these sudden business trips. He goes out early in the mornings sometimes in New York. He mentioned something about signing on the dotted line. What if he's – oh, God, that's exactly what he asked me to do when we first me. What if he's got some new ingénue tied to him with another silver chain?'

'Well, he wouldn't come out and tell you, would he?'

I pull the button right off its moorings. 'You mean he's a born deceiver, just like you?'

'No, no, not my brother, not in a million years, oh, God, I'm sorry, Serena. Stop it! I'm joking!'

'Well, for once in your life grow up!' I punch him with both fists. 'And now he's disappeared for the whole night. This is supposed to be our romantic break in Paris! Pierre, when I ask him where he is he brushes off my questions—'

Pierre stops my hands in mid-air and pushes me gently down into one of the armchairs and sits down in the other. He sits forward with his blazer across his legs, fiddling with the collar. His dark eyes are every bit as intense as Gustav's, but I can't read them. I wonder if, despite his tough words in the car earlier about being the man with no heart, he is hiding the embers of feelings that still burn inside.

'I have no idea what he's up to but I can swear, on every honey-gold hair on your beautiful head, that Gustav would rather cut his legs off than cheat on you, and even if hell froze over, it still wouldn't be with Margot. You're better than this. Don't let her turn you into a terrified, suspicious—'

I'm going to have to put my trust in Pierre now, however bizarre that sounds. I'm not convinced he's entirely over his infatuation for me. He'll always be a chancer. But he's making a good fist of putting the madness behind him, and the stark truth is that as I can't contact Gustav I have no one else to turn to.

'Just speak to him, Pierre. Go find him.'

'No need. This is all my fault.' Pierre pauses. 'Again.'

I sigh heavily. 'What do you mean?'

He stands and walks over to the bed and sits on the snowy sheets.

'The nasty part of me should be overjoyed by this.' He picks up the shoes and cradles them in his big hands. 'The old me would be stoking up these irrational fears until you were mine for the taking, and hang the consequences.'

'So what have you done this time? Why is it your fault? Why does Gustav keep sloping off?' My voice is shaking now as the emotion starts to spill over. Icy fury, but the desolation isn't far behind. 'And what were you doing standing outside my door?'

Pierre picks fluff off his blazer, and to my astonishment I see an embarrassed smile breaking on his wide mouth.

'I left something behind.'

I stare at him. There is barely any light now in the room. Only the fuzz of city lights and a couple of spotlights illuminating the façade of the hotel.

He smooths his hand over the sheets. 'It was me. I was in here earlier. Gustav texted me and asked me to come up and check a document he'd left behind and read it to him over the phone. It made no sense to me. It was about property, and it was all in Italian. His forte, not mine. Then I had a little bounce on the bed. It's superior, isn't it? I couldn't resist testing the thread count.'

'The thread count? There's spunk on the sheet, Pierre. You revolting little perv—'

'Bring it on, Serena. I can take it. At least you're attacking me, not him. I was just trying out the mattress. Twelve hundred count, pocket-sprung, multilayered fillings. I'm a geek when it comes to beds.'

'Oh, come on. You're really taking the piss now!'

He gives me a sideways glance, sparking with mischief yet challenging me to believe him.

And that's exactly what I want, too. He's spent all evening persuading me to believe in him, that he's sorry, and that he's mended his ways, and I'm ready. It may not be the conversion of St Paul on the road to Damascus. He may not be the new man he claims to be, to have turned from sinner to saint quite so comprehensively, but I have to give Pierre a chance. What's more, I'm tired of all the doubting and fighting. Doubting and fighting is Margot's game. I just want everything to be calm, and easy, and for my fiancé to come back to me.

'Anyway, this gorgeous chambermaid comes in just as I was lifting the sheet to check the Belgian damask cover. Tall. Blonde—'

I can't help smirking. 'She Belgian, too?'

He sniggers. 'I was going to say easy. What can I say? It was the work of moments. Then I had to come and meet you over at the château. I assumed she would clean up afterwards.'

I can bear to look at the bed again now. In a whole different light. 'So you haven't come up here as an excuse to be alone with me?'

'I told you, Gustav asked me to let myself into your room and read some dreary document to him over the phone. I won't tell you what I was fantasising about when I took a good snoop round these sultry surroundings, but I was more than up for an encounter with a saucy chambermaid when she sashayed in with her furniture spray, I can tell you. But tricking you again?' His eyes burn into me for a moment, but then he shakes his head, digging the heels of the shoes into the palm of his hands. 'Not even *I* am that crass.'

'And you're not covering for Gustav?'

'Listen to yourself. Princess Paranoia. I am not covering

for him. This is embarrassing enough without involving my brother. You see, those shoes—'

'Are Margot's! I know, because I told you she was prancing about in them at her apartment!'

'Christ, do you never shut up? She wears Jimmy Choo. These are Ferragamo. I'm a designer, remember? And they're mine. Don't look at me like that! Shoes are part of my arsenal when I travel, but I don't wear them. They're only a UK size five. I have a fetish. I like to be covered in some kind of clothing in bed. But I like my women to be naked, wearing nothing but a pair of impossible-to-walk-in shoes.'

We both stare at the bed, and at long last a different scenario plays out. The masked woman being ravished by the masked man in the gondola finally fades away. That man is now on his back being straddled by a white, blonde, red-shoe-wearing chambermaid.

I snort. 'You carry them with you?'

'When I'm on the prowl, yes. Which is why I came back up here. Silly girl told me she'd left them by the bed.'

He puts the shoes together on the floor. There's a long pause. A soft wind blows around the balcony, ruffling the tulips. I look out of the window, aware that Pierre's eyes are on me.

We both speak in unison.

'I miss him, Pierre.'

'I could always stay.'

I walk to the chair where my jacket is hanging, and hold on to the back of it. I look at the pale denim material, the fraying collar. My camera is on the table, waiting to be examined. I look up at Pierre Levi, and catch a look in his eyes of a hungry boy staring at a cake. But I can't feel fearful or annoyed. I just feel flattered. And I know, of the two of us, I'm the one capable of hurting him.

'Best you go, P. But thank you.'

He stands up and pulls on his blazer. 'Please don't tell Gustav. About the bed. The chambermaid. And particularly not about the shoes.'

He walks across the big, wide room. On his way past a tall lamp he switches it on, and instantly the dark room softens into friendliness. He bows like a soldier and steps out into the corridor.

'That's something I can hold over you, then, isn't it? Oh, and Pierre? You forgot something!'

He darts inside the room like a shot, an eager smile playing round his lips. He may have lost hope of having me, but he hasn't lost the desire. The smile turns into a grin as I hold out the red shoes.

'By the way, you just called me P!'

I push him out of the door. 'Maybe it'll become a habit, who knows?'

I give him the shoes and we both burst out laughing.

CHAPTER EIGHT

The car drops me in the Boulevard de Clichy. Right outside the Moulin Rouge theatre, in fact.

Gustav isn't here yet so I ask the driver to wait. I look up at the famous façade. The association with Pierre is unavoidable. The burlesque show I photographed for him back in February was modelled directly on this very venue and its colourful history. And at last I can see that show for what it was. The vision of my future brother-in-law, and his entertaining, sexy spectacle.

Anyway, I'm continents away from midtown Manhattan and any machinations, misunderstandings and menaces. I'm sitting in a French film company limousine after another hard day's graft at the château. And with Pierre's help, I've even managed to turn Margot and her red shoes into a bad joke.

I see Gustav striding along the noisy street lined with cheap shops, and I get out of the car, dismissing the driver. I want to run to him, but instead I watch him, his long legs in indigo blue jeans, his ripped torso in a dark blue T-shirt with another paler one underneath clinging to him as he hurries towards me. I stand and wait, my whole body smiling with joy.

189

And soon I'm in his arms, searching those shining black eyes for the love I feel for him, and feeling it in the way he's squeezing me tight, nuzzling into my neck.

'Let's not go in there,' Gustav murmurs, moving his mouth round to mine.

'Let's go back to the hotel?'

'You horny devil. I could have you right here in the street!' He laughs, pulling me as people push past.

We start to walk through the place des Abbesses towards rue Drevet.

I pause at the foot of the steep flight of stairs leading up to the *butte de Montmartre*.

It's on the tip of my tongue to probe a little, to ask him where he's been, but I remember Pierre's assurances. And just as quickly, I push Pierre out of my mind again. Why spoil a beautiful moment?

'Come on, *mademoiselle*, I'm hungry, so allow me to push this cute butt of yours up to a little place I know.'

We start the long, steep climb and emerge on the place du Calvaire.

'Here?' I ask, pointing at Le Plumeau with its tempting fenced-in terrace and solemn cello player, but Gustav shakes his head and pulls me on through the crowds, down the Bis rue Norvins and through a tiny door which looks from the outside as if it might be the entrance to a dusty old shop. But Le Vieux Chalet turns out to be an adorable restaurant, an oasis of calm amongst the tourist trails. We walk into a small, enclosed garden full of greenery. There's just one other couple in here, looking as happily surprised as I am. You can hear nothing but the tinkle of hanging glass candle-holders and the twitter of birds in the trees. A distinguished man greets Gustav and takes our order before leaving us alone.

The late May sun filters through the new leaves on to my skin.

The filet mignon melts in our mouths, the tarte Tatin, heavy with added cream, pricks my taste buds, and the rich Bordeaux makes me sleepy.

'*Now* can we go to bed?' I ask Gustav, licking a spot of gravy off the corner of his mouth and earning a glare from an elderly customer tucking a white napkin into his collar. 'I don't like it when you go away. I've been surrounded by sex and seduction at the château for two whole days.'

Gustav laughs and kisses me, once, twice, then comes back in for a long, searching third kiss before signalling for the bill.

'Let's take a little walk first.'

I stand up and sling my little sparkly cream cardigan loosely over my shoulders.

'I don't need to work up an appetite. I want you in me, now!'

Gustav chuckles and scoops my hair out of the collar and lets it drop down my back. The two old men wave us out into the narrow streets of Montmartre, and the door shuts softly behind us.

'*Patience, chérie.* Come on. There's somewhere I want you to see.'

We wander through the overcrowded place du Tertre, past the artists painting on-the-spot caricatures and portraits of easily fleeced tourists. We go to sit on the steps in front of Sacré Coeur with its panoramic view of the city. The sun is really warm now on my back, even though the steps are slightly damp.

'You wanted to show me this view?' I mumble as the damp from the steps begins to chill my legs. 'I have been up here before, you know.'

'But not with me, darling. I just wanted to sit here with you for a moment. Everything takes on a fresh new hue when I'm with you.'

Just then my phone trills. 'It's a text from Polly. She must have got a signal at last.'

191

'Can you reply a little later?' He pulls me close to him and waves his arm over the panorama in front of us. 'You never pay attention to important things when you're young, do you? Did you know I once started to train as an architect? How amazing would it be to create a space for human beings to live and work in – or an entire city? See how uniform Paris is. It was a slum before Haussmann recreated it. It took fifty years to complete his vision.'

'Didn't he have some idea about everything being the same height?' I ask, lifting my camera to peer through the viewfinder.

Gustav buries his nose in my hair. 'That's what gives it its charm. He had human beings in mind, not battery hens like the concrete monstrosities that went up in England after the war. Every apartment building in Paris was to be seven storeys high. Every façade was built in this golden limestone, which often came from right under the city. I'll take you underground one day. You can walk for miles, you know. And he even decreed that every second and fifth floor would have a wrought-iron balcony and every lead roof was to slope back at forty-five degrees.'

I can't resist zooming in on the rooftops below us, the tiny windows set up in the grey attics. Some have small boxes outside with herbs and flowers growing in them. I long to be able to peep inside the *ateliers*, and see artists or dressmakers or cooks at work.

I lower my camera as a terrible thought strikes me. Through those windows I could just as easily see two parents drunkenly slumbering in bed. A teenage Gustav, tiptoeing down the stairs or scaling the balcony to go out on the town although expressly forbidden. A toddler Pierre, wandering through the apartment in his dressing gown. The flare of a match, and the gathering flames.

Gustav sits up rigidly beside me, as if he can read my

mind. I lean against his shoulder and wait for a moment. 'So, is it the jeweller you're going to show me? The wedding rings? It's a long walk over to St Germain, but I'm game if you are.' I point across the city, past Notre Dame, over the Pont Neuf to the Quartier Latin. Maybe now he'll tell me where he's been. But he's silent. 'You look very serious, G. What are you thinking?'

He looks back at me, and kisses me on the nose. 'Getting married is a serious business, Serena! The rings are still being sized. I can't wait to put yours on your finger! But no. That's not where we're going this evening.'

Again a tiny shiver of anxiety runs through me. Why won't he tell me? Why won't I ask him? I press myself close to him so that I can feel the flex of his muscles as we walk together.

We stroll round the north side of the Sacré Coeur and into residential streets that become quieter the further we go. Then as we start to descend, we leave the private mansions corralled behind iron railings and return to areas lined with those seven-storey apartment buildings. Beneath the apartments are boutiques, cafés and little shops displaying lingerie or delicious cakes or brightly coloured bottles in the window.

Finally we come down another flight of steps with a central handrail commanding yet another stunning view of the city. At the bottom, Gustav suddenly turns right through an arched gateway, down a cobbled alleyway, and leads me into a secluded courtyard surrounded on all sides by newly scrubbed façades with long double windows and balconies hugging their privacy.

One of the buildings in the corner is still being cleaned. It's blanketed in dirty blue tarpaulin which is sprayed in places with graffiti tags, but as we pause in the middle of the peaceful courtyard the top corner of the shroud, right up by the roof, starts to come away. We dodge back in case it falls on us, but as it drops towards the ground it's caught and folded by a builder waiting on the next level of scaffolding. A guy is moving along the roof, systematically releasing more plastic, crackling panels of blue until the shroud is removed and the metal skeleton of scaffolding is revealed.

'It's the anniversary of the fire that killed my parents,' Gustav remarks hoarsely as we crunch on to what looks like the remains of a pile of rubble. 'Every time I'm in Paris I come to look. Pay my respects, I suppose. And I say a prayer. Sometimes I hope it will remain charred and scarred like a relic. Other times I wish it was all restored. And now it is. It's a home again for someone.'

'I'm sorry, darling. I had no idea.' I put my arms round him, but he keeps glancing around the courtyard then back down the tunnelled alleyway where we came in. 'Is it just a coincidence they are disrobing the building, or did you know this would be happening today?'

He rubs his chin across the top of my head and folds me close to him. I can feel the tension in his body. The memories of that night still haunt him. When he came home to find the apartment filled with smoke, his parents dead, and his little brother wearing a cloak of fire.

'Actually, the construction company have kept me informed about the restoration. I wanted you by my side when they unveiled it. Is that silly?'

I rest my face against his chest and feel his heart thumping beneath my cheek. A little faster than usual, but still so loud and vital.

'Of course not. I'm honoured to be here with you. But I'm not the right person. At least I shouldn't be the only person, G. This isn't my story. It's yours and Pierre's. Shouldn't he be here, too?'

Gustav sucks in his breath. I look up and see that he is smiling.

'My *signorina*. If you weren't so cute and lovely, I'd think you were a bit of a witch yourself. Because, well, because what you just said is absolutely right. He didn't mention it when I asked him to meet you at the château, did he? The real reason he's in Paris?'

'He never got round to it, no. He was more intent on mending fences between us. I wasn't particularly happy to see him, but we made progress, G. Ultimately your brother cares about you more than anything else in the world.'

'Mission accomplished, then. I'm sorry if it upset you, but it was the ideal opportunity. I didn't want any more awkwardness between you. Now we have something else to put to rest. Pierre should be here by now. I asked him to meet me.'

He glances over my head, and right on cue there is the reflection of his brother, growing behind me from a dot in the distance to a shadowy outline against the dark shine of Gustav's eyes.

'I thought this was just going to be you and me today. I've missed you while you've been on your mystery mission.'

'But as you said, he needs to be here, too. Forgive me for surprising you with all this, *cara*.' Gustav is distracted now. 'But this place represents another part of my life. This was our home. And look! They've rebuilt it at last. It's fresh, and new, and ready to start again, just as Pierre and I have rebuilt our relationship. That why I needed him here today.'

I can see I'm about to lose Gustav, temporarily. His mouth parts in a half-smile, and I turn to follow his gaze. Pierre pushes out from the now exposed main entrance to the building. He's wearing a bright yellow hard hat and another blazer, this time an old striped one like they wear at Henley Regatta. His transformation from rock star to English gent is complete.

He turns to shake hands with one of the builders, and then hesitates in the makeshift shadow of the scaffolding.

'Fine. I'll play nicely,' I say quietly. 'Thanks to you forcing him on me the other day, we've made friends again. Tentatively.'

'There are no more rifts between us, are there, Serena?'

Pierre's low, gruff voice is right behind me.

His voice echoes around the quiet, enclosed courtyard. Some of the builders stop working to watch the three of us. The brothers stand side by side, close but not touching, Gustav taller than Pierre. Their hair is such different textures, one man bearded, the other not, but the black eyes are so similar, sparking with argument behind the fierce eyelashes, the fire gradually subsiding to a smoulder. They look at each other briefly, then both turn to study me for an intense, silent moment.

A flurry of birds tumbles out of a small tree in the centre of the courtyard, scattering some bright green leaves, and swoops out through the entrance gate, and as if the passage of their tiny wings has dislodged it, a scaffolding pole, and then another, rolls off the growing pile with a discordant clang.

We are all quiet for a while, and as the upper storeys of the old building are now revealed, we turn away from each other to stare upwards. There are four windows set into the eaves of the retiled grey roof, and four longer, grander ones lined up below.

'This is where I carried you out of the fire and laid you down, P, still rolled up in that rug.' Gustav points at the paving at his feet. 'I had to leave you with the neighbours, you were screaming in agony, while I tried to get back inside.'

Gustav swallows and covers his eyes with his hands for a moment. I walk a little way from them, and sit on a pile of wooden pallets.

Pierre takes Gustav's hand away from his eyes and pulls up the sleeve. On Gustav's wrist, on either side of his watch, is a fine web of white scarring.

'Look. Even your scars are a work of art! The only part of you that was burned. That's why you developed a taste for big, expensive watches. Whereas I have had to develop a taste for costumes, masks, deception. Shoes.' He winks at me.

Gustav's phone starts. He is about to press his thumb on the keypad to cut it off when he checks the caller ID. 'It's the agents in London. They must be calling about the sale of Baker Street. I think I should take this. Come, I'll walk. You two talk. I'll see you in the little bar round the corner. Le Coin des Amis.'

Gustav starts to walk out of the courtyard. Pierre eyes me warily, then steps over to offer a hand to pull me up.

Gustav has walked out into the street, talking quietly on the phone. He glances back at us, points the way towards the café and disappears from view.

I let my hand rest for a moment in Pierre's. See the strong fingers around mine. And suddenly I feel desperately sorry for him. I stare once more up at the restored building.

'Maybe you'll learn from everything that happened here. Your LA therapists would tell you to make it work positively not negatively. Like I'm still trying to learn from things that happened when I was little. For good or ill, the truth catches up in the end. So no more mischief, Pierre. I mean it. I'm here in Gustav's life to stay.'

I turn to look at him. He's staring not at me but up at the windows of his childhood home.

'We had a laugh the other night, didn't we?'

I smile.

'Honestly? Yes. It's a start. You're not the monster I thought you were. But I'm still getting my head round the new Pierre. I still want to believe wholeheartedly in him. So in an ideal world the best thing you could do is stay away for a while. At least from me. I don't mean to be unfriendly, and I know you can't do that for ever. Gustav wouldn't want it. He loves you, and wants you in his life. So for his sake, and ours, we'll make this work. And let's bury any bullshit that you couldn't help yourself because you were in love with me.'

Pierre doesn't reply. The palms of his hands are pressed together in front of his face as he turns finally from the building and starts to back away towards the street.

'It's true, Serena. I am in love with you. Or I was. Oh, God. I know I denied it. I know I said I was getting over it, but the truth is I'm not quite there yet. There are still spots left on the leopard. Because I was being economical with the truth. Isn't that what politicians say? All that stuff about being incapable of love? About nothing being in here?' He bashes at his chest. 'I lied. In all the mayhem, Margot drove me straight at you, and you knocked me sideways. Not just because you're so beautiful and spirited and talented and naughty and wise. Because you were unattainable. Gustav is so totally under your spell. I wanted a piece of it, too, but—'

I put my hand up as if to separate us. It's a feeble attempt to hide the blush scorching my face, but I have to do something. 'You can't ever say it, Pierre. You can't ever mean it.'

'I can. And I do. But see? The love word? It's gone. Poof.' He blows an imaginary dandelion clock in an unexpectedly fey gesture. Reminding me of his theatrical bent. 'My infatuation will never rear its ugly head again.'

The final pole of scaffolding crashes away from the façade of the building, and we both jump at the sound. The builders leap down off the lower platform. Pierre doesn't wait for any further reaction from me, but calls out goodbye to the builders, who raise their arms in farewell.

Then he turns and gestures for me to lead the way out of the courtyard.

'Give me a moment on my own,' I tell him, taking my

mobile out of my pocket. 'You go to Gustav. We'll talk again. Soon.'

He hesitates. Runs his fingers through his thick hair. I watch it curl round his fingers as if to keep them there. 'You're not even a tiny bit flattered?'

'You are bloody unbelievable! You put a toenail out of line, and you're toast,' I hiss, keeping my eyes fixed on my phone as I bring up Polly's text. 'What you can do, Pierre, if you love me, or did love me, is never, ever speak of your feelings again. Never mention Margot, or your vile plotting, or your games. If we can draw a line under all that, and really banish it, and really strive to get on, then I reckon we've a good chance of making this work. And one more thing. One day I want you to find a way of apologising properly to Polly. It's up to her what she does with your apology. And then maybe, just maybe, we can forget everything that happened.'

Pierre walks away to the entrance of the courtyard, and I start to relax. Then he stops, calls something over his shoulder. I glance up and find his eyes on me. A smile so wide and charming that it's tempting to think that something in that black heart of his might just be melting.

He says it again. 'So then maybe, just maybe, you'll let me call you sis?'

I flick my hands at him, then press Polly's number to call. The blush is creeping back. 'On your way, Pierre.'

'Rena?' squeaks Polly's little voice from the phone. 'That you?'

I close my eyes and sit down on a stone window ledge. I want to shut everything, even Paris, out of my mind for a moment.

'Just wanted to hear your voice, Polly,' I say, trying to keep my voice steady. I can never tell her what so nearly passed between me and Pierre. I can't even tell her what he

199

has just said to me. She warned me to be careful, and she was right. But this is something I have to keep from her, at least until enough time has elapsed so that she won't care any more. 'But you sound as if you're in a Turkish bath!'

She laughs her filthy ex-smoker's laugh that is like music now that it's come back. Maybe her heart is already mended.

'I am! I've only just got your text. We're at a *hammam* in the next village and I've got a signal! Right in the middle of nowhere. Imagine that, hon. Our own private massage parlour!'

There's some kind of warbling music in the background and nearer by some riotous female singing.

'Spa, more like? I thought you were in a retreat, spending your days drying raisins and sewing and washing other people's feet?'

'Who thought being holy could be such fun? And not a single hairy man in sight!' Polly laughs again. 'Why not come to Morocco and see for yourself? This place is like a convent, but in a good way! It's paradise, Rena! Listen, we've been into the souq in Marrakesh and we've got some stunning fabric here for your wedding dress. You set a date yet?'

'In pencil, yes. Gustav's got to sell this horrible house in London first, and then there's my new exhibition back in New York—'

She doesn't appear to hear me, because she comes back in the middle of a sentence '—duchesse satin slip with some gorgeous Chantilly lace netting on top. Yeah, so get your ass over to Morocco! We ought to measure you up before you go and get pregnant or something!'

I run my hand over my flat stomach and laugh. 'Is it OK if I bring my fiancé?'

'Sure. He's going to be my new cousin, after all. But men aren't allowed in here. He'd have to stay in the male visitors' quarters outside the ashram. And he can't see the dress.'

200

The builders nudge each other and wink at me as I settle down to a gossip with my faraway cousin, and by the time they have packed up the pallets and poles and tools and I've walked down to the bar, Gustav is settled, alone, at a small table outside, nursing a stubby tumbler of cloudy *pastis*.

'Pierre says goodbye. He had to go.'

Gustav stands up as I approach and hands me a glass of red wine. I nod and take a long sip. I can feel every muscle unfurling, my shoulders easing as we sit for a moment staring down the hill at the lights blinking over the city of Paris.

Then we turn to each other, lean our foreheads together, and start speaking at once.

'Let's go to Morocco!' I say.

'I've got to go to London,' says Gustav.

We sit back, laughing. 'You go first,' I say.

'Something's cropped up. Well, two things, actually. The Baker Street buyer insists on meeting me at the house before we exchange contracts. The agents say that means before the end of the week.' He eyes me from under his straight black brows. 'And when I mentioned it to Pierre he asked if he could meet me there in Baker Street. He wants to see the contracts for the sale signed so he knows the house is gone for good. Also, it's his birthday this same week, and while we're with the lawyers there are other family documents he's entitled to see once he turns twenty-five.'

I put my hand over his. 'That's fine. If you can wait for a couple more days, I can finish the commission, get the contacts of the château shoot over to Alain the director, then I'll come to London with you.'

'You never cease to amaze me. The way you were with Pierre, after everything he's done. He told me how well you got on the other night when he collected you from the château. How gracefully you took his apology when you were alone in the courtyard just now.' He lifts my hand and runs his mouth over it, flicking his tongue over the tender skin. 'I'm more grateful than you will ever know that you didn't make me choose between you and him. It's what plenty of women would have done. And then I'd have lost him again.'

'I'm not the angel you think I am, honey, but I'm not that diabolical, either.' I run my hand over his face. 'I never had a proper family. How can I sit here and take yours away from you? I'm not going to pretend it'll be easy being around him. But we're getting there. If he behaves himself, and if I grow up a bit. So long as you and I are together, everything will be all right.'

He smiles and signals for the bill. 'How about you see it this way. You've got a new brother. Troublesome, admittedly – sometimes a real pain – who has to be kept on the straight and narrow. And I've got a new cousin. Talking of whom, seeing as P and I have dull legal matters to deal with in London, why don't you take the chance to visit Polly while I'm there? But if I'm going to be parted from my beautiful girl for a few days, I need to get you back to the hotel and into bed. Now.'

Paris is coated in night as we linger on our roof terrace a few hours later, looking out over the humming city.

'That was the most expensive chanterelle risotto I'll ever eat,' I say, pushing my plate away and holding out my empty wineglass for more.

'Well, I'll finish your almond tart then, shall I, while you have another glass of this obscenely expensive Pouilly Fumé and show me what you've been doing at the château.'

We scroll through the images, both still and moving, of *Les Liaisons Dangereuses*. His favourite, and mine, is the slow-motion film in the shuttered bedchamber of the toy boy Danceny throwing La Marquise down on the white bed. I freeze the frame where she has just landed amongst the soft pillows, her hair flying backwards, her throat arched in invitation.

I tap the image. 'She says she knew you in London?'

He stands up and stretches. 'Maria Memsahib. She was waiting tables in Marylebone High Street when – well, Margot spotted her and roped her into coming to Baker Street where she was part of the scene for a while. She was one of the tasty extras Margot offered to her clients. She was in that orgy film, too. But before you ask, darling, I never slept with her.'

'I saw her before, Gustav, when I was strolling on the High Line, the night you gave me the gallery. Actually she was one of the passers-by who saw us making out in the window later that evening.' Before Margot delivered that feather. I don't say it out loud. I move the frame on to the part where La Marquise is flipping herself on top of the boy. 'She's gorgeous, isn't she?'

I look up at him. He is biting his lip and trying not to smile.

'Isn't it the red-blooded male who's supposed to say that? You fancy her, Serena. And who wouldn't? She's the go-to sexy temptress. Part Brazilian, part Moroccan.'

'Which reminds me. I'm not sure I should go to Marrakesh after all. I want to stay with you.'

'We've both got business to attend to, Serena. It won't be for long. And I'd be as much use as a chocolate teapot when it comes to trying on wedding dresses.'

He lifts me out of my chair and carries me towards the huge bed. He throws me down into the soft sheets just as La Marquise was dropped like booty from a treasure chest. He turns the lights off, leaving just the lanterns and candles alight out on the terrace, selects something from the playlist and starts to take off my clothes.

I lie back, open my arms and legs, and let him undress

me as the song *Je t'aime*, slightly slowed down and remixed, starts to moan through the room.

'Talk dirty to me, Gustav, like the man in the song.'

'*Je t'aime, chérie*,' he growls, pulling his shirt off and shaking his hair free. '*Je vais, et je viens.*'

I admire the carved outline of his shoulders and arms in the candlelight, the ripple of muscle down his ribcage. I feel soft and lazy and tired tonight. Pampered like a princess, full of food and wine, and cradled by the city of romance.

All too soon we'll be parted and that doesn't feel right. I know all that worry and uncertainty will start up again. At least this time I know he'll be in London with Pierre and not on another mysterious mission.

I reach up and pull him down on top of me, licking up his neck, over the pulse beating there, over the strong, bristled jaw and smiling cheek, and then I press my lips on his until his mouth opens and I cling to him, kissing him hard as if to suck the life out of him before I hiss into his ear, '*Embrasse-moi!*'

As he kisses me, he pushes my breasts together, runs his thumb over my nipples, sending the instant electricity through me, sparking messages down to my ready wetness. I smooth my hands over his sides, down over his butt, and dig my fingers into it to make him buck with pleasure, and then, like La Marquise, I flip over so that I'm on top of him, pushing my breasts at him, still gripping to make him longer and harder, feel the blood pumping through it until it's taut with desire.

'*Maintenant. Viens*,' I order him, rising up on my knees in a parody of prayer and holding myself in place, a few inches above him.

He grins, his black eyes gleaming in the semi-darkness as he takes hold of my breasts and tugs with his teeth on first one nipple, then the other.

'Try saying it even dirtier.'

I balance myself on all fours and slowly lower myself so that he slides, hot and hard, into my soft, warm wetness. I arch myself so that he is sucking on me, hard, and as I plunge down I groan into his silky hair.

'*Baise-moi.*'

CHAPTER NINE

A fertile or green spot in a desert or wasteland, made so by the presence of water.

I glance up from my guidebook. Wasteland is the word. The surroundings haven't altered in aspect since we left the airport nearly an hour ago. I expected to land in an alien, hot, dusty world of tropical groves, with bending palm trees, groups of pretty tiled buildings, camels, donkeys and waving children, with the burnished walls and towers of Marrakesh dominating like a blockbuster backdrop.

But when I pointed excitedly at what I was certain was the famous minaret of the Koutoubia Mosque rising to greet me over the flat topography, the taxi driver hawked up phlegm along with a dry cackle, spat out of the window, jerked his thumb at the rise of the majestic snow-topped Atlas mountains in the distance and shouted, 'Another day, maybe. Today we go south!'

My fault for not doing the research, or even looking at a proper map. Polly did say she was living in a retreat out in the desert, not a chic little riad in town. Even so, I gaze longingly at the receding metropolis as we bump and rattle remorselessly along this straight, true road between flat, sun-baked fields, dark-green olive groves punctuated by the odd lemon tree, past building sites and ramshackle villages, until the ground starts to rise and with a resigned crunch the old car is forced to change down a gear or two.

I know Polly wanted to get away from it all, but this is like being admitted to a correctional facility. A high-security one at that.

The Kasbah Karma heaves into view. It's washed in lovely serene shades of umber and pale pink, but it's still a sturdy mud-brick fortress, standing by itself on its own hillock. It could almost be a mini Marrakesh, I think hopefully, as the taxi stops and toots the horn outside vast beaten-metal gates. They swing open with no apparent human intervention.

The car inches forwards into the middle of a hot, enclosed courtyard opened up by arches leading to curving staircases and tiled corridors. The driver doesn't even kill the engine. He just holds his hand out for the fare, and as soon as I and my luggage are deposited, he reverses out into the barren countryside and is gone in a screech of tyres and choking dust.

There is total, utter silence in here, apart from the faintest tinkle of bells, the cacophony of hidden cicadas and the running plash of the stone fountain in the middle of the courtyard. No one appears from the shadows to greet me. Perhaps they're all sunbathing, or cooking, or meditating, or praying, or whatever they do here.

The distance between me and Gustav is too far. It's warm, beautiful, peaceful here, but this solitude envelops me like a blanket. I am suddenly, ridiculously alone. Except that somewhere, unless the taxi driver is having the last laugh, my cousin Polly is waiting for me.

The heat sings in my ears. I glance up into the burning blue of the sky and see the faintest trace of an aeroplane's trail. Gustav and I are on different continents now. Not for long, but we've got our own families to deal with before we're back together again. Our own pasts to knit together.

I don't want to trundle my little case noisily across these smooth tiles, so I pick it up, glad that Gustav persuaded me to buy some light, floaty clothes suitable for a hot, Arab early summer rather than a mild, Parisian late spring.

I stop in the shade of the first archway and look across a second courtyard. There's an open vista beyond of smooth green gardens, clusters of flowers and lemon, orange and pomegranate trees, the tall, straight trunks of palms standing like guards around the lawns, and beyond the grounds the now familiar stony glare of the mountains reminding us that we humans are only as strong as the shelters we build.

The aroma of herbs and flowers and the piquancy of lemon grass and citrus fill the air. Small mosaic pathways wind between the neat beds and lead up to a series of carved wooden screen doors. These are set at intervals in the walls, which in this courtyard are washed a kind of peppermint green. Some of the doors are closed. Some hinge open into a hidden interior of dark violet shadows.

Siesta. That would explain the silence.

A white curtain billows from the furthest, widest doorway, and a woman draped in dark red muslin steps out of the shadows into the burning sunlight. She is staring down at her bare feet as she brushes her long, auburn hair. No, not auburn. It's the dark-red colour of the French marigolds that Crystal grows in a window box outside the drawing room of the Mayfair house. It even has blonde tips, just like the marigold petals. The sun catches the smooth waves as it ripples over her arms, and then the woman throws her head back so that her hair waterfalls down her back. It's even longer than mine. She taps the hairbrush thoughtfully against her mouth as she glances towards the expanse of garden with its handsome palms and what I can now see is a large swimming pool.

Then she turns in my direction. We stare at each other for a long moment. Her eyes are set wide apart and are emerald green. Gustav says my eyes are emerald green, too.

'*Ahlan weh sahlan*,' her voice murmurs eventually through the silence.

I shake my head, not understanding. She spreads open her arms as if to embrace me.

'*Bienvenue*. Welcome.'

I feel like I've seen her face before. The chiselled, high cheekbones and curving, mournful jaw. Those green eyes, outlined in kohl so that she has the look of Queen Nefertiti. The heavy eyebrows settling again now that she's greeted me. She could have stepped out of a Pre-Raphaelite painting.

She still holds the hairbrush against her mouth like a microphone, as if she's about to sing a song. Maybe that's it. I must have seen her in a magazine, or she's a film star. I tug like a teenager at my T-shirt. Polly never said anything about this being rehab for celebs.

The lady gives a very slight smile but doesn't come any closer. The red chiffon of her gown drapes over her, clinging to her curvy figure and long legs. With her eyes still on me, she stretches her arm and points the hairbrush out towards the garden to show me that's where I must go.

'Thank you,' I murmur, stepping awkwardly along the little path with my case. As I draw level with her, she produces a little jewelled glass from a low table behind and offers it to me. It's *citron pressé* or some kind of cold sharp juice, and I'm so thirsty I drain it. Smiling, she takes the empty glass, and then my suitcase, and points the hairbrush once again towards the garden, and before I can thank her, she has retreated back into the shadows.

I see Polly before she sees me and my chest goes tight

with love. She's sitting cross-legged on a flat turquoise cushion, wearing a loose primrose-yellow sari and reading while absently running her fingers through the water of the large pool. She's filled out a little. Not a scrap of make-up, but several pairs of silver earrings dangle from new piercings in her ears, and her white blonde hair, cropped severely short in the winter when she was so unhappy, has grown out to a choppy bob. She looks five years younger.

A situation or place preserved from surrounding unpleasantness. A refuge or haven.

Now I know the meaning of the word 'oasis'.

'I have to go to my meditation class in a moment,' Polly murmurs a long time later, as we lie side by side on the futon in her lemon-washed chamber. I stare up at the beamed and latticed ceiling of eucalyptus where the long struts of a wooden fan stir the soupy air. 'I've already spoken longer than my allotted hour today.'

'Allotted?' I stir sleepily and sit up on my elbows. We have spent all afternoon catching up on three months' worth of news. The doors are open on to the courtyard, and a very slight breeze is stirring the curtains. Just across the courtyard I can see other figures emerging from their own arched doorways and gliding out of sight. 'Who says?'

'Me. We can choose. There are no rules here. Just, like, guidelines. Suggestions.' She rolls away from me and stretches her long white limbs. 'And I mostly choose silence.'

'I'm in a real live ashram.' I wave two fingers in the air making a hippy peace sign. 'Far out, sister!'

'OK, cynic. Think what you like. I'm happy here. And you're lucky to be here, too.' She tweaks my hair and stands up. 'Now, come on. I've cuddled you enough to know you are for real and now I can't wait any longer. Come and see all this beautiful material I've got for your wedding dress.

210

Look. Some panels of duchesse, georgette, some Chinese shantung, even some chiffon. I've got to hurry up and pin this on to you before I'm summoned.'

She pads across the beautiful tiled floor. The entire kasbah was refurbished not long ago and she's told me that all the floors are tiled with contemporary variations on the zellij technique using pressed cement. Her floor is inlaid with cadmium yellow enamel chips. Polly opens a carved wooden wardrobe, and takes out a hanger draped in white material.

'Tell me more about this urge for silence,' I say, sitting up stiffly. 'Isn't it a bit creepy with no one speaking to you? I was certainly spooked when I arrived.'

'There is speaking, honey. Just not very much. There's other ways of communicating, as you'll discover. I reckon the reason you felt peculiar was because you were displaced from the big bad world and your big bad fiancé. But you'll soon find that once you enter this place the silence isn't restrictive. It's liberating. There's so much noise and hassle out there.' She takes my hand and pulls me in front of the long mirror. 'You can see why those Carmelite nuns take that vow and retire from the world altogether. In fact, Angelique herself was going to be a nun—'

'Angelique? Is she—?'

'Our chief guru.' Polly goes into hairdresser mode, lifting my hair away from my hot forehead and twisting it into a Heidi plait to garland my head like a coronet. 'You'd think that with nothing to do or say for hours on end all your thoughts would hammer away at your head, but they don't. The less airspace you give them, the quicker they disperse.'

'You are sounding more tripped-out by the minute,' I tease. I hold my arms out and let her wander round me, pinning the currently shapeless piece of fabric to me and

211

transforming it into a garment. 'So you're saying all our normal worldly concerns cease to matter?'

'Exactly. Apart from food, drink and love, what else do we need? Money, I suppose.' She pulls a couple of pins from the cushion on her wrist, and my waist reappears. 'I'm designing a few garments for some local boutiques, actually, but the ashram earns its shekels by making and selling aromatherapy oils.'

I groan. 'This isn't a drying-out clinic as well, is it?'

'It's a clinic where you learn to celebrate life at its most pleasurable! Right. I'll need to get some sari material to lay over the lining, but then again it all depends on what kind of wedding you're going to have. England, or tropics? Snow, or sunshine?'

I lift my hand and turn it slowly. The diamond ring winks at me, tamed in this hushed, dull light. 'We haven't booked anywhere yet, but we're thinking we'll have it at Halloween?'

'Not too long to wait.' Polly stands back and looks at me. 'Church or beach?'

'It wouldn't feel right for me if it wasn't in a church. But do you know, I haven't a clue how Gustav would feel about that. I don't even know if he's Christian!'

'Probably pagan, knowing him! But I'm surprised you haven't discussed it.' Polly pins the fabric into a dart above my waist. 'Is that because he's been wed before?'

Her words stab at my heart. There's a brief, unwelcome reminder of the little chapel in the mountains above Lake Lugano.

'What's the ashram theory about people who exist and shape our lives outside these walls?' I ask, trying to deflect the question, as Polly shapes the fabric around me to give me uplifted breasts, swelling beneath a draped bodice. 'Do they cease to matter, too?'

'Only the horrible ones. The bullies and the bitches and

the bastards.' Polly leans her pointed chin on my shoulder in the way she used to when we were kids, really sharp until I stopped talking nonsense. 'Hush my mouth! Do you know it even feels sinful to say bad words like that in here?'

A gong sounds somewhere outside and there's a slip-slap of feet past the door.

My cousin stands back and surveys me, and I sashay in a circle for her.

'Are you not allowed any sinful thoughts?' I ask her as she reaches inside the wardrobe again and pulls out a diaphanous roll of lacy chiffon. 'I mean, you know, no naughtiness? No sex?'

Polly smiles mysteriously and holds the chiffon across my breasts like a kind of shawl. 'This place is all about cleanliness, Serena. Of body and mind.'

'No fun, in other words. Basically you're a bunch of nuns.' I bite my lip and turn back to the mirror. Now is not the time to mention anything about Pierre, for instance, and what he tried to do to me, or how we're cautiously making friends. 'No men, you said. What about the men's visiting quarters?'

'There are no men's quarters. I was lying when I told you that on the phone!' She bursts out laughing. 'Your Gustav would have had to stay miles away in Marrakesh. Seriously! This is a women-only haven. Not because we hate men, but because we've all loved too much, like that self-help book. Every new recruit mentions heartbreak in their introductory talk. It's mentioned, and then it's gone, and we commence this new, female way of life.'

'Will you stay here for ever?'

'I can't imagine any other existence for the moment.' Polly pins the rest of my hair into loose waves. 'It's such bliss shutting the door. And what I didn't expect is how absorbing life is when it's just girls. It's pretty intense at times. Some

213

of us have become – a little too close. But mostly it's easy, and fun, and you know what? I don't care if I never see a thumping great hard-on ever again!'

Her laughter is infectious. 'You're bubbling over, Pol, yet you're so chilled at the same time. But what about sex? You used to be up for it all the time! Don't you get frustrated sometimes?'

We let a few moments pass, our foreheads pressed together, just like when we were kids, sharing all our secrets on the windy beach beneath the house on the cliffs.

'Once or twice I've – it's like the song, Rena. I kissed a girl. And I liked it!' Polly keeps her pale-blue eyes steady on mine, but her pixie face is slowly turning pink. 'Oh, it's not encouraged, but it's not forbidden either. There's intimacy during the massage and spa sessions, and sometimes the touching goes further. And these Moroccan nights are very long, and very hot! Maybe Angelique should pay a little more attention. This is a retreat, not a convent, but maybe she should add a vow of chastity to our other promises of loyalty and learning. We're here to purify ourselves, after all.'

'You sound like an irrigation system!' I giggle. 'As if you're all arid fields, or clogged-up plumbing!'

'A brilliant analogy! Descaled, all our pipes shiny and clean again!' She grins. 'I'm just content with the here and now. It's so peaceful without men. They push and prod and penetrate, don't they? Whereas we have all come here actively seeking peace. The last thing anyone wants is to break the harmony, and if they did they would be turfed out. Even so, if Angelique thinks any of us are getting unhelpfully close to another girl she separates us for a while.'

'Unhelpfully? Hmm.' I let her wrap a different cut of fabric around my face like a veil, to test my colouring. 'I couldn't live without my man.'

She tips her head on one side.

214

'Gustav is the centre of your world, I know that. Soon he'll be your husband. But don't give me that innocent look, girlfriend. I've a feeling you've tried it with a girl once or twice. In that Venetian convent, I shouldn't wonder!'

I shake my head, refusing to look at her now. 'Not with the nuns. But yes, I've had one or two, you know, encounters since I've been in New York.'

She fusses round behind me to pin the chiffon into my hair to make a bridal veil. She turns me towards the mirror so she can tweak at it. 'Encounters? Does Gust— I mean, does anyone else know?'

'Gustav is always with me. He watches. Sometimes he joins in. He wanted me to experiment, have adventures. Crikey, listen to me banging on.' My skin prickles with embarrassment. 'This place is like a confessional!'

'You've always been able to tell me anything!' She shakes my shoulders. 'So what exactly has my little cousin been up to while I've not been keeping an eye on her? Lesbians? Threesomes?'

I hold my arms out while she takes out some pins in the darts and seams and replaces them. She pulls the dress in tight around my body so that I look like the kind of curvy sculpture perfume makers might fashion a bottle out of.

I decide to keep to the subject of girls. Mentioning Pierre's antics would not only be hurtful, it would be pointless.

'Both of the above! A couple of times. Well, three?'

Polly has pins in her mouth now, and merely nods eagerly, turning my head to face forwards.

'There was this job when I was taking some pre-wedding shots of a supposedly virginal bride, and it turned out she and her bridesmaid had been a couple for years. They couldn't keep their hands off each other, then they dragged me into bed with them and one of them deflowered me, too, with her fingers, and made me come.'

215

'Who would have thought it!' Polly snuffles with laughter and takes the remaining pin out of her mouth. 'And the next time?'

'Well, that was with some dancers from Pierre's theatre. They ambushed me after we'd finished shooting the burlesque show and they used my camera to film the whole seduction.' I stop abruptly. 'Oh, God, Polly. I shouldn't mention men. Especially not him.'

She eases the pin into the material, turns her back for a moment. I can tell by the way she snatches a fig out of the fruit bowl that she's trying not to react.

'I can't believe you've had all these experiences without telling me.'

'We weren't exactly on speed dial at the time, and since March you've been incommunicado, remember?' I watch her biting into the dark pink flesh. 'And it wasn't always very pretty. Do you think all this girlie experimentation is just some sort of crisis? Me showing off?'

'I think it's Serena Folkes stepping into the limelight, seeking attention after a life of being forced into the shadows, with a man who is prepared to support everything she does.' Polly leaves the fig half eaten on the table. 'But it's how you're going to fight off Margot that interests me.'

'Well, I'm trying. She owns this new place, the Sapphix Bar, and when I went along willingly with some of her dancers it turned out she wanted to make me do something stupid and degrading in front of her punters, and in front of Gustav. But I brazened it out. We did a shadow dance behind this curtain with some strap-on dildos.'

Polly and I gape at each other in the mirror. The word dildo is all too graphic, especially in a world where men, and their appendages, are not welcome.

'So no need to be scared of her any more. You showed her that you're the beautiful, spirited princess, and she's the

216

wicked, bitter witch. So did that make her abandon her vendetta or whatever it is?'

I shake my head, pick up the abandoned fig, and bite into it.

'Gustav seems to think so, but Pi— we've been warned that she's dangerous. Obsessed with getting rid of me. Since that first horrible meeting when she sent that feather to entice us to the old apartment, she's still turning up uninvited, like Carabos at the christening. She ruined the Weinmeyers' private view. I even thought – I found these red shoes, and I thought she'd been in our hotel room in Paris!'

'What? Sleeping with Gustav, behind your back?' Polly shakes her head at my reflection in the mirror. 'He would never – he worships you!'

I stare at that familiar face, so calm and content now compared with the unhappy, mixed-up state she was in back in New York. This is the real Polly. When I was a child, stuck in that house on the cliffs, she would arrive on one of her treasured visits and whisk me away for a few days. I relied on those missions of mercy. I needed her to put me straight, tell me how to cope, keep me safe.

I wipe fig juice off my chin. 'Even so. I think he's wrong. She'll never go quietly.'

'Not even now she's seen the diamond ring?'

'Especially now she's seen it! It's given her ammunition. In her sick mind she's convinced Gustav will crawl back to her, but he loathes her. Even if he wasn't engaged to me, he would be revolted by her. He says she looks nothing like she used to.' I finish the fruit and look around for somewhere to throw the peel. 'My theory is she's had some kind of work done. Like those old-fashioned facelifts that are supposed to make you look younger, but just make you look like a death's head. Her mouth is all puffy, and her eyes are slanted like a cat.'

217

'So she doesn't have a snowball's chance in hell! It's about time you realised you knock everyone else into a cocked hat!' Polly steps back and surveys the drape of the fabric on me. 'You're strong enough and gorgeous enough to fight off any number of evil plots. You'll be fine, Mrs Levi!'

We both laugh.

'I'm dealing with it. One by one, I sort them out. Pierre was the worst, even without Margot's influence, but he's come to heel with his tail between his legs.'

'Like the dog he is.' Polly turns away abruptly. 'Don't forget it's because of him that I had to remove myself.'

'I'm sorry. But look where you ended up! The best place ever. You are positively blossoming. If it wasn't for Gustav, honestly, I would happily give it all up and come to live with you here.' I put my hand on her arm. 'But let me just say one more thing about Pierre and then I'll shut up. He's genuinely sorry. About everything. There is a heart under all that swagger. And I've made him promise that one day he will apologise properly for the way he treated you. He's got pretty dark issues from his past, but he's also acknowledged that his association with Margot could have proved fatal. For all of us.'

There's a long pause in the hot room, and total silence from the courtyards outside.

'He should set up his own ashram. For dark, damaged men. But enough of him, Rena.' Polly presses a button on an iPod that's plugged into some speakers on a nearby sideboard. A melancholy female singer, accompanied by equally despondent trumpets and violins and drums, starts to sing in Arabic.

Wenta fein, weh hobi fein?

'This is Om Kalsoum. Famous Egyptian singer. She's saying where are you, and where is my love?'

Polly finishes pinning the fabric and starts making little

dots and dashes all over me with a marker pen. I stand rigid as a mannequin, terrified I've offended her by mentioning Pierre. But then she tries to draw a moustache on to me and we collapse into giggles.

'Anyway, just wait for the Moroccan massage, honey! You'll forget all about the slugs and snails and puppy dog's tails!' she gurgles as I try to snatch the pen away from her. 'And I was teasing you about being pure in body and spirit. We do have wine! Barrels of it. Later on, we'll give you a tasting. We make our special vintage from the vines. Angelique calls it *La Religieuse,* after her failed calling. I designed the label for her. It's a picture of a cute little nun getting pissed in a vineyard.'

I laugh. 'Angelique, Angelique. Her name is like the madam of an upmarket escort agency! I reckon you all have a massive crush on her.'

She slaps at me then spins me round in my column of white silk, and we are still giggling helplessly when the curtains over Polly's doorway billow open and the lady herself steps inside. She raises her fingertips to her mouth and gasps in admiration when she sees us spinning in front of the mirror.

'Angelique! Meet my cousin Serena!'

Polly flies across and brings her over to where I'm hovering awkwardly. Up close Angelique is younger and even more arresting to look at. Her large eyes blink lazily as she studies you. Her skin is kissed by the sun, and even though she radiates a motherly warmth, the smattering of freckles across her nose, similar to mine, give her a girlish quirkiness I hadn't noticed earlier.

Her smile fades as she looks not at me but directly at my reflection in the mirror. '*Helwa awi, habibti.*'

I blush and glance across at Polly, who translates. 'That means "very beautiful".'

'Arabic's my language of the day. I'm your original hybrid, you see. French-born, ran away to England for a while, briefly in Rome, but now I've lived in North Africa for too long.' Angelique smiles and runs her hand over my hair. 'You may be a princess in that dress, but we all have our tasks, so I've come to ask if you'll help in the kitchen while you're staying with us?' She strokes my cheek and then glides out of the room again.

A velvety twilight has settled over the feminine gardens, and multicoloured fairy lights set on twigs and planted into the flowerbeds illuminate the pathways.

The romantic surroundings make me long for Gustav again. I try to devote a lingering moment to him, but all other thoughts are gone. Evaporated. The energy has drained out of me, and with it all the tension. I feel heavy, yet empty. Full, yet light as a feather.

'Pol, what does *habibti* mean?' I ask, as my cousin settles a primrose-yellow veil over her hair and, to my astonishment, runs some clear lip gloss over her lips.

'You'll have to watch out. The others might get jealous. Angelique must like you, because she's never used that word for any of us.' She winks at me. 'It means *darling*.'

The sun lies in heavy yellow stripes across the sparkling floor. I'm alone in Polly's huge bed and it must be nearly midday by now. There is that silence again, but after two days here I've learned to welcome it. I lean over the pillows to pick up my mobile phone, but there's no signal here.

As if anticipating my intentions, Polly has left a note.

Morning, lazybones. I'm in the vineyard this morning, and then I'll be at the hammam. *Join me there later. You can get a signal there if you absolutely can't live without speaking to Gustav. But first you are needed again in the kitchen.*

220

I wander through the first courtyard and, instead of walking out through the garden to seek Polly in the vine-yards, I'm drawn by the smell of cooking. Stretching away to the right is a long pillared pergola edging another courtyard. This walkway is shaded by more of the ashram's famous vines. It's where we dined last night on a meal of stuffed vine leaves and salad prepared by me and a pair of lively Greek twins.

'There she is! My handmaiden! Hello, *habibti*!'

I'm wondering if I can get out of chopping yet more tomatoes when I see that sitting cross-legged next to Angelique on a huge cushion at the far end of the verandah is Maria Memsahib. A heap of tomatoes and red onions and aubergines and jars of preserved lemons and herbs are in front of her, and she's holding up a large knife.

'My God! *La liaison dangereuse!* Good morning, Madame la Marquise! What on earth are you doing here? What about the film? Why aren't you at the château?' I pad uncertainly over to the two women on my bare feet. I feel even more naked in my floaty pale apricot kaftan as I recall exactly what Maria was up to in that shadowy bedroom. I'm trying to reconcile that hungry sex kitten writhing between her two lovers with the quiet, calm goddess settled on a large cushion and watching me now. But I like it. It's comforting, and easy, like everything else here. I'm loosening and opening like a petal in this hot, quiet place.

Maria grins as I approach, her fiery black eyes resting on me as if she never wants to look away. How can I forget that look, shot at me across her naked shoulder as she rode her young lover in the château?

'Valmont announced an unexpected finale, so the cage has opened and the cast has dispersed. Like so many migrating birds. It's going to be sensational when it's released. You weren't to know, but I happen to own this place. And a certain someone may have asked me to look after you while he's in London.'

Angelique glances from her to me, a slight frown between her elegant eyebrows as she returns to chopping coriander.

'Gustav, do you mean? You've spoken to him? Oh, tell me how he is. *Where* he is. I can't get a signal to speak to him!' I sit down opposite Angelique and she hands me a chopping board. 'Are we allowed to talk while we cook?'

'Not really. And definitely not about him, I'm afraid. This is a place of reflection. Even I have to muzzle myself when I visit.'

Muzzled or not, Maria's fingers deliberately brush mine as she hands me some red onions.

'Angelique, I realise who you remind me of! There was this girl nicknamed Rapunzel in some old Parisian photographs of the *maisons closes*,' I remark, letting some of the onions roll away from me. 'We saw similar ones in the erotica museum in Paris last week. She might be a French prostitute?'

Angelica's knife stops halfway through the flesh of a huge pomegranate.

Maria steadies the pomegranate. 'Angelique isn't speaking today. Maybe we should be quiet, too, Serena?'

'I'm so sorry! That sounded really crude! It's just – oh, God, I've put my foot in it, haven't I?' I go down on my knees and scrabble for the escaping vegetables. 'The photos were tinted to look vintage, but the pictures were only taken in the 60s. This Rapunzel, she was waiting, staring all mournfully at the photographer. She could have been a model, of course. But still it made you want to rescue her.'

Angelique's knife slams right through to the chopping board. She turns one half of the pomegranate upside down and starts to bash the tough skin with a wooden spoon to empty the ruby-red seeds into a glass bowl. Then she stands up, her curtain of claret hair covering her face. She opens her mouth, closes it again, bows, then glides away.

I try to get up to follow her, but Maria stops me.

'Leave her be, *mademoiselle*. You hit a nerve, that's all. Her French mother used the name Rapunzel when she was a hooker.'

I sit down again and pick at the flimsy golden skin of the onions.

'Polly's going to kill me. I've broken the rule about not mentioning men, and I've managed to insult the boss! I mean, the other boss!'

Maria hands me a knife. Her sudden silence surprises me. I look up at her. The vines overhead dapple her ebony hair with leafy shade so that she looks as if she's wearing a crown of light.

'It's a good thing you're not planning to join the commune full time, then, isn't it? You and I are the cats amongst these pigeons. I leave Angelique in charge of the admin and the anima in this place. I'm all about carnality, not spirituality. I just supplied the venue, and the funds. So you and I? We are simply passing through. But we still have to leave the past outside the gate.'

I blush and focus on chopping the onions, keeping my knuckles against the rocking blade.

'I wish I didn't have to leave my camera as well. Angelique confiscated it.'

'This is a place of safety for the world-weary, that's why.' Maria gives a low laugh and tips boiled water on to couscous in a huge earthenware bowl and covers it with a cloth. Then she pinches up a bunch of mint, closing her eyes briefly as she inhales the aroma. '*La petite voyeuse* would like to watch the girls in here?'

'I'd love to photograph the beautiful, exotic setting, but yes, I'm intrigued to know what goes on behind these muslin drapes.'

223

'Not much is secret here. Everything is open. Everyone can walk wherever they like, be with whoever they like.' Maria waggles the sprigs of mint, winking at me. 'Maybe you and I can spend some time together when they are all at prayer or whatever they do, yes?'

A burst of laughter comes from somewhere over the lawn and there's a series of huge splashes as a handful of naked girls jump into the pool.

'I thought you owned the place. Do you not know exactly what goes on?' I ask cheekily, throwing the sliced onions into the sizzling olive oil. 'Or did you only come here to watch over me?'

'I always carry out my duties, especially when Gustav Levi asks me to. And yes, I do own the place. My family lived here when it was a kasbah. Nearly twenty years ago I planned to convert it into a hotel, but Angelique approached me to help her found this ashram. There are no major profits to speak of, but I don't need the money. I need to feel I'm doing good for others, even if I only provide the bricks and mortar.'

'It feels like a nunnery to me.'

'So think of Angelique as the Mother Superior and me as the chaplain! Come to me any time, *habibti*. I will gladly hear your confession!' She lifts the cloth off the couscous and tips Angelique's pomegranate seeds into it before forking it through.

'Anyone less like a nun or a priest I cannot imagine!' I giggle as the steam rises between us. 'You're the one with the sins to confess!'

'They are coming to eat, so *halas*.' She shreds mint leaves over the couscous. 'Enough. No more talking for now.'

The girlish laughter in the distance lowers into quiet talking as various figures, in floaty dresses in all the colours of the rainbow, appear from doorways and arches and come out of the little white pavilions erected in the far corners of the garden for massage and treatments.

Maria hands me a flagon of wine and a tray of roughly blown stubby glasses stained with blue and gold, and a group of girls, including Polly, pushes through a curtain of vines to join us.

'So you've found your mother figure,' Polly remarks, sitting down and nudging me sharply in the ribs. 'But I'm going to have to prise you apart now. It's silence for the rest of the day.'

I have no idea what time it is, or even what day. I know that nearly a week has passed since I arrived at this ashram. I haven't been able to speak to Gustav, although in the *hammam* I did pick up one voicemail left the day we flew out of Paris, telling me he had touched down in London, he was missing me, and giving me the flight details of his return to New York next week.

And I know that the powerful, fruity homemade wine we have been drinking is making me languorous and heavy. Angelique is still in her vow of silence, but every so often I feel her eyes resting on me, and if ever there is a space on a cushion next to her, she beckons me to sit. So whatever I said out of turn is forgiven and forgotten. And I'm learning to keep my mouth shut.

Maria and I are together more, though, working in the kitchen or swimming in the pool. We talk a little about *Les Liaisons* and the promotional tour she will soon begin, but as soon as I touch on how she met Gustav and what went on in the house in Baker Street, she refuses to be drawn.

'Talking about that stuff is not in the spirit of this place,' she murmurs, and no amount of teasing or cajoling will get any more out of her. In any case, any talk of London or Gustav or Margot disturbs the peace that has settled on me since I came here.

But now it's siesta or meditation time. The others have dispersed and I'm lying face down on a massage table where Maria told me to come and wait for her. I rest my chin on my hands, staring through the gap in the white curtains of my personal little pavilion, heavy with the aroma of incense from the tapers burning on the mats all around. The treatment areas are deliberately placed at a remove from the main buildings, facing away from the earthly delights of the kitchen, the swimming pool, the art room so that all I can see from here are a few rows of vines, the village where they have the *hammam,* and then the rise of the grey-blue mountains.

All I can hear is the trickle of sleepy piano music coming from inside this tent. Outside, there is no sound but the splash of water and the twitter of tiny bright-blue birds.

A pair of hands lands on my shoulder blades, pressing me hard down on to my front. Because I'm not expecting it, the breath is pushed right out of me. I feel as if I'm going to go through the spongy couch, straight through the ground, and as the pressure releases so all my resistance evaporates. There is a pause. Ice-cold gel is squirted on to my back, and then the heel, the palm, and the knuckles of someone's hands start to work on me.

It might be one of the young, silent, dark-skinned girls in special golden shift dresses who flit about the grounds and the courtyards, bringing food, drink, towels and clean clothes, plucking flowers from the beds to decorate the rooms, and massaging the inhabitants.

But I know it's not. My body twitches with a sudden, fierce, forbidden desire.

My cheekbones dig into the towel, my body rocking, and gradually the surface of my skin starts to tingle in places my masseuse hasn't even reached yet. The oil slicks up and down my arms, back to my shoulder blades, and along the knobs of my spine. The blood starts to drum in my ears, drowning out any other sounds.

'What's this? Still tense even after all my efforts to relax you?'

Maria's husky accented voice murmurs in my ear. Soft, damp lips run along my temple, and I feel the tickle of her long, tangled black hair brushing over my shoulder. There's her dreamy, musky scent in the air.

'You're making me fidgety!' The breath is pushed out of me as she presses me down into the mattress again. 'And I'm missing Gust—'

'Don't say it. Don't think of anyone or anything except me, and what I'm doing to you. Not your fiancé. Not your cousin. Not even Angelique. They have all gone into one of their trances. It's just you and me this afternoon.' The hands massage each knob of my spine, right down to my butt, and then start to smooth up my sides, over my ribs. 'Are you going to resist, or will you let me woo you?'

'Woo me?' I ask, trying to twist round. What did she say to me at the château?

I saw how you looked at me. There is more you would like to try, but you hide it.

'You talk too much, *habibti*. We're not in Paris now.' A soft blindfold is tied round my eyes, blocking out the soft white light. Blocking out everything except the hands touching the swell of my breasts, then pulling away, down over my hips, and then gently pulling my legs apart. 'Just concentrate on the pleasure that is coming.'

Her hands run back and forth over my hips, and down the backs of my legs, and warmth oozes through me, yet my whole body is at the same time exquisitely sensitive. When she touches the crease at the back of my knees, I kick out involuntarily, and my thigh comes into contact with her leg.

'Why did Gustav want you to watch out for me?' I try to clench my legs together when her hands feel their way between my butt cheeks, but her knee comes up and parts my thighs. 'What does he think might happen?'

'Margot reared her ugly head and gave you a fright and he really didn't want to leave you. But he has a lot on, and he knows I'll keep you out of harm's way. He also knows I will have fun with you because I'm allowed in here and he isn't.' She is kneeling up on the bench. I feel something soft brush across my back, and back again. 'I'll do *anything* for that man of yours. And he'll do anything for you, Serena.'

I tighten inside. She's naked. Those are her breasts brushing across my skin. Her big, brown breasts with the hard, brown nipples that I saw pushing into the young man's mouth in the loft in Manhattan. The same luscious La Marquise who was straddling the young boy Danceny at the château last week, all the time her black eyes flashing at me. Wanting me.

I prefer women. That's what Maria said to me, back at the château. It was meant to reassure me that she wasn't after Gustav, but it resonates more now as a blatant flirtation.

Her breath is on my face, her lips pressing as her hands continue to stroke, and now it's less of a massage, more a blatant touching up, and now, oh, God, she's lifting me so that she can stroke my stomach and work down from there, down between my legs, hitching my hips up towards her. I have no strength to struggle or wriggle away, hell, I don't want to resist her. Her hands pull me so that I'm rubbing up against her, arching myself so that I can grind across her legs, I'm spreading myself open for her and now she's on top of me, the length of her warm body over mine, her body starting to rock against me, wetness slicking over my butt

228

cheeks, she's kissing me everywhere, hands everywhere, and I'm sinking rapidly into my own trance.

'Maria, I don't know, is this allowed?' I groan helplessly, just as she starts to turn me over. I grapple for the blindfold, but she takes my hands and holds them tight. 'What if the others—'

'They are gone for hours, and anyway, I can do what I like, *chica*.' She turns me over as if I'm something warm and delicious she's just taken out of the oven. 'Absolutely anything.'

I croak, trying to form some words even while the scented blackness of the blindfold seems to empty my mind.

'I'm here to rinse your mind clean of everything, and everyone. So hush. It's time for silence.'

She seems to be balancing herself astride me, and now I feel the tickle of her hair as she bends down and parts my mouth. She explores it with her long, wet tongue, probing until I relent and start to suck at it and nibble at her big, luscious lips.

My whole body fizzes with excitement. I'm splayed beneath her like a feast. She stops kissing me and squeezes some more cream or gel on to my breasts and starts to fondle them, circling the plump flesh, squeezing it, no pretence at massage now, and I give into it, arch myself, feel my nipples prick up hard against her hands. She chuckles and massages the area all around before pinching the nipples. Now there are teeth on them, biting, making me moan with growing pleasure.

She rocks against me and our dampness starts to mingle. The slowly accelerating rhythm of the pleasure she is taking from my body fills me with a hot, desperate desire. I shake my hands free and grab at her hips, pulling her so that we can move against each other. I dig my fingers into her bottom, edging one finger up towards her centre to show her I know what I'm doing, and I know what she wants. She moves back and forth as she sucks on my breasts.

And then her fingers are doing the same. One hand cradles my breast, but the other moves down between my legs, pauses, then her fingers trace the hidden crack and probe inside like her tongue probed my mouth and I gasp and tighten myself round her, pulling her against me, pushing my own fingers up inside her and she's so soft and scented, panting now, so womanly as we writhe against each other, and just as I push my fingers harder up, she locates my hidden spot and I cry out as she manipulates it with one of her fingers, no idea which one, and it's just then that I start to imagine her with other women, how often she's done this before, and that thought argues with a fierce determination to be the best she's ever had, so I start to fuck her and laugh out loud as I feel her body squeeze to keep my fingers inside her.

Little tongues of pleasure start lapping at me, too, as she pumps rapidly into me. Her thumb still plays me until I'm arching and bucking and the ecstasy is radiating through me and we tumble off the bed on to the cushions arranged all over the floor, our legs and arms wrapped tight, that big luscious mouth of hers locked on to mine as we roll over each other. I snatch away the blindfold in time to see her eyes go misty as she starts to come.

She falls on to her back and I fall on top of her, twisting and gripping her as our moans recede against the softly flapping sides of our pleasure dome.

'Surprised I could tear you away from two whole halcyon days with the Memsahib to come shopping with me, Mrs lover lover.'

Polly links arms with me as we walk through the narrow streets of the souq in Marrakesh, past stalls selling the pointy-toed slippers called *babouches,* leather, straw or canvas bags, bolts of cloth, bottles of perfume, blue and green painted ceramics, and everywhere multicoloured triangular pyramids of cinnamon, cumin, harissa, paprika and a myriad other spices.

'Sorry, Pol. I know we've only today and tomorrow together before I fly home.' I blush bright red and pluck at the neck of my silky copper-coloured T-shirt. My ordinary casual clothes feel strange on me now. 'She's a force of nature!'

'You think Gustav will be happy you were tasting a bit of girl-on-girl soon as his back was turned?'

I'm not in the mood for joking. I can't quell the churning of anxiety that started as soon as we left the ashram to come into town. I expected my phone to go crazy the minute we were in range of a signal, but this almost total silence is killing me.

'He organised it! And I'd report back if I could get hold of him, but I can't even get voicemail now. There was one text, then a couple of blank ones, and a call that was just a kind of scraping sound. Now his line is dead. I'm getting worried. I wonder – would you be really pissed off if I found a travel agent and got an earlier flight home?'

'Where to? New York, or London?'

We stop by a stall selling piles of silk scarves, some wigs made from real human hair, and every kind of gel and serum. I realise I haven't thought this through. If everything has gone according to plan, Gustav will be on his way back to New York tomorrow. But if something has gone wrong, he'll still be in London.

A text chirrups and I nearly drop the phone.

I let go of Polly's arm. But my heart plummets as quickly as it jumped, because it's not from Gustav. It's from Pierre.

Don't leave the ashram. Stay with Polly until we come for you.

I stare at the message. What the hell does Pierre mean? I don't know if it's from Paris, or London, or LA, or even Morocco. But what I can tell is that this order, or warning, is dated six days ago. Just like the non-texts from Gustav.

'That's henna,' Polly remarks, unaware of my panic. She's pointing at a green powder in a big sack. 'Our Angelique uses it to dye her hair that glorious colour.'

I text back quickly. *Too late. Am in the souq and about to book earlier flight. Where to? London or NYC? Blank texts from Gustav. GET HIM TO PHONE ME!*

The phone is hot in my hand. I grip it tight, willing it to ring. I need to hear Gustav's voice. Even some kind of explanation from Pierre would help.

Polly has wandered a little way down the street. I pick up a little hessian sack of the henna.

'You mean that's not her natural colour?'

Polly is looking at some chunky silver jewellery strung across a little pinboard. 'She was a redhead once, but she admitted that she was growing a little grey at the temples. She's old enough to be our mother. Or at least, our much older sister.'

I take a swig from my bottle of mineral water and shuffle along to the next stall, which has mirrors and small carved teak tables at the front. The world around me is noisy and crowded and too busy. I just want my phone to ring.

Through a gap at the back of the shop, I can see into a cavernous workshop. Rows of heavy carved wooden doors are stacked against each other or side by side, as if ready to open.

'So what made her leave the convent and fetch up in the Moroccan desert, do you think?' I ask, groping through a display of hanging carpets to find Polly. 'What commitment-phobe let that lovely woman slip through his fingers?'

Polly runs her fingers over the dark-red embroidery of a

kilim rug. The stall seller leaps forward to start haggling, and she grins and swerves past me to get away. She turns down a side street I didn't even know was there.

'Something happened in that convent.' Her voice retreats down the alleyway. 'We don't know what or who, but she never took her final vows. A naughty priest, maybe? Another nun?'

I go to follow her but stop when my phone trills with an incoming text, this time from Gustav's number. My hands are shaking as I read it.

Change of plan. Staying in London. Don't bother to come. Enjoy your freedom!

I frown at the screen, scroll down, but there's nothing more. No mention of Morocco, no jokes about meditating about him, no asking after Polly and the wedding dress. No endearments. No messages of love. A cold fist squeezes my ribcage. There's something cold and final in the tone of the text. As if he's saying goodbye.

I start texting back, aware that the stallholder is standing in front of me. The *kilim* rug that Polly was admiring is now hanging over his arm.

A little brusque, darling? Everything OK? Will meet you in Mayfair. Loving you until then.

'*Mademoiselle*, very good price. Pure cactus silk!' The stallholder lays the carpet out at my feet and invites me to stroke it. What have I done wrong? What's the matter with Gustav?

'*La'a, shukran!* No, thank you!' I press 'send', but the signal has gone again. Message failed. I hold the phone up in the air and it trills into life again. Without checking the number, I answer it frantically.

'Gustav! Darling! Is that you? Speak to me!'

There's a heavy sigh at the other end of the phone, a cough, then what sounds like a microwave beeping in the background.

233

'Serena. Sis. Ish Pierre.'

I nearly throw the phone across the alleyway with fury. 'Oh, stay out of it, P! You've been drinking! Get Gustav on the line!'

'He's not here. You need to get back to. The ashram. Danger. Go back to Polly and we'll get you – someone will get you.'

The single beep in the background goes into a two-tone wail, like the alarm that goes off at the supermarket when someone is shoplifting.

'Please, Pierre. Stop with the weird scaring. I've no time for your warped sense of humour, especially when you're pissed. I need you to get hold of Gustav for me. His phone isn't working, and I'm worried. I miss him. I need to tell him I'm coming over to London.' I clamp the phone to my ear, still searching the crowd and the stalls for Polly. A cold hand brushes over me again, despite the heat. 'Is Gustav on another of these mysterious trips? Is that why he isn't picking up?'

Pierre groans. 'I'm not drunk. It's these drugs.' A woman calls his name from across a noisy space. 'G's in London, but he can't. His head. Trouble. Get back to the ashram – wait!'

'You're breaking up!' I'm yelling now, and people are staring. 'So I've said I'll get a flight as soon as I can. Tell him to sort his phone out and I'll meet him at the Mayfair house!'

The carpet seller barges up to me again, pushing the carpet into my face.

'Take American dollar!'

I spin away from him and step straight into someone standing behind me.

'Hey, Pol, why did you rush off like that?' I splutter, as the person catches me and holds on to my shoulders. 'I need to book that flight right away!'

'Well, how about that?' someone says. 'Of all the souqs in all the world.'

Standing in front of me, grinning and running his fingers through his overgrown blonde curls in a *faux* Hugh Grant-like gesture is Pierre's American friend Tomas. The guy who Pierre and Margot thought might be the one to wreck me and Gustav.

'Sorry, I can't deal with you right now. Every time we come face to face there's trouble. Just leave me alone! I've got to get to the travel agents!' I struggle to get free, peering down the tiny path where I thought she disappeared and calling frantically. 'Polly! Where are you?'

My voice sinks into the pitted stone walls and worn steps. There's a sharp bend at the far end where she must have gone.

'Polly's here too? This is such a stroke of luck. We've so much to talk about.' Tomas still blocks my path. He pushes his mirrored sunglasses up on to his head casually, as if we have just collided doing the weekly shop. 'You could tell us where Pierre's got to, for a start. We were hanging out at The Standard Hotel back in February and he was badgering me to get him membership of the Club Crème – remember that bucks' night at the club? He would have moved heaven and earth to get in, once he heard what we got up to!'

'Don't remind me.' I glare at his wide, blue, blank eyes. 'Pierre told you to do that to me, didn't he? Lick me in front of all your mates. You think it was a bit of fun, but it was part of a plot with Gustav's ex-wife to split us up.'

'The heat's getting to you, girl. Have you any idea how crazy that sounds?' Tomas takes my arms in a firm grip. 'I have no idea what you're talking about. I told you, I haven't seen Pierre for months! He left the Big Apple without a word. Back up a second. Don't tell me he's here in Marrakesh as well?'

235

I waggle my mobile in his face. 'That was him on the phone. But I don't know where he is at this precise moment. He was working in LA, then he came over to Paris, then they were meeting their lawyers in London—'

I rush down the alleyway to look for Polly. Tomas follows me, even pushing ahead to peer round the corner. He shakes his head.

'So you're with Pierre now? This is giving me motion sickness! Your life sounds a little out of control.'

'I'm not with Pierre. My life is fine. Everything's fine.'

'Not from where I'm standing! Sounds like your engagement to Levi Senior got called off?'

'Oh, please. Wouldn't you just love that? Nothing's been called off. It's all good. Everything was lovely. I was in the ashram, all chilled, and now just – I'm in a state because I can't get hold of my fiancé and he's leaving strange texts and I'm lost in the middle of Marrakech and my cousin has disappeared. Oh, God, where is she?'

I retrace my steps to the main market street, back to the carpet shop and the spices. Tomas tries to take my arm again.

'Calm down – Serena, wasn't it? You'll only get more lost if you start to panic.'

'Look, I can't talk right now. I need to find Polly, and then I need to find a travel agent to change my flight!' Tears are rising up and blocking my throat. 'And I need to get a bloody signal!'

This part of the souq is suddenly crowded with people and donkeys and bikes, children with school satchels on their backs, gangly youths huddling round to light cigarettes. Two tall Berber women in black *djellabas* glide by. From the shadow of their pointed hoods, the only part of them visible beneath pretty yashmaks is a pair of huge amber eyes, outlined with thick black kohl pencil.

'Polly will be fine. We'll sort this out. Look, give me your phone. They'll have a connection at my place.' He takes it from me and grabs my arm. 'I'm staying in this fantastic riad. It's just a few blocks away. Well, you know what I mean. Not blocks. Corners.'

I push him away, run up and down this stretch of alley, people jostling past me, the bags and carpets and lamps all bashing at my head as I search frantically for my cousin.

But Polly's nowhere to be seen.

CHAPTER TEN

The devil or the deep blue sea? It has to be the devil.

After wandering in circles for what seems like hours, after searching every overstuffed stall in this warren of streets, after following Tomas as he gives a description of my cousin to anyone who will listen and peers down every dingy alleyway, our shouts for Polly are drowned. The racket of the market clangs and rushes in my ears.

'She must be on her way back to the ashram.' I adjust my camera and bag, which are digging into my shoulder. I'm drenched in sweat and I half lean, half fall into a rail of T-shirts. 'I need to get a taxi, Tomas.'

'It's a bit of a walk from here, but I can take you to the edge of the Medina.' He stares at a sign in flowing Arabic script. 'Where do you want to go?'

Dots are sparking in front of my eyes. Every time I try to focus on him, bits of him are missing, like his shoulder, or one lens of his sunglasses.

'Home. Or maybe I should go to the ashram.' Pierre's strange words on the phone come back to me, urging me to return there, but I push them aside. 'Actually, scrub that, it's better if I go straight to the airport.'

'You have your passport with you? No? Didn't think so.'
He starts walking under the road sign. 'So we'll do this the
sensible way. You come with me first, charge up your phone
and get a clear signal. Then you can call Polly and check
exactly where she is. Make a proper plan. Meanwhile, if
you'll just let me—'

He stretches out his hand gingerly, and places it on my
forehead.

'As I thought. You're burning up.'

'What are you now, a doctor?' But even as he says it I
realise how hot I am, panting for breath like a dog. 'It's
May in Morocco, for heaven's sake. Of course I'm hot!'

'Actually, we're into June now.'

And that's when I burst into tears.

So I give in, and Tomas, keeping his hand on my arm, leads
me away from the busy touristy streets and into a warren of
ever-narrowing alleyways. I have no idea where we are. Just
a faint instinct that we are walking north, away from the
central square of Jemaa El Fna. We must be on the edge of
the Medina because we pass the odd gateway to the outside
world, glimpse cars rushing by, or happen upon a sudden
opening of space and light as a mosque or shrine shimmers
into view. And then we turn into more apparent dead ends.

Marrakesh is like a North African version of Venice. My
camera bounces on its strap against my hip as Tomas picks
up his pace. If my head wasn't pounding, my mind racing
with a muddle of questions, I would want to dawdle and
capture the tantalising glimpses of life behind the carved
mushrabiyya screens. We pass what is basically a cave where
an ancient-looking man is hunched over an open fire, beating
holes into metal sheets to fashion lanterns. Another alley is
lined with pastry kitchens, where young boys are tossing lacy
pancake wafers in the air, or standing in pools of blood
hacking chunks of halal meat off the bone.

When we pass what looks like the window to a store room and I see several rows of neatly brushed and combed schoolchildren chanting the ABC at their plump teacher, I can't resist snatching my camera out of its bag and taking several shots as the teacher draws an apple, a ball, a cat on the tiny blackboard nailed to the rough teal-blue wall.

The call to prayer winds up from a nearby mosque, the muffled holy voice wavering skywards like a snake charmer's rope. Tomas turns down the shortest, darkest alleyway yet, and just as I think there's nowhere to go but the thick stone wall forming a dead end, he stops in front of a low, splintered wooden door set into a crumbling pink wall, which looks as if it simply opens into a coal shed.

'You must be thirsty, Serena. We'll get you a nice cold glass of something,' he says, rapping on the door. 'Just take off your shoes.'

The door creaks open on big iron hinges and I nearly fall down several steps. Tomas bolts the door and locks it, and then walks ahead of me into a large square courtyard, open to the sky, surrounded on all sides by tiered galleries twined with roses, jacaranda, bougainvillea, orange blossom and the tiny white petals of jasmine. The mingled floral scents are so heavy and powerful that my head throbs even more.

The walls, arches, ceilings and floor are all tiled in a kind of silvery finish, inlaid with occasional flashes of ruby red and cobalt blue.

'That's *tadelakt* tiling,' Tomas remarks as I stand and stare round me. Everything is far too bright. 'My excuse for staying here for so long. I'm supposed to be studying Moroccan plastering and tiling techniques to export to my interior design business back home in the US.'

'How far away that seems right now.'

I leave my sandals by the door as instructed and follow him along one side of the courtyard, which is formed into a row of alcoves each furnished with low bench seats upholstered in striped silver and white cushions. Lounging on these benches are couples or groups who mostly look like hippy travellers, wearing thin cotton shorts or vests or flowery dresses with long dreadlocked hair. All the girls wear thick silver anklets round their bare feet, and have pretty sequinned veils over their faces, which have the incredibly sexy effect of making their features tantalising, and their eyes huge and inviting.

Tomas points to the bare female legs. 'Those anklets are called *khuul khaal*. They represent purity and the binding of marriage, which is ironic considering what goes on here. The female guests wear them to show that they intend to go along with the ideology of the riad.'

'To keep tabs on them, more like. They look like electronic tags,' I mutter.

The girls blink sleepily at me and drape their legs over the nearest male.

It occurs to me that these slackers ought to be out sight-seeing, or trekking in the mountains, but they are mostly asleep or drowsily sucking on hookah pipes. Some are sketching or reading. In the furthest alcove a guy wearing a ripped vest over a gold sarong stands on his own, playing a beautiful, swooping melody on a flute. The acoustics of the riad are perfect, like the choir stalls of a church, and the music is pure and clear.

'So how long have you been staying here, Tomas?' I glance up at the various arches and screens around the courtyard. 'It looks more like someone's home than a hotel.'

241

'Oh, long enough. I'm practically a native. You'll be all right here while I go to the study?' He takes the phone out of his pocket. 'I'll go plug this in.'

He shows me to a low wooden couch beside the little oblong pool and then disappears through one of the arches. A couple of dark, thorny trees with closed white flowers stand in terracotta pots. I reach out and touch one of the leaves. The sap prickles on my finger and a strong, intoxicating wave is released. There's something peachy in the scent, something else, sweet, nutty. Almonds. I breathe it in and my aching head starts to swim even more. Isn't that the smell of Agatha Christie's poison of choice – arsenic?

The silvery courtyard, lit by the matt infusion of white light coming through a veil draped above the roof space like a sail, starts to dip as if we're on a ship. I sit down hastily before I fall.

Tomas has reappeared by my side. He takes my camera before it clatters to the floor and puts it on the carved wooden table beside me. He sits down very close, stretching out his long legs in white jeans. I try to focus on him. He's the same preppy, slightly pasty New Yorker he ever was. This sunburned bum look doesn't suit him.

'My phone charged yet?' I ask. My voice sounds faint, as if I'm talking in my sleep.

'Give it a good twenty minutes.' His arm rests on the back of my seat and I find myself staring at the gold hairs on his skin. Now that we've stopped rushing about, and we're inside this quiet, luxurious haven within the pink city's walls, my mind stops flapping about like a caged bird and settles on one excruciating memory.

This man and I were together in a private room a few months ago, in the Club Crème in Manhattan. We were cavorting in front of a smirking, appreciative audience of

242

men at their bachelor party. I had been taking photographs, as commissioned, and was high on the attention and the sleazy atmosphere of the club. I was up for anything. This guy's hand, with the golden hairs, was gripping my legs to open them. This head, with its slightly sweaty curls, was buried between my thighs. His tongue was on me, licking. If Pierre told Tomas to target me like that, I played straight into his hands. Not only was I allowing it, I was cajoling him to do it, in front of all his mates, until Gustav walked into the room and the dirtiness of what I was doing hit me. I pushed Tomas off me but still went ahead and fingered myself in front of them all!

A tall slim girl with sheets of long blonde hair, wearing a tiny pair of bright-orange sequinned shorts and a belly dancer's tasselled brassiere, appears from nowhere. She balances a round tray on her fingertips, and presents two glasses edged with *lapis lazuli* filigree and filled with some kind of clear liquid. Tomas runs his hand up her leg and points at one of the glasses. Without thinking, I knock the liquid back, thinking it'll be lemon juice or iced mint tea. At first I taste nothing, and then I realise I've swallowed some kind of strong, spice-infused vodka.

'Thanks, gorgeous. Meet Serena Folkes. She's the hot English photographer making waves in Manhattan and oh, my goodness, I see the rock on her finger now. So it's really true. Meet the fiancée of Gustav Levi!'

The girl sinks down and drapes one long leg over his, swaying her head to some music on her iPod. Although she doesn't respond or even register that I'm here at all, I recognise her immediately. It's the long, rangy limbs and neck, and those huge cartoon eyes above her powdery veil, but without the stage make-up and spiky false eyelashes her eyes look blank. *She* looks blank.

'Chloe? It's me. Serena! From the *Serenissima* gallery?

We were at the Sapphix Bar together just a few weeks ago!'

But still she doesn't answer. My voice has become thick and rough, and her name sticks like a fur ball in my mouth. In fact, neither of them seems to hear me. Tomas strokes her idly, fingertips sliding inside her tiny shorts. I remember Pierre Levi touching my cousin Polly like that, sprawled across the suede sofa in our apartment on New Year's Eve, just like Tomas is sprawled across this sofa now. Chloe starts to move against his fingers, but still her eyes stare blankly into the shifting blues and greens of the pool. Just like Polly seemed that night, this girl looks as if she's been drugged.

Tomas tops up the glasses and continues his monologue. 'So the plan is still on, that you'll marry Gustav Levi and you'll be lucky old Pierre's sister-in-law? My God, how's he going to cope with that? He'll go out of his mind! I've never seen a guy so hopelessly in love with someone he can't have.'

I sit up straighter and try to focus on Tomas, but he's splitting into two. I don't feel sick exactly, but my head feels as if it's about to fly off my neck. Tomas looks as if his blonde hair has suddenly turned black and oily, like a gangster. And Chloe's legs and arms have become rubbery and see-through, like a glass octopus.

'Just give me back my phone so I can call Polly to meet me here, or you can take me to the nearest taxi rank.'

'Sure, in a minute. It's still charging.' Tomas glances at my camera. 'So, where were we? Oh, yes. Pierre. Well, poor guy didn't get to first base with you, did he, though he said he was determined to try. Obviously he didn't try hard enough, because, oh, my, if he'd seen you doing that sexy stripper dance in the Club Crème he'd have known you're just an easy little slapper, like all the others.'

'So much for the good Samaritan. Why are you being so

offensive?' I tug at my blouse, which is sticking to my skin. I feel hotter than ever, despite the cool courtyard and the drink. 'Sorry. That wasn't very grateful of me. It's just – Pierre and I understand each other now.'

Chloe uncurls her leg from his and stands up. I want to call her back. I don't want to be on my own with Tomas. But my jaw feels locked. She steps away across the courtyard towards a curved staircase, picking up her feet like a show pony, and water seems to be lapping all over the floor now, like the *acqua alta* that rises from the lagoon in winter and floods all over Venice.

'No need to be touchy, Serena. I'm just remembering the good times. I mean, how could I forget your performance that night at the club, now that you're sitting here in front of me again? I think an action replay might be called for, don't you? It was easy enough for me to get a taste of you at the club, wasn't it? I was so close to making you come with my tongue, remember that?'

'I just – that was a wild phase I was going through. I don't want to be reminded.'

Tomas crosses one leg over the other and runs his finger over his lips. He has apparently just sprouted a full, piratical beard. He's turning into Pierre. I rub my hand over my eyes and realise my eyelashes are wet with tears.

'So what's Pierre's problem? Horny devil like him didn't even succeed in feeling up his own sister when she was there for the taking? Sorry, that was a Freudian slip, eh? I should say sister-in-law.'

'Please, Tomas. I just need to make that call. I need to get a ticket. I need Polly. You know Polly? She's your friend? She'd love to see you. Just give me my phone!'

'All in good time. Don't get so worked up,' Tomas murmurs, leaning forward to stare at me. 'We're just so pleased we got you here at last.'

It must be later than I thought, because dusk is falling, dropping right into the middle of this courtyard, and all I can see of him, like the Cheshire Cat, is his grin.

My eyelids feel as if they are weighed down with stones and someone is sewing them closed, and then everything goes dark.

It's not just my eyes that are weighted and my head that is banging like a drum. When I wake up, or think I'm waking up, my ankle bone grates against something hard and cold, as if I'm shackled, too. I struggle up on to my elbows and force my eyes open. The darkness around me is hot, close and still, but there are pinpricks of light around me, flickering.

For a moment I lie still. I'm obviously seriously ill. Or something's come adrift in my eyes or in my brain, like a cataract or a slipped retina. But it's OK. Gustav's here. He's got me tied with the silver chain, that's all. Just like old times. Any minute now he'll lean over me, push me back against the bank of pillows or cushions I've been lying on, he'll make sure I'm totally naked, then he'll run his mouth over me, and then his hands, and then he won't be able to stop himself because the sight of me lying so still beneath him will make him rock hard with wanting.

Then I realise I'm alone, in a strange dark room.

I'm shivering and sweating as I lie back. Wisps of hair are sticking to my neck and I'm wearing nothing but some kind of slip. It's not mine. My clothes have been taken off me.

The digital letters of Pierre's text glow across my mind.
Ashram.
Danger.

Cold fingers of panic grip and galvanise me now. What did he mean? Was he just teasing? I try to calm down. I'm still feverish, that's all. Pierre sent that text just before I lost Polly in the market, so he had no idea I was in any kind of trouble. In fact, when I speak to him or Gustav they'll probably be relieved that I bumped into Tomas.

I sit up straighter. My eyes are clearing, but then I realise that it's because light is coming into the room through a keyhole-shaped doorway. It's a muted light, not the bright outdoors of the ashram. So I wasn't imagining it. I may not be in *danger*, whatever Pierre meant, but I'm still stuck at the riad. Which at the very least is bloody inconvenient.

Someone's pulling back a curtain, or a screen. I must be up high, in one of the riad bedrooms, because through the archway I see the ornate railings that run round the galleried floors, the plants and flowers twining and cascading, and the plash of the pool is now far below.

A little lamp goes on in the corner of the room, and to my relief I see Chloe pacing round the carved screen that surrounds my bed. I realise that the little pinpricks of flickering light come from wavy goatskin lanterns placed around the tiled floor.

I heave myself upright again, swing my legs over the edge of the bed. I'm not shackled, but that grating feeling is a heavy anklet that Tomas or someone has seen fit to clamp round my foot. And I don't like it.

'It's so incredible to see you, Chloe. And incredible to see where you've been staying. But hey, I can't stop. This is all very nice but I need to get my phone and my clothes and be on my way. You can help me, can't you? You're my only hope before any more time runs away with me!' I give a bright laugh to enhance my easy façade. 'How about we catch up over a coffee or a beer? You must know some cool places near here. But first, could you find my phone for me?'

'Why do you need a phone?'

I swallow, and lace my fingers together to stop them shaking.

'The thing is, Chloe, I only came here to get it charged up. But I'm in a real hurry now. I don't think Tomas realises how important it is for me to find my cousin. She'll be wondering where I am. It's time I was off.'

'I don't know where your phone is.' She glances round the stark room. 'We all switched ours off when we got here, and I've no idea what they did with them. It's all free love and free everything here. Why would I want to make a call? Everyone and everything I want is in this house.'

Her words are euphoric, but beads of sweat are breaking out on Chloe's forehead. She's not wearing the veil today. Her lovely blonde hair is tied up in a stringy, messy knot. Either there are some serious substances doing the rounds in here or she must have had the same dodgy drink as I did earlier.

'Tomas wasn't very nice to me, actually Chloe. And as for that disgusting medicine—'

'That wasn't medicine. We all drink it. That's the cocktail he gives us to keep us mellow.' She pulls a strand of hair out of its loose knot and starts chewing it. 'Oh, he's a dreamboat. You'll love it here.'

I resist the urge to jump up and shake her – I've got to keep her on side if I'm to get out of here anytime soon. Instead I cross one leg over the other, swinging my weighted ankle. The jangling of it against the bone keeps me alert.

'So this is the holiday you said you were owed, Chloe? It's amazing. When are you flying back to New York?'

'Don't you love these anklets? Our personal passes! You shouldn't look so freaked out, Serena. You're perfectly safe here.'

'I'm not freaked out, Chloe. I'm just pissed off.' I count

248

slowly to five. 'I'm very grateful and all that, and you may love it, but I'm not supposed to be here.'

'Nonsense. This is the best place in the world. An endless free vacation.' She runs her hands over the silver anklet circling my leg then lifts her own long brown leg to show me hers. 'Why would I want to go back to New York? Tomas and I are going to live here forever.'

The clearer-headed I feel, the more robotic she sounds. I stand up and walk unsteadily over to a mirror. My hair has been fixed in a messy knot like hers. My face looks sweaty like hers, too. I look awful.

'Remember you brought your portfolio to my gallery, Chloe? I never got the chance to take a look, but when I've got all my stuff we could go back to the US together and you could show me.' I say it softly, as if I'm coaxing a child, leaning against the wall because I still feel dizzy. 'How is your talent ever going to be recognised if you're hiding it?'

'We spend all day painting and drawing and singing right here. You could take some fantastic photographs of all the naughty things happening, because there are no doors, except the main one. Otherwise it's only curtains and *mushrabiyya* screens. That word means "not see". But you *can* see, if you peer very closely.'

'What day is it, Chloe? How long have I been here?' I take a step towards the door, aware of how high and tight my voice sounds as renewed impatience threatens to blow my cover.

'Not long. You came here yesterday afternoon and slept all last night and most of today.'

'I've been in this place more than 24 hours? My God, this has cocked up everything! Polly will be going out of her mind with worry! Why didn't someone wake me?'

'You weren't well. You had some kind of fever. You still look awful.'

'Well, I *feel* awful, but I can't linger. So I'd love it if you could show me where to find my phone, because you all might be having a nice holiday here, but I've got places to go, people to see, and also my cousin will be worried sick. I don't want to bother Tomas. He's probably stoned and forgotten about me. So help me out, hun. If I don't go now I'm going to miss my plane.'

'You haven't booked the ticket yet, he says. Or got your passport. Oh, and you won't get out. The main door is usually locked.' She looks steadily at me, but the brief glimmer of life I just saw in her eyes has snuffed out again. Her pupils are so dilated that her blue eyes look black. She gets up with a sigh and wanders towards the door. 'I'll just go find Tomas.'

'Oh, we don't need to tell him, do we? If you're not going to come with me, surely you can find my belongings and just quietly let me out? That would be great.' My legs start shaking with fatigue. I sit down on the bed and feel the weight of exhaustion descending on me again. 'Because I'm ready to go home.'

When I wake up after another long sleep, I realise from the way my head feels rinsed and fresh that another night and day must have passed. As far as I can tell, Chloe hasn't come back. Eventually I sit up. I'm still dirty and sweaty, but I feel tons better. Enough to make sure I've got my camera. Enough to be seriously annoyed. I've been left all alone in this strange, disconnected place by a man who may have helped me out of a tight spot, but now that I'm better, I need to get back to the real world.

Most of all I need to find Gustav.

I step out of the pretty bedroom and on to the landing. The sun canopy up above has been rolled up and the night sky is now a square of purple velvet. The moon is a perfect sickle surrounded by dots of stars. It's so beautiful it looks like a Venetian ceiling.

The courtyard below is lit by flickering candles, but it is deserted. I can only hear the murmur of voices coming from various places around the riad, and the odd burst of gentle laughter. I give myself a mental shake. The fever has lifted, both physically and mentally. I'm still desperate to get out. Polly will kill me when she catches up with me, but this strange pocket of a place doesn't seem so menacing now. After all, a switched-on New Yorker like Chloe wouldn't swap her existence for something nasty or illegal. It's just some kind of hippy commune. When I get my phone I'll find dozens of messages from Polly, an explanation from Pierre and some loving reassurance from Gustav. And then I'll get my ass over to London, or New York, or wherever he wants me to be.

I call softly into the silence. 'Tomas? Anyone?'

I'm drawn along the landing by the murmur of voices, and up a winding staircase which leads out on to the roof. The terrace is set out like a bar, with striped tents heaped with cushions arranged around the central atrium, low seats and tables with multicoloured, scented candles flickering.

The slight breeze on my cheeks cools me as I stare out at the jumble of rooftops where the washing lines and cooking pots and potted plants of each house are all dominated by the round white eye of a satellite dish.

Under a striped tent at the far end of the terrace I can see the source of the murmuring sounds. There is movement, and as I draw closer I can see there's a couple, no, three people, writhing on the cushions. I remember Chloe's invitation to spy. I'll take a couple of brief photos if the scenario presents itself, but decide to keep my distance. It could be the owners, after all, assuming all their guests are out.

Through the long lens I can see the long-haired boy I saw earlier playing the flute. He's lounging on his elbows. Two girls are swaying around him, pushing him down and pulling down his shorts to smother him with oils. The girls are already naked, except that both of them are wearing their filmy yashmaks, trimmed with sequins. They look fresh and alert and their eyes, heavily painted, are bright.

The Arabian version of a Venetian mask is somehow all the kinkier by comparison.

I take a picture and the quick flash distracts them. The huge female eyes ringed in blue kohl spot me. I can see no smile or facial expression, but both girls wave across the roof, then one of them takes the boy in her hands and starts to massage him into hardness. The other girl crawls over his face.

I take another picture. I can't resist. I know I'm in a hurry but this is the kind of surreal set-up I thrive on. There will be a soft moonlit wash to these shots. The secretive kinkiness of this evening compared with all that laid-back vibe of the daytime is seductive. It looks as if it's not just the living that's communal. Everyone seems at liberty to do what the hell they like, with whomever the hell they like. No wonder I can't drag Chloe away.

On the other side of the terrace, a boy in another tent is just entering his girl from behind. She, too, is veiled, and gazes calmly at me as my camera wanders up her limbs, over the formation of their two bodies. They pause for my benefit before retreating into their dream and going at it. None of them looks surprised to see me.

I turn back to the staircase. I really need to find my phone and my clothes, but I'll see if I can sniff out a few more scenes to film on my way down to the main door. I'm on to an incredible voyeuristic theme. Similar to those

Parisian photographs of the prostitutes awaiting their punters, and the actors in the château. But brought up to date. A modern *Arabian Nights*. An exotic, subversive new exhibition is forming in my mind. I could even get Chloe to contribute, if only I knew where she was.

But as I glance around this balmy rooftop, with its swaying potted palms, the velvet sky and the distant mountains draw my eye and I come to my senses. Somewhere between here and that horizon, Maria and Polly are pacing and fretting in the ashram, wondering where I am.

My throat goes tight. However lovely this riad is – if you're in the mood – I long, more desperately than I've longed since I was a child trapped in the house on the cliffs, to be gone. To be far away with my Gustav.

A burst of party laughter reaches me from the street below. The thought of Polly, of Gustav, clings where the others have fallen away.

They'll be wondering where I am.

I leave the lovers and run down the staircase. But I've no idea which of the keyhole arches punctuating the gallery leads to my room. I peer into the warm darkness of each one, see nothing, hearing only the faint sounds of breathing or whispering.

This must be it, on the opposite side of the gallery. I recognise the large red lantern flickering outside. The curtain has been pulled aside just as I left it. But there are voices behind the screen concealing my bed. A man's deep voice murmuring, then laughing.

Goddammit. I'm going to have to walk right in. All very well photographing copulating couples with the protection of my camera. Quite another trying to pull my belongings out from under their hot, sweaty bodies.

I step into the room. It is not in darkness as it was before. The cupboard has fallen open and the fluorescent internal strip light spreads its garish gleam into the room. A square of light flickering by the fireplace comes from a small television, as does the murmuring and moaning.

Maybe I'm in the wrong room, but I can't resist having a look anyway. There are clothes tightly packed in the cupboard which don't belong to me. Dresses and shirts and business suits which look too formal or dressy for the hippy vibe going on here. I grope along to the end. The last hanger falls off with a rustle of cellophane and a white shirt drops into my hands.

I gasp out loud. Who have I been kidding, rushing around staring at everything through a lens, letting my passion for photography blind me to why I'm really here?

The tentative calm of the last half-hour is splintered like glass.

Because on the shirt is a silver tiepin engraved with the initials GL.

Why is it here? Does that mean Gustav is here? The hopeful question dissolves as soon as I ask it, because wafting off the shirt and the cellophane, getting behind my eyes, that cloying, sickly scent is seeping into everything, just as it seeped through that garish apartment in New York.

This is the wedding shirt that was in Margot's apartment, only now it's wrapped in the same protector used by Gustav's dry-cleaner in Manhattan. My hands shake as I check the sleeves. I can't remember whether it was the left or the right that the cufflink was in before, but it no longer matters. Because there are two cufflinks now. The matching pair. The odd link that Gustav kept has been retrieved from his cigarette box in our bedroom and reunited with its twin.

There's a burst of female laughter from the television, and then a deep voice as familiar to me as my own.

'So this is a lovely surprise, but – hey, you little minx! Get this off my eyes!'

The shirt drifts like a corpse to the floor. I step closer and there is Gustav, close up on the video. He's smiling, but he's wearing a leather executioner-style mask which covers his head and his eyes but leaves his mouth free. A lock of his glossy black hair has somehow escaped and fallen over one eye.

A mosquito dances past me. I bat it away and peer closer. This is a video shot in Baker Street. It must date from when he lived there. I recognise the bare panels and plasterwork behind him. Tomas or Chloe or someone who knows I'm here must have gotten hold of it, and the shirt, but how? Why? Is it for my benefit? Could this be Pierre's doing? Does he know I'm here? Has he set this up for some reason? Or is it another warning?

Danger. Ashram. Go back to Polly.

'This is to teach me for leaving you, isn't it?' Gustav chuckles on the screen.

My mind is whirling, torn between the voices of the two brothers. The filmed Gustav, and Pierre's inexplicable text and garbled phone call.

Nausea tightens and loosens in my stomach like a fist. Gustav's voice is so clear that he could be right next to me. He's fixed inside that television, still married to Margot.

Don't look. Don't look. Polly's voice, pleading with me.

I back away blindly. I'm his fiancée and this video reminds me that, at this moment, I don't know where he is or who he's with. I bash my shin painfully against the coffee table, and as I bend to rub my leg, I notice the antique copy of *Les Liaisons Dangereuses* which Gustav gave me in Paris. I frown. It should be in my luggage, back at the ashram, but maybe it dropped out of my bag in the souq and Tomas retrieved it. I'm surprised he didn't stash it away with my phone. He probably thought it was some old tat.

I pick it up absently, slipping my finger into the page where Gustav wrote the loving inscription I've committed to memory.

Serena. Ma chérie. Ma femme.

'These handcuffs are too tight.' Still smiling, the Gustav on the video tries to twist round. 'Unlock them, darling. I'm happy to play. But no punishment.'

There is a pause on the film. The diesel engine of a black cab rumbles down Baker Street. Nothing has changed. Ten years ago taxis sounded the same. People walked, shopped, ate, visited the Sherlock Holmes museum nearby. But that was Gustav's old house. His old life, when he called someone else 'darling'.

Back in this riad in Marrakesh, the only sound I can hear, apart from the sickening thump of my pulse, is the whine of that mosquito. I swipe at it and it spirals into the candle and frazzles to a crisp.

I haven't got time to work out why this film is playing. I need my phone. I need to get home to Gustav. I need to contact Pierre and ask him what he meant about not leaving the ashram. And where the hell Gustav is now.

Footsteps approach along the landing. Small, tripping female steps in some kind of clacking heel, accompanied by the thump of slower, masculine ones. No one wears shoes here, and certainly not high-heeled, clacking ones. Instinct and fear make me hide.

I crouch down behind the *mushrabiyya* screen, but that places me close to the TV where my fiancé is so far away in time and space, smiling as his ex-wife prepares him for a sex session.

His gorgeous, sexy mouth, the one that knows exactly which parts of me to kiss, the mouth that was running over me and passing grapes between his lips to mine just over a week ago in our luxurious eyrie in Paris, looks just the same. Relaxed, open wide with amusement. He hasn't aged one jot in the last ten years.

And there's such tenderness in his face. The tenderness I thought was reserved for me. His tongue is running across his teeth because he's anticipating something really good to happen.

He's enjoying all of it. Being tied up and blindfolded. That's how he used to be.

There's another pause. A pair of hands wearing black leather mittens appears from the side of the screen. They move over Gustav's hair, stroke down his face, his jaw. My stomach tightens as a black leather finger runs across his mouth, pushes into it, lets him bite it.

'They could walk in on us at any minute,' Gustav mutters to his invisible companion, but the finger presses against his mouth to silence him. 'Take these off, my love. I can do this so much better hands-free!'

Part of me prays that it's not her. That someone else is in this film with him. Maria Memsahib, Crystal, any damn woman. Anyone would be preferable to seeing him with Margot.

As he pulls at the handcuffs, the camera focus is pulled back slightly and now we can see all of Gustav. He's tied to a hook in the wall near the window, which is why he can't brush the hair out of his eyes, and he's wearing a business suit.

Also, he's wearing a scarlet tie. It's printed with tiny hearts in a darker red, so small you would only know they were hearts if you were pressed up close to him.

I gave him that tie for a belated Valentine's Day present this year.

Now Gustav looks like a stranger. Distant and

professional, like he did when I first knew him. I don't know this man. He's unutterably sexy. I know he has a beautiful, strong body beneath that formal exterior. But he's not mine any more. He's gone back to her.

Every one of my nightmares has come true. Every one of his promises has been broken.

Which makes my life over the last year utterly meaningless. Dashed by one malicious detail.

Margot's hands are pulling his shirt out of the waistband of his trousers and touching his flies, kneading the warm shape she has found, closing round it to make it grow.

I fall forward on my knees to study the date that is blinking faintly in the bottom corner of the picture. I drop the little book just as the leather mittens start pulling off Gustav's jacket. My fiancé grins and gives a theatrical shiver as his jacket flies off, followed by the tie.

This film was taken just ten days ago. The day he arrived in London from Paris.

The footsteps echoing on the tiled landing stop. Someone comes into the room, and when I see who it is I start sobbing with distress and relief.

'Tomas! Help me! Something terrible's going on! I need my phone and I've got to get out of here!'

'You can't go now! We're just getting to the good bit!'

A figure slides out from behind Tomas, blowing a plume of aromatic smoke from a long thin spliff. Like all the other girls in the riad tonight, the woman is veiled, but even with her face covered I would recognise those nasty cat's eyes anywhere. She pauses the video then bends to rip the cellophane off the discarded white shirt and drapes it over her arm.

'Welcome to my pleasure palace, Serena! Gustav is going to love it when he moves in. But oh dear. We're not looking after you very well, are we? You look absolutely dreadful.

Gustav would be revolted if he could see the state you're in.' Margot drawls into the silence. 'Want to take a look in my magic mirror? Puffy eyes, cracked lips, sweaty hair. Such a shame.'

I try to get up. My ankle bone digs into the silver anklet. 'It's that poison I drank.'

Margot pushes me back down and taps ash into a copper ashtray. 'Nonsense. That was merely iced tea with a pretty vicious twist. Admittedly, Tomas was a little careless with the dosage. Those little trees in the courtyard? Those are daturas. I've been cultivating their sap for perfume while I've been living here. Lovely scent, isn't it? But it can also be fatal. Mythology has it that witches used to take the drug so they could fly. But I prefer the idea of wronged wives using it to commit murder, which is why it's known as the jealousy tree.'

I realise that my mouth is parched and I couldn't get up even if I wanted to. 'What do you want from me?'

Margot steps over me and arranges herself on the bed like some kind of multi-armed and multi-headed goddess. A clinging black kaftan is slashed low between her high, full breasts, and slit up the sides of her legs, which she folds into a lotus position. Her snaky black hair is hidden by the folds of an elegant black turban. I can see that from afar she is still mesmerising. If I can't take my eyes off her, no wonder Pierre, and Tomas, and those other toy boys, are all in her thrall.

'What I want, Serena, is for you to fuck off back to whatever little backwater you came from. I want you to get it into your empty little airhead that Gustav is mine, not yours.'

I grasp the edge of the table. 'Gustav hates you, Margot. Really, really hates you for everything you did to him and his brother.'

'And that's just the way I like him. Full of healthy hatred.' She inhales deeply then whistles another plume of herbal smoke straight at my face. 'You wouldn't understand, Serena, but there's a fine line between love and hate, and he's always crossing it.'

I lift my left hand. The diamond ring picks up the flicker of the little candles. 'See this? We're going to be married.'

'You poor, deluded idiot.' I see the sway of her high, round white breasts under her kaftan as she lifts the veil to relight the joint. Her red lips purse around the filter, wet with her saliva. 'You think that ring is the answer to all your prayers, don't you? But all it means is that Gustav went to a shop one day and bought you a trinket to keep you in his bed.'

I push my hands between my knees to stop them shaking. 'That's bullshit. I'm his future. You're his ugly past.'

'Not what this priceless little piece of film says. Give it up, why don't you?' Two smoke rings float towards me and then split into wavy question marks. I keep my eyes on her hands, bony and old, rather than the swell of her breasts and that cruel, sexy mouth. 'That wedding's never going to happen. Just admit defeat. You're young. The world's your oyster. There are cute red-blooded males right here in this riad who are primed and horny and yours for the taking. I know. I've road-tested them all. But you and Gustav? So wrong. The minute you're separated you're led into all kinds of temptation, and sure as night follows day, he walks straight back into my arms.'

I shake my head. 'He would rather scratch his own eyes out than do that.'

'Still she protests, when the evidence is right here? I knew you'd be difficult, you little bitch.' She reaches underneath one of the pillows and tosses something across the table. 'This is why you'll never be speaking to him again.'

It's a mobile phone. As the blood drains from whichever part of me is supposed to keep me breathing, I pick it up. The screen saver is my self-portrait, the one we have hanging in our apartment in New York.

'That's Gustav's phone!'

'Mine, now. But what a stroke of luck, eh? These phones store all the information these days, don't they? That's how I knew you were in Morocco. Which ashram. Delightful to discover that even my old protégée Maria was detailed to keep you safe, by the way, even though she's singularly failed. And finally we knew when you were coming into Marrakesh. A combination of detective work, deception and devilry. Ears and eyes everywhere if you pay enough. Pierre made a big mistake to defect on me like that, but I needed someone he *would* talk to for information, and who better than his friend Tomas, who wandered into my Sapphix Bar one night.'

'Tomas told me he hasn't spoken to Pierre in weeks!'

'These mobile phones. Amazing how they keep us all connected, isn't it? One little call or text, and your world is, oh dear! Shattered! Once we'd located you in the market and organised that chance meeting, Tomas couldn't resist telling Pierre he'd just got his hands on you! He's not going to be cheated out of his prize this time. Pierre was going to set you up together in New York, but he wimped out of that plan, as we know. So our Tomas is going to go where no Pierre has gone before, and just to make sure no one can stand around arguing the toss he'll make a visual record of his own. We'll make sure all the information, and the sexy footage we're going to make of you and Tomas making out, will filter back to Gustav eventually.'

'That's not going to happen. Come on, Tomas. Why would you want me when you've got the gorgeous Chloe? This is all a crock of shit!' I stare at Gustav's phone and scroll through the incoming messages. 'Look! Gustav sent me a text!'

'Such defiance from the condemned woman.' Margot runs a nail down Tomas's leg. 'You really don't get what's going on here, do you? Tomas will do whatever I tell him to do, especially when it means putting you in your place. He's already hard just thinking about it. And as for Gustav trying to reach you, I'm afraid *I* sent you that text! Just to keep you off our backs.'

I stare down at the phone again. In my confusion I can't remember exactly what Pierre said in that muffled phone call, but it was *before* I bumped into Tomas. So he was trying to warn me.

I scroll through my increasingly anxious, unanswered texts as if somehow Gustav will magically answer them. 'No wonder he sounded so brusque. Oh, God, Margot. What have you done with him?'

'If a little text message hurts you so badly, wait until I've finished telling you – sorry, *showing* you – how much worse his behaviour is when your back is turned. Your Gustav and I have been celebrating the old times, as only we know how.'

The candles and the paused television screen light up her grinning face. Even semi-veiled she looks like a terrible, beautiful skull, and now I can see that her eyes look even more slanted and catlike than when I saw her in New York.

I hold the phone so tight I can feel it heating up in my hands. It's all I have of Gustav right now. That and the diamond ring.

'I'll do anything, Margot. Anything. Just tell me Gustav is OK.'

'You have nothing to offer me. Just watch the film. Trust me, you won't be offering yourself as any kind of deal or sacrifice for that man once you've seen this. You'll want nothing more to do with him.' She crosses one long, skinny leg over the other. 'You'll be begging to forget him. Maybe you'll finally see sense and go downstairs to play with boys and girls your own size.'

There is a sudden chorus of *muezzin* over the rooftops, calling the faithful from their minarets, a kind of syncopated summons as each is slightly out of step with the next. The mournful sing-song echoes over the city and up into the sky. Oh, I'm so far away from home.

Wherever home is.

Tears are spilling out of my eyes. 'All this time you've followed me?'

'Such hard work. But see the fruits of my labours! He's still so handsome, isn't he? Gustav, I mean, not Pierre.' Margot strokes Gustav's crisp cotton shirt. 'Maybe Pierre will get his heart's desire after all, once you've accepted that Gustav is mine again.'

My head is whirling. Two weeks ago Pierre was assuring me that Gustav would never be unfaithful. Then he was telling me to get back to Polly and a place of safety. But surely he can't have known how far Margot and Gustav had already gone?

'All those times he sneaked out early in the morning. Those mysterious business trips. That night in Italy? Gustav was with you?'

'Better and better! You had suspicions already!' Margot wriggles delightedly on the bed. 'So this video doesn't altogether shock you?' She runs the white shirt under my nose. 'I've got all his old shirts, ready for when he gets here. Of course, this is my favourite, the one he wore when we got married, but all these years the missing cufflink has pained me. But no more. Gustav has returned its pair. The cufflinks have been reunited, just like him and me!'

'He was supposed to be meeting the buyer of Baker Street.' I cough to try to erase the sick quiver in my voice.

Margot flicks at the silver cufflinks. 'Well, he did meet her. Because the buyer is me!'

Another mosquito must have found its way in here because she starts scratching her arm.

'He knew you were the buyer all along? He told me he only dealt with the sale through agents.'

'Details, details! No, he didn't know I was the buyer at first. But since the two of you came bursting into my apartment with the feather it's been so easy. I'll do *whatever* it takes. I'm even using the money Gustav gave me in the divorce to buy back my own house.' Margot gives a sudden wheezy cough and takes a little bottle of pills out of some hidden pocket. I notice that she has a rash of midge bites up one of her arms. 'I never wanted his money. Not really. I love that man. I loved that house. That life was ours, and we were happy. I want every single bit of it back.'

I try to stand, but Tomas comes and puts his arms round me, pulls me on to the bed.

'You should watch this,' he murmurs in my ear. 'There's more to come.'

'Yes! Enjoy the show! Gustav Levi, in our old house, with me, enjoying himself!' Margot gulps down a tablet with a miniature bottle of some colourless liquid. The Moroccan darkness seeping through the house is a smothering blanket. 'I've got him tied up just like I used to, and he's getting hard, just like he used to, see? That big wonderful part of him is about to be exposed. There's no trickery, Serena. Gustav was alone with me, being aroused by me, by these very hands!'

She waggles them like a clown. Just like she did when she was mocking her puppet Pierre. The nightmare is crystallising around me. The tangle of Pierre, Gustav, Margot. The unholy trinity. No way in for anyone else.

Tomas squeezes me harder. My breath is coming in tiny

bursts, like a bird that's fallen out of its nest. My hands rest on the carved sandalwood table, stretched towards the television. I am alert now. The blood tingles in my fingers and toes, my hair prickles on my scalp. I'm not sweating now. I'm aware that the night is hot and stuffy, but my skin is extraordinarily cool. This is what the fight-or-flight instinct must feel like. But which is it to be? Fight for my fiancé, who's already lost to me? Or flight? Back to – where?

Margot's black eyes are glinting at me above her veil so intently my skin goes up into goosebumps.

'I was going to let you watch the whole thing on your own, but I couldn't resist seeing your reaction!' Her eyes narrow triumphantly as Tomas plays the recording. 'Watch this, princess!'

The hands on the video undo the trousers and yank them down. Gustav bites on his tongue, trying not to grin too widely. He doesn't want to give too much away. He struggles with the handcuffs, makes a show of resistance, but he doesn't flinch as the mittens come back and pull down his boxers. Quite the opposite. He goes very still, obviously relishing the pulsing pleasure as the hands massage him to hardness until it's standing proud and stiff.

Nausea tips inside me to see the familiar softening in his face, his mouth murmuring something filthy at his companion that I can't hear.

Pleased with their work in arousing him, the hands play-fully smack his bare bottom and then they take hold of his hips and pull him back so that he is forced to bend slightly against the tug of the handcuffs. I must have lost concentra-tion for a moment, because there's a sudden sharp whisking sound on the screen, and although I don't focus in time to see it land on him, there's the unmistakable slap of a whip.

I stare at Gustav again. The smile has disappeared. His

head whips back in surprise, and an angry shadow crosses his face. 'For God's sake! What are you doing!'

Thank God. He is going to put a stop to this in a minute.

But this is Margot's cue to appear full-size for the first time in front of the screen, smiling and spinning in circles like a dervish for the camera before stopping dead and putting her finger to her lips as if I, the voyeur, am about to warn him.

She's behind you!

Within those peeling and panelled walls, far away in London, Margot has stolen my fiancé. She's dressed all in black leather, including a cat mask, studded collar and the black laced basque I tried on once, when I was snooping in the chalet in Lugano last autumn.

The white expanse of her throat and ribbed chest is bare and bony, and then there are the cartoon breasts, perched up high and round like hard, unripe fruit, their unnatural roundness accentuated by the black pointed cups of the basque.

Still prancing for the camera, she produces as if from thin air the thin black switch she has just used, with its delicate tail of fine leather tassels. She flourishes it, as if this is a circus act.

And like a circus master, or a mime artist, she steps forward, her face huge in the lens as she adjusts the camera slightly and pulls the focus closer in. Then she dances backwards and curls her fingers to beckon it, us, to come nearer, and to watch some more. She steps behind Gustav, who is sideways on to the camera. She keeps her eyes on us, the viewers, to make sure we are watching as she turns his bottom towards us and we can see the faint stripe already visible from the first strike.

Then with the merest flick of her wrist, she brings the whip down on him again, so hard that we can see the flesh

266

tremble beneath the blow. His head jerks back as the whip stripes its punishment across him and seems to sink down as if gouging into his flesh. What shocks me is that there is no shouting out or objection this time. His shoulders seem to sink, to submit to the whipping. There's a slump in the line of his spine that I've never seen before.

On the film, Margot unpeels the whip from the dent it has made in his buttock and Gustav bites his lip, so hard that blood starts to ooze from his lower lip.

I moan out loud as a third strike comes down. Again the chiselled planes and angles of his face lie still, the white teeth biting again into the already bloody lip. Tomas leans forward and presses the pause button for the second time.

'Need to see more, Serena?'

I shake my head, bending over as the nausea surges up my throat. Tomas sits back down, stroking between my shoulder blades.

'Too bad. Keep her there, Tomas. She has to see it all. How easy it was to get my husband back.' Margot shifts further up the bed, as if she can't bear to come any nearer to me. 'She will watch this film if it kills her.'

'Let me go!' My voice is muffled with tears. 'I just need to get back to Polly!'

I bat uselessly at Tomas. He holds me more firmly, winding one arm to pull me close to his tough, warm body, the other clutching my wrist, making my silver bracelet dig into my skin.

'Just let her finish this. I'm right here. I'll help you,' Tomas murmurs, his breath brushing hot in my ear. 'It's for your own good. You were never going to win the battle between those two. She was never going to give up. They will always end up together. And I'm right here to catch you. I'll show you how you can get your life back.'

'You can't force me to watch,' I growl, trying to pull

267

away. But he grips my wrists and pulls me against his chest. I can hear his heart drumming up against my spine.

'You might enjoy it. It's really dirty.' His mouth moves across my cheek. 'Margot's fucking good, you know. It turns *me* on, just watching!'

'That's because you've learned from the best, Tomas! Serena Folkes is your consolation prize, now that I have Gustav, but still you'll never find anyone who can match up to me. Just like poor Pierre.'

Margot laughs softly. The mention of Pierre brings back brief, snapping images, changing each time my tired eyelids blink, but instead of filling me with dread I welcome them. If I focus on him, I can forget what I've just seen Gustav doing. It's like peering through the tiny viewfinder of a toy camera I was given once. Each time you clicked the pretend shutter there would be a new picture. A snow-covered chalet. A camel in front of the Giza pyramids. A ballet dancer. All tinted in bright colours and tricking you into believing you were peering at something real.

So there's Pierre, or rather his mask, looming over me under the canopy of a gondola. Then he's in that courtyard in Paris, the scaffolding tumbling off the apartment building behind him like bandages off a wound. Then he's standing in a hotel corridor, holding up a pair of red shoes.

When I try to picture Gustav, he's contorted and fractured, as if there's a splinter in my eye.

'Pierre Levi did find someone to match up.' I try again to twist away from Tomas, but he yanks my hair hard to keep me in place. 'He fell in love with me.'

'A poor second, that's all. A cheap imitation. Keep hold of her, Tomas. She'll be yours for the taking when she realises she's lost.' Margot presses play then leans back as the screen flickers to life. 'If she doesn't want to watch, at least make her listen to every last gasp of pleasure!'

As if to interrupt her, Gustav's voice is harsh on the screen. 'I thought you understood my thoughts on punishment! No more bondage. No more whipping.'

The real Margot sitting beside me chuckles. Her screen self strokes the whip tenderly up Gustav's buttocks, tickles it round his hardness until it stiffens and jumps in response, then she trails it round to his jaw, runs it between his lips and flings it on to the floor.

'That's better, my love. Obeying me, for a change.' He nods and his mouth spreads open in a wide smile. 'I told you we don't need whips for our pleasure. So why don't you untie me so I can get my hands on you properly?'

I don't care any more. The tears are hot and thick and my sobs choking me as on the film Margot unlocks one of the cuffs, takes Gustav's hand, and places it on her own bare flank. She kicks at his legs so that he stumbles to his knees, pulling hard on the remaining cuff to keep his balance and slightly dislodging the hook in the wall.

I feel sick to hear the crack of his knees against the parquet floor, but as the truth of it sinks in, a strange, tingling numbness replaces the flow of blood in my veins. I have no energy to struggle or run, but Tomas tightens his arms around me just in case and I'm vaguely aware of his strength and heat. I'm even oddly glad of the restraint. Without it I might just crumble into little pieces.

On the film, Margot glances once more at the camera, smiles beneath her catlike mask, then she spreads open her thighs. And with all the class of a pole dancer she pushes her naked crotch into his face.

'Watch what Gustav does to me now,' Margot gloats, leaning forwards to study the action, her chin resting on her knuckles. 'Watch how hungry he is for me.'

On the screen, she weaves her leather fingers through Gustav's hair and pulls him closer, wriggling impatiently. I see his free hand running down from her bottom and catching on the top of the thigh boots. His fingers pluck at the tight leather, then move up again over the nearest white butt cheek, up the crack between. I see his other hand jerking at the cuff imprisoning his wrist. He's pulling the hook a little further from the old panelled wall. He pauses with his mouth and nose almost buried inside her. He seems to be sniffing for her scent.

That's his way. I know how he does it. He keeps the tension racked up until I'm begging him to do it. He teases his lover until the first electric touch ignites her.

Except that Margot is his lover now. Not me. He is running his tongue over his lower lip to moisten it, and he is going to taste another woman. Not me.

'Hey, take these silly gloves off. They're catching in my hair,' Gustav murmurs on the screen. 'I want to feel those lovely fingers on me. Your tiny wrists.'

I shut my eyes, and all I can hear from the screen is the slight metallic clink of the cuff as Gustav shuffles closer to her on his knees. As I'm about to cover my ears, too, I can also make out the loud rev of a car on screen, parking outside the house.

Margot's hand snakes out and turns my face towards the television as those moist licking sounds go on and on and on.

'See his mouth on me? Oh, so good feeling his tongue on me after six long years!' Margot is crooning. Her hand sneaks down between her legs. 'Hear that? How wet I am? Right now, as well as in that film. I'm as hot for him as ever. That's our thing, you see. We always did that afterwards, you know? When everyone had gone. He'd be on his knees licking me. His way of saying thank you.'

I have nothing left. Nothing except my sense of hearing to witness my fiancé's betrayal with his ex-wife. I can shut

270

my eyes, smash the TV, but the image of him on his knees with Margot's pussy in his face will forever be seared on my mind.

'Don't you just love it when he does that with his teeth? I call him my pet vampire. When he nips on your clit, ooh, makes you scream, doesn't it? Have to be careful when little brother's asleep down the hall, of course!'

Tomas presses close to me and chuckles in my ear. 'And how ironic is this? You pushed your fanny into my face just like that, at the Club Crème. Just think. If your boyfriend – *that* boyfriend, by the way, the one in the film who's lapping at his ex-wife – if he hadn't walked into the room that day you would have stood still and let me lick you till you came. Don't deny it. You were up for anything.'

'You tell her, Tomas. Time her halo slipped off.'

Margot leans back, and as she watches my fiancé Gustav licking her on the screen, her arm moves between her legs until she's bucking against her own hand.

'Seen enough?' she gasps. 'Or do you want to see the bit where I untie his other hand and he attacks me, so starved of a decent woman, the poor man, and then the bit where he has me, again and again, on that hard wooden floor, all the time crying out for me like he used to. "Margot, my darling Margot!"'

Her head tips back and her hips give a little final convulsing twitch.

'Shut up! Shut your yapping mouth!' I jump to my feet and kick at the television until the screen cracks and breaks apart with a satisfying, elongated smashing of all its parts. 'You win. Just let me go. I need to get back to Polly. And then I need to speak to Gustav, face to face.'

'The same face that was buried in me a few sweet days ago? Well, you can't. And he won't.'

Margot doesn't even look at the broken television, now

a scattering of black shards across the floor. She lights up a new joint, puffing blue smoke which hangs in ribbons in the stifling night air.

'He wouldn't just leave me without a word! What about the silver chain? The golden locket he gave me?' I start pulling at the diamond ring, but my fingers are swollen and hot and it won't come off. 'What about our wedding? He doesn't do anything without some kind of deal or contract. He at least owes me an explanation!'

'Oh, such indignation! You really are even more stupid than I thought you were.' Margot sighs and holds up her hand. 'Time to show you how deadly serious I am about getting rid of you. Hold her still, Tomas. Give me the scissors.'

Tomas holds me like a vice. The blades glint in the candlelight as she snips them in front of my face. I am so totally terrified that not one part of me is able to move. She really is going to kill me.

I fall back against Tomas, trying to communicate some kind of plea to him, but he only twists my arms more painfully behind my back. Margot puts her joint into the ashtray and opens the scissors.

'He calls you Rapunzel, doesn't he? Well, let's see how that particular fairy tale ends.'

She darts forward, and with one snip under the topknot she has cut off my hair.

I jerk backwards so quickly that the scissors are knocked out of her hands, but I'm too late. It's all gone.

'Just an ugly little runt beneath it all, aren't you? He won't look at you twice. So I'll spell it out for you one more time, Serena dearest, if you'll just stop snivelling. There's no more Gustav. No more boyfriend. I met with my husband in London. Behind your back. We had rough, nasty sex just like old times, in our old house. *Behind your*

272

back. And by the way, he also knows I'm showing you this film. He doesn't *care*, Serena. He was a bit cross when I stole his phone, but *tant pis*. He doesn't give a flying fuck what you think. Because he's mine again.'

A red mist literally drops in front of my eyes and I lunge towards her, my hands out like claws, my teeth bared. Tomas tries to pull me away, his arms tight around my waist again, but I pull against him, trying to get close enough to hit her. She shifts back into the pillows, putting her hands up, but instead of hitting her I kick at the little book on the floor.

'So why isn't he with you now? It's been ten days since you – since that film!' I yell, my voice infuriatingly strangled. 'What have you done with him?'

'I could tell you he's got business to tie up in London, you know what a workaholic he is, but that would be lying. He didn't want to come anywhere near you, that's why he's not in this room tonight. All you need to know is that he's waiting for me.'

'Where? I asked you where?'

I kick at the book again, and the pages flutter open.

'Tomas! Pick that up!' Margot tosses her joint into the ashtray. She tips another handful of pills out of the bottle and swallows them. Whatever she's taking only makes her black eyes glitter all the more, her face grow even whiter, despite the Moroccan sunshine that beats down day after day. 'You stupid, stupid girl!'

'Where is he, Margot?'

She slams her hands down on the bed.

'He doesn't want you to find him!' She takes the book off Tomas and folds it open against her breasts. 'He doesn't love you or want you. He never did. How could he love you, a little ginger alley cat, when he has me? He didn't want to let me out of his sight, but I said I had to show you the film personally. I knew how much I would enjoy

273

putting you through that, because I am so very mean, but I also wanted to make sure you knew exactly what the score is now.'

'And what *you* don't get is that I love Gustav. He's done the worst thing he could possibly have done, and I can't forgive him. But I have to see him!' The sobs choke me and Tomas puts his hands on me again. 'Just one more time!'

'How the hell did he put up with you and your whining all this time? You are making me tired. So tired.'

'At least give this back to me!' I grab the book off her and open it to the page where Gustav's italic writing flows.

Margot doesn't bother to read the inscription. She falls back against the cushions, her eyes fluttering, but then they snap open and are as black and poisonous as ever. She drops the mobile phone on the floor. 'Oh, for God's sake, Tomas, take her away!'

'You still want me to keep the riad locked?' Tomas asks, pulling at me and lifting me up into his arms as easily as if I'm a bouquet of flowers. 'She stays here?'

'Until I say otherwise, yes. She's all yours. Get her drunk or something. Do whatever you want and keep doing it until she comes to her senses.' Margot picks up the SIM card from the wreckage of the phone and throws it into the candle flame. 'And make sure you record every minute of it. I want something graphic and unforgettable to show Gustav.'

'This can't be happening!' I start to sob. 'We were getting married!'

'This says not.' She taps the book, the black sapphire glittering like a beetle shell. 'Take a look at what my husband has written.'

'Gustav bought this for me in Paris just two weeks ago. This shows how wrong you are about him. About all of this!' I snatch the book from her, the leafy pages fluttering

274

uselessly as I struggle to open it. 'Whatever you may think you're showing us on this film, he wrote me a loving message, and you can't erase that. He called me his wife.'

I run my fingers over the ink inscription, somehow hoping to feel still the warmth of the hand that wrote it.

'Let's hear the loving message he wrote to you, then, shall we?'

I look down at the words, written in our special book. It's the same date. But not the same book, and not the same message.

This one says *Margot. Ma petite amie. Ma femme.*

Margot scratches at the bite on the inside of her arm. She scratches so hard that she draws spots of blood.

'See? The wedding is off.'

CHAPTER ELEVEN

I struggle and kick, but Tomas carries me down to the next landing. Over the balustrade I can see that Chloe and the others have been out somewhere but are piling into the candlelit courtyard, pulling off hooded cloaks but wearing long see-through kaftans similar to Margot's, in jewel-bright colours. They are still veiled, which gives them an ethereal look as they settle down to pour clear liquid from the spouts of elegant silver pitchers straight into each other's mouths. Chloe must have taught them the technique from those tequila-drinking sessions in the Sapphix Bar. They drink and smoke and start swaying their heads to a sound that is barely music, just a kind of low drumbeat.

Chloe lifts her head, but she is not looking at me. She is glaring straight at Tomas.

'She's jealous because you're with me tonight.' Tomas grins down at her. 'Take no notice. She knew the score when we came here. Free love. No exclusivity.'

I try to catch her eye. I have to make some kind of connection, however fuzzy, with this girl. Chloe glances at my hand, the fingers clawed desperately to hold the balustrade. She meets my eyes. She must be able to see what's happened. Surely there's something there, a gleam behind those huge blank eyes. Recognition? Hope? Fear?

I lean away from Tomas and mouth it. 'Help me, Chloe.'

'Let's get you to the reward room.'

Tomas carries me down a short passage and into another room, bigger than the one I was in before. The big bed has been turned back, the white pillows plumped up, and the clean, pressed sheets are so inviting. It has been lit with some more lanterns, goatskin stretched across wavy iron frames and pierced with holes so that the candlelight shines through. Although the air is warm and fragrant with an incense so strong my head is swimming again, I start to shiver uncontrollably.

'I've lost him, Tomas. I've lost Gustav!' I sink down on to the bed and the tears take over.

Tomas pulls the curtain across the entrance, and the music and voices from the courtyard trail upwards. He takes his shirt off and drops it on a chair, then fiddles with what looks like a CD player in the corner. Various little red and green spots light up on the silver casing, but he doesn't seem to have noticed that the music hasn't started. He comes back to the bed and holds me against his chest while I sob until my throat is red raw.

'You're safe with me.'

He smiles and pulls me towards him. He starts stroking my back and my arms and then his fingers are under the flimsy slip, wandering across the warm skin on my stomach. I feel my body quiver in response.

'I'm so tired, Tomas. Please leave me alone,' I murmur, trying to push him away. I raise my hands to feel my shorn hair, but I daren't. 'I meant it the first time you asked me, and I mean it now. If I can't have Gustav, I don't want anyone.'

He's strong, and heavy, and now he's pushing the negligee up over my breasts.

'You've been promised to me, Serena. And I know how dirty you can be. God, Pierre will go mad with jealousy when I show him the next instalment!'

'I'm not some kind of trophy. I said get off!' I try to cover myself. 'All those kinky things, I only do them when Gustav is with me.'

'Well, I'm here, not him. And you don't have to do anything. Just lie back. It's my turn now!' He rips off one of the spaghetti straps. 'And we're going to film it all, just to make sure Gustav gets the picture!'

Tomas is too strong for me, pressing me down into the pillows. I'm dizzy, and sick, but my mind is whirring like an overwound clock. Suddenly it clicks into place.

'Not here. Let's get away, and then we'll do whatever you want. Let's find Polly! You could have her, too!'

Tomas shakes his head and glances across the room. I'm so stupid. I thought Tomas had been fiddling with a CD player when we first came into the room. But that's not what it was. It's a movie camera, ready to create what Margot called his visual record, and the record button is on. He starts to rip my slip upwards from the hem.

'I'm going to have to stuff this into your mouth if you don't shut up!' he growls. 'I know Polly's given up sex.'

'For God's sake, Tomas!' I punch out at him. 'I knocked you back before, and I'm sorry, but I'm not going to let you force me. If it's sex you want, why don't you just walk down the landing and ask Chloe?'

'Quit yapping!'

I have to find the words to get through to him. 'I'm your friend! You're Polly's friend! You're supposed to be helping me!'

'You're not my friend. You're the bitch who rejected me,

and now you're the bitch with rubbish hair. I'll have you, because you've got a beautiful body. But no one else will want you now.'

My blood is throbbing in my ears, behind my eyes, almost deafening me. And my mind is working fast now. 'OK, OK, so if I give in, you know, if I let you do it, you'll help me escape?'

His blonde curls shake over his eyes as he pauses. This tangle-haired, sweaty look doesn't suit him. He's become the same dead-eyed, directionless dude as everyone else in this riad.

But whatever substances he's on, they haven't affected his strength.

'You don't do deals with me, Serena.' His lips are wet and thick as he starts to kiss down my neck. 'Sluts like you can't say no to a guy three times and get away with it.'

As he reaches behind me to lift the negligee over my head, I am dimly aware of a phone buzzing.

'That'll be Gustav!' I croak desperately, still stupidly wishing he'd call me. But Tomas leans across me and knocks the phone to the floor.

'Nope. That's my phone, not yours.'

The slip has come free and I feel the release of my breasts as they fall into his hands. I squirm and try to twist away, but that just pushes my breasts harder into his hands. He pinches both nipples until they are sparking with the kind of hot pain that will soon, very soon if I'm not careful, transmit pleasure to the rest of me.

'Christ, Tomas, look at yourself! You can have anyone you want. Chloe's crazy about you! This is all wrong, and you know it!'

His eyes are blank, wide and staring. 'This sex film is going to be such a turn-on!'

He pins my arms over my head so that he can lower his

blonde head over me. He snuffles his warm wet mouth over my breasts. He gets as far as grazing one sore nipple with his teeth, making me flinch and squeal in disgust, and then, like curtains opening over a brightly lit stage, I see it all once again, Gustav and Margot together on that screen. Horrific. Sickening. And so is what's happening right here. This guy is crazed with drugs, has a camera running, and he's about to rape me.

Swearing and cursing, I wrench my knee up and kick Tomas right in the balls and so damn hard that he screams, as they say, just like a girl.

I roll away and scoop up the phone. It's a text from Pierre.

Lay one finger on Serena and you're dead. We're getting her out.

I try to call him back, but he must be in some kind of trouble of his own because I just get voicemail again. I turn my back on Tomas as I text back.

I'm OK, P, but you have to hurry.

Several veiled figures jostle in the doorway. I tense, ready to strike or to run, and then I see Chloe stepping into the room.

'What have you done to her hair?' she gasps at Tomas, her vacant blue eyes finally registering me over the flimsy yashmak.

'How long have you been standing there?' I ask her, scrabbling to cover myself and grab my camera. Everything else is still missing. My phone. My clothes. My money.

'Long enough to see what he was doing to you. But I thought you wanted it. You know, that you were getting into the spirit of the riad. I didn't realise you were trying to fight him off,' she whispers, pulling off her veil. 'Thank you, Serena.'

'I didn't do it for you. Christ! You're welcome to him,' I mutter, swiping the little movie camera off its stand and taking it with me as I stumble to the door. 'I'm getting out of here before she catches me, and so should you. They'll totally brainwash you. Or worse.'

She crouches over the writhing figure of Tomas. The other two girls take hold of me from behind, hissing instructions through their veils. They are still wearing their outdoor cloaks.

'Come with us. Quick. With any luck, Margot's asleep, or in one of her drug-induced trances, but we don't want to be here when the police arrive.'

'You were absolutely sure of the facts when you called them?' asks the other one. 'Are they able to execute an arrest warrant all the way from London?'

'I'm no lawyer. But even if there's no extradition treaty they can get her for abduction and robbery right here in Marrakesh. You saw those kids. Some of them look under age. Add on the drug offences and they'll throw the book at her.'

They throw a hooded cloak over me to cover my semi-nakedness and pull me from the room. But as we run along the gallery, those tight, quick footsteps in their high heels clack across the roof above us, matching our progress, tapping slowly at first from the far side of the terrace where the striped tent was, then speeding up, running towards the staircase.

Margot's not asleep. She probably never sleeps.

'Get me away from her!' I sob,

The courtyard downstairs looks so peaceful with its cascading flowers, arched alcoves and glassy blue pool. How can Margot have created a haven so lovely on the outside, so ugly behind those screens? The other guests, or captives, are either asleep on the cushions, their veils and cloaks thrown aside, or they've crept away into the shadows to touch each other up in private.

The two hooded inmates hustle me across the courtyard

281

towards the main door. I glance up at the rectangular purple space of sky, as if any minute Margot will flap down from the roof terrace like a bat. But she doesn't appear. Nor do Tomas or Chloe.

The bolt slides back with a rusty screech. The hood is pulled down over my head so that I'm plunged into suffocating darkness, and I'm dragged away down the alleyway.

I don't know what is more petrifying. Falling into the hands of two new kidnappers and being dragged blindfold through the labyrinthine streets of Marrakesh, bashing my shoulders and elbows as we whisk round first one corner then another. Or the fact that my abductors have suddenly halted, when we don't appear to have gone very far, and are shoving me into what, from the echo of our footsteps and the dankness seeping through my cloak, must be some kind of cellar or storeroom.

I cower against the damp wall, imprisoned in my shroud. The riad was frightening enough, but now nobody, friend or foe, knows where I am. The drumming of my heart sounds like a boot kicking a body. There is urgent whispering close to me. My ears prick like a cat's. Something awful's going to happen. I'll never see Gustav again, or Polly, I can feel it. I'll never get the chance to put my hands round Margot's throat and squeeze—

Hands rove over my head. I flinch backwards and try to scream, attract attention somehow, but the cloth is sucked into my mouth and muffles me. Someone grips my shoulders to keep me still. The hood shifts across my face and panic surges through me again.

'My God, did you see her sweeping down from the roof terrace just as we got to the door? She nearly caught us!'

I take the thick, rough cloth of the hood and yank it away from my face. Although it's the middle of the night, the one lantern dangling above us seems blinding.

The two hooded figures are standing a few feet away from me. We're in some kind of dark corner. There's water running down the bricks. As I try to inch away, the figures swivel round and remove their hoods and veils, and when I finally see their dear, familiar faces, I crumple on to the cold, damp ground. My captors are Polly and Maria. I have never been so glad to see them.

'Oh, my God, your hair! She went at you with scissors! That madwoman could have killed you! No, no, babes, don't cry! We'll fix this!' Polly kneels down to fling her arms around me, tangling us both in the folds of our cloaks. 'Listen to me. We didn't meant to scare you, but there was no time! This disguise was the only way to merge with the others and get into the riad. It was Pierre's idea! Honestly, if anyone's scared half to death it's me! How do you think I felt when I turned round in the bazaar and you'd vanished? I'd only gone off to haggle for some earrings!'

I can't calm down. I can't stop shaking. 'I was lost, Pol. It was stupid of me to go off with Tomas, but it seemed like a coincidence, him popping up like that. I wasn't exactly overjoyed to see him, all I wanted was to find you and contact Gustav, but I was like a headless chicken by then, and Tomas seemed genuine. Even friendly. I thought he was helping me. I had no idea there was some kind of plan to abduct me.'

'Margot's had this luxury harem going for the last six years, apparently. Ever since she abandoned Pierre in that flat in New York and came to live here. She entices all those beautiful young things off the street wherever she finds them, promises them a free holiday then drugs them with some old witch's potion so that they're constantly high and constantly horny. The only thing she expects in return is that they pleasure her and each other, girls and boys alike, whenever she demands it!'

283

I lift my head sharply. 'They're all still in there, still high and horny. But I don't care about them. They were just cannon fodder while she waited for Gustav.'

'Maria, tell her what's been going on!' Polly glances across at Maria, my other rescuer.

Maria's chocolate eyes are unusually grave as she pulls us both to our feet. 'She was always a conniving bitch, but the word is she's losing it. Physically and mentally. I think that's why she's become so outlandish in her games and lies. Those house guests told us that she's addicted to some really strong medication and keeps disappearing back to New York for surgery of some sort. There's something wrong with her.'

Helpless rage surges through me.

'There's nothing wrong with her! She's done exactly what she set out to do, way back before Christmas. She's got Gustav back, and just to make sure I'll never touch him again, she's shown me every graphic detail of how she did it and then cut my hair off. So. Now I'm all alone again!'

'Don't be daft, honey, this isn't my feisty mare talking! You're not alone!' Polly shakes me, hard, glancing again at Maria. 'And you're safe! Margot could have really hurt you! You've had a lucky escape.'

'But it's such a terrible mess!' I try to focus on her lovely familiar face, those swimming-pool eyes the same colour as the hood, but everything is jumping and shaking around me. 'I don't know what to do, Pol. I've nowhere to go! I can't go back to London. Or New York. I loved him, Polly. He was my world, we were going to get married, and now he's gone!'

'Calm down. You're getting hysterical!' Polly pulls me close to her. 'Read my lips, Rena. Gustav hasn't left you. He's desperate to speak to you!'

'Don't give me that bullshit! Don't say his name!' My

voice is rising to a scream. 'I've seen on Margot's film how *desperately* that bastard wants to speak to me!'

'Be quiet, for God's sake! They'll come straight here and find us if you make that noise!' Polly shakes me. 'Listen to me, Rena. You've got it all wrong. Pierre texted me and explained everything—'

'Pierre told Tomas he was coming for me!' I pull at my hair and squeal in horror when I touch the ragged strands around my ears. 'Where is he? Is Pierre safe? He can tell me where Gustav is!'

Maria spins me round and presses her hand over my mouth. She wraps her other arm round me and brings me up very close, fixes her brown eyes on me, wide, unblinking, to calm me. I can see my wild-eyed reflection in the pools of her eyes.

'He can't come. He sent us. Now stop. Stop. You're upset, and hysterical, and no wonder. But you have to hold it together. We'll get you to the airport if that's what you want but I want you to breathe very deeply until you are calm.'

I stare back at her. My jaw feels rusty as I close my mouth. I grit my teeth in an effort to obey her command, and after another moment Maria removes her hand from my mouth.

'Can I trust you to be quiet now and listen to your cousin? You're scaring her.'

Polly is white. 'I've never seen you like this, Serena. Not even when you were a frightened little kid!'

'Well, she's done exactly what those people did to me when I was a kid, hasn't she? Cut off all my hair. And she's taken my Gustav. So yes, I'm scared out of my wits, Pol.' Hot tears rinse away the rage as I reach out for her. 'Help me. What do I do now?'

'You be quiet, and you listen to me.' Polly takes my hands warily. 'This situation was so serious that I actually found myself communicating with Pierre Levi. The night I lost you in the market, he got hold of the ashram's admin number to check you were safe, and when Angelique admitted you hadn't come back with me, Pierre told her he'd had this gloating voicemail from Tomas! If it wasn't for Pierre having details of the riad, and Tomas being such a weak link in Margot's web, you'd still be in there! They could have hurt you. Transported you overseas. Or worse – I had to believe him, Rena! It's been nearly three days! You and Gustav were both off the radar! We even thought you'd buggered off back to America on a whim. Then when I was dithering and not wanting to take his calls, Pierre went mad, going on about how precious you were, threatening to fly over from London to get you out of there himself. Maria told me not to be so stubborn. So I listened to Pierre, and did what he said, because I didn't want him coming here. I'm not ready to see him just yet.'

'So Pierre Levi meant every word he said to me in Paris? He loves me. He saved me.' My whole body starts shaking with sobs. 'Pity he couldn't have saved Gustav.'

'Don't even start down that road. It's too long.' Polly leans her forehead on mine. 'But Pierre's been coordinating all this like James Bond, all enigmatic messages and broken mobile signals.'

'And you were Miss Moneypenny?'

Right on cue, Polly's phone bleeps. She glances at Maria, who takes hold of me, and then, draping the hood back over her head, Polly steps into the alleyway to take the call.

I stare at Maria. 'I don't know what to do.' I can't breathe as the sobs squeeze at my ribcage again. 'I loved Gustav with all my heart, and now he's broken it!'

'Hush, *habibti*. You're making yourself ill. Everything will become clear.'

Polly ducks her head back into the alcove. 'We can get her to the airport now.'

286

'No, no, I can't, they've stolen my money!' My voice rises dangerously again. 'And my phone!'

'It's OK, honey. We've got your passport. But we're running out of time!'

I shrink away from her and flatten myself against the wet wall.

'Don't take me to the airport,' I whimper. 'I've nowhere to go!'

There's a brief pause. Heaven knows what they're thinking or saying, but then Maria puts her hood back on and arranges mine over my head. I fit myself into the folds of her tall, warm, curvy body as we step out into the street.

'That's it, Serena. You're exhausted, and you need rest. You're coming home with me.'

The sun is treacle on my skin. I shouldn't be out here, but I love the burning sensation. June is getting too hot for tourists to visit Morocco, but over the last few days the heat has melted me, little by little, until I'm reduced to the very last traces of humanity. I have a pulse, and all my senses, but apart from that I'm a scooped-out shell, washed up on this white towel, beside this big blue pool.

Heaven on the outside. Hell inside.

The others are all meditating in the prayer room at the moment, and there has been a vow of silence ever since we got back here. And that means everybody. Polly, Maria, Angelique now she's come back. And me.

The silence together with the emotional absence have been perfect therapy. Several times since we returned to the ashram they've tried to talk to me, and they've been near me when I need them, but the minute they mention Gustav or Pierre the hysteria rises in me again and I press my hands over my ears. I want to be alone. I probably look and sound demented, but I don't want to hear it. Any of it. I know what I saw in

287

that sickening film, and it's enough. My brain won't take in any more.

I can see the pain in their eyes, the confused, silent messages flashing between them, but it's not up to them to be pained or confused. I'm wrung out. No more lies. No more questions.

Polly sat me down as soon as I was calmer, forced me to look in a mirror and tidied up what was left of my hair. There's nothing for the straighteners to get a grip on, so my curls have come out to play. They hug my cheekbones and tuck in close to my neck. I look like a downcast flapper girl and it's much cooler to have short hair in the heat. But who cares what I look like?

They've given me a small room beside Polly's and I'm in there most of the time, alone, and asleep.

I tried the meditation last night, but it didn't work. I knelt down on the rush mat in the lovely scented chamber with the other girls in their floaty garments, their bouncy brushed hair, their serene faces, but my mind was like a hive, buzzing with hideous voices, hideous images scrolling endlessly, one after another. Freeze-frames of Gustav and Margot in the house in Baker Street. Her hands, running through his hair. The whip, slicing into his bottom.

His beautiful, blindfolded face pressed against her, sniffing for her intimate scents.

There's something wrong with her.

But worse even than that are the unbidden images that inhabit my head, tick-tock, like some kind of water torture. With my eyes open. With my eyes shut. The bodies of Mr and Mrs Levi, moving, sliding, thrusting together. Sometimes I imagine them in the hot shadows of the roof terrace in Marrakesh. Sometimes I see them in our bedroom in the London house, beneath the portrait Gustav once sketched of me.

288

By now they could be humping in the huge bed in our Upper West Side penthouse, New York City spread out beneath them. Have they packed up her whips and bottles and scarves and toys and brought them uptown from her seedy apartment?

I think of Gustav's big hands, cupping Margot's buttocks as she rides him. His hardness pushing into her, making her clap her hands in total, joyous triumph.

The thought has even crept across my mind that Gustav sent their old friend, Maria Memsahib, not to look after me but to distract me while they kept their earth-shattering rendezvous in London.

'So you've broken your vow of silence to offer me this ridiculous theory?' Polly grumbled when I shook her awake this morning. 'Maria has told me that she and Gustav were friends in the bad old London days. So I reckon Gustav was more anxious about being separated from you than he admitted. Maria was the obvious person to keep a lookout as she co-owns the ashram. She can pitch up here for R and R without explanation. The cherry on the cake was that she got to introduce you to some earthly delights while the rest of us were scrubbing our souls. And I daresay she got Gustav's blessing for that, too.'

'Whatever. I don't want to talk about him any more.'

I sank into the bed beside Polly. A sharp object dug into my side as I lay down. Polly whisked her hand away, but not before I'd spotted her phone.

'It's barely dawn, Rena. Go back to bed!' Polly shoved the phone under her pillow and lay back, closing her eyes. 'Look. Everything will be OK, I promise. But I can't say anything more. I'm not allowed—'

'Allowed? Who's told you to be so bloody mean? Who's pulling your strings? Who keeps texting you? This is a different phone. Is that how you've suddenly got a signal?'

289

I tried to roll her sideways to get at the phone. 'It's Pierre, isn't it? I need to speak to him. Or are you – you're not thinking of getting back with him, are you?'

'Last man on earth. And I've told you. No men in here. No signal,' Polly mumbled sleepily, pushing me away. 'Rena. Please. I shouldn't have said anything. In any case, I can't talk to you when you're so paranoid. No, don't you dare get cross with me. You're distraught after what you've seen, and I understand that. But trust me on this. Everything will be all right in the end.'

Now I'm stretched out in the sun, melting into the stones. Maria Memsahib chuckles softly in the air above me. 'It will soon be time to go. You have to find the answers that are waiting for you on the other side of that gate. And Angelique needs that little room for some new recruits who are arriving this evening.'

A shadow crosses my closed eyelids.

'Everyone's life goes on, even when mine is falling apart.' I lift my hand wearily in greeting. 'I can't stay here for ever. I know that. Maybe a gentle but firm dose of reality is the medicine I need.'

The snap of a sunshade tells me I've hit the nail on the head. A cool hand drifts across my forehead. I smell the fragrant oil the ashram produces from Angelique's crop of jasmine and roses, alongside her potent wine. I don't open my eyes, but I know it's Maria, and she's sitting very close. If I stretch my hand I can stroke her silky sari.

'Not one mosquito bite,' she murmurs, lifting my hand. 'Such perfect, creamy skin.'

I blush as her fingers run over me. 'They hate my blood.'

'And mine.' Her fingers pause. 'I'm leaving today, too.'

I frown, and sit up as a thought strikes me. 'You'd have thought after living here for six years Margot would have sorted out insect repellent. Yet she had bites all up her arms.

So bad it was like a rash. All evening she kept scratching at herself.'

'You're going to make yourself ill again talking about her, but I do have a theory.' Maria pours out a glass of cranberry juice. 'It's an allergic reaction to all that medication.'

I take the glass and stare into it, remembering the horrible drink Tomas gave me. 'She had buckets of pills. But how did you know?'

Maria tucks a strand of hair behind my ear. 'She was already an addict when I knew her back in London. She was a piece of work anyway, but the drugs only exacerbate the problem, especially as age catches up with her.'

'Well, Gustav will be her carer now.' I hold my glass out for more. 'I need to speak to Angelique. If I leave today, I need to know when I can come back.'

I run the glass over my hot cheek and gaze out over the garden and out to the vineyards, wavering in the heat haze.

'This isn't the right place for you and me. We have too much to do.'

I shake my head, hot tears rising in my eyes like bubbles in a boiling pan. 'I don't know where to start.'

Maria's fingers close around mine. There's no sound except the fountain splashing at the end of the pool and a couple of lovebirds swooping out of a tree with a whirring of feathers and a flutter of disturbed leaves. A bell starts chiming in the courtyard over the wall, signalling the end of meditation, but neither of us moves, or speaks.

'We've left you alone as long as we could, but now you're ready. Polly's waiting for you.' Maria stands up and pulls me with her. 'Time for the next part of your life to begin.'

The late-afternoon sun is sliding behind the palm trees that guard the garden as I step outside the beaten-metal gates of the fortress with my bags.

Polly has agreed to travel back to London with me. We'll go and huddle in her little flat near Tower Bridge until I get my bearings and work out what to do with my life. But instead of the scratched taxi that brought me here, she's sitting in the driving seat of a silver Land Rover Discovery.

'This is a bit swanky just to take us to the airport, Pol. Where did you get this?'

'Who said anything about the airport?' She drums her fingers on the steering wheel and I notice that she's still wearing her pale-blue meditation sari, rather than clothes for London. 'The car belongs to Angelique. She doesn't just lounge about twanging her harp all day, you know. How do you think she markets and sells the wine?'

As I throw my bags in the trunk, I see Maria standing in the shadows of the gate, watching me. I move out of the burning sun and into her embrace and stand there for a long time.

'Will you be OK?' she murmurs into my hair.

'I would be if I could stay here.' I nod, sniffing the heady scent wafting off her. 'But I'll manage. I always have. I'm not hysterical or crazy any more. I was so alive when I first came here two weeks ago, but in these last three days or so since you rescued me from the riad I've just become numb. That way no one can hurt me. It's my default position when things are too terrible to contemplate. I learned the hard way when I was a kid, hiding in the cupboard under the stairs.'

'That's what worries me.' Maria strokes my hair. 'You're in your cave, licking your wounds, but you know you can't withdraw completely. You need to get your mojo back.'

'I want to pretend like the past year never happened. Polly's been trying to talk me out of it, but if I can't stay here I'm thinking of going back to that enclosed convent in Venice. At least see if they'll let me stay for a while.'

'You can't do that. And they won't accept you. There's too much light inside you. Your beauty, your talent. Your smile, when you find it again.' Maria pulls away. 'And there's so much joy waiting for you out there.'

I catch a glimpse of anxiety in her face before she resurrects her wide, sexy grin.

'You've been fantastic, Maria, but you're wrong. I can't imagine ever feeling happy again.'

'If this wasn't supposed to be a holy kind of place, I would offer you gambling odds on that right now.' She kisses me on the lips. No tongue this time. 'You will be happy, Serena. Sooner than you think.'

Polly shifts the car into gear and roars away from the kasbah while I'm still buckling my seatbelt. I watch the red and pink adobe battlements and walls receding through the dust cloud she's created. Even the palm trees seem to be waving. And, nearly hidden by the haze, Angelique comes to stand beside Maria and raises her hand in farewell.

'I'd forgotten what a lousy driver you are. We'll be dead before we've even taken off.' I sit back in the comfortable leather seat, and then something strikes me. 'Polly, what's going on? Where's your luggage?'

She turns on to the main road and checks her reflection in the rear-view mirror. 'I hate horses.'

'Who said anything about horses?'

She accelerates along the smooth surface for several miles. I stare at her, not at the passing landscape, until she explains herself.

'OK, I admit it. It's a trick. You've been so scarily inside yourself that we reckoned we had to fool you into leaving, although it was true that Angelique needed the space for some new recruits. And before you get angry and say I'm ditching you when you need me the most, I'm doing this for

293

your own good. You need to get back in the saddle, Rena, and the sooner the better.'

I try to swallow the fear surging inside me. I slap at her slim white arm, making her bangles jingle. 'Very funny. Very symbolic.'

'Oh, no, this is for real. Real horses. Real saddles. That's why I'm not joining you on this particular safari.' She peers at the road ahead, whistling tunelessly. 'Now, open the glove compartment, will you? There's a little present in there. So I won't ever lose you again.'

A neat little iPhone is in there, with the Pollyesque touch of a jade-green leather cover which will match the leather jacket I have in my luggage ready for the English weather. I scroll through the contacts. My phone is still in the riad, but somehow Polly has managed to put in most of my old numbers. All except Gustav's.

'So does that mean you're not coming to London with me, either?'

'Honey, this is my home now. Apart from when I'm with you, I've never been happier. Angelique's going to train me up to be one of her guru counsellors. But it won't be long before I see you again, will it? I've always had your back, and that hasn't changed. I'll be wherever you need me, when-ever you need me, but—'

'I can't do this alone, Polly. Can't you just take me back?' We can both hear the panic in my voice, but she keeps right on driving. 'Pierre's been a star, but I can't have anything more to do with those Levis. It's not just me who's suffered. Pierre was a bastard to you, too. It was never meant to be. Gustav's history, I know that. I need to get back to London, I know that. I need to get on with my life. I know that, too. Just not today, OK? I'm not ready.'

'Rena. Listen. You know I love you and care about every single thing that happens to you.' She glances in the mirror and indicates to turn off the main road. 'But this is something I can't do for you. Believe me, you're more than ready for what's ahead.'

'The first step is to stop saying his name.' I kick my feet up on the dashboard. 'It's like a dagger, every time.'

As I flatten my hands on my knees, the diamond ring sparkles defiantly in the westering sun. I reach to pull it off, as I have done every day. It starts to slip up towards my knuckle. But Polly reaches across and stops me.

'Leave it on for now. And if after today everything is still as bad as you say it is, well, you can always sell it!' She smirks as we drive up a long, bumpy track. We are winding through rocky hills which undulate like sand dunes, but we're not in the Sahara. The landscape is hard grey stone with dry grass scoring the ground like thinning hair.

On the rise in front of us there's another kasbah, similar to, but much smaller than, Angelique's. Its sturdy walls and single tower are washed in the same dark pink, and pricked by windows latticed with the familiar Moroccan ironwork. A pathway winds between a collection of smaller buildings and one or two nomad tents, the colourful canvas flapping in the approaching evening breeze.

Polly stops the car, and we listen to the engine ticking for a moment.

'OK, so this isn't the airport.' I peer through the windscreen. 'And you're not coming with me. So what is this encampment? Another retreat?'

'It's called La Paix. The place where you stop ranting and give yourself a break.' She unbuckles her seatbelt and turns to me. She is smiling. 'This is the part of the journey you have to make on your own.'

Now that I'm trying to savour every little detail in the moments before we're parted again, I can see that my cousin looks a million times better than when I last saw her at the opening of my gallery in Manhattan back in March. Centuries ago, it feels like. Everything about Morocco, about life in Angelique's ashram, suits her. And even though she knows I'm in such pain, and she's tried to help me, she doesn't share it. Not deep down. She is calm, and happy, and I can't begrudge her that, however eccentric it seems to me. I'm being gently prised out of her new life. I can't hang on her coat-tails any longer.

'That stuff about making the journey on my own?' I tease, coughing to ease the tightening of my throat. 'Is that one of your new guru counsellor mantras?'

She slaps at my leg with the back of her hand. 'Don't take the piss. There's nothing far out or funky about this next bit. What you're about to experience is totally real. You'll see. You'll be bowled over. Now get out of the car. He's waiting.'

I glance outside the windscreen. Sure enough, an old man in a long white robe has materialised beneath a palm tree and he's holding the tasselled bridle of a beautiful Arab mare.

'Your steed awaits. You've been lolling around with us for far too long.' Polly puts on a kind of sergeant major's voice. 'We need to get the blood pumping again, girl!'

We squeeze each other until we can't breathe, half giggling and half crying. I climb slowly out of the car, clutching my bags and my new phone. Polly doesn't dawdle. She slams her foot down, waggles her fingers through the window and is gone.

The paralysis returns as soon as I'm alone. It's creeping like ivy through my body.

'*Excusez-moi.*' The old man sniffs apologetically and takes my bags while I stand in the dust. I've shut down. It's the best way to be. God knows what I'm supposed to do next, but being numb and dumb will do for now.

The palomino horse nudges my arm, and, as I stroke the

curving bone of her aristocratic nose, hints of earlier sensations flow into my fingers, like blood into a wound. She bats her long eyelashes at me. Even the warm mammal smell of her pale crème Anglaise coat and the linseed oil on the polished leather of the tack relax me.

The man returns with a pair of riding gloves and a big scarf. He taps at the diamond ring before concealing it with the gloves, then makes a wrapping motion with the scarf around his head to indicate protection against the strong dusty breeze coming off the distant hills.

'*La bas*,' he says, pointing directly into the setting sun.

He holds the stirrup for me. I slide my foot in and swing my leg easily over the horse. I find my seating, thread the reins through my fingers, then the man clicks his teeth and the horse moves smartly from a standing start into a swift trot, her hooves striking the small stones of the track, which bounce and knock against the trees and bushes as we set off into the desert.

Once I'm settled in the saddle, I lean over the pommel. The mare starts to canter, lifting her head joyously, her white-blonde mane flowing like pale silk out to one side.

I try tweaking at first the right rein, then the left, just to see if I have any control, but the horse pays no attention. She just keeps right on ahead, aiming for the sun. Anyway, steering is useless when you have no idea where you're going. The one-two-three, one-two-three rhythm of her canter is steady and soothing. The blood is pumping round my body. My knees and thighs are beginning to strain with gripping when the ground curves and rises into a steeper hill, forcing us to slow down.

The lowering sun is dazzling directly into my eyes now. All I can see is an orange flare spreading across the sky like fruit cordial spilt across a tablecloth. I can't see the ground, only feel it beneath us. My horse shifts back down to a fast trot, still barrelling upwards, still aiming directly for the sun as if the idea is to catch it before it falls.

Just as the ground becomes rockier and steeper and I assume we'll slow or stop, or turn back, my horse tosses her head and lets out a greeting neigh, because there, silhouetted on the next horizon against the fiery sky, is another horse, and another rider.

I take the reins in one hand and shade my eyes with the other. There could be a group of riders around here somewhere for all I know, maybe on the other side of this hill, but the one in front of me seems oblivious to everyone. He could be one of those statues of an Army general about to lead his troops into war. The horse, also an Arab breed with shiny black coat, is pawing the ground impatiently.

I pull on the reins, desperate to turn my horse around. Desperate, also, to turn my back on the low, burning sun and rest my eyes. But the mare doesn't respond. She just pushes on, her head dipping eagerly, like a rocking horse, as we approach her friends. So this is our destination. This must be where the horse was told to go.

We're already within hailing distance, but the only people doing the talking are the two horses, who snuffle at each other. I decide to pretend I don't understand if this other tourist tries to engage me with conversation. I don't want to hurt my horse's mouth, but I yank one last time on the reins. She slows down slightly, but the other horse rears on its back legs. It shoots out of view as if a crevasse has cracked open beneath it.

My screech of alarm makes things worse. It spurs on my horse. She quickens her pace, stretches her neck, and now we're following, we've reached the place where they were standing and the ground does fall away on the other side, but not as steeply as I feared, which is a good thing as we have now broken into the rapid one-two, one-two relentless rhythm of a gallop and we're flying into the dust thrown up by the other rider.

My heart is banging in my chest, in my ears, my knees locked against the sides of my horse as we follow the other two crazily rocketing towards the sun. My horse wants to be with them. No doubt about it. Maybe this is her mate up ahead. Her mate, and her master.

'Stop!' I yell, at my horse, at the other rider. At the world. 'For God's sake, can't you slow down?'

I can't see for the dust in my eyes and I'm sobbing now with fear and panic. Every muscle is flexed and fixed to keep me on her back. The others remain about eight lengths in front of us, and cutting through the fear is the realisation that I'm relying on them to guide me back. Otherwise I will be lost out here and no one will ever find me.

Just as my knees lose their grip and start to bang against the saddle, and just as the sun slips down behind the black ridges ahead of us, and just as I'm storing up any number of punishments and tortures for Polly or Maria or maybe even Pierre who arranged this mad escapade, the rider in front wheels in a wide semicircle, and to my astonishment there, up ahead, is the proud little kasbah again, steady on its own hill, lording it over the scattering of houses and tents.

My horse alters her stride with a leg-change that jars right up my coccyx. We swerve down into a canter, and the canter slows into a trot as we follow the other two into a dip hidden from the other buildings. A large red and gold tent is strung beneath a cluster of palm trees, and a fire is burning in a pit in the ground.

The other rider jumps off his horse as it's still moving and marches towards the trees, pulling at the scarf that's been wrapped, like mine, around his head. I don't see his face, but I should have known it was a man, swinging his dick through the desert like that.

299

I slither off my horse and bury my face in her silky mane for a moment, but she stamps her foot and lunges towards a water trough for a well-earned drink. Now I can see that the bridle is just a head collar. There's a pretty sequinned fringe across the forelock band, and plenty of shining metal. But no bit between her teeth. No wonder she didn't respond to any of my commands.

I don't know or care what the other person is doing. I just need to get my breath back. I bend over my knees, shaking like a leaf.

'Your horse is just like you, Serena. Uncontrolled. Wayward. Refusing to obey. But still utterly breathtaking.'

The deep voice, catching with emotion. Just loud enough to cut through the rasping of my breath. Just low enough to make me lift my head instinctively.

Gustav is standing a little distance from the tent. The gauzy twilight has already dropped over us, so that, apart from this circle of light, the rest of the world is concealed by the surrounding battlements of hills and trees. He's looking down at the fire and the flames jump and illuminate the fine angles of his beautiful face.

I try to move, but all I can do is stare at him. I have never known agony like it. I'm a starving woman looking at the favourite dish she can never taste. A force field, wavering with heat, is pulling me towards him. But he's not my Gustav any more, is he?

That's the face that kissed me goodbye at Paris airport after we hadn't slept all night, exploring every corner of each other in every corner of that huge hotel bed.

That's the face that since then has been buried between his ex-wife's thighs.

I wait for the numbness to return. Please let it come soon. My legs, still knocking at the knees, are feeble twigs. My heart, from racing like a jackhammer, has stopped beating

300

entirely. I open my mouth, shut it again. Try to turn away. I lift my hand towards my horse in some kind of effort to get back on and ride away. But I can't move.

'Say something, darling,' he says, eyeing me warily as if I might bite. 'Say hello, at least?'

'Go. To. Hell.'

He drops his head sideways as if I've struck him. Every line of his cheek, jaw, mouth drops, like the sun just now, falling out of the sky. He rakes his hand through the strands of black hair that are blowing across his eyes, but I can't read that gesture any more. Does it mean he's groping for the final lie to top his monumental betrayal? Is he confused by this seething, spitting Serena who has replaced the sweet, smiling one? Is he realising that whatever magic he hoped to weave by dragging me across the desert and scaring me half to death wasn't going to work?

'So she's done it. You've seen her nasty little film.'

I nod. What else can I do? My head is the only part of me that will move, and even that feels as if the glue has crumbled away.

'Tell me how to get as far from you as possible.'

There's a pause. I keep my eyes on the track where we galloped just now. I garner every ounce of strength I have to start walking.

'Look at me, Serena. Please look at me.'

I shake my head, so violently that my ears sing. I grope in my pocket for the little iPhone, and realise I've left it with my other belongings with the old man. My feet scrape through the dust as I try to get away from Gustav, and a tiny scorpion, camouflaged apart from the black hook of its tail, skitters so quickly out of an invisible hole beneath my feet that it looks as if someone is tugging it like a toy with a string.

'Turn around, *cara*. They told me you were in a terrible

state and wouldn't talk to anyone. So I thought it was easier just to get myself over here. Look at me, Serena. I'm pleading for my life.'

I keep my back turned, but I can't help glancing over my shoulder. The firelight is leaping across his face and the first thing I see is that his left eye is black, bruised and swollen half-closed. The discolouration extends over his nose, and there's a rectangular white dressing covering his left cheek.

My hands fly up to my mouth.

'Margot did this to me. We were fighting. We were not getting back together.' His mouth is swollen and cut, too, which is why he's speaking so quietly. 'I don't understand why you've blanked me. It was all there, on the film. You must have seen it?'

'What I saw on the bloody film was Margot whipping you. I saw you smiling and laughing and calling her "darling". You were on your knees, and then I saw your mouth on her, and I saw you licking her.' I keep my hands over my mouth in case I start to spew. 'So you can gallop back to wherever she's waiting for you, and let me go.'

His hands are held upwards towards me, as if he's holding something heavy but precious.

'That's not even half the story. She tiptoed up behind me and put her hands over my eyes. I thought she was you, Serena. I thought you'd come to Baker Street to surprise me. That's why I was happy, and laughing, and saying "darling".' He stops. 'Did you hear me say her name?'

I shake my head.

'You went to London without me, just like all those other secret trips and meetings. You met her in the house in Baker Street, and you ended up fucking her on the parquet floor.'

Gustav pushes the imaginary object through the air towards me.

'Did you see us doing that? On the film? Did you see me fucking Margot?'

I stare at him. For some reason his use of that obscenity, so rare for either of us, conjures up not what I saw on the film but a bright, glaring image of him and me the last night in Paris, play-fighting in our hotel room, teeth and nails making tiny scratches and nips to mark each other, our skin smooth and damp, his hardness in my hands, in my mouth, then our laughter subsiding into sighs of love as he pushed inside and filled me, our moans of desire abandoned as we came together.

'Did you, Serena?'

'Don't you dare shout at me!'

'Darling, I'm sorry, this is agony, but I'm just – I don't want to waste any more time. What did you see on the film, exactly, after she'd whipped me? You heard me tell her to stop?'

'You're bullying me, Gustav! Why can't you just let me go?'

He takes half a step through the dust.

'I won't stop until I've proved myself to you.'

'You want me to go over it all, frame by horrible frame? You really are a cruel, heartless bastard!' Angry tears fill my eyes and throat. 'OK. Here we go. What I saw was your hands on her bare bottom. Your mouth, your tongue on her body. I saw you licking her, and then—'

'And then I got her to take her gloves off. And that's how I stopped her. I don't understand – what else did you see?'

Gustav is close enough to touch my arm. I try to shake him off, but his fingers close round, and oh, the warmth from him, the firmness of his grip. I stare at his fingers.

'Nothing. There was nothing about you calling a halt. She was practically hopping about with glee, urging me to watch every terrible second. The forthcoming attractions,

303

apparently, were you giving it to her, hard, on the floor of your matrimonial home. You think I'm so pathetic that I'd torture myself watching that? In front of her? I wish I could say I was too proud, but it's nothing to do with pride. There was nothing left of me by then. And there's nothing left of you. Because I smashed the video.'

Gustav bows his head to study my hands, as if he's never seen them before.

'My girl! Normally I'd applaud you for one of your impetuous gestures, but not this time. You smashed the film just at the point when I knew I'd walked straight into a trap. Just as she knew you would, well before her trickery was exposed. She knows those torture techniques by heart. The psychology of winding your victim up to breaking point. The timing. Except she doesn't use it to extract information. She plants it. Like knotweed in a rose garden. She knows exactly what to say, how to say it, even how long it will take before you snap.' He pulls the riding gloves off, drops them to the ground and touches the diamond ring, running his fingertip over the facets, which still shine as brightly as the day he gave it to me. 'All smoke and mirrors.'

My hands are limp, dead, as he touches me. 'I'll never know now, will I?'

'You will, because I'm telling you the truth. And I'll move heaven and earth until you believe me. I've been phoning Polly several times a day, to speak to you. But she told me you wouldn't communicate with anyone, least of all me. You were in this terrible, mute state. Oh, my darling, the thought of it! We decided you couldn't take any more trauma, let alone hear what had really happened in London. Of course I wanted to fly here immediately, but I couldn't because of this.'

I sneak a peek at his bruised, swollen face. As he glances up, something deep inside me starts to stir.

304

'I still can't bear to look at you,' I mutter, managing to pull my hands away. I step across to the tent, where pretty red sequinned cushions are piled up on low sedan seats around a table flickering with tealights and brass plates laden with food. 'Margot Levi is your girl. She's got what she wanted, and what *I* want is for you to let me go.'

'If you still want to leave in five minutes, I will call the old man over, and that will be the end of it. But just give me that time to explain. It was a lie. She didn't feel like you, Serena. She didn't smell like you. That's why I got her to take her gloves off, and bingo. No silver round the wrist. You still wear the bracelet, even though we unclipped the silver chain back in Venice. And when she released one of my hands so I could touch her neck – no golden locket.'

I pick up a soft samosa from a pile on a plate and bring it towards my throat, where the golden locket still nestles.

'Talking of precious jewellery. Explain the cufflink. The one you kept, even though you told me you had thrown it away.'

'What are you talking about?'

'I found it in your cigarette box, the one where you keep your treasures.'

'The box full of useless tat that I haven't opened since we moved into the apartment? Why are you talking about cufflinks?'

'Because there was only one in the wedding shirt Margot had in the apartment in New York, but by the time she brought it to the riad the other one was there, too. You must have given it to her to complete the set. You must have been together.'

Gustav leans heavily against one of the struts supporting the entrance to the tent. The black eye makes him look like a thug with a patch.

'I will answer this madness because I need to root out all

these seeds she's sown in your mind. And then all I can do is pray that you believe me. I did dispose of that cufflink. The rather melodramatic gesture of throwing it into Lake Lugano, if you must know. I doubt even she could have dredged it up. So whatever you saw in the cigarette box was a replica planted – no doubt by Pierre back at New Year – in the knowledge that after enough provocation you would go rummaging for it. And then, because Pierre was no longer onside, she got in and stole it back.'

The firelight is behind him, the velvet sky is above and my heart aches with sadness. His proud face is so battered. I have a terrible urge to rip off the dressing and see what jagged red mark she's left on him. I know it would hurt. I want it to hurt. I want to give him a *soupçon* of what I've been feeling. But I won't touch his scar, or kiss it, or try to make it better.

'And you expect me to believe that.'

'I'm *begging* you to believe it. Take a good look at me, Serena. Margot would have killed me if Pierre hadn't got to Baker Street in time. Breaking into apartments is chicken feed for him.'

I let the golden locket fall back against my chest and put the samosa into my mouth. I bite into the soft pastry and the spiced meaty filling bursts on to my tongue. For the first time since Maria and Polly rescued me from the riad, I realise I'm ravenous. I want to eat, and keep eating, until I'm sick. Keeping my eyes on him, I next pick up a little pitta bread filled with *fuul*, a bean mixture.

'Pierre is the only positive thing to emerge from this mess. Who knew he would turn out to be the better brother?'

'Sarcasm doesn't suit you, Serena.'

For the first time, Gustav's voice hardens, and I flush in response. It's not the heat of anger this time. More the prickly heat of shame, because someone has taken a hammer to the

306

picture I thought I was seeing, and the shards are tumbling in slow motion through the air to land in completely different places.

'Infidelity doesn't suit *you*, either. I'm not your Serena any more.'

The glare in our eyes fades, but the heat behind it doesn't.

'We have two minutes left of this conversation,' Gustav says, stepping inside the tent less tentatively, and lowering himself stiffly on a low divan on the opposite side of the table. 'The new Serena will just have to listen to me for a bit longer.'

He lifts a tall glass of wine off the tray and without thinking I accept it. Despite his bashed face, that edge of authority is back in his voice. And it's sending tiny licks of desire through me, even though I hate him. I hate him.

There's a fine line between love and hate, and he's always crossing it.

'Two minutes. Right.'

Already the idea of leaving him here in the desert, getting my bags and going off into the bleak night to a bleak future, is starting to hurt.

'You're right about Pierre. He's been pivotal in all this. I know he's in love with you. And as I said right at the start, I don't blame him. How could I? When I'm mad with love for you myself?' Gustav sits back in his seat. 'His infatuation was nearly the death of us, but it's also proved to be our salvation. It's down to his quick thinking that you and I are still here.'

'And I'll thank him personally when I next see him. Maybe I'll even put him out of his misery and give him what he's been pining for all these months. But if he's such a hero, why isn't he here?'

Gustav turns to stare out at the stars. His bruised side is towards me, and now I have a mad urge to touch his poor cheek.

'He would have come for you himself if he wasn't in hospital with a smashed pelvis and two broken legs.'

My body is too hot from the fire, and the tent, and the wine. The numbness, the anger, even the tension, are seeping away like water into the parched ground.

'Oh, my God! What's he done this time?'

'Pierre knew Margot was the buyer of Baker Street. His final deception was keeping that from me. He misjudged her completely. He assumed that selling the house would be the end of it. He never dreamt she'd go to the house in person. So when he rang the agents for a key, and they told him she had taken one, he rushed over there.' I can see a slight easing in his face. He knows I'm listening now. 'He got there in time to find her trying to break my face with the unlocked handcuffs because I'd just told her what a mad, deluded bitch she was.' He tips his injured cheek towards me. 'That's the last thing I remember.'

Finally, finally, it falls into place. 'My God, G. I should have been there with you!'

Gustav shakes his head. 'I couldn't even protect my own brother. I wasn't there for him, Serena. Again. I let him down. Again.'

'What do you mean?'

'It was my idea to meet him in London. To hand over his inheritance. He had no idea because the conditions were that he wouldn't be told until he reached the age of twenty-five. But I never got the chance.' He picks up a bunch of huge black grapes and starts stripping them off the stalk, one by one. 'Crystal and Dickson arrived and took me to get patched up. Pierre stayed and searched the house, but Margot was waiting for him outside.'

'You're scaring me, G. What do you mean, you never got the chance?'

He runs his hand over his eyes. One of the grapes drops off the table and rolls across the floor.

'She drove her car at my little brother. It was his birthday, Serena. And she did it because I'd just told her that I was going to marry you as soon as I possibly could.'

A sudden breeze, warm like someone's breath, finds its way into the tent, making the candle flames all bend sideways.

'She told me the wedding was off.' I start to shake and I can't stop. 'That woman had me prisoner, Gustav. She had a pair of scissors. Anything could have happened.'

At last, he's beside me on the cushions. I curl away for a minute. I'm not sure I have the strength, or the weakness, to be close to him again. But how can I not? That's like the sun saying it hasn't the strength to rise in the morning.

'And if you had been harmed, I would have killed her with my bare hands. But she's not as clever as she thinks she is. She used our phones to track us down, but it was Tomas who led us to you. Pierre wrung out of him exactly where in that maze of a city the riad was, so Polly was able to find you.' He pulls me towards him. His face may be scarred and bruised, but his arms are strong as ever. 'But now nobody knows where Margot is.'

I look up at Gustav as a new, terrible thought strikes me. 'This is all my fault. If you hadn't met me, if we hadn't got together, got engaged, none of this would have happened. Pierre wouldn't be in hospital. And you—' I run my fingers over his forehead, stopping above his swollen eye.

'Me?' He grabs my hand and turns it to kiss the palm of it. 'I would be lost. Empty. My life would be totally meaningless if I hadn't met you.'

And then I'm in his arms again. His hands are tangled in my hair, his lips are moving gingerly over my head as he presses my face into his chest. I can hear his heart battering beneath my ear and it's like a message, an urgent message.

This is my man. He's mine. Margot so nearly succeeded

in turning me against him. How could I have listened to the venom dripping from that crooked mouth?

Never mind forgiving her. I'll never forgive myself.

I came within a hair's breadth of losing the love of my life.

In a minute I'm going to kiss him and then, if we're strong enough, this night is going to end with him deep inside me again.

'We've wasted so much time, G. I've been in utter darkness since they got me out of the riad, thinking I'd lost you.' I look up at him. 'Polly knew what had happened to you. Why didn't she tell me?'

'Polly told me that you'd seen Margot's film and you were out of your mind with grief and fury every time my name was mentioned, so in the end I asked her not to say anything. Ordered her, if I'm honest. Me and my stupid pride. I hoped she'd keep you calm until I could tell you all this myself. But I've been out of it for more than a week. That woman had stolen my phone. I shudder to think what messages she sent you. Dickson and Crystal tried to call you, but your phone wasn't picking up either.' He closes his eyes. 'How close we came, yet again, to losing everything.'

'I'm so sorry she hurt you like this.' I run my fingers tenderly over his bruises and brush my lips across his mouth. 'But why all the Lawrence of Arabia stuff with the horses?'

'You looked so beautiful when Polly dropped you off earlier. So sad and lost. I panicked. I thought you would refuse to listen. Never forgive me. And look at me. Christ. I'm hardly Lawrence of Arabia now, am I? Utter stupidity to go galloping about like that. My face is aching like hell. I'm going to have to change this damn dressing.'

I can see a seep of blood. The sudden bloom of red contrasts with the equally sudden whiteness in his face. I pull the scarf off my head to dab at it and my hair springs into damp curls.

I flush and close my eyes tight. He'll hate it. If I close my eyes he won't be able to see me.

There's a pause, and then Gustav's fingers are running through the new little waves, lifting my hair away from my scalp.

'Polly told me what Margot did with those scissors, Serena, but you are as beautiful as ever. More so, if that's possible. Because you've come back to me.'

He stands up and staggers through a curtain. I follow him into a dreamy chamber furnished with a big bed heaped with red pillows and sheets and draped with a mosquito net. Tall glass lanterns stand about the sandy floor, and stone steps lead down into a bathroom that's been hewn out of the surrounding rock. Modern chrome and glass units surround a sunken bath where petals float and more candles flicker.

The other side of the chamber is open, and a silver crescent moon is riding up the sky.

Gustav steps down into the bathroom and leans on the square basin, tiled in pink and grey. We stare into the mirror. We are both an absolute mess. Our hair is dry and windswept, dirt and dust are smeared in rings round our eyes, and I'm not wearing a scrap of make-up.

Gustav peels down the white dressing.

A long, jagged scar runs from the corner of his eye, across his sharp cheekbone, then, like a hairpin, it doubles back towards the bottom of his ear. The line of it across his cheek has dried into a narrow surface scratch, but the lower part has been stitched. It looks angry and sore, and beads of blood are oozing from between one or two of the stitches.

He starts to dab at the wound, wincing as the antiseptic stings. I take the cotton wool from him and start to do it for him.

'At the riad, Margot told me you were waiting for her,' I say, staring at the savage mark Margot has gouged into her

311

ex-husband. 'Well, you're here with me, G, thank God. And she's – where the hell is *she*?'

His black eyes close briefly in pain. Even his good side has shadows carved into it, violet with exhaustion. But that flicker of vulnerability makes me move closer and wind my arm round his waist.

'That's just it. They don't know where she is. We've got security at the hospital in London. And security with me here, actually. I even asked them to plant someone in the ashram to look after you when Maria said she would have to leave and you were asking to stay there for good.'

I shake my head in disbelief. Someone's been watching me. Watching us. Gustav has had to go to all these lengths to keep that woman away, but it will never be enough. She'll always track us down.

Eyes and ears everywhere if you pay enough.

I glance out of the tent to where the palm trees are bending elegantly to the command of the evening breeze. Gustav says we're safe. So why can I not stifle the idea of someone with evil intent slipping through the shadows outside this circle of fire?

'She had this book in the riad, Gustav. *Les Liaisons Dangereuses*. Bought at the same sale in Paris. You'd written a love note to her in it.'

'Tomas or whoever she got to track us was even better than I gave him credit for, then.' He stares at me, but his eyes don't waver. 'She has hoarded countless letters and notes from me over the years. That note was forged.'

A cloud passes over the sky and disappears.

'My darling, we're safer at this precise moment than we've been for months. Certainly since Christmas.' Gustav clears his throat. 'The police went to the riad, but she'd gone. She's slipped through the net.'

'Holy shit. Polly mentioned the police, but I paid no attention. Why were they involved?'

312

'*Chérie*, this isn't a game any more. Margot Levi is a wanted woman on the run. She kidnapped you in broad daylight and held you against your will. I'm scarred for life, and my brother's in hospital.' Gustav holds the new dressing away from his face and we both stare at the deformity scoring his beautiful face. 'This is grievous bodily harm, at the very least. With intent. As for Pierre? She could have killed him.'

We are both silent as I finish cleaning the wound. I decide to leave the loosening stitches that will drop out soon, and carefully cover it again with gauze and a fresh white dressing. He stares at me in the mirror, and we both speak at the same time.

'But he'll be OK?' I ask.

'Pierre will be OK,' he says.

We laugh quietly at our synchronicity and Gustav pulls me close again. 'We Levis are indestructible. He'll be knee-deep in sexy nurses by now. Talking of which—'

He tips my face up to his, and the dirty, dangerous gleam in his eyes lighting up his white face as he runs his lips across mine sends a surge of desire through me.

'Who knew you had the healing touch, Serena?'

I pull him back into the warm, dark bedroom. I sit him down on the bed and pull off his dusty boots, his socks, his crumpled shirt. There are bruises on his neck and left shoulder where Margot must have caught him with the sharp edges of those handcuffs when he couldn't defend himself. I swallow the surge of anger, crawl on to the bed and kneel up behind him, bending to kiss the scratches.

As my lips make contact with his warm olive skin, I realise how much I've missed him.

But not yet, not yet. I arrange him so that he's sitting straight but relaxed, his hips and shoulders aligned, and then I start to knead the knots of muscle and sinew under his

313

skin, tight as bailing twine through his body. He tries to look at me.

'Eyes front, *signor*,' I whisper in his ear, his silky hair tickling my face. 'You move when I tell you to move.'

'We've not been apart that long. When did you learn to massage like this?' he murmurs, his head falling forward as if it's too heavy, his black hair covering his face. Making him look for a moment like a doomed martyr.

'A few sessions with Maria Memsahib is all it took. I daresay it's her party trick to get girls into bed,' I murmur back. 'Not sure that's what you intended when you sent her to look after me? But she did look after me, ooh, deliciously. Turns out she has many skills in her repertoire.'

'Sounds like you have more sins to confess to me, *signorina*,' he groans, as I rotate his head firmly. I give it a tweak. 'You can't help yourself, can you? You're still so naughty.'

'I said, no more talking.'

My body heats up with desperate longing now I have my hands on him once again, but I keep it slow, oh, so slow as I come round to the front and push him down into the pile of snowy pillows beneath the mosquito net and start to unbutton his tight-fitting jodhpurs.

His hands wind up into my shorn hair, and my scalp tingles as he plays with it, but I'm not going to be deflected. Leaving his trousers still loose on his hips, I stand up to wriggle out of my jeans and kick them into the corner. He grins as I unbutton my blouse and slip it off to show him that all I have on now is my underwear. The lingerie he bought me in Paris, in pale-green and cream lace.

His tongue runs across his lower lip as I sway in the candlelight then turn my back to unclip the bra. This striptease is like the very first time I was in his London house. The first time I danced for him. The first time I took him in my mouth.

314

'Lie back for me, but whatever you do, don't you dare pass out,' I order him, yanking the jodhpurs right off, then his boxers, reaching out for him as his glorious length, already hard, springs up into my hands. I settle myself on his legs, just in my little green lace knickers. I lean forward, and the soft round end of my prize bumps blindly against my cheek with a jumping life of its own.

His hands slide under my hair. He can still wind it round his knuckles to pull me closer, but because it's so short now it hurts, waking my lust. He slips smoothly inside my mouth. So long. So hard, despite his tiredness, his injuries. It jumps over my tongue. His hands close over my ears so now I can only hear the thick pulsing of my own blood.

He pushes into my mouth hard, right to the back of my throat. My man is desperate for me. Desperate for release. The first time I sucked on him like this, after dancing for him in his house, was the first time I'd ever given head to any man.

Polly was in my mind then, just as she's trying to get in now, directing proceedings. She did this when we were teenagers, sitting on the beach in Devon with a peeled banana and pushing it down her throat. Guys love you to swallow, she said, biting into the soft bend of the poor fruit so that it almost squealed with pain. How I giggled and spluttered.

If you swallow, they'll be your slave for ever.

I pull him out carefully.

'I have one other question, Gustav. Those times you were away, or at meetings, and I didn't know where you were?'

'You're asking me that? Now? When I'm in your mouth about to explode?'

I rest my teeth on him, ready to bite.

'I've been working on a wedding gift, but it's not complete yet. That's the truth, on my life. On your new head of hair.

315

Pierre and Polly, Crystal, Dickson, they'll all back me up, but please don't ask me to spoil the surprise!'

I nip at him enough to make him wary, then suck him into the wetness. What goes around comes around. This is like the very first time. He bucks and starts to grow even more.

The first time I sucked Gustav Levi he turned me away when I offered to sleep with him. Well, that's not happening tonight. His obvious, thrusting pleasure is turning me on too much. I'm already too wet. Gustav's big warm hands are jammed over my ears. He's stiffening and swelling in my mouth as I suck. His hands tug at my head, moving my mouth up and down, he's rougher now, yanking at my hair.

My mouth loosens, lips losing their tight grip. I start to nip the taut surface, daring myself to hurt him.

He moans. His grip on me grows weaker and elation surges through me again. He thrusts deeper into my mouth. I will myself to exercise control for a little bit longer and start to fondle the soft balls, reacquainting myself with the feel of him, taking possession of every inch. He's filling my mouth. He's pushing at the back of my throat, forcing my mouth down over the velvety surface.

I nip once, nip a little harder, then suck, but suddenly he groans and falls away from me.

'Am I hurting you, darling?'

He shakes his head, a sleepy smile on his lips, battered yet so beautiful against the white pillow. His serious face has settled into dark shadows. Some healer I turned out to be.

As I lean over to kiss him, he suddenly grips my hips with all his old strength and slides me on to the hardness I've prepared. My body clenches tight as he enters me. But I don't want to be the dominant one swooping down on him right now. It doesn't feel right when he's so bruised and fragile.

Understanding that, he rolls me so that we're face to face,

316

the soft bed giving beneath us. I hook my legs around him so that we're pressed together, so tight. So tender. The angry lust that burned him up in the last few weeks has ebbed away. We start to rock, eyes closed, mouths pressed together, damp, barely breathing. How did I ever think I could live without this? Without him?

We rock together in the dreamy red bed under the Moroccan stars. Our sweet rhythm has never been so gentle. He's hard and hot inside me, I'm squeezing him so tight, yet if he thrusts too hard I'll come. Every touch or sensation threatens to make me explode. And I'm already crying.

'*Chérie?*' he whispers, throbbing urgently inside me. 'You want to stop?'

'Quite the opposite! I'm on fire!' I rub his nose with mine, feel a tear running down it. 'But I'm scared. Of loving you so much. Of ever losing you again.'

'You'll never lose me. We're together for life.' Gustav runs his finger under my eyes, tastes my tears. 'No need to be scared.'

'Well, I'm scared of hurting you. Your poor face—'

He kisses me, takes my hips to rock my body away from his, then pulls me hard in against him again. I gasp as he plunges up inside.

'Hey, my face may be hurting, *signorina,* but you'll just have to be gentle with the rest of me,' he says with a chuckle. 'How do you think scorpions make love?'

I shake my head, unable to stop myself moving against him, unable to stop the ragged gasps tumbling from my lips as that delicious deep pressure grows and grows inside me, heating us both.

'I don't know, you crazy man, but you're going to tell me anyway.' I pummel at his back and he responds by tipping his hips and thrusting more forcefully, to lock himself inside me.

My tears are still hot, but the release as they flow is ecstatic. I've missed him so much. I'm so sorry for the bereft girl I was a few hours ago. His body inside mine feels so good. The hand inside the glove.

The tears add to this ache of pain and pleasure. Gustav licks them off my cheek then draws back, tenses, teasing me, all the muscles in my thighs tugging him back where he belongs.

'So tell me, lover,' I gasp. 'How *do* scorpions make love?'

Tears are softening his face now, too. He pushes, hard, and when he's safely inside I explode with wonder. He doesn't stop moving until we come together, our mingled moans and the tears at what we've nearly lost rising like smoke to dissipate into the starlit sky above.

'Very, very carefully!'

CHAPTER TWELVE

New York is sweltering in a July heatwave. It's almost as hot as it was in Morocco last month, but at least there you could rest in marbled courtyards or under the spreading arms of a palm tree. Here, from quite early in the morning, the heat beats up through the pavements, comes at you sideways off the brickwork buildings, weighs down from the burning sky. I've started to gauge which are the best awnings on my route, or the best struts of the High Line, to seek shade.

Sometimes on the way to the gallery, despite the fact that it means he's disobeying Gustav's orders, I get Dickson to drop me off at one of the Hudson River piers so that a walk along the river can shake off the lethargy that has been creeping up on me since we got back from Marrakesh.

If it's the heat, then it doesn't seem to affect these New Yorkers.

On the wide straight sidewalks they march shoulder to shoulder, crossing like a determined herd at the intersections, eyes and minds always forward, focusing on the working day ahead. Down here by the piers they use any free time to hone their bodies as they run, or improve their team spirit as they play volleyball on the grass or the man-made beaches. Even families are taking this weather seriously, getting out elaborate picnics now that temperatures are rising.

Sometimes Dickson drops me in the heart of Chelsea so I can stroll through the quiet streets and peep through the tall windows of family homes or apartments, seeking out celebrities getting their kids ready for school or having coffee with equally shiny people.

I haven't mentioned feeling out of sorts to Gustav because when we're together I'm in utter bliss. I love padding barefoot through the apartment, breakfasting on our wrap-around balcony or heading out on a balmy evening to catch some jazz at the Carlyle Café. At work I'm enjoying the intense concentration of being closeted away with Crystal, studying the shortlisted portfolios for the *Serenissima* gallery's Young Talent exhibition.

Maybe I'm running on half a tank like this because my low-grade paranoia is presenting in physical form. The other morning as I got dressed, I noticed dull jabbing pains in my sides, my ribs, in my breasts, everything hurting as I lifted my arms to put on my bra . Gustav doesn't know about that. He continually tries to reassure me, like he did before, that there's no danger, but I know he's instructed Dickson to stay within a few yards of me at all times. Sometimes I sense someone is following me as I wander along Eighth Avenue, darting from doorway to doorway like a thief in the night. Once, I even hid in the lobby of the Chelsea Hotel when I was convinced that Margot, in owl-like Jackie Onassis sunglasses, wide-brimmed hat and a full-length white belted raincoat despite the heat, was standing beside me at the flea market, picking through a clattering collection of old picture frames.

Sometimes I fancy the *muezzin* are still calling from the faraway rooftops of Marrakesh.

Crystal is already there when I arrive late at the gallery. It's the day before the private view. The dizzy spells and aching have become permanent fixtures, but the iron pills the doctor prescribed for anaemia haven't helped. Now there's an increased stabbing pain and swelling in my left breast, and bone-numbing fatigue.

The only thing that helps, until I've got through the day and home, is power-napping in the back office and mouthfuls of dry ginger cookies, baked by none other than my old client Mrs Robinson, who I bumped into one morning when I'd shaken off my minder and was wandering in her neighbourhood feeling poorly. So the journey to work now regularly includes a stop at Ma Robinson's to top up my supply.

Crystal is click-clacking along the white walls of the gallery with her clipboard, checking the positioning of each of the paintings and photographs. Every so often she whisks her pen out from behind her ear and squiggles a hieroglyphic on the paper.

'I'm getting a distinct feeling of *déjà vu* seeing you at work,' I remark, leaning in the doorway as Dickson, having delivered me straight to the gallery this time, drives smoothly away. 'If it wasn't for the heat outside making those sidewalks bubble, and having the air conditioning on full blast in here—'

'And the fact that we're in Manhattan, not London' – she adds, tucking the clipboard under her arm – 'we could almost be back in the Levi Gallery last November, hanging your debut exhibition. I know, Serena. I think of it often.'

Crystal regards me with her black button eyes, which, together with the perpetually white deadpan face, are the only features that have remained the same in her lizard-like metamorphosis through the months. Instead of the black pencil skirts and severe chignons, she has gone into Audrey Hepburn mode, in a crisp white poplin shirt tied at the navel (which is pierced with a tiny ruby), houndstooth-checked pedal pushers and high-heeled slingbacks which she walks in effortlessly. The only inconsistent element in the ensemble is that instead of a 50s-style ponytail, she has cropped her jet-black hair in sympathy with my unexpected chop, except that hers stands bolt upright, punk-style, like a brush.

She straightens the exhibition's main picture very slightly. It's not one of mine. We've decided to intersperse my Manhattan and France work and the Moroccan studies at random intervals amongst the main event, because this show isn't about me. It's about fledgling talent.

This main exhibit is one of the photographs Chloe brought in here that cold spring day when she and her mates used her portfolio as a cover for carrying me off to the Sapphix Bar.

Crystal and I have argued well into many nights, when I'm much more alert, as to which photograph deserves centre stage. But I'm the owner of *Serenissima*, and I'm convinced that *Synchronised Swallow*, Chloe's photograph of a row of lush, red-painted mouths, each one opening to take in its individual elegant stream of tequila, like so many oversized, oversexed baby birds, will stop passers-by in their tracks.

I walk up to Crystal as she bends to examine one of my photographs, taken in the market in Marrakesh just before Tomas escorted me away. It's a shelving display of multicoloured ceramics. A tiny pale-yellow bird sits in the midst of them, and just out of sight, a door, painted the same pale yellow, is ajar to reveal a stack of raw, unpainted clay pots and plates.

'If I haven't thanked you enough for looking after the shop, Crys, then I'm an ungrateful – my God! What's that new scent you're wearing today?' I reel away from her, holding my hand over my nose. 'I don't mean to be rude, but –!'

'It's not new!' She sniffs, waving her wrists in the air. 'It's my usual. I never wear anything else. It's *Cristal,* of course, by Chanel!'

'It just smells different today. Like flower water left too long in a vase?' My skin prickles and goes cold. I assume it's because we're now staring at the smudged watercolour of the Zattere waterfront that Pierre Levi painted in Venice.

Crystal draws herself to her full rigid height and is about to snap something quite rightly indignant in reply when my stomach uncoils like a fire hose. Hot nausea rushes up my throat, my mouth flooding with saliva. I double over and make a run for it, vaguely aware that the gallery door has just opened.

The gallery feels even colder than before when I stagger back a few minutes later. Crystal hasn't moved from her position beside Pierre's painting, but standing with her, biting her thumbnail, is Chloe.

'Hey, Serena! You OK?' she whispers anxiously. 'You look terrible!'

'Maybe a cup of coffee, Crys?' I whisper, sinking on to the chair behind the desk and trying to look like the proud owner of this gallery.

Crystal frowns slightly and gives Chloe a little push towards me as she goes out to the office to boil the kettle.

Chloe sits on the white leather chair on the other side of the desk as if I'm about to interview her. She's no longer the dishevelled, doped-up, weeping creature she was when I left her in the riad over a month ago. She's back to her old self. Sleek, tanned, her golden hair tied in a high ponytail, and she's wearing a pink and white striped crop top and tiny white shorts.

'I didn't mean to shock you. You've been so kind to me.' She fiddles with her hair and crosses her shapely legs. 'You must think I'm the pits after what happened in Marrakesh.'

'Hey. You did nothing wrong. You weren't to know you were walking into one of Margot Levi's power plots. You just thought she was giving you a lovely free holiday along with a lovely free man.' I try to focus on Chloe. There are dots obscuring my eyes and a high-pitched singing in my ears. Like Margot's mosquito. Why have I been so slow to work it out? This illness must be down to that vile drink I was given at the riad. 'How is Tomas, by the way?'

Chloe bites her thumb again and rubs her hands up and down her perfectly waxed shins. 'Angry. Ashamed. And AWOL.'

'So long as he isn't still under her spell.' I shake my head blearily. 'Maybe he's gone to London, to see Pierre?'

'We'll track him down, Chloe,' Crystal says, clattering about in the back office. 'But that's not why you're here today. We wanted you to make sure everything's shipshape for the show tomorrow night, didn't we, Serena?'

'Yes, but before we do – I have to ask this because it's another thing making me ill. Margot's not only deranged, Chloe. She's dangerous, too. I was hoping you might know, or maybe Tomas when he makes an appearance, where she is? You know the police are after her—'

Chloe nods. 'She vanished from the riad right after your friends rescued you. We were all questioned, but none of us had a clue what was going on and we were just chucked out. I don't see how she can be on the run for long. All those drugs she takes – she gets the shakes. And this skin complaint she got on her arms and her neck, like acne – some kind of allergy. In the end it was all over her. The first time he saw her up close, without a veil, Tomas thought it was some kind of pox. It's horrible, and it's come on really fast. Like one of those flesh-eating tropical diseases.' She slides her hands across the desk and I cover them with mine. 'The Sapphix Bar closed overnight, so you don't need to worry. I doubt she's here.'

Crystal reappears with the cafetière, cups and some ginger cookies on a tray. 'Even if she is, they won't catch her. Because she'll have changed her identity.'

'Her identity?' I ask, glancing up at her. 'What do you mean?'

'If you've been a knockout beauty like she was, you'll never get over losing your looks. You'll fight it.' Crystal puts down the cafetière and folds her arms across her narrow chest. 'Six or seven years ago, make-up and wigs were all she needed when she wanted a disguise. And an assumed name. But you can't disguise old age, can you?'

'Except with surgery.' Chloe glances from Crystal to me and back again, then drags her hands against her hairline and pulls her pretty face tight. 'Tomas said her butt and boobs belonged to someone half her age.'

'She had those done long ago, in London. Such a good surgeon even Gustav didn't suss it out when they were married. Sorry to mention it, Serena.'

'Tomas was her favourite. She knew how I felt about him. She should stick to people her own age, then, whatever that age is.' Chloe scowls. 'I don't know how she did it. Probably because she never came out during the day. Only at night, so they couldn't see her clearly. But still, the boys, they were all, like, half-witted when they were anywhere near her. The night after we arrived at the riad I caught her and Tomas having a fuck-fest on the roof.'

Chloe stops. I keep my eyes on her, pressing my hands over my stomach.

'It's only a matter of time before they do more work on her face. And with all the top-up treatments, she'll end up looking like someone else.' Crystal pours a strong Americano into my favourite *tasse*. 'She won't know when to stop.'

'When she saw me watching, she beckoned me over to join in.' Chloe goes on talking as if we're not there. 'If you want your Tomas, she said, come in here and get him!'

'And did you? Join in, I mean?' Crystal pours in the dash of cream that I like. 'Please tell me you didn't.'

Chloe pulls at some loose threads trailing from her tiny shorts. 'We all did whatever she told us. But I wish I hadn't. She told me to take my clothes off, said I could suck him off, but he was still inside her, I tried to pull him off her, but – do you know what? I know where he's been now. I don't want him any more.'

'Bravo. I can understand that,' murmurs Crystal, patting Chloe on the shoulder. 'Poor Tomas. He won't even know he's tainted for life. But you? Plenty more fish in the sea.'

The conversation is becoming too much. The graphic image the poor girl has painted in my head, Pierre, tainted, Tomas, also tainted, both of them inside Margot, and both of them trying to get inside me. I lift the cup to my lips. Whatever Crystal has put in my coffee smells like horse dung. I slam my hand over my mouth.

As I rush to the bathroom for the second time, I hear Crystal say calmly, 'Could you mind the shop, please, Chloe? I'm taking Serena to the doctor.'

So we're standing in a lift, rushing up through a tall building somewhere east of Central Park.

'It's just the heat getting to me, Crystal. I never knew New York could get so hot in July. Or more likely it's some stupid bug I picked up in Morocco,' I grumble, leaning against the metal wall, which vibrates soothingly against my spine as the lift shoots us upwards. I try, and fail, to read the labels describing various surgical departments and medical procedures as we whizz up to the heavens. 'What is this place, anyway?'

'The Peter Abelard Clinic.'

'Does Gustav know we're about to have a very expensive, and wasted, consultation?'

'They deal with every possible medical and surgical complaint known to man. Anyway, Gustav told me to bring you here. He'll get to us as soon as he can, but he's on the other side of town at the moment.' Crystal takes my hand in her own gloved one and I'm too astonished by the rare gesture of affection to resist. 'We need to get you right, lady. I can't be holding the fort for ever, you know. You have to get back to running your gallery.'

The lift stops and spits us out on to a powder-blue carpet. We're in a quiet, cool reception area high up in the clouds, with huge windows shaded from the blistering sun, squashy blue sofas everywhere and piles of glossy magazines. To my astonishment one of my photographs faces us as we emerge from the lift.

It's a panorama of the Amalfi coast at sunset, with the apricot spill of Positano cascading down towards its regimented beach. Three topless ladies old enough to know better are lying rigid as mummies, oiled like anchovies and lifting their sunglasses to stare at a muscle-bound hunk packing up parasols.

'In any case, there could be something really serious going on, which is why we're on the twenty-second floor. Tropical diseases.' Crystal nods calmly. 'My diagnosis is dysentery. Or cholera. In which case, the private view is off, because I daresay you'll have to be quarantined.'

On cue, my stomach heaves, and I charge through a wide white bathroom door conveniently placed right next to the lift.

Two hours later we are in a different department, on a

different floor, pressing the button marked G for ground. Crystal looks at me, and I look at her. I can see her clearly for the first time today. I'm no longer nauseous. I'm still weak, and light-headed, but none of it matters. If she wasn't holding my hand, I'm certain I'd float right up to the top of the lift and she'd have to tug me down like a balloon. But I've just drunk some sparkling grape juice and gobbled two small, sugary doughnuts handed to me by a small, sugary doctor, and those have worked wonders on my knackered body.

'You fell asleep in there, right on the examination couch,' Crystal remarks, as the lift descends from cloud nine back to earth. 'You didn't even hear what the doctor said at first.'

I close my eyes and lean back against the warm, humming wall. 'That's why Gustav pays a fortune for this place. Such incredibly comfortable couches. Such lovely warm hands.'

We step out of the lift, stop and peer, for the tenth time, at the small square white envelope Crystal is holding. She leads me away from the group of people trying to barge into the lifts. We flop down on another set of squashy blue seats. She takes a printout from the envelope, and we both snuffle with shocked laughter, like a couple of schoolgirls gawping at a heartthrob.

'Where is that Dickson?' Crystal lifts her phone to her ear.

'Why can't we walk back, at least some of the way? I'm fine now. In fact, I'm all jittery. I can't sit still – we've got so much to do, Crys!'

'It's Crystal. You're not coming back to the gallery today. You need all your strength for the private view tomorrow. It won't look good if you throw up all over Park Avenue, and in any case, I'm not strong enough to carry you,' she replies, tapping the phone as if sending Morse code. 'Gustav would never forgive me if I dropped you.'

I slip the paper back into the envelope, hand it to her and

walk over to the window. There's a huge arrangement of lilies set on a glass table. It reminds me of the only ornament Gustav had in his office at the London gallery. It was a vase so huge you could have climbed right inside and taken a shower in it. I swerve away from the flowers because their scent is sickly.

But at least I know, now, what's wrong with me.

There are slatted blinds to hide the VIP patients from the prying eyes of the real world, but I don't care how exclusive this clinic is. I don't care who sees that I'm a patient in here. I'm just over the moon that I'm not dying.

'Come and sit down, Serena. We have to discuss how to break this news to Gustav,' murmurs Crystal, her calm voice carrying, even though she's on the far side of the bank of lifts. I start back towards her obediently, but before I can reach her, the lift doors open.

The three doors in a row remind me of the little weather house which sat in the window of the house on the cliffs when I was a child. It's the only item I took from there, and it sits now in the kitchen in Gustav's London town house. On hot days, a little door opens like a cuckoo clock, and a wooden man wobbles out. On rainy days, it's a little wooden woman.

A human couple emerges from the far lift door, followed by a burly male nurse in unflattering green scrubs. The man and woman are pressed tightly round a newborn baby and, like a shoal of fish, the three of them flow along as one, as if they've all been sewn together. The nurse watches them until they reach the revolving door, then checks his pager and stomps away.

A group of grey-haired patients in dressing gowns, looking hot and bothered, poke their heads out of the middle lift like chickens in a coop, then dart them in again. They press the buttons at random as if the floors have changed since the last time and they can't work out how to go up or how to go down.

I assume there's no one in the lift nearest to me because the doors are about to shudder closed again. But then a lone figure steps out. She's dressed very oddly, considering the heat, in a crumpled linen Edwardian dustcoat buttoned to the neck. The antiquated style is emphasised by the kind of circular wide-brimmed bonnet a beekeeper might wear, complete with full face-veil, but as the patient steps out of the lift, she lifts the veil, presumably to see where she's going.

I see the expression of horror on Crystal's face before I register the reason. She is rising from her chair. She freezes, her eyes fixed on the woman lifting the veil. As it rises off her face, my eyes are drawn to the fresh white bandage binding the nose and cheeks like a highwayman's mask, but then I notice the lips beneath the bandage. They are blueish, cracked, puffed out like a fish, yet somehow pulled down to one side. There's a web of angry red scars covering one cheek, while the other is the same waxy white as the bandages.

But it's the black, slanted eyes that are unmistakable, even though they have been stretched at the corners and the eyelids above the tightly wound bandages are red and swollen.

I think of Gustav's scarred face, the dressing speckled with fresh blood, the rawness still gouged in his cheek.

Crystal and I have drawn together. We must look like sentries, posted one on either side of her, because the woman glances first at Crystal, who is in her line of sight, and then she turns painfully towards me.

I take a breath, smoothing my hands over my stomach. Whatever she has to say, I have plenty more. But there's no expression in that ruined face, and no sound comes from her, either. The trout lips part stickily.

Margot jerks into life like a marionette and takes a rapid step towards the doors.

'Security!' shouts Crystal, sticking out her pointed toe. Margot falls on to the nearest chair, an ignominious tangle of coat and hat, bandages – and an astonishingly ugly pair of orthopaedic sandals. People back away from all of us, muttering and taking photos with their phones. But I remain right where I am.

Crystal speaks quietly to the security guard who has appeared then motions me to wait by the reception desk and goes over to Margot. She pulls the woman upright into a sitting position, adjusts her clothing, even straightens her bonnet and drops the veil back over her face. All the while she is speaking, but I can't hear what she's saying. Her lips move silently, and Margot lets her manhandle her, staring intently like a drunk person trying to look sober.

The security guard must have called 911 because already in the distance comes the familiar whoop of the NYPD, echoing and bouncing off the towering trunks of the urban jungle. Still, Crystal is mouthing words into Margot's face. The two women, once such close friends, stare at each other for another long moment. Now Crystal carefully opens the white envelope we were given upstairs, holding up her finger for Margot to pay attention, like a conjurer surprising his audience at a children's party. 'Twixt finger and thumb she takes out the flimsy piece of paper.

Margot lifts her veil to peer at the paper. Reads the patient's name and date, printed at the top. She rears back and lifts her hand as if to slap Crystal across the face, but Crystal's arm flashes out like a tentacle, catching Margot's in mid-air.

And that's the position they're in when the fully armed cops arrive a couple of minutes later, tear into a hushed clinic full of sick people and adopt a defensive crouch.

'For once she's finding out what handcuffs are officially for,' remarks Crystal as she comes quickly across to me. I fall against her and her arm comes round my waist, strong

331

and solid. I should be laughing, or even smiling with relief, but instead I burst into tears and watch as they arrest Margot Levi.

Gustav arrives just as his fugitive ex-wife is about to be bundled out through the revolving door like a misdirected parcel. There is a ghastly moment of utter stillness. They are face to face one more time. Her parting gift to him is still etched in his cheek, the scar faded but forever. He turns his back to her, his head bowed as he speaks quietly to one of the officers.

Margot juts forward to say something, and from this sideways angle I see that those are not surgery scars on her face. They're pits, and lesions.

She caught smallpox and went into hiding because her beauty was ruined.

To Gustav, she no longer exists. He steps aside as the cops take her out and place her in a car. His black eyes find me where I'm propped up against the reception desk and he puts his fingertips to his lips. He's too far away. There's too much space between us.

Crystal leads me across to him, holding out the white envelope. He opens it, stricken with dread, even though she's smiling and patting his arm. In slow motion he registers what he is seeing, then his mouth drops slightly open, then he sweeps his hair back off his face, and then his black eyes lift to mine again, burning with amazement, melting us both with tenderness.

As for me? I do what every rough tough tomboy heroine would do in the circumstances.

I pass out cold.

'And so here we are again. Another private view. Another array of talent. And I'm delighted to be sharing my great new space with some new artists who are already snapping at my heels!'

I hear my voice, speaking as I'd rehearsed it, but it sounds like someone else talking. I'm in a total daze, yet the only substance to pass my lips has been a pretty strong cocktail of vitamins.

Gustav is standing beside me and I'm sitting on the gallery desk swinging my bare legs and sipping fizzy apple juice. I am counting the minutes until he and I can be alone again. I've been in bed most of the day, so this mental haze is due in part to sleep and laziness. Gustav hasn't left my side since the scenes at the clinic yesterday. I've promised him I'm fine. But once I've given my speech I'm happy to leave the rest of the evening to Chloe and Crystal.

'All of the exhibitors here tonight are brilliant, and a hugely promising raft of talent for the artistic future of this city, but I particularly wanted to flag up Chloe, who created the central piece of this exhibition, and I also wanted to chide her two fellow dancers, yes, you two skulking in the corner. Word to the wise. Don't dress as sugar-plum fairies if you're travelling incognito. And don't be too shy to admit that at least three of these photographs are in fact yours. Also, we're thrilled to include work from the degree show at the art school, and those students are here with their tutor. Finally I'd like to draw your attention to the dreamy Venetian watercolours of my brother-in-law Pierre Levi, who can't be in New York tonight.'

Gustav takes my hand and kisses it, and then he stands up and raises his glass.

He clears his throat. 'This is a very special occasion for the new stars of *Serenissima*. But it's also a special day for my fiancée and me.'

Crystal taps Gustav's hand warningly with her pen. I shake my head frantically, but he ignores us.

'For the many amongst you that we consider to be friends, I want to take this opportunity to announce that this beautiful girl and I, just today, have finally set a date for the wedding!'

Everyone starts to clap, and then stops. 'Well, go on then, Levi!' yells Mr Weinmeyer. 'Put us out of our misery! When is it?'

Gustav looks at me. No point trying to stop him now. His handsome face is alive with excitement, colour running along his cheekbones. The jagged scar makes me love him all the more.

I sometimes think I'm going to drown in love.

'Well, we've been telling everyone it's going to be Halloween, which would have been the anniversary of when we first set eyes on each other in London, but we want to bring the date forward because—'

I put my hand on his leg and squeeze. On the other side of him, Crystal has raised her eyes to heaven.

'Because I love Serena Folkes so damned much I can't wait that long. So it's going to be next month, and when I get round to booking it I'm afraid it will be a semi-elopement, without the secrecy, because we're in a rush and I want to fulfil her dream of getting married on a beach. Somewhere exotic. Somewhere hot. Preferably somewhere Caribbean, or Italian—'

'Actually, there's been a change of plan, darling.' I stand up.

The colour drains from Gustav's face. Crystal takes out a Japanese fan and starts flapping it in front of hers. They think I'm calling the whole thing off.

'I still insist on an extremely expensive, exotic beach for our honeymoon, but I've decided, because Pierre is still in a wheelchair and can't travel from England, that we should get married in London.'

Everyone claps again. Crystal snaps her fan closed. Gustav takes the glass out of my hands, curls my fingers over his knuckles and bends over them to kiss them, and when he lifts his face, I see the rare, priceless glint of tears in his eyes.

'And even though it's sure to be raining in London in August, *that*, ladies and gentlemen, is why I love this woman so much. And I'm going to make her cross now, because she says it's too soon to say, but as a lot of our best friends and patrons are here I can't wait another single second. The real reason we're in a rush to marry is that six weeks ago I was lying under the Moroccan stars with this beautiful creature, and now she's pregnant. With our twins!'

I can still hear the applause and the cheers as Dickson guides the Porsche Cayenne away from the little gallery and directly on to Tenth Avenue to drive us home. We sit back in the car watching locals and tourists idle along the clogged, airless streets.

As we approach the west side of the Lincoln Center, Gustav lowers the window. The mellow song of a saxophone, clean and clear and out in the open, floats into the car.

'You're feeling OK to get out here, Serena? There's something I want to show you.'

I stretch luxuriantly in the car seat, lifting my sky-blue silk dress and letting it float back over my legs. 'You know what, *chéri*, for the first time in weeks I feel great. Really full of life.'

Gustav smiles and taps Dickson on the shoulder. 'So give me the lowdown, Dickson. Is it lindyhop tonight? Or the hustle?'

Dickson pulls over, ignoring the honking of frustration from the drivers behind him, and stops the car. He shifts the rear-view mirror so we can see his grey eyes staring at us. There's an unaccustomed crinkle of amusement at each corner.

'Lindyhop was last night. Tonight it's salsa meets charanga, if you can manage it. Crystal's favourite.'

I burst out laughing. 'What are you two banging on about? I can't understand a word you're saying!'

'Thanks, Dickson. We'll meet you in an hour. I don't think we'll be staying for the late-night silent disco.'

Gustav pulls me out of the car and we are plunged straight into a jostling crowd of brightly dressed, chattering people being drawn like magnets into a wall of Latino jazz. We walk off the pavement and through to the main plaza of the Lincoln Center. There's a stage up at one end, lights, booths, amplifiers, musicians – and an extremely camp instructor wearing high-waisted trousers, cummerbund and frilly white shirt, who is taking an obedient line-up of dancers through their paces. The workmanlike space has been transformed into a giant alfresco ballroom.

We check our bags and sashay into the swirling, smiling, swinging crowd, half skipping, half swerving round the other dancing couples to find a place. Gustav holds me close as if I'm made of porcelain.

'Welcome to the Midsummer-Night Swing, my love!' he shouts when we reach the centre of the action. 'Time to celebrate!'

He turns to me, pulling me up close against his body as the music trills and trumpets through us. He starts swinging his hips, licking his lips naughtily, then he puts his hands on me and pushes my body into a spin so that he can catch me and twirl me under one hand.

I can see why dancing started off as a human kind of mating dance. This glittering kaleidoscope of colour and sound has become Gustav's natural habitat. He looks dead sexy in those well-cut, butt-hugging trousers, showing off the Latin hip action I never knew he possessed. But my teenage nights of hesitant salsa dance classes in the village pub haven't been wasted, either. At one point we clear the floor and have people clapping and yelling around us as we move in perfect harmony, tight together, then spinning away again.

As our eyes fix on each other in the midst of that crowd, our hot bodies pressed and gyrating to the rhythm, my desire for him, teased and tossed about recently by feeling so sick, starts to return with a kind of gruff, animal urgency to it. And he knows it, because as we dance, my silk dress flying up round my thighs, the snapping fire of lust in his eyes is as bright as a traffic light.

After an hour of dirty dancing I start craving another fizzy drink. Gustav parks me by the central fountain, starts to walk away, then turns back. Lifts his arms like wings.

'You have never looked so beautiful, darling. Something secretive and shaded in your eyes, yet such a bright glow. I'm amazed the whole world can't see it.' He comes back to me and tips my face upwards for a kiss. 'I want you so badly. Right now, girl. Soon as I get you home, do you think we could—?'

'I'm pregnant, honey. Not sick.' I smile against his mouth. 'So long as we do it like those scorpions. You know, very, very carefully?'

He grins, standing back and raising his arms again as if he's about to take flight. Then he backs away into the still swirling crowd in search of refreshment. I watch the other people. Some are ordinary couples shaking their booty. Some are professional dancers. Some are shy singles, approaching other singles for a dance or two, sticking like glue to each other for the rest of the night or separating, unsuited, never to see each other again.

I'm just warming myself by the fire of my own happiness when I realise Gustav's been gone a tad too long. A frisson runs through me, leaving me chilly and tired, despite the soupy warmth of the evening. I search the crowd for his black glossy hair, his long legs striding back towards me, but I can't see him anywhere.

Now there's no nausea. Just pinpricks of cold, hard anxiety.

Then the music fades to a twang of guitar strings and a couple of cheeky trombone notes, and the lead singer of the salsa band taps the microphone up on the stage.

'Hey, guys and gals, my old jamming friend Gustav Levi has something to say to you all!'

The bandleader waves his trumpet, and there he is, my Gustav, up on stage like a rock star, running his hands through his black hair and grinning sheepishly, still breathing hard from spinning me round the dance floor.

His eyes are fixed on me, and he points the microphone over to show everyone where I'm sitting. The dancers, reluctant to tear their eyes away from the gorgeous gypsy up on the stage, nevertheless follow the line of his eyes to where I'm flushed scarlet, sitting on my hands by the fountain.

'That's Serena Folkes over there, everyone! My beautiful fiancée!' Gustav cries, the giant speakers around the plaza squeaking slightly as if they can't contain his excitement. 'One of the few things she doesn't know about me is that I used to play trumpet. I haven't picked up an instrument for ten years. Somehow, back then, the urge in me died. But I took her to see Herb Alpert the other day. Oh, she's too young to remember "Rise" and all those other great tracks, but it sure inspired me, because, well, here I am, full of music again. And because she's my muse, I'm going to embarrass her, slow it right down and play this smoochy Garfunkel number.'

His eyes are on mine the whole way through, except when a phrase carries him away and they close for a moment, shutting out the light. But I can still watch his mouth on that trumpet, the lips that kiss mine, that run over my body at dead of night.

The guys in the audience look somehow belittled as their women sway their hips exaggeratedly, unconsciously puffing out their breasts as they gaze at my Gustav. He's the guy who the men all want to be, and the women all want to be with.

As he holds the final note and everything around me wavers and blurs through the threat of yet more tears, everyone claps and cheers, shrugging in slight confusion as they swing first towards him, then back towards me. I wipe my eyes and make a glugging gesture at Gustav, followed by a get-the-hell-off-that-stage gesture.

But he shakes his head, pointing at his feet in an I'm-staying-right-here gesture. He lifts the microphone again.

I only have eyes for you.

CHAPTER THIRTEEN

It's late August in London, and although someone else will be taking the photographs today, I'm still viewing my life as if it's through a lens. Framed by this car window, the capital looks lovely. It's summer, and unusually warm for England, but it's not as steamy and frantic as New York. It's not as dry and dusty as Morocco, either, or as crowded and canal-odoured as Venice. At the first glimmer of sunshine and heat, the cafés and pubs have planted out their chairs, tables and striped umbrellas like so many shrubs and flowers, so the side streets have a continental, holiday feel, even though it's only mid-morning.

'None of them have a clue. Look at them! They're working, shopping, eating, drinking, sightseeing, planning what to do tonight. They have no idea that my life's about to change.'

I press my nose up against the tinted glass as Dickson takes the Lexus in a second circuit round the garden square outside Gustav's house. I say Gustav's house, because it still feels like *his*, not ours. And although we first met in this square, and it's pretty cool being within spitting distance of Soho, Bond Street and Piccadilly, we'll be leaving soon. Not only is the area pretty dead once the shoppers and diplomats and gallery owners have gone home, but the house itself represents the limbo between his past and his future with me.

'How about putting this place on the market and moving further west, after the wedding?' I'd remarked on the night we flew in from New York. I was tying my silky kimono printed with splashy violet flowers round me after a quick shower and sitting on one of the barstools in his vast white kitchen. 'I don't mean moving out of London. But I fancy Holland Park, or South Kensington. Oh, God, hark at me! Princess Serena! Can we, though, Gustav? Could we afford to live there? The kids could go to the French Lycée one day, and be bilingual, just like their daddy!'

Gustav was threading chunks of chicken, marinated by Dickson in lemon, thyme and Riesling prior to our arrival, on to skewers so we could cook a quick kebab before we keeled over with jet lag.

He glanced up at me, grinning, his dark face contrasting with the pure white chef's top he'd put on.

'You made enough money from those exhibitions and commissions to pay for a place in the Boltons, did you, madam? But sure. Why not? When we have some time, let's sit down with our spreadsheets and count up the pennies.'

'Pennies? Since when did you become so tight-fisted? Not only do you own this place, and our eyrie in Manhattan, but the Weinmeyers have just paid handsomely for the house in Baker Street. Lock, stock and several smoking barrels!'

'The proceeds of which go straight to Pierre, darling, as you know. But it's all worked out brilliantly. By flying over here personally to sign the transfer documents, the Weinmeyers have earned themselves an invitation to the wedding. They were so keen to have a London base, and it made perfect sense, since they acquired all that erotic footage earlier this year, to buy the very location where it was filmed. But I made them sign one proviso.'

'Oh, honey! You and your contracts!' I tried, and failed, to open a packet of breadsticks. 'Even negotiating with old friends there are terms and conditions. You haven't asked Ernst Weinmeyer to give me away, have you?'

'That's not his job. There's only one person who can do that.' Gustav took the packet from me and ripped it easily with his teeth. 'But as far as the house is concerned, I would rather have sold it to strangers, if I'm honest. Anyway, I've asked them to edit that damaged film loop. It's an almost completely different film now that they've deleted every single image of—'

He rammed a lemon wedge on to the end of his skewer and laid it with the others to sizzle on the hot griddle before washing his hands.

I flattened my hands on the white counter between us, and he pushed the griddle to the far gas ring. He folded his warm fingers round mine, fingering the diamond ring to calm himself down.

'Say it. You can say her name, now that she's gone.'

We stared at each other, waiting for the grinding weight of her presence to loom up and drag at us. But there was nothing. Not a flicker of dread or doubt inside me, and no fear or anger or hatred inside him either. I could tell from his eyes. Her shadow no longer flitted behind his face.

'It's like the clear, clean air after a lingering, destructive storm, you know? Knowing that she dropped dead in a prison infirmary before they could deport her. Necrotising fasciitis. A hideous flesh-eating condition, creeping through and destroying an equally hideous person. The symmetry with La Marquise and her smallpox is uncanny. They say she picked it up during one of those surgical procedures. Though I reckon it was one of those Moroccan mosquitoes.

She never faced her comeuppance for trying to kill Pierre, but it's the rough justice she deserved. Margot is dead.' We both glance through the doors, which have been opened to let in some summer air. There's the faint aroma of oregano, basil and thyme from Dickson's herb garden, and the perfume of roses. 'There. I've said it. Anything that belonged to her has been sold and given to charity. Now I want to forget she ever existed. She will never torment us, or herself for that matter, ever again.'

We watched the pale amber of the street lamps outside the garden wall glow into life as the late London evening took hold. After a few moments Gustav turned to tossing the salad.

'Going back to the topic of paying for our next abode, there's one thing you're forgetting.'

I leaned forward and dunked a breadstick into Crystal's home-made guacamole. I licked the dip off the tip of the stick, then slowly nibbled up the crumbling length of it, making Gustav's eyes spark once more with amusement and desire, despite his exhaustion.

'What's that, my love? That you're the sexiest, naughtiest, most fertile woman in the world?'

I laughed and poked at him with the stick, which snapped and fell into his glass of Chablis.

'Not just that. I'm also an heiress from when I inherited the house on the cliffs, if you recall. I was a woman of means before I even met you! What I'm saying is, I have my own money. So with it all put together I've enough to buy a nest somewhere classy and warm.'

Gustav turned the kebabs over, releasing the aroma of lemon and thyme.

'Great minds thinking alike. If you open that big envelope, you'll see that I've beaten you to it.'

Inside was a glossy brochure showing a group of dove-grey

houses with ridged red tiles scattered over a hilltop outside Siena. The bird's-eye view shows the honey-coloured stone turrets and courtyards, the glittering blue rectangle of a swimming pool, sloping terraces of vines.

And stamped across it in red letters the word 'sold'.

I could already feel the warm sun on my back, taste the Chianti. See the rosy sunset, smell the oregano and rosemary, hear cicadas and the church bells tolling over the fields.

'You're telling me those early-morning meetings and trips and the night in Italy were all about this? You've bought a villa?'

'Not just a villa. An entire hamlet!' He picked up a smoking kebab stick and pushed the cooked chicken off it on to a big white plate. We speared the chunks straight into our mouths. 'An early wedding present for you, *signorina*. It was like a dagger in the heart when I realised that you thought I was cheating on you. My God what a year this has been! But I couldn't keep it secret any longer, because I need you to cast your eye over it. It's going to be a fantastic project. It can be an artist's retreat, or a cookery school, or a wedding venue. Or if it's going to be a home just for us, then we'll need a lot more babies to fill it!'

I held one more juicy chunk in my mouth, chewing deliberately, licking buttery juices off my lips. 'Hmm. And talking of babies—'

Gustav paused, his skewer held in front of him like a microphone. 'What is it, *cara*? Too early for them to kick. Are you all right?'

I put my skewer down, slid off the stool and held out my hand.

'Oh, my love. I am more than all right. That jet lag has miraculously cured my morning sickness. And made me horny!'

His black eyes glinted with amusement as he popped the

last bit of kebab into his mouth and followed me through the kitchen and up the stairs.

Halfway up I leaned against him. 'If we're going to be leaving this house soon, maybe we should make sure we celebrate every corner of it.'

His arms were round me, tender yet strong, keeping me safe as we leaned over the banister to survey the red-lacquer-painted hallway and the pinprick spotlights edging the skirting boards.

'Funny to think of that tangle-haired creature coming to the house for the very first time, last autumn, all wet from the rain.' He breathed in the scent of my hair. 'That was the first time you touched me. You danced for me, and then you sucked me, remember?'

'On your orders. Yes, of course I remember. I wanted you almost as badly that night as I do now.' I pulled him on up the stairs and across the wide landing into our huge bedroom. 'I was furious that you didn't seem to want me.'

Above the bed hung the sketch of my face that Gustav made at my first ever private view. He was watching me that night across the gallery while I talked about the concept of the exhibition. My face in the sketch is turned sideways, half smiling as I speak passionately about the nuns I'd spied in the convent in Venice.

I was relieved that my old self wasn't staring at us now as I wandered over to the bed, lay down on the huge Oxford pillows, and started to peel open my kimono. Starting at my throat, the silk slithered over my breasts, setting up little shivers over my skin and tightening my nipples in answer to the desire waking up inside me.

'I was a troubled soul who needed rescuing, but I wasn't ready to throw myself over that particular cliff.' Gustav's dark face was flushed with lust as his eyes travelled slowly over my gradually exposed body. 'But I'm cured. I want you now, *signorina*.'

I lay there for a moment longer, luxuriating in the dark gleam of adoration in his eyes as he slowly unzipped his jeans. He kicked them off along with his boxers, releasing the hardness that was already jutting forward impatiently. I smiled and crooked my finger.

'Good. But I'm giving the orders tonight.'

He knelt on the bed, still wearing his shirt half-buttoned in his haste to get to me, and laughing softly I pulled it off his shoulders and tossed it across the room to tangle in the heap of my travel-worn clothes.

Then I opened my legs, the kiss of silk kimono still on my arms. I was soft and yearning down there, I could feel the moistness as I parted myself for my lover.

Gustav crawled over me, pushing my thighs wider apart. He didn't just focus on what I was offering him. He looked over my stomach, studying my breasts, which no longer ached so much, but had swollen with pregnancy. Just his eyes on me made me squirm with longing for him, a kind of fierce, primal lust that must have been something to do with keeping my mate close to me now that he'd impregnated me. But I lay there, letting him worship me with his eyes, feeling like a queen.

Then he pinned my legs down, wide apart, dipped his head, and his lips closed around me, sucking my hot pussy.

He was doing something amazing with his mouth. Massaging my pulsing sex, and as his lips squeezed and sucked, his tongue roamed up between the lips, insinuating up the tight wet crack and sliding inside, probing, tasting me, until he reached the tender burning clit.

I moaned and juddered violently as he tapped and flicked and then licked me. His hands came round and lifted my buttocks so that I was pressed into his face. So dirty and naughty and sexy, yet so reverential, too. Like he was supping a rare, delicate feast. I gasped in excitement and encouragement.

Gustav was worshipping me silently, holding me completely still on my bed. I watched him sucking me. He seemed totally mesmerised. His hands manipulated my bottom as he sucked, pressing my butt cheeks very lightly as if testing my ass for reactions, but even though I was supposed to be in charge, it felt more like a warning not to move. Hell, I wasn't going anywhere. I was lying there being licked and pleasured, my head tipped back in a kind of melting ecstasy, my own tongue flickering obscenely like a porn star as he worked at me. The more I challenged myself to stay absolutely still, the more intensely every flickering sensation was heightened.

A wave of exhaustion took me by surprise just as my stomach coiled and tightened with excitement, but I roused myself. My self-control ebbed away, the climax gathering so close to the edge. Gustav was sucking, hard, and I bucked against his face, unable to stop myself, but I had to stop, I had to. I wound his hair in my fingers and tugged at his head. Eventually he pulled away gently and very reluctantly.

'Fuck me now, Gustav,' I breathed, and the order was soft this time.

His mouth released me with a delicious wet sound. As I slid down on to my back, he licked my juices off his lips.

His hands came away from my bottom and I placed them on my big aching breasts. My nipples pricked up hard with desire. I wanted to feel that gorgeous mouth sucking on them. He smiled and his lips closed round one sharpened nipple and the sparking flesh around it. I felt the nipple scrape on the roof of his mouth, and then he bit it, and it hurt, already hypersensitive, ready to feed those babies I suppose, and I screeched with delight and crushed his face into me, scrabbling to hold the other breast, heavy and warm as I pressed it against his cheek and rubbed the second nipple against his mouth until he turned to nibble on that one too.

I arched my back to push my breasts into his face and took hold of his big cock. I guided it to slide into the shadowy dampness. The sensations of his mouth and teeth on my nipples, the hardness throbbing in my hands, got me even hornier. If I hadn't been so heavy with exhaustion, I would have made him do something really dirty like take me up the arse.

But there was all the time in the world for that. So instead I rubbed the blunt tip across my hidden clit, wet and singing from where his tongue had been.

Oh, God, I nearly came there and then at the touch. I was so worked up now.

I moaned and writhed, rubbing him again and again across me, feeling him bump against my clit, keeping the movement as delicate and slow as possible while his face disappeared between my breasts, his hands roaming, caressing, those lips kissing and sucking.

And then I wriggled down beneath him so that he pushed easily into me and thrust up inside, not grinding greedily and pumping but filling me, taking me in every sense of the word. Both of us, coming home.

I was so tired now that I just floated there, his hardness filling me and resting inside me. He's perfect for me. The right shape, touching the right places in the right way. He was plugged into me, closing me in, not going anywhere. Yes, owning me. And he is all mine. I hovered there, squeezed him tight inside until I was ready to move. He didn't move either, just waited, locked in there, lying on me, slightly raised on his hands so as not to squash me, and then he started – not to move exactly, or thrust, but to pulsate, to *vibrate*. God, this was something else. He wanted to be so gentle and careful with me, he was just vibrating inside me. Slight, tiny, imperceptible, shivering pulses, but steady enough and strong. Growing stronger, like a light burning brighter, keeping me alert, awake, in our warm dark bedroom

And so it took a while. Because this incredible vibration increased so slowly, and so slightly, and my body tightened round him so slightly in answer, we inched in sensuous slow motion towards our climax. He was rearing over me as he was overtaken by the shared ecstasy, dipping his mouth to suck on my nipples, then resting on his hands, watching my face as we grew wilder. My head fell back on to the pillows, my breasts rising proudly in the darkness as our bodies started to melt together. I was going faint with ecstasy and he had one more small surprise to rouse me, inching his finger between my buttocks and jabbing up into my ass. It opened softly to let him in, and, as his finger started pushing hard up there, I lay back, just gave in, limp, exhausted, yet on fire deep inside, and my fiancé took me harder, pushing me up the bed, into those pillows.

We rocked, faster, faster, and then the climax flared and bloomed, throwing us together, arms and legs wrapped round each other like limpets.

'These babies,' Gustav murmured, his voice tickling my ear as sleep pressed me into the pillows. 'Who will they look like, do you think?'

I laughed softly and closed my eyes. 'Like the puppies in *Lady and The Tramp*. The boys will look like you, dark and naughty and sexy, and the girls will look like me.'

'They could never be as beautiful as their mother.'

And then we descended from the hurly-burly of the chaise longue into the deep, deep peace of the marital bed.

'You say your life is about to change as if it's a bad thing. You want all those people in the streets to get the bunting out?

Bring on the dancing girls?' Polly lowers the antique lace veil over my face. Now I'm seeing London through a delicate swirl of embroidery. 'You're the one who wanted to marry Gustav as quickly as possible. No fuss. You said you wanted to be able to count your guests on the fingers of one hand.'

'All of which is true. I can't wait to be Mrs Levi!' I reply, taking her hand. Our joined palms feel a little damp in the lace gloves. 'What I mean is, I feel sorry for anyone who isn't me. I don't mean to sound smug. And I don't mean you, obviously. I mean I wish they could all have an inkling of what a happy day this is – how good this feels. I'm marrying Gustav Levi.'

'Stop it. You're getting me started.' Polly dabs at her eyes and I turn away from the car window to look at her. On this hot summer's day, she still manages to look like a snow leopard. Pale skin, white blonde hair grown long enough to plait the delicate gypsophila flowers through it, and all brought to life by the sapphire glitter of her eyes.

'God, I'm selfish. Ever since you arrived from Marrakesh all I've done is fuss over altering the dress, packing for this secret honeymoon, wondering if I'm allowed a glass of champagne at my own wedding reception – I've barely considered your feelings. You weren't anxious about seeing Pierre again, were you?'

'Babes, I'm only human. I wasn't wild about seeing him again. But I am in another zone these days, thanks to the ashram, and it was a good idea of yours to get us to meet up on our own the other day. I've accepted that he wasn't some great love that I've lost. Me and Pierre were a flash in the pan. More importantly, he's your brother-in-law. Which makes him something, and nothing.' She breaks into a smile and tweaks my nose. 'And not even *I* can feel threatened by a guy on crutches!'

I laugh. 'He might realise what *he's* missed, though, Pol.

Maybe he'll be bowled over by how sexy and gorgeous you look today!'

'That ship has sailed, and while we're busy gloating, I can tell you it feels bloody fantastic to be able to say that and mean it!' She squeezes my fingers. 'I'm different from that neurotic nutcase back at New Year's, Rena. I'm a shining light of acceptance and calm. Angelique has taught me how to heal myself. She's taught me how to lay my hands on others, too – oh, shut up, I don't mean sexually, hey, stop giggling!'

But it's too late. I'm clutching her hands and we're half laughing, half crying as Dickson guides the car, bedecked with white ribbons, onwards through the streets of Mayfair.

Polly taps him on the shoulder. 'Time to get this bride to the church on time, I reckon, if I'm ever going to give her away!'

The only positive thing that still chimes from my childhood is the security of knowing that if I step inside a church or chapel I will know peace. Those people who called themselves my parents used to take me every Sunday, and although even as a tiny child I could see how breathtaking was their hypocrisy, I ceased to care, because it was the one time in the week that they had to be civil to me, and the one time, until I was old enough simply to leave home, that I could escape into my own spiritual world.

When I told Gustav this and asked if he'd mind getting married in church, he was overjoyed. He hasn't stepped inside a church since his parents died.

The car glides up Mount Street and stops in front of the pretty Gothic façade of the Catholic church. As soon as it stops, I'm overwhelmed with the urge to rush inside. Dickson only just has time to leap round and open the door for me, and Polly only just has time to scramble after me to lift the train of my dress out of the dust, before we're dashing up the path into the cool arch of the porch.

Inside the church I can hear the organ playing the soft strains of *Jesu, Joy of Man's Desiring*.

'I daren't look, Polly. Is he here?'

She peers through the wooden door, then steps further inside to look. My sense of smell is still acute, though the sickness has subsided. Honey-flavoured French polish and candle wax waft from the interior, mingled with heavy incense being prepared in the thurible. The priest comes towards me to murmur a few words, the smell of fresh soap on his hands.

Then it's just me and Polly again. She straightens my veil, fluffs up the white tulips and greenery in my bouquet.

'My hair OK?'

'Perfect. All these hormones have made it longer and thicker already. But I've put a serum in it so it's brushed back and smooth as glass. You look like an absolute princess.'

She touches her favourite nude gloss to my lips.

'Why have you got that funny look?' My voice is hoarse with nerves. 'Is it because you've seen Pierre? Did he see you? He's the best man. Has he got the rings?'

'Yes to all of the above. But the poor guy. He doesn't look great.' Polly puts her finger on my lips to hush me, blinks and fiddles with her little vanity case. I realise she can't say any more because tears are sparkling like diamonds in her eyes.

'He's in a lot of pain still,' I remark thoughtfully. 'You know, he gave Gustav back their father's watch as a surprise gift the other night? G didn't have a stag night. Just the two of them spent the night at the house while you and I were being pampered at Champneys. Maybe that accident has changed him, after all.'

'Maybe *you've* changed him.' Polly sweeps one more coat of mascara on to my eyelashes. 'Babes, he's your brother-in-law. He's part of your life. I get it. I'll cope. It's fine.'

'What about Gustav?'

She does the other eye and frowns, holding the wand up like a conductor's baton. 'What about him?'

I nearly stamp my foot, except that I'm wearing very high white satin mules and I'll snap the heels.

'I asked you before. Is he here?'

She just smiles and opens the door wider. The church is shadowy and cool, but a shaft of sunlight is arrowing in from the high stained-glass windows in the side aisles, shining a spotlight directly at the tall, straight-shouldered back of my bridegroom. Pierre is standing beside him, slightly shorter, and listing sideways on one of his crutches. The brothers are wearing identical black morning coats, and their black hair shines in the sunlight.

I stare at the back of Gustav's head, willing him to turn round and watch me walk up the aisle towards him. I take one step forward, and the organist plays the opening bars of Schubert's *Ave Maria*.

The hairs on the back of my neck rise as the music pierces me. Polly and I take another step into the nave. Pause.

'They're all here. A small but perfectly formed collection of well-wishers.'

I hold back a moment, staring at the back of Gustav's head. Polly presses close to me, running her hand over the just visible swell of my belly under the swish of ivory chiffon.

'Time to marry your prince.'

She falls behind me and I walk up the flower-decked aisle. As soon as he hears my first footstep, Gustav turns round. His black eyes are the brightest thing in this sunlit church, drawing me towards him. All around us are the people who have done something to shape our lives in the last year. In no particular order. Crystal and Dickson, side by side in matching Lincoln green like Robin Hood and Maid Marion.

The Weinmeyers, big and blonde in blue. Maria and Angelique in peach and tangerine.

Up in the choir stalls, Chloe and her henchwomen are singing like angels.

Polly is slipping into the pew next to Pierre.

The two little ones are tucked inside.

But all I can see is him. Gustav Levi.

My prince.

Can the heat of passion thaw a
frozen heart?

*Can the heat
of passion thaw a
frozen heart?*

melting
ms
frost

kat black

Prepare to be seduced in the sexiest
romance of the year.

A quaint suburb. A quiet little reading group. A very naughty reading list . . .

Passions will be awakened at...

the **naughty girls'** book club

'Deliciously addictive'
Justine Elyot

sophie hart

Chicklit with a saucy twist, passions will be awakened at The Naughty Girls' Book Club . . .

Follow Avon on
Twitter@AvonBooksUK
and
Facebook@AvonBooksUK
For news, giveaways and
exclusive author extras

A V O N